The Sergeant's Cat

Outsider in Amsterdam
Tumbleweed
The Corpse on the Dike
Death of a Hawker
The Japanese Corpse
The Blond Baboon
The Maine Massacre
The Mind Murders
The Streetbird
The Rattle-Rat
Hard Rain
Just a Corpse at Twilight
Hollow-Eyed Angel
The Perfidious Parrot

Janwillem van de Wetering

The Sergeant's Cat

Collected Stories

To Isis and the Beeper

༄

Published by Soho Press, Inc.
853 Broadway
New York, NY 10003

The Amsterdam cops: collected stories / Janwillem van de Wetering.
This paperback edition published under the title The Sergeant's Cat
(A Grijpstra & De Gier mystery)

ISBN 978-1-61695-698-1
eISBN 978-1-61695-691-2

1. De Gier, Rinus (Fictitious character)—Fiction. 2. Grijpstra, Henk
(Fictitious character)—Fiction. 3. Detective and mystery stories, American.
4. Police—Netherlands—Amsterdam—Fiction. I. Series.
PS3572.A4292A8 1999   99-23243
813'.54—dc21   CIP

Printed in the United States of America

10 9 8 7 6 5 4 3 2

The Sergeant's Cat

Table of Contents

The Deadly Egg

The siren of the tiny dented Volkswagen shrieked forlornly between the naked trees of the Amsterdam Forest, the city's largest park, set on its southern edge: several square miles of willows, poplars, and alders growing wild, surrounding ponds and lining paths. The paths were restricted to pedestrians and cyclists, but the Volkswagen had ignored the many no-entry signs quite legally, for the vehicle belonged to the Municipal Police* and more especially to its Criminal Investigation Department, or Murder Brigade. Even so, it looked lost and its howl seemed defensive.

It was Easter Sunday and it was raining, and the car's two occupants, Detective-Adjutant Grijpstra and Detective-Sergeant de Gier, sat hunched in their overcoats, watching the squeaky, rusted wipers trying to deal with the steady drizzle. The car should have been junked some years before, but the adjutant had lost the form that would have done away with his aging transport, lost it on purpose and with the sergeant's consent. They had grown fond of the Volkswagen, of its shabbiness and its ability to melt into traffic.

But they weren't fond of the car now. The heater didn't work, it was cold, and it was early. Not yet nine o'clock on a Sunday

---

* The ranks of the Amsterdam Municipal Police are, in descending order, chief-constable, commissaris, chief-inspector, adjutant, sergeant, constable-first-class, constables.

is early, especially when the Sunday is Easter. Technically, they were both off duty, but they had been telephoned out of warm beds by Headquarters' communications room. A dead man was dangling from a branch in the forest; please, would they care to have a look him?

Grijpstra's stubby index finger silenced the siren. They had followed several miles of winding paths so far and hadn't come across anything alive except tall blue herons, fishing in the ponds and moats and flapping away slowly when the car came too close for their comfort.

"You know who reported the corpse? I wasn't awake when the communications room talked to me."

De Gier had been smoking silently. His handsome head with its perfect curls turned obediently to face his superior. "Yes, a gentleman jogger. He said he jogged right into the body's feet. Gave him a start. He ran all the way to the nearest telephone booth, phoned Headquarters, then Headquarters phoned us, and that's why we are here, I suppose. I am still a little asleep myself—we are here, aren't we?"

They could hear another siren, and another. Two limousines came roaring toward the Volkswagen, and Grijpstra cursed and made the little car turn off the path and slide into a soggy lawn; they could feel its wheels sink into the mud.

The limousines stopped and men poured out of them; the men pushed the Volkswagen back onto the path.

"Morning, Adjutant; morning, Sergeant. Where is the corpse?"

"Shouldn't you know, too?"

Several men said simultaneously, "We thought maybe you knew. All we know is that the corpse is in the Amsterdam Forest and that this is the Amsterdam Forest."

Grijpstra addressed the sergeant. "Do you know?"

De Gier's well-modulated baritone chanted the instructions. "Turn right after the big pond, right again, then left. Or the other way round. I think I have it right; we should be close."

The three cars drove about for a few minutes more until they were waved down by a man dressed in what seemed to be long blue underwear. The jogger ran ahead, bouncing energetically, and led them to their destination. The men from the limousines brought out their boxes and suitcases, then cameras clicked and a video recorder hummed. The corpse hung on and the two detectives watched it hang.

"Neat," Grijpstra said, "very neat. Don't you think it is neat?"

The sergeant grunted.

"Here. Brought a folding camp stool and some nice new rope, made a perfect noose, slipped it around his neck, kicked away the stool. Anything suspicious, gentlemen?"

The men from the limousines said there was not. They had found footprints—the prints of the corpse's boots. There were no other prints, except the jogger's. The jogger's statement was taken; he was thanked and sent on his sporting way. A police ambulance arrived and the corpse was cut loose, examined by doctor and detectives, and carried off. The detectives saluted the corpse quietly by inclining their heads.

"In his sixties," the sergeant said, "well dressed in old but expensive clothes. Clean shirt. Tie. Short grey beard, clipped. A man who took care of himself. A faint smell of liquor—he must have had a few to give him courage. Absolutely nothing in his pockets. I looked in the collar of his shirt—no laundry mark. He went to some trouble to be nameless. Maybe something will turn up when they strip him at the mortuary; we should phone in an hour's time."

Grijpstra looked hopeful. "Suicide?"

"I would think so. Came here by himself, no traces of anybody else. No signs of a struggle. The man knew what he wanted to do, and did it, all by himself. But he didn't leave a note; that wasn't very thoughtful."

"Right," Grijpstra said. "Time for breakfast, Sergeant! We'll have it at the airport—that's close and convenient. We can show our police cards and get through the customs barrier; the restaurant on the far side is better than the coffee shop on the near side."

De Gier activated the radio when they got back to the car.

"Male corpse, balding but with short grey beard. Dentures. Blue eyes. Sixty-odd years old. Three-piece blue suit, elegant dark grey overcoat, no hat. No identification."

"Thank you," the radio said.

"Looks very much like suicide. Do you have any missing persons of that description in your files?"

"No, not so far."

"We'll be off for breakfast and will call in again on our way back."

"Echrem," the radio said sadly, "there's something else. Sorry."

De Gier stared at a duck waddling across the path trailing seven fuzzy ducklings. He began to mumble. Adjutant Grijpstra mumbled with him. The mumbled four-letter words interspersed with mild curses formed a background for the radio's well-articulated message. They were given an address on the other side of the city. "The lady was poisoned, presumably by a chocolate Easter egg. The ambulance that answered the distress call just radioed in. They are taking her to the hospital. The ambulance driver thought the poison was either parathion, something used in agriculture, or arsenic. His assistant is pumping out the patient's stomach. She is in a bad way but not dead yet."

Grijpstra grabbed the microphone from de Gier's limp hand. "So if the lady is on her way to the hospital, who is left in the house you want us to go to?"

"Her husband, man by the name of Moozen—a lawyer, I believe."

"What hospital is Mrs. Moozen being taken to?"

"The Wilhelmina."

"And you have no one else on call? Sergeant de Gier and I are supposed to be off duty for Easter, you know!"

"No," the radio's female voice said, "no, Adjutant. We never have much crime on Easter Day, especially not in the morning. There are only two detectives on duty and they are out on a case, too—some boys have derailed a streetcar with matches."

"Right," Grijpstra said coldly. "We are on our way."

The old Volkswagen made an effort to jump away, protesting feebly. De Gier was still muttering but had stopped cursing. "Streetcar? Matches?"

"Yes. They take an empty cartridge, fill it with match heads, then close the open end with a hammer. Very simple. All you have to do is insert the cartridge into the streetcar's rail, and when the old tram comes clanging along, the sudden impact makes the cartridge explode. If you use two or three cartridges, the explosion may be strong enough to lift the wheel out of the rail. Didn't you ever try that? I used to do it as a boy. The only problem was to get the cartridges. We had to sneak around on the rifle range with the chance of getting shot at."

"No," de Gier said. "Pity. Never thought of it, and it sounds like a good game."

He looked out of the window. The car had left the park and was racing toward the city's center through long empty avenues. There was no life in the huge apartment buildings lining the streets of the old city—nobody had bothered to get up yet. Ten o'clock and the citizenry wasn't even considering the possibility of slouching into the kitchen for a first cup of coffee.

But one man had bothered to get up early and had strolled into the park, carrying his folding chair and a piece of rope to break off the painful course of his life, once and for all. An elderly man in good but old clothes. De Gier saw the man's beard again, a nicely cared-for growth. The police doctor had said that he hadn't been dead long. A man alone in the night that would have led him to Easter, a man by himself in a deserted park, testing the strength of his rope, fitting his head into the noose, kicking the camp stool.

"Bah!" he said aloud.

Grijpstra had steered the car through a red light and was turning the wheel.

"What's that?"

"Nothing. Just bah."

"Bah is right," Grijpstra said.

They found the house, a bungalow, on the luxurious extreme north side of the city. Spring was trying to revive the small lawn and a magnolia tree was in hesitant bloom. Bright yellow crocuses set off the path. Grijpstra looked at the crocuses. He didn't seem pleased.

"Crocuses," de Gier said, "very nice. Jolly little flowers."

"No. Unimaginative plants, manufactured, not grown. Computer plants. They make the bulbs in a machine and program them to look stupid. Go ahead, Sergeant, press the bell."

"Really?" the sergeant asked.

Grijpstra's jowls sagged. "Yes. They are like mass-manufactured cheese, tasteless; cheese is probably made with the same machines."

"Cheese," de Gier said moistly. "There's nothing wrong with cheese either, apart from not having any right now. Breakfast has slipped by, you know." He glanced at his watch.

They read the nameplate while the bell rang: H. F. MOOZEN, ATTORNEY AT LAW. The door opened. A man in a bathrobe made out of brightly striped towel material said good morning. The detectives showed their identifications. The man nodded and stepped back. A pleasant man, still young, thirty years or a bit more. The ideal model for an ad in a ladies' magazine. A background man, showing off a modern house, or a minicar, or expensive furniture. The sort of man ladies would like to have around. Quiet, secure, mildly good-looking. Not a passionate man, but lawyers seldom are. Lawyers practice detachment; they identify with their clients, but only up to a point.

"You won't take long, I hope," Mr. Moozen said. "I wanted to go with the ambulance, but the driver said you were on the way, and that I wouldn't be of any help if I stayed with my wife."

"Was your wife conscious when she left here, sir?"

"Barely. She couldn't speak."

"She ate an egg, a chocolate egg?"

"Yes. I don't care for chocolate myself. It was a gift, we thought, from friends. I had to let the dog out early this morning, an hour ago, and there was an Easter bunny sitting on the path. He held an egg wrapped up in silver paper. I took him in, woke up my wife, and showed the bunny to her, and she took the egg and ate it, then became ill. I telephoned for the ambulance and they came almost immediately. I would like to go to the hospital now."

"Come in our car, sir. Can I see the bunny?"

Mr. Moozen took off the bathrobe and put on a jacket. He opened the door leading to the kitchen, and a small dog jumped around the detectives, yapping greetings. The bunny stood on the kitchen counter; it was almost a foot high. Grijpstra tapped its back with his knuckles; it sounded solid.

"Hey," de Gier said. He turned the bunny around and showed it to Grijpstra.

"*Brwah!*" Grijpstra said.

The rabbit's toothless mouth gaped. The beast's eyes were close together and deeply sunk into the skull. Its ears stood up aggressively. The bunny leered at them, its torso crouched; the paws that had held the deadly egg seemed ready to punch.

"It's roaring," de Gier said. "See? A roaring rabbit. Easter bunnies are supposed to smile."

"Shall we go?" Mr. Moozen asked.

They used the siren, and the trip to the hospital didn't take ten minutes. The city was still quiet. But there proved to be no hurry. An energetic bright young nurse led them to a waiting room. Mrs. Moozen was being worked on; her condition was still critical. The nurse would let them know if there was any change.

"Can we smoke?" Grijpstra asked.

"If you must." The nurse smiled coldly, appraised de Gier's tall, wide-shouldered body with a possessive feminist glance, swung her hips, and turned to the door.

"Any coffee?"

"There's a machine in the hall. Don't smoke in the hall, please."

There were several posters in the waiting room. A picture of a cigarette pointing to a skull with crossed bones. A picture of a happy child biting into an apple. A picture of a drunken driver (bubbles surrounding his head proved he was drunk) followed by an ambulance. The caption read, "Not if you have an accident, but when you have an accident."

De Gier fetched coffee and Grijpstra offered cigars. Mr. Moozen said he didn't smoke.

"Well," Grijpstra said patiently and puffed out a ragged dark cloud, "now who would want to poison your wife, sir? Has there been any recent trouble in her life?"

The question hung in the small white room while Moozen thought. The detectives waited. De Gier stared at the floor, Grijpstra observed the ceiling. A full minute passed.

"Yes," Mr. Moozen said, "some trouble. With me. We contemplated a divorce."

"I see."

"But then we decided to stay together. The trouble passed."

"Any particular reason why you considered a divorce, sir?"

"My wife had a lover." Mr. Moozen's words were clipped and precise.

"*Had,*" de Gier said. "The affair came to an end?"

"Yes. We had some problems with our central heating, something the mechanics couldn't fix. An engineer came out and my wife fell in love with him. She told me—she doesn't like to be secretive. They met each other in motels for a while."

"You were upset?"

"Yes. It was a serious affair. The engineer's wife is a mental patient; he divorced her and was awarded custody of his two children. I thought he was looking for a new wife. My wife has no children of her own—we have been married some six years and would like to have children. My wife and the engineer seemed well matched. I waited a month and then told her to make up her mind—either him or me, not both; I couldn't stand it."

"And she chose you?"

"Yes."

"Do you know the engineer?"

A vague pained smile floated briefly on Moozen's face. "Not personally. We did meet once and discussed central heating systems. Any further contact with him was through my wife."

"And when did all this happen, sir?"

"Recently. She only made her decision a week ago. I don't think she has met him since. She told me it was all over."

"His name and address, please, sir."

De Gier closed his notebook and got up. "Shall we go, Adjutant?"

Grijpstra sighed and got up too. They shook hands with Moozen and wished him luck. Grijpstra stopped at the desk. The nurse wasn't helpful, but Grijpstra insisted and de Gier smiled and eventually they were taken to a doctor who accompanied them to the next floor. Mrs. Moozen seemed comfortable. Her arms were stretched out on the blanket. Her face was calm. The detectives were led out of the room again.

"Bad," the doctor said. "Parathion is a strong poison. Her stomach is ripped to shreds. We'll have to operate and remove part of it, but I think she will live. The silly woman ate the whole egg, a normal-sized egg. Perhaps she was still too sleepy to notice the taste."

"Her husband is downstairs. Perhaps you should call him up,

especially if you think she will live." Grijpstra sounded concerned. *He probably was*, de Gier thought. He felt concerned himself. The woman was beautiful, with a finely curved nose, very thin in the bridge, and large eyes and a soft and sensitive mouth. He had noted her long delicate hands.

"Husbands," the doctor said. "Prime suspects in my experience. Husbands are supposed to love their wives, but usually they don't. It's the same the other way round. Marriage seems to breed violence—it's one of the impossible situations we humans have to put up with."

Grijpstra's pale blue eyes twinkled. "Are you married, Doctor?"

The doctor grinned back. "Very. Oh, yes."

"A long time?"

"Long enough."

Grijpstra's grin faded. "So am I. Too long. But poison is nasty. Thank you, Doctor."

There wasn't much conversation in the car as they drove to the engineer's address. The city's streets had filled up. People were stirring about on the sidewalks and cars crowded each other, honking occasionally. The engineer lived in a block of apartments, and Grijpstra switched off the engine and lit another small black cigar.

"A family drama. What do you think, Sergeant?"

"I don't think. But that rabbit was most extraordinary. Not bought in a shop. A specially made rabbit, and well made, not by an amateur."

"Are we looking for a sculptor? Some arty person? Would Mr. Moozen or the engineer be an artist in his spare time? How does one make a chocolate rabbit, anyway?"

De Gier tried to stretch, but didn't succeed in his cramped quarters. He yawned instead. "You make a mold, I suppose, out of plaster of Paris or something, and then you pour hot chocolate into the mold and wait for it to harden. That rabbit

was solid chocolate, several kilos of it. Our artistic friend went
to a lot of trouble."

"A baker? A pastry man?"

"Or an engineer—engineers design forms sometimes, I
believe. Let's meet this lover man."

The engineer was a small nimble man with a shock of black
hair and dark lively eyes, a nervous man, nervous in a pleasant,
childlike manner. De Gier remembered that Mrs. Moozen was
small, too. They were ushered into a four-room apartment. They
had to be careful not to step on a large number of toys, spread
about evenly. Two little boys played on the floor; the eldest ran
out of the room to fetch his Easter present to show to them. It
was a basketful of eggs, homemade, out of chocolate. The other
boy came to show his basket, identical but a size smaller.

"My sister and I made them last night," the engineer said.
"She came to live here after my wife left, and she looks after the
kids, but she is spending the Easter weekend with my parents
in the country. We couldn't go because Tom here had measles,
hadn't you, Tom?"

"Yes," Tom said. "Big measles. Little Klaas here hasn't had
them yet."

Klaas looked sorry. Grijpstra took a plastic truck off a chair
and sat down heavily after having looked at the engineer, who
waved him on. "Please, make yourself at home." De Gier had
found himself a chair, too, and was rolling a cigarette. The
engineer provided coffee and shooed the children into another
room.

"Any trouble?"

"Yes," Grijpstra said. "I am afraid we usually bring trouble.
A Mrs. Moozen has been taken to the hospital. An attempt
was made on her life. I believe you are acquainted with Mrs.
Moozen?"

"Ann," the engineer said. "My God! Is she all right?"

De Gier had stopped rolling his cigarette. He was watching

the man carefully; his large brown eyes gleamed, but not with pleasure or anticipation. The sergeant felt sorrow, a feeling that often accompanied his intrusions into the private lives of his fellow citizens. He shifted, and the automatic pistol in his shoulder holster nuzzled into his armpit. He impatiently pushed the weapon back. This was no time to be reminded that he carried death with him, legal death.

"What happened?" the engineer was asking. "Did somebody hurt her?"

"A question," Grijpstra said gently. "A question first, sir. You said your sister and you were making chocolate Easter eggs last night. Did you happen to make any bunnies, too?"

The engineer sucked noisily on his cigarette. Grijpstra repeated his question.

"Bunnies? Yes, or no. We tried, but it was too much for us. The eggs were easy—my sister is good at that. We have a pudding form for a bunny, but all we could manage was a pudding. It is still in the kitchen, a surprise for the kids later on today. Chocolate pudding—they like it."

"Can we see the kitchen, please?"

The engineer didn't get up. "My God," he said again, "she was poisoned? How horrible! Where is she now?"

"In the hospital, sir."

"Bad?"

Grijpstra nodded. "The doctor said she will live. Some sort of pesticide was mixed into chocolate, which she ate."

The engineer got up; he seemed dazed. They found the kitchen. Leftover chocolate mix was still on the counter. Grijpstra brought out an envelope and scooped some of the hardened chips into it.

"Do you know that Ann and I had an affair?"

"Yes, sir."

"Were you told that she ended the affair, that she decided to stay with her husband?"

"Yes, sir."

The engineer was tidying up the counter mechanically. "I see. So I could be a suspect. Tried to get at her out of spite or something. But I am not a spiteful man. You wouldn't know that. I don't mind being a suspect, but I would like to see Ann. She is in the hospital, you said. What hospital?"

"The Wilhelmina, sir."

"Can't leave the kids here, can I? Maybe the neighbors will take them for an hour or so . . . yes. I'll go and see Ann. This is terrible."

Grijpstra marched to the front door with de Gier trailing behind him. "Don't move from the house today, if you please, sir, not until we telephone or come again. We'll try and be as quick as we can."

"Nice chap," de Gier said when the car found its parking place in the vast courtyard of Headquarters. "That engineer, I mean. I rather liked Mr. Moozen, too, and Mrs. Moozen is a lovely lady. Now what?"

"Go back to the Moozen house, Sergeant, and get a sample of the roaring bunny. Bring it to the laboratory together with this envelope. If they match, we have a strong case against the engineer."

De Gier restarted the engine. "Maybe he is not so nice, eh? He could have driven his wife crazy and now he tries to murder his girlfriend, his ex-girlfriend. Lovely Ann Moozen, who dared to drop him. Could be. Do you think so?"

Grijpstra leaned his bulk against the car and addressed his words to the emptiness of the yard. "No. That would be the obvious solution. But he was distressed, genuinely distressed, I would say. If he hadn't been and if he hadn't had those kids in the house, I might have brought him in for further questioning."

"And Mr. Moozen?"

"Could be. Maybe he didn't find the bunny on the garden path; maybe he put it there, or maybe he had it ready in the

cupboard and brought it to his wandering wife. He is a lawyer—lawyers can be devious at times. True?"

De Gier said, "Yes, yes, yes . . ." and kept on saying so until
Grijpstra squeezed the elbow sticking out of the car's window.
"You are saying yes, but you don't sound convinced."

"I thought Moozen was suffering, too."

"Murderers usually suffer, don't they?"

De Gier started his "Yes, yes," and Grijpstra marched off.

They met an hour later, in the canteen at Headquarters.
They munched rolls stuffed with sliced liver and roast beef and
muttered diligently at each other.

"So it is the same chocolate?"

"Yes, but that doesn't mean much. One of the lab assistants
has a father who owns a pastry shop. He said that there are only
three mixes on the market and our stuff is the most popular
make. No, not much of a clue there."

"So?"

"We may have a complex case on our hands. We should go
back to Mr. Moozen, I think, and find out about friends and rela-
tives. Perhaps his wife had other lovers, or jealous lady friends."

"Why her?"

Grijpstra munched on. "Hmm?"

"Why *her?*" de Gier repeated. "Why not him?"

Grijpstra swallowed. "Him? What about him?"

De Gier reached for the plate, but Grijpstra restrained the
sergeant's hand. "Wait, you are hard to understand when you
have your mouth full. What about him?"

De Gier looked at the roll. Grijpstra picked it up and ate it.

"Him," de Gier said unhappily. "He found the bunny on the
garden path, the ferocious bunny holding the pernicious egg. A
gift, how nice. But he doesn't eat chocolate, so he runs inside
and shows the gift to his wife, and his wife grabs the egg and
eats it. She may have thought *he* was giving it to her; she was
still half-asleep. Maybe she noticed the taste, but she ate on to

please her husband. She became ill at once and he telephoned for an ambulance. Now, if he had wanted to kill her, he might have waited an hour or so, to give the poison a chance to do its job. But he grabbed his phone, fortunately. What I am trying to say is, the egg may have been intended for him, from an enemy who didn't even know Moozen had a wife, who didn't care about killing the wife."

"Ah," Grijpstra said, and swallowed the last of the roll. "Could be. We'll ask Mr. Moozen about his enemies. But not just now. There is the dead man we found in the park—a message came in while you were away. A missing person has been reported and the description fits our corpse. According to the communications room, a woman phoned to say that a man who is renting a room in her house has been behaving strangely lately and has now disappeared. She traced him to the corner bar where he spent last evening, until two A.M., when they closed.

"He was a little drunk, according to the barkeeper, but not blind drunk. She always takes him tea in the morning, but this morning he wasn't there and the bed was still made. But she thinks he'd been home, for at a little after two A.M. she heard the front door opening and closing twice. He probably fetched the rope and his camp stool then."

"And the man was fairly old and had a short grey beard?"

"Right."

"So we go and see the landlady. I'll get a photograph—they took dozens this morning and they should be developed by now. Was anything found in his clothes?"

"Nothing." Grijpstra looked guiltily at the empty plate. "Want another roll?"

"You ate it."

"That's true, and the canteen is out of rolls; we got the last batch. Never mind, Sergeant. Let's go out and do some work. Work will take your mind off food."

⌇

"THAT'S HIM," THE landlady with the plastic curlers said. Her glasses had slipped to the tip of her blunt nose while she studied the photograph. "Oh, how horrible! His tongue is sticking out. Poor Mr. Marchant. Is he dead?"

"Yes, ma'am."

"For shame, and such a nice gentleman. He has been staying here for nearly five years now and he was always so polite."

Grijpstra tried to look away from the glaring pink curlers, which pointed at his forehead from the woman's thinning hair.

"Did he have any troubles, ma'am? Anything that may have led him to take his own life?"

The curlers bobbed frantically. "Yes. Money troubles. Nothing to pay the tax man with. He always paid the rent, but he hadn't been paying his taxes. And his business wasn't doing well. He has a shop in the next street; he makes things—ornaments, he calls them—out of brass. But there was some trouble with the neighbors. Too much noise, and something about the zoning, too; this is a residential area now, they say. The neighbors wanted him to move, but he had nowhere to move to, and he was getting nasty letters, lawyers' letters. He would have had to close down, and he had to make money to pay the tax man. It was driving him crazy. I could hear him walk around in his room at night, round and round, until I had to switch off my hearing aid."

"Thank you, ma'am."

"He was alone," the woman said, and shuffled with them to the door. "All alone, like me. And he was always so nice." She was crying.

"Happy Easter," de Gier said, and opened the Volkswagen's door for the adjutant.

"The same to you. Back to Mr. Moozen again—we *are* driving about this morning. I could use some coffee again. Maybe Mr. Moozen will oblige."

"He won't be so happy either. We aren't making anybody

happy today," the sergeant said, and tried to put the Volkswagen into first gear. The gear slipped and the car took off in second.

They found Mr. Moozen in his garden. It had begun to rain again, but the lawyer didn't seem to notice that he was getting wet. He was staring at the bright yellow crocuses, touching them with his foot. He had trampled a few of them into the grass.

"How is your wife, sir?"

"Conscious and in pain. The doctors think they can save her, but she will have to be on a stringent diet for years and she'll be very weak for months. I won't have her back for a while."

Grijpstra coughed. "We visited your wife's, ah, recent lover, sir." The word "recent" came out awkwardly and he coughed again to take away the bad taste.

"Did you arrest him?"

"No, sir."

"Any strong reasons to suspect the man?"

"Are you a criminal lawyer, sir?"

Moozen kicked the last surviving crocus, turned on his heel, and led his visitors to the house. "No, I specialize in civil cases. Sometimes I do divorces, but I don't have enough experience to point a finger in this personal case. Divorce is a messy business, but with a little tact and patience reason usually prevails. To try and poison somebody is unreasonable behavior. I can't visualize Ann provoking that type of action—she is a gentle woman, sensual but gentle. If she did break off her relationship with the engineer, she would have done it diplomatically."

"He seemed upset, sir, genuinely upset."

"Quite. I had hoped as much. So where are we now?"

"With you, sir. Do *you* have any enemies? Anybody who hated you so much that he wanted you to die a grotesque death, handed to you by a roaring rabbit? You did find the rabbit on the garden path this morning, didn't you, sir?"

Moozen pointed. "Yes, out there, sitting in between the crocuses, leering, and as you say, roaring. Giving me the egg."

"Now, which demented mind might have thought of shaping that apparition, sir? Are you dealing with any particularly unpleasant cases at this moment? Any cases that have a twisted undercurrent? Does anyone blame you for something bad that is happening to them?"

Moozen brushed his hair with both hands. "No. I am working on a bad case having to do with a truck driver who got involved in a complicated accident; his truck caught fire and it was loaded with expensive cargo. Both his legs were crushed. His firm is suing the firm that owned the other truck. A lot of money in claims is involved and the parties are becoming impatient, with me mostly. The case is dragging on and on. But if they kill me, the case will become even more complicated, with no hope of settlement in sight."

"Anything else, sir?"

"The usual. I collect bad debts, so sometimes I have to get nasty. I write threatening letters; sometimes I telephone people or even visit them. I act tough—it's got to be done in my profession. Usually they pay, but they don't like me for bothering them."

"Any pastry shops?"

"I beg your pardon?"

"Pastry shops," Grijpstra said. "People who make and sell confectionery. The rabbit was a work of art in a way, made by a professional. Are you suing anybody who would have the ability to create the roaring rabbit?"

"Ornaments!" de Gier shouted. His shout tore at the quiet room. Moozen and Grijpstra looked up, startled.

"Ornaments! Brass ornaments. Ornaments are made from molds. We've got to check his shop."

"Whose shop?" Grijpstra frowned irritably. "Keep your voice down, Sergeant. What shop? What ornaments?"

"Marchant!" de Gier shouted. "Marchant's shop."

"Marchant?" Moozen was shouting, too. "Where did you get that name? *Emil* Marchant?"

Grijpstra's cigar fell on the carpet. He tried to pick it up and it burned his hand, sparks finding their way into the carpet's strands. He stamped them out roughly.

"You know a Mr. Marchant, sir?" de Gier asked quietly.

"No, I haven't met him. But I have written several letters to a man named Emil Marchant. On behalf of clients who are bothered by the noise he makes in his shop. He works with brass, and it isn't only the noise, but there seems to be a stink as well. My clients want him to move out and are prepared to take him to court if necessary. Mr. Marchant telephoned me a few times, pleading for mercy. He said he owed money to the tax department and wanted time to make the money, that he would move out later; but my clients have lost patience. I didn't give in to him—in fact, I just pushed harder. He will have to go to court next week and he is sure to lose."

"Do you know what line of business he is in, sir?"

"Doorknobs, I believe, and knockers for doors, in the shape of lions' heads—that sort of thing. And weather vanes. He told me on the phone. All handmade. He is a craftsman."

Grijpstra got up. "We'll be on our way, sir. We found Mr. Marchant this morning, dead, hanging from a tree in the Amsterdam Forest. He probably hanged himself early this morning, and at some time before, he must have delivered the rabbit and its egg. According to his landlady, he has been behaving strangely lately. He must have blamed you for his troubles and tried to take his revenge. He didn't mean to kill your wife; he meant to kill you. He didn't know that you don't eat chocolate, and he probably didn't even know you were married. We'll check further and make a report. The rabbit's mold is probably still in his shop, and if not, we'll find traces of the chocolate. We'll have the rabbit checked for fingerprints.

"It won't be difficult to come up with irrefutable proof. If we do, we'll let you know, sir, a little later today. I am very sorry all this has happened."

"Nothing ever happens in Amsterdam," de Gier said as he yanked the door of the Volkswagen open, "and when it does, it all fits together immediately."

But Grijpstra didn't agree.

"We would never have solved the case, or rather *I* wouldn't have, if you hadn't thought of the rabbit as an ornament."

"No, Grijpstra, we would have found Marchant's name in Moozen's files."

The adjutant shook his heavy, grizzled head. "No, we wouldn't have checked the files. If he had kept on saying that he wasn't working on any bad cases, I wouldn't have pursued that line of thought. I'd have reverted to trying to find an enemy of his wife. We might have worked for weeks and called in all sorts of help and wasted everybody's time. You are clever, Sergeant."

De Gier was studying a redheaded girl waiting for a streetcar.

"Am I?"

"Yes. But not as clever as I am," Grijpstra said, and grinned. "You work for me. I personally selected you as my assistant. You are a tool in my expert hands."

De Gier winked at the redheaded girl and the girl smiled back. The traffic had jammed up ahead and the car was blocked. De Gier opened his door.

"Hey! Where are you going?"

"It's a holiday, Adjutant, and you can drive this wreck for a change. I am going home. That girl is waiting for a streetcar that goes to my side of the city. Maybe she hasn't had lunch yet. I am going to invite her to go to a Chinese restaurant."

"But we have reports to make, and we've got to check out Marchant's shop. It'll be locked; we have to find the key in his room, and we have to telephone the engineer to let him off the hook."

"I am taking the streetcar," de Gier said. "You do all that. You ate my roll."

Six This, Six That

Quite a pleasant summer morning, Adjutant Grijpstra thought, *with nothing amiss, except that wasp. The outsize bug hums in an irritating manner and is armed with a poisonous sting. What do I know about wasps? Do they attack without warning? Maybe not; maybe they only go for you when you bother them. How do I not bother the opponent? By sitting quietly. While observing, I will see the connection of cause and effect. How the wasp got here in the first place, and how he will leave again, maybe, because the window is open.*

In the same room, on the third floor of Police Headquarters in Amsterdam, opposite the adjutant, sat Sergeant de Gier, feet on his desk, head against the wall. He also observed the wasp. The sergeant's hands were out and ready. De Gier waited. The wasp dove, straight at the sergeant.

Whap.

"There you are," de Gier said. "One enemy removed." He flicked the striped corpse into the wastepaper basket. "At your service. You're welcome."

"Is that the way we're going now?" Grijpstra asked. "Violence in the early morning? Would that be the solution? Does the opponent have to be flattened? Without the slightest consideration?"

"Indeed," de Gier said. "I analyzed the situation and acted at once. Ever been stung by a wasp? This morning that didn't happen. No painful swelling, no throbbing. On the contrary, you're now experiencing a continuing feeling of peace of body. Be happy and thankful."

There was a knock on the door. A well-dressed middle-aged man entered. The detectives got up and shook the man's hand. De Gier found a chair for the client. Grijpstra found paper and ballpoint. "Yes, sir, what can we do for you?"

The man dried his skull with a silk handkerchief. An expensive watch glittered on his hairy wrist. "My name is Vries; I have a complaint."

"Go ahead," Grijpstra said.

The man talked with authority and confusion, in a civilized but nervous manner. Grijpstra wrote; de Gier listened. "That's it?" Grijpstra asked five minutes later. The man nodded. Grijpstra cleared his throat. "Allow me to tell you what I think I've understood. You work for the supermarket chain Zwart Incorporated. You're the chief accountant. Your company has profitable outlets all over the country. Your number one store is right here in Amsterdam, in New South, our fanciest suburb, where the well-heeled live on choice and rare foods only. Before your last checkup the store did well, but now it doesn't. Money seems to have disappeared."

"Millions, Adjutant."

"How much exactly?"

"Two-point-eight million, Adjutant."

"How did you arrive at that figure?"

"Look here," Vries said. "We know what we're buying, right? We know what overall profit percentage we're making, right? So we know what our sales should be, right? Sixteen-point-eight million."

"And the actual sales were?"

"Fourteen million."

"A small mistake perhaps?" de Gier asked. "Accountancy involves bookkeeping, does it not? Did you check the books properly this time? Did you look at the right side of the page?

Administration is always off. Have you been reading the paper lately? Take the government's budget, for instance—billions come and billions go. A billion is a thousand million and you're talking about a mere two-point-eight."

"Do me a favor, Constable," Vries said. "Spare me your amateurish gibberish. Every figure has been chewed and digested. Don't tell me how to look at figures. My computers don't make mistakes and my deduction is correct. Theft is a crime, and you work for the police."

"Theft means a hand reaching in from outside," de Gier said, "and the hand is connected to a masked face under a cap. What we have here is something else—embezzlement, I would say. An employee makes off with money that has been entrusted to him. Embezzlement is worse than theft, for it's nasty and sneaky. It therefore ranks higher on our list."

"I didn't know," Vries said.

"But you do know that your complaint is not related to violence," Grijpstra said. "Who sent you to us? We're Murder and Manslaughter. You're in the wrong room."

"Never mind," Vries said. "I was in the right room before and waited an hour. I demand prompt action. Zwart Incorporated is a pillar of our society. We provide work and feed the people. You're just sitting here. Do something, Adjutant."

"One moment." Grijpstra lifted his phone and dialed a number. "Is that you, Inspector?"

"Yes?" shouted the inspector. "Yes? Yes? *Yes?*"

"Your client strayed into our room, sir. Some lost millions. Do you have a minute? Can I bring him in?"

"A minute?" shouted the inspector. "Minute what? Minute where? Nothing but fraudulence in the land and we're short-staffed. The tax department has lost its safes, the rent-a-cars their cars, the building companies their building materials, and the pension funds their pensions. Railways just phoned; they've lost ten miles of track. My files are stacked to the ceiling. Yesyes. *Yesyes.*"

"A bit busy, sir?"

The telephone cackled and coughed.

"Put the phone down," de Gier said. "I saw the inspector in the canteen just now. He was pouring coffee on his trousers, for he had dropped and broken his cup. He'll be taken away soon and will have leave for the duration."

Vries got up and looked out of the window. "Are you going to do something or not? If not, I'll be going, but not through the door." He looked down. "It's high enough." He lifted his leg and rested it on the windowsill. "Please give me a push."

"Are you all right, sir?" Grijpstra asked.

"Isn't suicide within your duties, Adjutant? Will my death instigate your investigation?"

"Sit down," Grijpstra said. "Tell me what you have done about this case so far."

Vries ticked off his fingers. "Checked programs. Compared results with other stores. Completed stocktaking. Followed flow of incoming goods. Checked cash registers. Screened all members of staff. Worked in the store myself."

"You found nothing?" de Gier asked.

"I found something, a difference of two-point-eight million guilders." Vries produced a calculator from his pocket and placed it on Grijpstra's desk. He pressed its keys. "See how much two-point-eight million is? Lost in a year. You know how much that is in a day? Divided by three hundred? Sundays and holidays discounted?"

De Gier read the result. "Nine three three three three point three three three three."

"A hundred thousand a day," Vries said. "Bit of a leak, I would say."

"Illegal," Grijpstra said, "but rather abstract, don't you think?"

"A mere falsification," de Gier said. "Not our field, Mr. Vries. We'll pass on your complaint if you can't find the time to wait, and I can promise you that a colleague will take your case. A specialist, I'm sure. We're all specialists here. How can we be of use to you if your complaint isn't our specialization? I assure you, sir, we know nothing about groceries."

Vries pushed the sergeant aside and replaced his leg on the windowsill.

"Please," Grijpstra said, "give this another thought. Perhaps it's unnecessary to inflict violence on yourself. Are you sure there is no violence in this complaint?"

"Yes," de Gier said. "Any fights in your office? Someone disappeared perhaps? A secretary maybe? Left an incomprehensible note and never showed her pretty face again?"

Vries thought. "Gennep never showed again."

"Murdered?" Grijpstra asked. "The name means nothing to me and I do have a memory for the lost and unfound."

"Accident,"Vries said. "May this year, on Mallorca. We didn't even know he was vacationing out there. A bachelor, in charge of buying machines for the administration. Slipped off a cliff."

"Were we informed?" Grijpstra asked. "I assume we weren't. Did the Spanish police issue some statement?"

"*Accidente*, Adjutant, that's what we were told."

"Tell us about this Gennep," de Gier said.

"These things shouldn't be said," Vries said, "but I can do without Gennep. He was a maker of messes. He also bought too much. I picked up after him, as far as I could. Gennep didn't know the alphabet. His files were a disaster."

"Purchasing invoices referring to computers and such?"

Vries nodded.

Grijpstra studied his notes. He tore a fresh sheet from his notebook and wrote down in an artistic hand the figures $16.8 - 14 = 2.8$. He held up the sheet. "Like this or not like this?"

"Like that,"Vries said.

"I suggest you leave us now," Grijpstra said. "You may hear from us soon. We'll take on your case."

"Catch the embezzler," Vries said, and walked toward the door. "Please. My boss is a devil who haunts all my moves. He breathes on me during the day and telephones at night. I can't go on like this. I'm going crazy."

De Gier closed the door. "He's crazy now, don't you think? Even so, accountants seem to have a way with figures. My brother-in-law is an accountant, and he can add a page of telephone numbers, in his head, straight from the book. What do we make of this tale? A mistake after all? The electrons got stuck in the conduits so that the profit evaporated in a loose condenser in an odd nook of a computer? How can a deli-supermarket in New South not make a profit?" The telephone rang. The sergeant listened and spoke. He put the phone back and put on his jacket. "Something to do. A drowned bum in the inner harbor. The man is known to us and to most of the local bars. Coming to have a look?"

"No," Grijpstra said. He glanced at his watch. "Ten in the morning—there's still some working day left. I'm going to sniff about and will meet you at the supermarket's office at three in the afternoon."

De Gier left. Grijpstra contemplated. Meanwhile, he looked at his equation: $16.8 - 14 = 2.8$. Figures. Who would know about figures? What do figures show? Aren't they mathematical symbols? Symbols that can be rubbed off a piece of paper? Who rubbed out two-point-eight million guilders? Who blew away a sum of money sufficient, if conservatively invested, to last a luxurious lifetime? And who was still blowing, rubbing, hiding, embezzling?

Who knows about figures? He opened the telephone book and found the Free University's number. "The chief of the Mathematics Department, please." A female voice answered.

"Hello?"

"This is the police, ma'am. Are you a professor?"

"I am."

"Adjutant Grijpstra, Murder Brigade. I would like to speak to you. What would be a good time?"

"Two o'clock," the lady said. "Elize Schoor is the name, the room is 212."

"PROFESSOR SCHOOR," GRIJPSTRA said. "Here is a store with a yearly turnover of fourteen million, but it should be sixteen-point-eight million, as the total purchases and the profit margin are known. What does that mean to you?"

She's attractive, Grijpstra thought. *She has a lovely face. A professor in her early thirties. Step right up, step right up. And while you get closer, listen to her voice. Isn't it pleasantly low, warm, and sympathetic?*

"It means," Elize Schoor said, "something. You may call me Elize. I'm rather fond of dignified, heavyset, old-fashioned-looking gents. Are you married?"

"Yes, Elize."

"Happily?"

"No, Elize."

"I wasn't either, but I'm bored with celebrating celibacy now." She wrote. "Look here. Do you see the equation? There is an unfavorable difference, of two-point-eight million."

"Elize," Grijpstra said heavily, "I had reached that point myself. Please move on a little."

"You see the factor?"

"Factor, Elize?"

"Agent," Elize said. "There's a fixed agent at work here, who's unmasked by the equation. Isn't logic wonderful? Sixteen-point-eight divided by two-point-eight is *six*. Six times the difference equals the original amount. The factor is now known—*six*. Are you following me?"

"Six times this?" Grijpstra asked slowly. "Six times that?"

She frowned and wrinkled her dainty nose. "The layman's vagueness, the amateur's vagary. Logic is hard, since Newton, although since Einstein it has softened a great deal." She bent toward him. Grijpstra inhaled her perfume. "Do you know, Adjutant, that the connection between cause and effect may no longer be valid?"

"So where does that take us?" the adjutant asked.

"Where we were in the beginning." She smiled. "Nowhere, Adjutant."

"Can you calculate nowhere?"

"Hardly." She smiled. "But isn't it better not to pinpoint the illusion? Didn't logic limit us too much?"

Grijpstra flapped his hands gently.

"You don't believe me, Adjutant?"

"But Elize? Common sense?"

She laughed softly. "Do you know how Einstein defined common sense? The conglomeration of prejudice formed before the student's eighteenth year."

Grijpstra got up.

"Must you leave so soon?"

"I move on a flat surface," Grijpstra said. "Within limited time. When the agent is caught, I would be honored to have dinner with you. Would that be possible?"

"Time," Elize said, "in a flat space. That's how hurry is created. From the Past through Now to Later. While Nowhere is timeless." She raised her voice a little. "I cannot stop you. I have no better advice. *Six,* Adjutant; the key is the figure six. Maybe you shouldn't multiply, you might also divide."

"Six," Grijpstra said. "Right. I thank you, Elize."

She walked him to the door. "And when you have your answer, we'll share dinner; that's fine. My place will do?"

"I'll phone," Grijpstra said. He hesitated at the door.

"Six," the professor said. "That's one plus two plus three. Or one times two times three. A holy figure in the kabbala. The Star of David has six points. Kepler thought that six was the essential figure. Ever heard of Johannes Kepler?"

"No, Elize."

"Sixteenth century. An astronomer. We thought then that there were only six planets, and Kepler thought that the relation of their various distances from the sun would hide the key to the universe. He kept calculating with six, and not quite in vain, although his supposition was false."

"Is that right?" Grijpstra asked.

"You know nothing about mathematics?"

"Two parallel lines," Grijpstra said heavily, "intersect in the infinite."

"Your line and mine," Elize said, "and all the others, too. You do have something there. Many a mathematician started with less."

"Bye," Grijpstra said, kneading the door handle.

He walked along a long corridor. "The incalculable," Grijpstra said to the emptiness that surrounded him, "is the enemy that I despise. There has to be clarity, especially at the end.

"And there is," Grijpstra said as he drove to the supermarket, "even before the end. We can rely on facts; if we couldn't, our very existence would be at stake."

Grijpstra parked. "It's three o'clock. De Gier is here, the splendid fellow. When de Gier says he'll be somewhere at three, he'll be somewhere at three."

De Gier wasn't there.

"Twice three is six," Grijpstra said, entered the supermarket, and asked a clerk to take him to the manager's office.

"Jansen," the manager said. "At your service. I was expecting you. The administration telephoned this morning. The police will arrive to take a look. You came alone?"

Grijpstra nodded.

"You heard about the missing sum? There is nothing missing and nothing is amiss. This store flourishes and makes a sizable daily profit. The administration has gone mad. Please sit down, Adjutant."

This is a suspect? Grijpstra thought. *This kindly fellow with the name of the company embroidered on his uniform? This friendly compa-triot with his open face? His close-cropped hair? His blushing cheeks? His clear blue eyes? This trustworthy soul running a spic-and-span store? Why am I wasting my time?*

"Mr. Vries says . . ." Grijpstra said coolly.

"I know, I know." Jansen pointed at his forehead. "An idiot, with permission. I make profit and he makes trouble. It's been like that for months. But there's nothing wrong. The goods come into the store in trailers, and the goods leave the store in brown paper bags. The money the clients give us flows into the registers, and the total is banked at the end of each day. Whatever the computer says is checked by me: Okay, there may be a difference, the ladies who work the registers are human. Half a percent too little today, half a percent too much tomorrow."

"Two-point-eight million," Grijpstra said coolly, "is not half a percent this way or that."

"Nah," Jansen said cheerfully.

"You've worked here long?"

"Thirty years."

"Five times six?"

"Beg pardon?" Jansen asked.

"The figure six? Does *six* mean anything to you?" "What?"

"A sixth of your turnover is lost, it seems."

"Nah," Jansen said. "Is craziness catching? Mr. Vries is nuts, but you still seem sane."

"Can I look around?" Grijpstra asked.

The adjutant counted the girls who arranged packages on shelves. There were six girls, but they were joined by a seventh. He counted the boys who were opening cartons. Three boys. He counted the shelves and the counters, the tables and the cupboards. Too many. The store was busy and getting busier. Pressed by customers from all sides, he counted the registers. There were five registers. Ladies pushed carts against his shins, toddlers climbed over his feet, a passing baby drooled on his sleeve. He looked down into the blouse of a lady who had bent over. Two. He was stabbed by a loaf of French bread. One. A lady grabbed eight bottles of hot sauce. A fat gent swept two candy bars off a shelf. Whoever buys three cans of bean soup gets a fourth as a present. *What am I counting here?* the adjutant thought. *I'm too stupid for this type of job. I have never been able to solve puzzles with figures. Six this, six that? There are no sixes in this store.*

Mr. Jansen came by. "Found anything, Adjutant?"

"I'm leaving," Grijpstra said.

"I'll take you through the back way," Jansen said. "Too much of a crowd up front today. Can't get through in a hurry. Only one set of doors and six streams of clients converge at that point."

"Whoa," Grijpstra shouted.

Jansen stopped in his tracks.

"Six?" Grijpstra asked.

"Sure, Adjutant, look for yourself—six registers, right?"

"I just counted five," Grijpstra said. "I didn't see the sixth because it was blocked by that stack of cartons."

"We've got six registers," Jansen said.

"Can I have a minute with you, in your office?"

Adjutant and store manager faced each other in the office. "You know," Grijpstra said, "I do believe you were lying to me just now."

"Me?"

"You." Grijpstra tore a cigar from its plastic envelope. He tried to blow a ring, in vain. The ragged cloud made Jansen cough.

"Me? Why should I lie?"

"I may seem clever," Grijpstra said cheerfully, "but I had help, professional help from a professor. Did you tell me just now that nothing could be wrong?"

"Nothing is wrong," said Jansen.

"Five times right, once wrong," Grijpstra said triumphantly. "Ha-ha. How simple."

"I don't follow, Adjutant."

Grijpstra observed the moist end of his cigar. "Yes."

"You claim I'm a crook, Adjutant?"

"Only a suspicion," Grijpstra said. "I suspect you of murder. You're under arrest. Don't say anything from here on if you don't want to say anything from here on. Whatever you say now may be used as evidence against you. You can phone your lawyer later on from my office. Take off your dustcoat and put on your jacket. We'll be going."

"Murder?" Jansen whispered.

"I'm sorry," Grijpstra said. "I suspect you of embezzlement, too, of course. I forgot that for a moment because embezzlement is something else. I work for Murder. You see, there are six registers here, but only five connect to your computer. That will be proved in due course, by an expert, an electrician, I suppose."

Jansen smiled. "What nonsense, Adjutant."

"You have another solution?" Grijpstra asked. "One-sixth of your turnover never reaches the terminal. What does it reach, if not your pocket? It has to go somewhere and you're in charge."

"And the murder?" Jansen asked.

"In May," Grijpstra said, "you were on holiday."

"Correct."

"Mallorca?"

"No," Jansen said, "hiking, here in Holland."

"Alone?" Grijpstra asked. "With a backpack? Surrounded by nature? You slept in a tent? A trip we can't check on?"

"Indeed."

"You were in Mallorca," Grijpstra said, "with your accomplice, a man by the name of Gennep. The very same Gennep who didn't file his invoices properly. The very same Gennep who bought too many registers for this store. He bought six, but connected five."

Jansen was silent.

"Just a minute," Grijpstra said. "*You* were the accomplice. Gennep invented the trick. You were a mere pawn. But he needed you, of course, for you had to empty out that sixth register at the end of every working day. Without you the plan couldn't work. So you got your share. Half, isn't that right?"

"Really," Jansen said.

"Are you married?"

"No."

"Neither was Mr. Gennep," Grijpstra said.

"So?"

"I can see it clearly now," Grijpstra said. "Two bachelors, unfettered by family chains, stealing together. And one glorious day you would both take off. Each with half the loot. It wasn't enough for you, was it now? So you kicked your friend Gennep off that cliff. You pointed out the view, Gennep turned away, and you actually kicked his ass."

"Homemade riddles," Jansen said, "homemade answers."

Grijpstra got up. "Not at all. The Spanish police made an accident report. I plan to go to Mallorca myself. You two must have been camping somewhere; there'll be a record. Camps keep names. I'll prove you and Gennep were there together. What did you do with the money?"

"What money?"

"Two-point-eight million guilders," Grijpstra said patiently, "and a lot more has been added to that meanwhile. Three million by now? There'll be papers in your home. You must have bought dollars and made wire transfers to foreign banks. There'll be receipts. Maybe you keep accounts on tax-free islands."

"Sit down," Jansen said.

Wasn't he quick, Grijpstra thought. *Never saw him take that gun from his drawer.* "Put that down," Grijpstra said firmly. "You're making things worse. Threatening a police officer who's in the exercise of his duty."

Jansen got up and locked the door. The lower part of the door was plywood, the upper part glass. Jansen's pistol was still aimed at Grijpstra. "Into the cupboard, Adjutant. I'm going to bind and gag you now. We'll be closing soon, and you won't be found until the cleaners arrive tomorrow morning. Can I have your gun and handcuffs, please?"

"You cannot," Grijpstra said. "You're under arrest and you stay under arrest. Are you quite right in the head?"

Jansen tapped his temple. "Quite sane, thank you. People do underestimate me, however. Take Gennep now, he wanted to go on until we had a total of five million, but that would have taken too long. I have more than half that now, for we both paid into the same account. I can sign alone and I'll be doing that tomorrow. The true criminal works alone. Once I'm across the border, which will take a few hours, I'll be as free as a bird. Let's have your pistol and your handcuffs now."

"Shall I tell you something?" Grijpstra asked. "You may pretend what you like, but you really wanted to be arrested."

Jansen stared.

"You don't even know that yourself, do you now?"

Jansen kept staring.

"Listen. Didn't you draw my attention to the sixth register yourself? Hadn't I told you already that I was fascinated by the figure six?"

Jansen gaped.

"Subconscious guilt feelings," Grijpstra said. "We see it all the time. Suspects propel themselves straight into our hands. Now put that pistol down and follow me."

"I'll have to kill you," Jansen whispered. "You leave me no choice. I'd rather not, but if I do, there's no risk. The pistol doesn't make too much of a bang and it's noisy in the store now; no one will notice. Last chance, Adjutant. Your weapon and your cuffs. I'm not going to fight you; I can kill you from behind my desk."

"No," Grijpstra said.

Jansen released the safety on his pistol and closed one eye.

There was a knock on the door.

"Not now," Jansen shouted.

Someone rattled the handle of the door.

"Go away," Jansen shouted.

De Gier came through the door, following his raised foot, which had splintered glass and plywood.

"Careful," Grijpstra shouted.

De Gier wasn't careful. He jumped on top of Jansen. The sergeant's left arm knocked up Jansen's right. The pistol fired at the ceiling. De Gier grabbed Jansen's arms and twisted them together. Handcuffs clicked. "You're under arrest."

"He's been under arrest for a while now," Grijpstra said. "What kept you so long?"

De Gier picked up the gun, shook out the clip, and dropped both parts into his pocket. He picked up the suspect and put him on a chair. "Complications delayed me. The bum in the harbor had been beaten up by other bums. I had to find the others. There were witnesses, but they kept wandering off. All tied up and taken care of now. Sorry, Adjutant."

"Bah," Grijpstra said. "I counted on you."

"You can't count on anything," de Gier said. "You should know that by now."

"AREN'T WE GREAT?" de Gier asked, leaning against the counter of a bar in the inner city. "Complaint received in the morning, suspect arrested in the late afternoon. Unheard of these days, but we took it in our stride."

"No," Grijpstra said. "That'll be two more jenevers, bartender, please."

"I'm closing," the bartender said, "and as you are what you are, you'll be taking your time. Two more and that's it."

"How do you mean, 'no'?" asked de Gier.

Grijpstra drank and ordered two more. "Armed and threatening suspects should be talked at, not jumped. A quiet conversation usually leads to a complete confession."

"I was just in time," de Gier said.

"They never shoot at me," Grijpstra said. "I'm too nice. The professor thought so, too—I'm having dinner with her tomorrow."

"Tell me about the professor."

Grijpstra explained.

"Wow," de Gier said sadly. "Then what will you do? After dinner, I mean."

"Coffee?" Grijpstra asked. "Cognac perhaps? Help her wash up? Help her keep her distance?"

"You'll be chaotic again," de Gier said enviously, later that night. "You can do that so well. If you keep that up, you'll dance away from your own fate. True existence is true illusion, and you're the only one I know who has learned to ignore what circumstances seem to be offering for free, or am I idealizing you again?"

"You better not drive home," the bartender said.

"But don't you *see?*" the drunken sergeant asked. "If we can undo logic, like the adjutant will do when he refuses the beautiful professor, we free ourselves from self-inflicted chains and . . ."

"I'll have one, too," the bartender said, checking his watch. "Just let me lock the door."

"The wise," the sergeant said, "only *seem* to behave unwisely, but . . ."

"I'm truly unwise," Grijpstra said sadly. "We'll have three more."

De Gier was mumbling. "To undo logic . . . to refuse fate's gifts . . . to accept chance . . . if only we dared . . ."

"Three more," the bartender said.

"Common sense," Grijpstra said, "is my only motivation. To

see what's what. The professor is so beautiful. I will not drag her down to my level."

"Poor Grijpstra."

"No, no, you see that wrong. On the contrary. When I'm alone, I'm safe. Strengthened by common sense, following the line of logic, adhering to the law, reasoning clearly, moving in a straight direction reaching B from A . . ."

"You really think you're doing that?"

"I do." Grijpstra smiled modestly. "But I do need help from time to time, from people with more sense, like that graceful professor—from you even, for you're so quick." Grijpstra sighed. "She presented me with the figure six."

They stumbled home together. It was early in the morning. There was no one about. "To be certain is good," Grijpstra said. "I'm certain at times. Like now. Nothing can happen to us now. When emptiness surrounds me, there can be no threat. I so like to be sure. To go home in a void. Can you follow me so far?"

"No," de Gier said. "And I don't agree either. Chaos is all around us. Anything can happen and it will, as you'll see."

Grijpstra pulled his arm out of de Gier's. It was time to say good-bye. He stumbled and embraced a lamppost. His feet slid away and he pulled the lamppost toward him. The lamppost fell, on top of Grijpstra.

"WHAT?" THE COMMISSARIS asked the next morning.

"The lamppost fell on top of Grijpstra, sir," de Gier said. "The adjutant was drunk and failed to step aside. The lamppost was quite heavy. Grijpstra suffered three bruised ribs. The ambulance picked him up."

"And?"

"He's in the hospital, sir, doing fairly well."

"Lampposts don't fall over," the commissaris said.

"This one did, sir. Dogs, you know?"

"Hm?" the commissaris asked.

"Urinated," de Gier said.

"Are you withholding information?" the commissaris asked.

"I do believe in the unexpected," the sergeant said, "although there's always a reason afterward. Factors combine in an unpredictable pattern, but there will be a connection if you follow the pattern in reverse. There are a lot of dogs in that particular part of the city and they all seem to prefer that particular post. Urine contains acid, and enough acid will eat through the heaviest metal. It can take a while, in this case a hundred years perhaps, but once the adjutant grabbed that particular post at that particular moment, he had to bruise three ribs."

"So?" the commissaris asked.

De Gier spread his hands.

The commissaris began to smile. "I see your point. Our very own Grijpstra comes along, believing only in the obvious, but behind the obvious hides the nonobvious, and it's just as true?"

The commissaris laughed.

De Gier frowned furiously.

"Poor Grijpstra," the commissaris said, "but he did solve his case."

"By chance," de Gier said.

"And choice," said the commissaris. "But what else can we choose but chance?

The Sergeant's Cat

"A shot in the night," Sergeant de Gier of the Amsterdam Municipal Police was saying as he put on his jacket, "does break the routine rather pleasantly." He faced the mirror next to the door and arranged his silk scarf. Adjutant Grijpstra agreed and pushed the sergeant aside. The adjutant held up his left arm and attempted to smooth the fold under his armpit. De Gier raised his arm as well. "My bulge is worse. The new gun is too large."

In the elevator, Grijpstra smiled. It had been a quiet evening, with coffee in the canteen and friendly conversation with colleagues. De Gier complained contentedly next to him, still on the subject of the new oversize gun. Grijpstra acknowledged his assistant's objections, repeating them in part. The new service handgun was the Walther P-5, and although it was lightweight and aimed well—very well, up to two hundred meters, so Grijpstra stated—the weapon suited the plainclothes detective badly, for it was too long.

"And too wide," said de Gier. "All right for the uniformed branch—they show the gun—but we're supposed to hide it."

The elevator door opened, offering a view of a sterile corridor wherein neatly dressed constables marched to and fro. Their bright blue tunics contrasted sharply with the light grey corridors. A lady cop came along on long slender legs, her bosom gently bouncing. Her hair was long and blond, curling from under her small round hat. Grijpstra observed her approvingly. He was working on a painting at home in his spare time. The painting had been sketched in outline and now needed color. The policewoman had lilac-colored lips. Grijpstra had chosen the shade for one of the flowers in the foreground of the painting.

She nodded at Grijpstra and greeted de Gier. "Hi, Rinus."

"Hi, Jane," said the sergeant.

"Jane?" Grijpstra asked when they crossed the inner courtyard of Police Headquarters. "Isn't Jane a somewhat prosaic name for such a luscious woman? Where are we going?"

De Gier got into the unmarked car and opened Grijpstra's door. He waited until Grijpstra had forced his bulk into the car's interior. "What's wrong with Jane? It's a good name. She's a good woman, too. We're headed for the southern suburbs."

The car stopped at the first set of traffic lights. Grijpstra tore at the cellophane cover of a cigar. His eyebrows were still raised as he looked at the sergeant again.

De Gier made the car surge forward, following bicycles whose riders were impatient and wouldn't wait for the lights to change. "The shot in the night was fired in Ouborg, an exclusive area for the well-heeled."

"And Jane?"

The car was half on the sidewalk, speeding to pass clogged traffic, and de Gier had to pay attention. Finally he reached a square offering more space. "Jane?"

"You said she's a good woman," Grijpstra said patiently. "How do you know? Did you try? With success?"

"Not yet." De Gier avoided more traffic lights by crossing over to the part of the boulevard reserved for streetcars, ambulances, and patrol cars. "I think she's good, but it might just be that she's not prepared to prove my point." He looked at Grijpstra triumphantly. "A shot in the night." He hunched his shoulders and lowered his chin so that he could look up and admire tree branches adorning a starry sky. "It's a lovely night, but ripped apart by a shot. That's what the lady on the phone said. She lives next door, in another small palace. She also said that a car drove away after the shot had been fired—an expensive car, silver-colored. She didn't note the license number." The unmarked car sped up again. "And she heard a woman scream."

"What do you know," Grijpstra said, and glanced over his shoulder. "And look at that."

De Gier looked into his rear mirror. A patrol car had detached itself from the parking lot in front of a suburban police station and was following them, flashing its lights, its siren howling.

"Ignore them," Grijpstra said, sucking on his cigar. He checked the speedometer. A hundred kilometers an hour. He listened to the scream of tires. He nodded.

"You're nodding," de Gier said. "You usually complain when I drive too fast. Are you changing?"

"Everything changes," shouted Grijpstra. He had to shout because the patrol car was now riding next to them.

De Gier braked.

"Why?" Grijpstra wondered aloud. The patrol car stopped ahead and two cops tumbled onto the pavement.

"Because their car is brand-new and ours is falling apart," de Gier said. "Old cars don't drive very fast. They were cutting me off."

"Ho-ho-ho!" the cops shouted. "Speeding, dear sir? And failing to stop when followed by a patrol car flashing its lights, with its siren howling. Are you blind? Are you deaf?"

De Gier showed his police card. Grijpstra loosened the microphone from under the dashboard and held it up by way of proof.

"Detectives, eh?" the cop on the left said.

"Can we come, too?" asked the cop on the right.

"Something nice?" the cop on the left asked.

"Be our guests," de Gier said, "as long as you don't make so much noise. It's close. Ouborg. Do you happen to know where that may be?"

The patrol car guided them. The address was in a lane overshadowed by plane trees, with spacious homes on each side. A windmill stood behind the trees, artistically cutting the night sky with its sails.

A lady came running toward them, waving her arms.

"I DON'T THINK that's legal," one of the cops said a little later.

"That's breaking and entering," the other cop said. "You need a permit, signed by a commissaris."

"The hell," de Gier said, hammering on a window with the butt of his gun. "I've looked through the side window and I've seen a lady on a bed. She has no clothes on and she's bleeding from the head."

"That won't work," Grijpstra said, "the new gun is mostly made of light plastic. It won't break glass. Use this rock."

"JANE," GRIJPSTRA SAID.

"I beg your pardon?" asked de Gier.

"She looks like Jane," Grijpstra said. "Very much like Jane, and she's dead. Sit down, Sergeant. You always faint when in the presence of a corpse. Ah, it's suicide, see? She's still holding the gun. There's a glass. She had a drink first and then she shot herself through the temple. But why is she naked?"

"Can I phone?" one of the policemen asked. "I know Headquarters' secret number."

The other cop wandered about the room. "Posh," he commented. "That painting is by Edward Hopper, a famous American, worth a year's wages—two maybe. Look at the books. The collected works of a number of geniuses, at fifty guilders a volume. What would that antique couch cost?"

"The house alone costs a million," Grijpstra said. "Yes? What is it, Sergeant?"

De Gier stood in the open door to the garden, nicely silhouetted against the dark, clear sky, flanked by small poplars. He was a tall man, narrow-waisted, wide-shouldered. His mustache was modeled on those of high-ranking cavalry officers a hundred years back. His eyes were large, brown, softly pleading. His cheekbones were pronounced, his hair thick and curly. He looked good framed by the open garden door until he staggered and grabbed a post.

"Don't look at the lady," Grijpstra said. She had been attractive, but she was bleeding now and her eyes stared strangely. "Did you see anything worth noting?"

"Yes," de Gier said. "There's a car in the garage and it's burned out. It was a Camaro, I think, or a Corvette, resembling a fish of prey. Chevrolet makes those cars, for the rich and happy people."

"S o   w h a t   d o we know?" Grijpstra asked three hours later in the car on the way back to the inner city, driving quietly through empty streets, silent but for the chirruping of birds and the squeak of a paperboy's roller skates.

"That the lady is dead," de Gier said, "and that the doctor isn't pleased. The fingerprint gentlemen aren't pleased either." He held up a finger. "The doctor seems to think she was drugged." He held up a second finger. "The fingerprint gentlemen checked her hand. They think she didn't fire the gun. If she had, the porridge they smeared on her palm would have discolored— because of the fumes of the exploding cartridge, mixed with her sweat and the oil of the gun."

"Modern methods," Grijpstra said unhappily. Grijpstra was an older man, in a forbidding three-piece dark blue suit softened a little by thin white stripes.

"Adjutant," de Gier said, "we do have modern methods and they're sometimes known to work. If the corpse didn't kill herself, then somebody else did. The murderer shot her and took her hand afterward and inserted the gun in it."

"Why did she take her clothes off?" Grijpstra asked. "Did she make love to the killer? The doctor wasn't sure."

"He used modern methods, too, our killer," de Gier mused, "and then he drove away in his silver-colored car. But we have found that the lady's lover is also the owner of the house. He's a man by the name of Wever and he doesn't drive a silver car. He hasn't been home for a few days. And we know the lady's name, which is Cora Fischer."

"Drive on," Grijpstra said. "I don't want to go to Headquarters. The building is bleak at this hour, in the early morning."

"Where would sir like to be driven to?"

"To an all-night café on a picturesque canal where we can drink gin and beer and smoke black cigars. If we get drunk, we'll leave the car and stagger home."

"RIGHT," DE GIER said. "Here's your beer and here's your gin and here's my coffee."

"Is there cognac in your coffee?" Grijpstra asked. "What a lovely café this is. Behold the heavy rotten beams supporting a smoky ceiling. Take a look at that criminal-looking bartender and that small crowd of hopeless alcoholics. Isn't Amsterdam a beautiful city?"

"There's cognac in my coffee," de Gier said. "Let me wish you good health. Cora Fischer. First she was loved and later killed. This is a choice crime and I'm glad I work for the police. And you know, she looked rather relaxed. I hardly think there was a fight. Was she drugged or not?"

"I'M NOT QUITE sure," the pathologist said some six hours later. "Sit down over there, Sergeant. The autopsy will supply us with tangible information. I haven't seen you here before. Are you sure you can take it? I'll have to cut and saw."

"He can't take it," Grijpstra said, "and I don't think I can either, but the law says there should be some officer of the law here to watch you. But the inspector is otherwise engaged, and the commissaris has been told to rest in the morning. Please go ahead."

"I'm going out for a walk," said de Gier. "It's a nice day and I hardly ever visit cemeteries. I'll walk about for a while and study flower arrangements on tombstones. I'll be back when you're done."

Grijpstra watched how the pathologist, in a white coat and a plastic apron, made the incision: two long cuts from the shoulders to the navel and a shorter one from the lower belly to the pubic area. Another doctor, a clone of the first, cut the scalp in order to bare the skull. One doctor cut while the other sawed with an electric gadget that sprayed sawdust against his mask. *Why don't I think of something else?* Grijpstra thought. *This is not appetizing. They are damaging her, as if she isn't damaged enough already.*

The lady's consort, Grijpstra thought, is called Wever, and he owns the villa, worth a million, which is about as much as I can make in twenty years. The man is extraordinarily wealthy, although he isn't an attorney, or a dentist, or even a registered accountant. He's rich because he owns illegal gambling houses and a drugs-and-sex joint in the fashionable little seaport of Noordwijk close by. His name is known to us, but we haven't been able to arrest him so far. He doesn't pay taxes because he cooks his books. He's a gangster, an evil spirit from the underworld. With the old police gun we couldn't shoot him because the bullets would have been stopped in his fat. With the new gun we could kill him easily, but we don't because that would be illegal. He's known to us because our undercover detectives visit brothels and are equipped with large ears. We've heard that about a year ago he took a new mistress, a certain Cora Fischer, the ex-model of a famous painter, the ex-star of art-loving society.

The pathologists handled their knives like indifferent but knowledgeable butchers. As they cleaned the parts taken from the body with fresh water bubbling from a hand shower and dumped them into dishes and bottles, one of them spoke in a loud, monotonous voice, reporting his observations to a clerk, positioned at a safe distance. "Liver," the pathologist said, "slightly enlarged and discolored." He weighed the liver and announced the figure. The clerk wrote the figure down.

Where was I? Grijpstra thought. Right. Cora impressed the arty and the affluent. But the famous painter tired of her and turned her out of his turn-of-the-century loft. She was without employment, but she was still attractive. Wever welcomed her, and Cora became the hostess of his club in Noordwijk and sometimes of his illegal blackjack joints. Or so said the undercover detectives who live in the underworld and whisper through telephones and slip letters under Headquarters' doors.

"Well?" Grijpstra asked.

"We still can't be sure," the second pathologist said. "We'll have to do some tests. She didn't inject, that's for sure, but she did sniff cocaine. She drank a bit too much and she smoked."

"Can I smoke?" Grijpstra asked.

"I'd rather you didn't."

"I think I will all the same," Grijpstra said. "This is a good cigar and I'm a bit nervous."

"I'll open a window," the doctor said, doing so. "Smoking can kill you, you know."

"Is that right?" Grijpstra said. "So what killed her?"

The doctor smiled. "A bullet through the head. No doubt about it. And her vanity. She was a lovely dame."

"WELL?" DE GIER asked.

"They're still not sure," Grijpstra said, "but there was alcohol in her stomach, mixed with sleeping draught. It's very pleasant out here."

"I saw three thrushes," de Dier said, "and a crow. Some chicka-dees, too, and a magpie. Some of the tombstones bear impressive poetry. And I saw a gent with a motor helmet under his arm, hiding behind sunglasses. He must have been a boxer, if his flattened nose is a clue, and is still an athlete judging by his bouncy gait. Look, there he is, riding away on a four-cylinder motorcycle."

Grijpstra looked. "That's a very large gent. Six foot six, I would think. What was he doing here?"

"I'm beginning to think I know," de Gier said. "He looked at me for quite a while with much interest . . . Does she still look like Jane?"

"*MISTER WEVER*," DE Gier said four hours later, "listen, and listen good. There are some facts. One of the facts is that your reputation stinks. Your gambling joints and your brothel are no good. You're a pimp and a drug dealer."

"Facts," Wever said, sitting uncomfortably on a straight-backed chair in Grijpstra's office, placing his hands on his knees so that the middle fingers rested on the immaculate creases of his tailor-made sharkskin pants, "should be proved. You've never proved anything regarding me. You haven't done that because no drugs have ever been found in the establishments I own. So what's all this empty talk, eh?"

"I'm telling you," de Gier said, "that you're a curse on our society. There's another fact." The sergeant held up a finger. "Your girlfriend was murdered—in your house, on your bed."

Wever showed the gold stuck in his whitish gums. "So what?"

De Gier said, "She didn't shoot herself—our modern methods say so."

Grijpstra nodded. "And someone had mixed a sleeping pill into her drink."

Wever adjusted his hairpiece. "So you claim. But why should I believe you? Why should the judge believe you? So Cora took a tranquilizer—she often did, she was a highstrung woman, you know. She worried a lot, whether I loved her or if I didn't. And I didn't, of course, because I have this other lady, in my club in Noordwijk, who is younger and more appetizing. I was spending nights with Yvette, so Cora shot herself."

De Gier had become angry. He was hitting his desktop with the flat of his hand. "And burned her own car? No, sir, *you* burned her car and later you had her killed. Now listen to me—"

"But what if I don't want to listen to you?" Wever asked. "You're impolite and I'm a gentleman of sorts. I wasn't home. Alibi, don't you know? Are you familiar with the word? She shot herself." Wever got up. He was a big man; he kept getting up.

"Sit down, Mister Pimp," de Gier said. "If you leave this office, you'll be arrested in the corridor, for not paying traffic tickets. And we'll close your joints."

Wever sat down. "What's wrong with my gambling establishments? Blackjack's okay. The court says so and the Supreme Court is about to confirm it. Blackjack has to be played with intelligence; that's why you could never play it. I wasn't home; I can prove I wasn't home. It ain't me."

Grijpstra looked up. "Can't you conjugate verbs correctly? Can't you do anything right?"

Wever got angry, too. Sweat trickled down his cheeks on its way to his many chins.

"What happened was this," de Gier said. "First you were proud of Cora. Because she was so lovely, and so famous. You installed her in your palace and she was the queen of your club—people pointed her out to each other. You bought her a car worth forty thousand. Clothes. Jewelry. She was a *nouveauté*. But after a while she wasn't anymore. But she was still around, costing money. You're a businessman in a way and like balancing things out. If you lose money you have to gain it back again. So—"

Wever put up his hands. Sunlight reflected from his varnished nails. "That's enough."

"Not at all," de Gier said. "We're after the truth. So what was Cora to do? She had to smuggle dope. The Camaro nosed into Paris and back again, once a week. Cora carried cocaine and heroin in her pants, in her cleavage. She slipped easily back and forth through the checkpoints, the Customs agents smiling at her. But then she wouldn't go anymore."

"No?" Wever asked. "Changed her mind, did she? Whatever for?"

"Let's not be funny," de Gier said. "She stopped smuggling your drugs because she realized drugs are bad for people. Cora was never a bad girl. You made her bad, but she wanted to be good again."

Wever sighed. *"Good?* That phony, hysterical broad?"

De Gier stirred his coffee. The room became quiet.

"Hello?" Grijpstra asked.

"Yes," de Gier said. "Then you destroyed her car a few nights back. The fire department came, but they couldn't save the Camaro—that classy car she liked so much, gone forever. Insured, but that didn't help her since you weren't planning on replacing it. You threatened her, right?"

"Right," Wever said softly. "Suppose, as long as we're playing this game together, that what you say is true. It isn't, but okay. Even if it were true, you can't prove I killed her. You can't because I didn't kill her. I wasn't home."

"*You* weren't," de Gier said, "but you sent your right hand— a gent by the name of Freddie. A big gent—bigger than you, but with a good build. You're horribly fat, you know. Freddie isn't, but he does have a fat head, and the chips in it aren't very complicated. Kill, you say, and Freddie kills. He gets into a silver car and shoots the lady. He also rides a motorbike, by the way."

"I'm going," Wever said. "You're not only wasting my time, you're spoiling it. I'll pay my traffic tickets on the way down. Good-bye."

"YOU WEREN'T REALLY angry?" Grijpstra asked.

"He was," de Gier said.

"Yes," Grijpstra agreed. "And I believe you're right. I don't particularly care for bluffing, but we sometimes have to do it. How could you know that Freddie is the motorbike rider."

De Gier shrugged. "I sensed evil in the man and checked our files. The undercover branch sent in a snapshot of Freddie once. We've got nothing on him, but we know he works for Wever. He doesn't go to cemeteries because he likes looking at tombstones. He's an artist in a way. He follows up on his work. Or maybe he's horribly crazy. Perhaps this was a special job for him, because Cora was such a beautiful woman. She was naked, remember? He had her, then he killed her. He felt a link that pulled him right to the cemetery—to me, the avenger. I'm an angel of light; he's a demon of darkness."

"A farfetched conclusion."

"Wasn't I right?" de Gier said. "Didn't you say so just now?"

Grijpstra murdered his half-smoked cigar with a spark-whirling stump in the ashtray. "I never went in for mysticism. It doesn't get anybody anywhere. You were right, certainly, but we're where we've been so often—nowhere. Wever wasn't home, he really wasn't. And Freddie will say that he wasn't in Ouborg either. There'll be witnesses in Noordwijk claiming that they were playing cards with him all night. And the silver-colored car was borrowed for the occasion, or stolen, or the license plates weren't right. No."

"Coffee and cake?" de Gier asked.

"HELLO, JANE," HE said in the canteen.

"Can I join you?" the female officer asked.

Grijpstra jumped up. De Gier fetched a chair. "You know," he said, "it wasn't wrong what I did. I got him rattled. I made waves in his soul. Didn't Newton say that action provokes reaction? I made him angry. Wever has lost his cool—he's got to slip up now."

"What are you two talking about?" Jane asked. "Don't I get any coffee and cake?"

"You're a sweetheart," de Gier said. "You're actually asking. Feminists get their own coffee. You're a real woman and a beautiful woman, too. I can hardly believe your beauty. You instill tender and protective feelings in my deepest mind."

"The sergeant," Grijpstra said, "likes to work on people's feelings."

"I love it," Jane said. She pushed back her chair and crossed her legs.

"You have good legs," Grijpstra said. "It's a pity I never paint human figures. If I did, I'd ask you to model for me."

"Model," de Gier said, returning with Jane's coffee. "Cora was a model. It seems that the universe is unlimited in its manifestations, but deeper reflection might show that everything is a variation on a single theme."

"What was that?" Jane asked.

"You look like Cora," Grijpstra said.

FOUR HOURS LATER de Gier's apartment buzzer buzzed. The sergeant put his cat on the floor, placed his book on the table, and opened the door.

"Evening," his visitor said. "My name is Freddie."

Freddie sat down. The cat jumped from the chair.

"My cat was sitting there," de Gier said.

"Stupid cat."

"Yes?"

"Listen here," Freddie said. "I've come to bring you money. Here you are." He put an envelope on de Gier's book.

"What's in that?"

"Ten thousand. There'll be more later, but then we will require your services. This is a present. You don't even have to *not* do something because you can't do anything anyway. You have no proof."

"You're not providing me with news," de Gier said.

"You're fuzz," Freddie said, "and fuzz is for sale. Because you're good fuzz, I bring you money straightaway. The fuzz we have so far is little fuzz. They're okay for a bit of information now and then, like so that we won't be there when you're preparing a raid. But it would be nice to have some big fuzz on the payroll, too."

"Yes?"

Freddie smiled. "Yes."

De Gier lit a cigarette.

"You're not offering anything?" Freddie asked.

"No," de Gier said. "You're unwelcome company. Maybe I don't want your money either. Maybe I'll shoot you in a minute or so. I don't want to fight you. This is a small apartment and we'll break the furniture."

"Once we start fighting," Freddie said, "I'll break you, too. The boss has lost his temper. You've been rude to him. The boss likes people to be polite and helpful. So he's not giving you a choice. You've got to work for us and you've got to take our money. If you refuse, we'll be nasty."

"Like what?" de Gier asked.

The cat walked past Freddie's leg. Freddie picked up the cat and turned it over. He slid a stiletto from his pocket. The point of the stiletto scratched the cat's chin. The cat purred. "Stupid cat," Freddie said. "I can open him up, like they opened up Cora today. But I won't sew him up again. I'll leave him here, open."

"Maybe you shouldn't do that," de Gier said.

Freddie pushed the cat from his lap. "Not yet, but I might later on if you happen to be disobedient. I'll kill your cat and your old mother and anybody else you care for. If I happen to be busy, someone else will do it. The boss is rich, unbelievably rich. He can buy anybody. And whoever he buys makes more money for him."

"Yes?"

Freddie grinned, slowly and completely. "Cocaine and heroin prices are going up again, and the customers carry the money in without the slightest prodding. There's no end to it. Money is good. It buys good cars and good trips. Look at my color."

"Nice tan," de Gier acknowledged.

"Bermuda. I was there last week. I'll go again. I've been in the Seychelles too and in Indonesia. You can take nice trips, too. You can use this money."

"Not a bad idea."

"I'm glad you agree." Freddie got up.

"Good-bye," de Gier said, and closed the door behind Freddie. He waited until he heard the elevator going down and sprinted down the staircase. He was outside before Freddie got out of the elevator.

"*Psst,*" de Gier said.

Freddie approached him with his legs astride and his fists up.

"Not here," de Gier said. "We don't want to make a spectacle of ourselves. Over there, in the park."

"You can't be serious," Freddie said.

They crossed the street together. It was late. The sky held few clouds. The moon cast delicate shadows on the lawns. Ducks in the pond woke for a moment and murmured sleepily. A swan bobbed, propelled by one foot. De Gier walked next to Freddie, his hand on his back. De Gier was tall, but he wasn't a giant. He exercised regularly, one evening a week, sometimes two. He had a black belt in judo.

Freddie was a giant. He also exercised regularly and he had a high grade in karate. He could split bricks. Freddie drank heavily, de Gier moderately. They both smoked.

"I'll take you apart," Freddie said. "But not altogether. The boss likes things to develop slowly. He warns first."

De Gier smiled. They passed a tree, and a thrush opened an eye and tried a slow trill.

"What's funny?" Freddie asked.

"That I don't give warning," de Gier said. He kicked and hit simultaneously. His foot hit Freddie's shin and his hand made contact with his belly button. Freddie almost fell. De Gier half circled him and extended an arm, holding his waist in a friendly manner. He shuffled sideways until his foot touched Freddie's, then he swung swiftly.

"Hey," Freddie shouted as he fell.

"Here you are," de Gier said, and closed Freddie's eyes with his fist. Then he hit him on the chin.

"YES?" THE LADY in charge of ambulance dispatch asked.

"In the Southern Park," de Gier said, "just north of the larger pond, there's a man on the gravel. He's been knocked down and he's unconscious."

"Did you phone the police?"

De Gier replaced the hook. "No," he said to the quiet telephone. "They know my voice."

He picked up the phone again.

"Yes?" Detective-Constable-First-Class Simon Cardozo, temporarily attached to the Criminal Investigation Department of the Amsterdam Municipal Police, said.

"Listen," de Gier said. "My cat has been threatened."

"Tabriz?" asked Cardozo.

"I have only one cat. Can she stay with you?"

"For long?" Cardozo asked.

"I'll bring her over now."

"I'll fetch her," Cardozo said. "You don't have a car. Give me five minutes."

A BURGLAR CYCLED into suburban Ouborg about two hours later. The burglar broke into the mansion where Cora Fischer had lived such a luxurious life. Nobody was home, and the burglar found a suitcase and filled it with clothes and jewelry. He cycled away again and was spotted by a cruising patrol car. The car didn't stop.

"Three o'clock in the morning?" the constable next to the driver asked. "A cyclist with a suitcase?"

"His lights were in order," the driving constable said. "You don't see that very often. A cyclist with working lights is okay."

"WELL, WHAT DO you know?" Wever said about nineteen hours later. "Bit of a fool, aren't you, Sergeant? Do you know that Freddie has been admitted to the hospital?"

De Gier sat on a low leather chair. He drank beer. "Nice place you've got here, but too expensive, I would think."

"Join us," Grijpstra said. "You interfere with my view of the musicians."

Wever sat down. He snapped his fingers. A girl brought drinks. She was a nice-looking girl in a miniskirt and high heels. She wasn't wearing anything else. "To think," Grijpstra said, "that Noordwijk was a rustic little port once and that there were sailors and fishermen in the cafés, smoking stone pipes through their beards. To think," Grijpstra said dreamily, "that their wives and girlfriends wore blue calico underwear right down to the knees."

"Listen," Wever said, "Freddie tells me he forgot an envelope in the sergeant's apartment."

"One of the reasons for our visit," de Gier said, and put the envelope on the table. Wever picked it up. A combo consisting of a pianist, a drummer, and a bass player played a European version of "This Here."

"Is your paneling rosewood?" Grijpstra asked.

De Gier observed the suspect. He saw that Wever had a soft face, not soft as in sensitive, but soft as in weak. *He had been doing too well for too long*, de Gier thought. *His spine is dissolving. He was a tough guy once but now his muscles are yellow fat.*

"Don't get up," de Gier said.

Wever's big fingers, flashing with diamonds, clamped onto the side of his chair. His buttocks rose off his cushion. "Why not? This is my place—I can do what I like."

"You're under arrest." De Gier sat. "Sit down."

Wever's body flopped back onto the cushion. "Arrest for what?"

"For serious suspicions. I suspect that you're dealing in drugs, that you make money out of prostitution, and that you allow your customers to engage in illegal gambling."

Wever's cheeks rippled. He gestured. Grijpstra watched the moist spots on the armrests of Wever's chair.

"Are you crazy?" Wever asked. "This is today. Today anything goes. What's wrong with keeping whores? I have a sex club here, not a brothel. Brothels are out. And so is the law!" He looked about him. He pointed at guests. "And why did you bring all these cops? Do you think I can't smell cops even when they dress up like real people?" He began to get up again.

"Down, boy," Grijpstra said. "Didn't the sergeant just tell you that you're under arrest?"

"I've got to go to the restroom."

"Need a sniff, do you?" Grijpstra said. "That won't help you now. Those days are gone. You've done too much. You even tried to bribe my colleague."

"Why not?" Wever asked. "Aren't you all corrupt these days? Even a commissaris can be bought. Corruption has become a way of life."

"Not quite," Grijpstra said. "The ten thousand is back in your pocket. Cat-threatening is bad, too—we'll have you for that as well."

"And," de Gier said, "you had your girlfriend killed. That's really going too far."

"Proof?" Wever asked.

"Quiet," de Gier said. "That piano player is good. Let me listen for a while. I'd like another drink, too . . . Miss?"

Wever didn't look happy, but the general atmosphere improved. The topless waitress brought a round of drinks, and then more. Wever was allowed a visit to the restroom under Grijpstra's supervision. The adjutant frisked his suspect and confiscated one gram of cocaine and a stiletto. The combo, encouraged by applause from the plainclothesmen and the other guests, improved. The pianist played meticulously, although he increased his speed. The drummer was also a percussionist, doing well on cowbells and wooden gongs. The bass remained steady, providing a strong beat.

"Some flute maybe?" Grijpstra asked.

De Gier produced a piccolo from his inside pocket, deftly joining its parts. He got up and repeated the main theme of the song. The audience cheered. De Gier tried an arpeggio, then improvised freely. The combo adjusted easily.

Grijpstra studied Wever. *He's afraid.* Grijpstra thought. *Things are going well. De Gier has set up the scene properly and we're getting close. But now . . . but now . . .*

The moment came. The revolving door introduced a tall but slender woman, a lady in the full glory of her beauty. Her hair had been elaborately arranged. She was dressed charmingly in a linen gown hand-painted with Chinese designs. Jewels bedecked her hands and neck. She sat down in the rear of the establishment.

De Gier still played his flute, encouraged by the musicians and the audience. Grijpstra waited. Wever looked about. He finally saw the woman. The light was dim—he could see the lady's general appearance but no fine details. "Cora," he whispered.

De Gier bowed and put his flute down. Grijpstra sucked on his cigar. He waved with his free hand. A young man with unruly curly hair and dressed in a threadbare corduroy suit got up and walked toward him. "Cardozo," Grijpstra said, "it's time." He produced a document, unfolded it, and handed it to Wever. "This is our permit to search the premises. You stay here."

Wever sweated, cursed, and muttered four-letter words.

Grijpstra waved again. Two men jumped up. "Sit here," Grijpstra told them, "and make sure the suspect doesn't move."

He and de Gier left the table as the two men sat down.

"YOU KNOW," DE Gier said a quarter of an hour later, "if we don't find anything, we've wasted our time."

"No negativity now," Grijpstra said. "We found the roulette, didn't we? Roulette is illegal. We have a charge."

"Nah," de Gier said. "The roulette wasn't being used. Wever'll provide some excuse. He can afford the best lawyers. Even the corruption charge won't stick. I want him for dealing in heroin—and for murder, of course."

They were in a large room, leaning against exotic wainscoting, their hands in their pockets, their chins on their chests. Plainclothes cops wandered about, picking up objects and putting them down again. "Adjutant?" Cardozo asked. "Detective-Constable-First-Class?" Grijpstra asked.

"Look," Cardozo said, pointing at an oak shelf above the open fire. "I noticed it," Grijpstra said, "That's a small statue of a reclining Eastern goddess. We've seen the type before. They're hollow and contain heroin when they cross the border, but by the time we see them, they're always empty."

"They're usually hollow," Cardozo agreed, "but that one is solid."

De Gier walked over and picked up the statuette. He showed it to the adjutant. "Cardozo is right—it's solid."

"Exactly the same type as the ones we've found before," Cardozo said, "in Chinese restaurants and junk stores and so forth. They've always been hollow, but we've found traces of heroin inside. This one is solid." He weighed it on his hand. "A litde over two pounds, I would say."

"Odd," said de Gier, scratching the statue.

"Careful," said Cardozo, "I tried that, too. The stuff flakes easily."

"Gypsum doesn't flake so easily," Grijpstra said.

"It isn't gypsum," Cardozo said.

"If you're right," de Gier said, "you have a fortune in your hands. A million maybe—at street level, that is."

"I am right," Cardozo said. "And we are in a retail outlet."

Grijpstra whistled—and the room filled up with cops.

"The treasure has been found," Grijpstra said. "Have all employees arrested and have extra staff alerted at Headquarters."

"The suspect downstairs," one of the men said, "seems to be suffering a mental breakdown. He's accusing himself of committing the murder of a certain Cora Fischer, and keeps pointing at our Jane."

SERGEANT DE GIER, about ten hours later, admitted that the course he had taken, and subsequently helped to direct, could be defined as irregular. He made his statement in the commissaris's office. The commissaris was facing him from behind his imposing desk. Grijpstra stood near the window, admiring a geranium in bloom.

"Yes," the commissaris said, "but that fellow Freddie had been threatening your cat, which is an extenuating circumstance. The results are excellent, fortunately. I hear that Wever has not retracted his confession."

"Freddie has confessed, too," Grijpstra told the geranium. "It seems that he's been under some stress that has weakened his nerves. He also objects to being called the murder weapon by his boss."

"Your cat is not too disgruntled?" the commissaris asked.

"She's doing well, sir," de Gier said. "Cardozo took good care of her and she's home again."

There Goes Ravelaar

It was a late-summer day, crisp under a pale sun suspended within a circle of lifting fog. An old-model Volkswagen, fat and round, purred happily through the Amstel Dike's curves, headed for the city's limits. The driver, a tall, lean man with an angular face adorned by curly hair and a huge handlebar mustache, admired a flock of ducks, coming in low above the river. As the car accelerated, the passenger, an older, heavy man, flapped his large hands while he woke up.

"Are we going anywhere?"

"The radio is talking about a fire and a corpse."

"Far away?"

"Close by."

Sergeant de Gier, assigned to the Homicide Department of the Amsterdam Municipal Police, slowed the car and pointed. A wild goose floated quietly between the cattails, its neck bent back sleepily, about to insert its head between warm wings. "Look, Adjutant, isn't that a nice inspiration for you? That bird has swum right out of one of your favorite Hondecoeter paintings."

"Not now," Detective-Adjutant Grijpstra said. "My mind is on duty." The adjutant stared ahead, focused on a large, spheric, pitch-black cloud, billowing slowly from behind tall trees. "You say that pollution ahead hides a corpse?"

De Gier swerved abruptly to the right. A fire truck clanging and hooting, passed them rudely. The Volkswagen maneuvered around a sloppily parked patrol car. It stopped. A constable, legs wide apart, had posted himself in front of imposing cast-iron gates. The sergeant got out. "It's us, your very own detectives. What's up?"

The constable scowled.

"Accident?" the sergeant asked kindly.

"Murder!" the constable shouted.

"Hear, hear," Grijpstra said, treading heavily on the driveway's gravel. "I urge you to keep calm, colleague." The adjutant beheld the large flames ahead with awe. "A most stately mansion."

"Not for much longer," the constable said.

"It'll be magnificently restored," de Gier said. "The city's architects are good at that sort of thing now; ancient square sixteenth-century merchants' palaces are all in vogue."

"Hop along," a fireman's bullhorn roared, "there are more fire engines on the way. Be off with your rust bucket at once, you hear?"

De Gier drove the car through the gates that the constable was now willing to open. Two big red trucks thundered by on either side. Firemen, red-faced under gleaming helmets, unrolled hoses.

"Why murder?" the adjutant asked, pulling the constable to the side.

"*Whammo!*" the constable shouted. "That's what we heard, me and my mate. Over there we were driving, quietly on patrol on the dike, and all of a sudden, *kerboom,* all the windows popped out, flashing sparks, flames, what have you. We shot right down the drive, looking for what's what. Got into the place to see if anyone could be saved but the little lady was quite done for— bits of her all over the place . . ."

"In the kitchen?" Grijpstra asked.

The constable's arms pointed vaguely. "Over there. In the house. Disgusting, I tell you."

"The gas range," the adjutant said. "Seen it many times before. Missus tries to light the stove, but the pilots are off. She never notices, the kitchen fills up with gas, she's doing something else now, comes back, lights a cigarette and . . ." The adjutant nodded at the flames licking out of the mansion's windows, mocking the pressurized water aimed at them from three trucks at once.

"Faulty pilots," de Gier said, shaking his head. "I'm changing over to electric."

"No, no, no," the constable shouted. "She was in a room, over there, up front. A bomb exploded. I heard it myself."

"You heard a bang," the adjutant corrected. "What else did you notice?"

"A bomb," the constable said. "Aren't people *bad?*"

"Oh, *there* I agree," Grijpstra said. "But all we have here is a bang that disturbs and an innocent corpse to follow. Anything else to report?"

"A fat, furry, short-tailed cat," the constable said. "The fire was getting worse but we could still be heroic, so me and my mate rushed about for a bit. There was a fireplace with a cat up the chimney, blown right out of its basket. We heard him holler. I pulled his bit of a tail, but he was stuck in too far."

Another constable became visible. He was talking to a lady. The lady ran along. De Gier ran along, too.

"Who was that?" Grijpstra asked, grabbing hold of the other constable. "The neighbor woman," the policeman said. "She was alerted by the bang. She's going home now to phone Mr. Ravelaar. The corpse inside would be Mr. Ravelaar's wife."

"A bomb," the first constable said. "Bad people killing good ones. How can they do it, Adjutant? Won't it come back to them in dreams?"

Grijpstra wandered off, away from the smoke and into the park. De Gier came running back. "Got any wiser, Sergeant?" Grijpstra asked.

"The cat blown up the chimney was called Max," de Gier panted. "Tubby little fellow, well equipped with brains. Sense of humor, philosophically gifted, like all good felines. Mr. Ravelaar, the fellow who lives here, has been contacted and is on his way in a two-horse Citröen. He's a lawyer."

"Does a baby Citröen go with this opulent elegance?" Grijpstra asked.

"According to the lady next door, Adjutant, we're dealing with crazy folks again. Missus inhabited the mansion while estranged Mister had to live in the servants' quarters. Missus is qualified as 'disturbed,' Mister as 'most definitely rather odd.'"

"A leisurely walk," Grijpstra suggested, "will provide clarity of mind."

The wind was pushing most of the smoke toward the river. De Gier stroked the bark of a huge tree. "This poplar must date back a hundred years, and those oaks over there could be older still; imagine dwelling in the midst of all this ancient splendor. What is that graceful little building ahead? The servants' villa?"

Grijpstra opened a door. "One garage—contents: one late-model Mercedes-Benz."

De Gier opened another door. "One steep staircase with a mahogany railing. Leads to an apartment? Maybe Mister's digs?"

They were walking again. "Artful arrangements of rocks overgrown with assorted mosses," de Gier said. "A rose garden, a greenhouse filled with a complete collection of orchids; more wealth, more beauty. Over there—an antique gazebo with a mushroom roof topped by a giant hardwood cherry. Our couple would take tea there, with cream cakes on the side."

"Cream cakes," Grijpstra said, "turn sour when harmony is lacking. However"—his arm swept around—"someone took loving good care of all this. Acres of high-class lawn. All sorts of herbs in splendid condition. Greek statues surrounded by neatly clipped hedges. No weeds."

"Wah," de Gier said.

"Wah what?"

De Gier frowned. "Filth ahead. *Yecch.* One muddy pond under a broken-down bridge." He held his nose. "Extreme decay."

Grijpstra rubbed his chin.

"Thinking?" de Gier asked.

Grijpstra smiled. "I often do."

"In the car you often sleep."

"Deep concentration is often mistaken for slumber." Grijpstra looked around. "Why this contrasting mess all of a sudden? A forgotten and dying nook in an immaculately kept park? Nobody has been near this filth in years. But why, eh, Sergeant? Ponds go very well with parks. If this were mine, I'd keep rare fowl."

"There were birds here once," de Gier said. "Over there: rotten coops and cages, and broken little ducks' houses on posts." He moved his hand dreamily. "Scarlet-beaked Mongolian geese, long-legged whooping cranes, multicolored gooney birds, a flamingo here and there." He slapped Grijpstra's shoulder. "The magnificence of our national Golden Age preserved in the here and now. Here is where your cherished Hondecoeter pulls up his silk stockings above his silver-clipped boots before knocking together another of those priceless pictures of his. Just like you pull up your sixty-five percent polyester socks before getting into the acrylic paints."

"Please," Grijpstra said.

De Gier patted his superior's ample back. "I'm serious, Henk. Your talent leaves me breathless. Remember the coot cock look-alike you whipped up on your last day off??"

The first constable came running. "The fire chief wants to see you two."

The constable brought along the stench of thick smoke, and flakes of ashes that attached themselves to Grijpstra's dark blue suit. He rubbed them into sooty stains.

"Report on the proceedings," Grijpstra ordered.

"The fire is under control. There's limited damage. But the lady is still dead."

"How's Max doing?" de Gier asked.

The constable shivered. "He finally popped out of the chimney."

"He's okay?"

"Not okay." The constable dropped his half-smoked cigarette and stamped it into the path. "They sprayed him full of foam, but the poor fur ball was fried solid." The constable snarled. "You better get the perpetrator. The neighbor lady showed again and analyzed what must have been going on here for years and years." The constable held up both hands. He shook one. "I now know *what*"—he shook the other hand— "is *what*."

"You do, eh?" Grijpstra asked. "That's not your business. Now refer your knowledge to proper quarters. Describe both sides of this equation."

The constable talked. De Gier summed up. "Prolonged domestic conflict on the left—premeditated violent death on the right."

"It's the prolonging that always does it," Grijpstra said. "I was married myself. Couldn't I imagine what would have happened if the connection hadn't been cut?" He mopped his cheeks.

"Could be self-defense?" de Gier suggested. "Missus pushes Mister into poverty, the servants' quarters. He has to do all the hard work. She lords it in the castle. He drives the second car."

The constable was observing another half-smoked cigarette. "I see," he mumbled.

"Changing sides?" de Gier asked. "What about the cat?"

The constable stamped on the stub. "Right. *Right*. So what does the despicable demon of a husband come up with? With a bomb. Planted inside. We saw the windows blown out. What did he care? There must be insurance."

"A bomb with a long fuse?" Grijpstra asked. "All the way to his city office?"

"Please," the constable said. "We have technology now. A mechanism?"

De Gier's head swayed rhythmically. "Ticktock, ticktock, ticktock."

"Or a radio device?" the constable asked, imitating an antenna with his raised arm. "Can't you see it? I see pure premeditation. Ravelaar must have listened to the weather forecast, too. Today the wind changed. It has been blowing the other way for weeks. With the wind the wrong way, he would have destroyed some good trees maybe, and risked the fire spreading to his own quarters."

De Gier pointed at something dark and dirty left out on the lawn.

"Yeah. Max." The constable nodded. "Wow, did that animal ever howl!"

De Gier leaned against a fence.

Grijpstra looked away. "A lawyer?" he asked. "An attorney? A master of our people-pleasing laws? A gentleman playing perverted criminal?"

"Gents are the worst," the constable whispered loudly. "They have to be real bad to stay on top. For us it's different; we've learned to be comfortable down below."

"Easy now," Grijpstra said. "As a noncommissioned officer, I'm half agent myself, and the sergeant here is an autodidact, intellectually inclined. Asphalt bunnies like you should not try to understand their betters."

The constable apologized. De Gier let go of the fence.

Adjutant and sergeant walked into the ravaged house.

"So what kept you?" the fire chief asked. "I come up with something interesting at long last and there's nobody around to see it. Oops. Bah."

Grijpstra stepped aside from something moist that had dropped from the room's high ceiling.

"Bit of Missus," the fire chief said. "The larger part has been scraped into the ambulance just now."

De Gier stumbled away.

"Can't stand it?" the fire chief asked.

"Tag along anyway," Grijpstra said. "I don't like to be lonely."

The fire chief displayed a small object.

Grijpstra peered. "Shard of grey metal?"

"Also known as a bit of deadly shrapnel," the fire chief said. "You have no idea how hard it is to prove intent when there's a fire. This may be my first chance."

"Shrapnel," Grijpstra said. "What does that call to mind? War? Grenades?"

De Gier came in again, holding a hand over his mouth.

The fire chief picked up another small object and gave it to de Gier. De Gier dropped it. The fire chief picked it up. "Too hot for you? It's just mildly warm."

"What is?" de Gier asked.

"Bit of brass, a piece of shrapnel. From a brass shell casing designed for a cannon. Brass is close to copper. Missus here must have been a great copper collector, for there are torn-up plates, jugs, pails all over the place. Came off those ripped-out shelves there."

"A shell casing?" de Gier asked. "From a big gun?"

"*Now* I see," Grijpstra said. "Someone shot up the house with a fully automatic cannon."

"Close," the fire chief said, "but not quite. The shell *casing* exploded, meaning the whole thing blew up, not in a gun's chamber, more likely on a shelf."

"How?" de Gier asked.

"Dunno," the fire chief said.

"By accident?" Grijpstra asked.

"Of course," the number one constable said. "An accident, what else? I'll tell you what happened. Missus sort of accidentally hit the shell with a hammer. No, listen here: she happened to find a nail, tucked it into the shell's detonator cap, *then* got it with the hammer. All by accident, like, just to see what would happen."

Grijpstra applauded.

"It's my hobby," the constable explained. "I sometimes like to figure things out a bit, when I have an odd moment."

"And would anyone by any chance know what sort of shell we are dealing with here?" Grijpstra asked.

"I'm not sure, of course," the fire chief said, "for I'm never sure of anything ever, but I'm somewhat sure that this here was part of an Oerlikon shell, for I was a soldier once and carried cannon shells around in cases."

De Gier nodded. "I found some once, in a terrorist's apartment. This long? This thick?" He made indications.

The constable nodded too. "About my size. No wonder it caused utter devastation."

"And why did this phallic object explode?" Grijpstra asked. "Did the fire set it off? So what set off the fire? Which is the chicken? Which the egg? Or shall we never know the sequence?"

"There he is," the constable said. "That must be Ravelaar, the suspect, who just sneaked out of the compact Citröen that just sneaked in."

"You take him, Chief," Grijpstra said. "When he has seen the victims, you can pass him along. We'll be in the gazebo."

"MR. RAVELAAR," GRIJPSTRA said twenty minutes later, "meet Sergeant de Gier. I'm Adjutant Grijpstra."

"Ha-ha."

"Beg pardon?" De Gier asked.

"I laughed," Ravelaar said. "Very sorry. Delighted to meet you both." He laughed louder. *"There goes Max!"*

"You're saying?"

Tears of joy ran down Ravelaar's puffy cheeks. He clapped himself on the polished skull. He leaned against the gazebo's wall and patted his round belly. The detectives waited. Ravelaar managed to master his emotions. "I do beg your pardon, but this is really very funny. Would you care for a drink? Follow me to my humble quarters?"

"Are you suffering from shock?" De Gier asked.

"Not at all," Ravelaar said, "but a pick-me-up will do us all good."

De Gier sat on a wobbly Gothic stool, Grijpstra rocked in the remains of a Victorian armchair, Ravelaar's weight made the springs of a reject Empire couch creak. "Throw-outs from the mansion," Ravelaar said. "Alicia kindly let me have them. Now they can be sent to the dump."

Grijpstra chose a lemon soda; de Gier selected a glass of water. Ravelaar poured into chipped mustard jars, filling his own with cheap jenever. "To an end," Ravelaar said, raising his drink, "to a beginning."

"There goes Max?" De Gier asked.

"Ho-ho," Ravelaar laughed. "Oh, dear. Not again."

"I don't quite believe we folly follow your line of reasoning," Grijpstra said.

"Alice in Wonderland," Ravelaar said. "English literature, an obscure quote."

"Tell us more?" Grijpstra asked.

Ravelaar smiled. "My wife, Alicia, also lived in a most different world."

His audience smiled, too. There was a long silence. Ravelaar got up and pulled a book off a shelf. "Here, let me find the passage." He flipped pages. "Alice is growing quickly and becomes stuck in a house. Curious animals come along; they're outside. A lizard is nominated as their scout, and the poor fellow is pushed down the house's chimney. Alice kicks it up again." Ravelaar wiped his eyes with a large handkerchief, "Oh, dear. Hee-hee. Here we are. The animals outside see Bill rocket into the sky and shout: *'There goes Bill!'*" He dropped the book. "Hee-hee!"

Grijpstra picked up the book and put it back on the shelf.

"You like that passage?"

"Adjutant," Ravelaar said, exercising supreme effort to become calm. "Adjutant, you will agree that this is a comical moment. To me it is the best scene in my most favorite tale."

"Not funny," de Gier said, "not in this context."

"Not even," Ravelaar asked, "when a real little devil flies into the sky, straight from Alicia's house of horror?"

"No," Grijpstra said.

Ravelaar's thin eyebrows danced in indignation. "Please. Don't tell me you don't appreciate what went on here. It all fits in nicely. Alicia's threatening presence becoming larger and larger, her kicking *me* out first. *There goes Ravelaar,* and all her subconscious animals laughed, and then her own wickedness took over, in the shape of Mighty Max, and then justice came about, and then, ha-ha . . . excuse me . . . *there goes Max?"* Ravelaar tittered expectantly. "No . . . ?"

"No," de Gier said. "Are you crazy?"

Ravelaar sat down. "No." He grabbed the bottle and refilled his jar. He drank.

De Gier checked the books on the shelf. His forefinger followed an orderly row of leather-bound volumes that contained a complete series of articles on the application of tax laws. "Your specialty, I presume?"

"Yes," Ravelaar said. "My profession. I deal in justice."

"So you aren't crazy?" Grijpstra asked.

Ravelaar massaged the smile off his face. "No. Not normally, and circumstances will excuse my present state of mind. You can forget that line of thought. Madness presupposes being able to prove that subject is a danger to others or himself. There are other conditions, too. An irregular life? I'm as regular as they come. Irresponsible behavior? I've always been known to pay my bills."

"Max died painfully," de Gier said.

"Good." Ravelaar grinned. "That hairy horror has pestered

me for years. You try and prune roses while a snarling and clawing varmint prepares his attack behind a bush. You take pleasure in neatly raked gravel when Misery Max translates your labors into the preparation of a giant litterbox. I ate stale bread; Mouthy Max lived on salmon and smoked eel." The jenever bottle gurgled angrily.

"So much for Max," Grijpstra said. "Your wife was blasted into death by an exploding cannon shell. Parts of her are still stuck to the mansion's living-room ceiling. How about that, sir? Are we having justice again?"

Ravelaar's fingertips tried to knead his drink's container.

"We could become technical," Grijpstra said. "A cannon shell in a magnificent mansion?"

Ravelaar smiled stiffly. "Good question. I've been asking that myself. I came up with an answer. Alicia was neurotic. She collected like a magpie. There was no end to her greed for gleaming objects. She haunted the flea markets and secondhand stores. She was particularly fond of brass. Some hooligan sold her a live cannon-shell casing. She happily displayed it on the mantelpiece."

"Where it exploded?" Grijpstra asked.

Ravelaar waved impatiently. "Wait. I am not done yet. Alicia liked to polish her wonderful possessions. She bought polish by the drum. Polish, polish, polish." He laughed, while both his hands rubbed air.

Everyone stared at each other.

"I see," Grijpstra said.

"But do you understand what you see?"

"Not quite," Grijpstra said. "Maybe it'll come to me after a while. Meanwhile could you tell me how old you are?"

Ravelaar got up. "Sixty-four springs have passed me by."

"Can you explain to me what you do for a living?"

Ravelaar bowed. "With pleasure. The office that will retire me next week fights the Tax Audit Bureau on behalf of clients. I am their most respected and underpaid slave. Senior inspectors, however, tend to accept my suggestions. If not, they know they'll be cruelly defeated. I prepare my cases carefully, approach slyly, my attack is lethal. I will miss making mincemeat out of them."

"Try us," Grijpstra said.

Ravelaar rubbed his hands, then winked.

"Let's go," de Gier said.

"One more little question," Grijpstra said at the door.

"I knew you would do that," Ravelaar said. "All authorities are trained the same way. Cajole suspect into dropping his defense, then strike." He caressed Grijpstra's arm. "Go on, Adjutant, let's have your unexpected sudden trip-up."

Grijpstra led the way down the little building's steep stairs. Outside, he looked around. "You take care of the park yourself?"

Ravelaar bowed. "Alicia wouldn't spend money on upkeep. This is a perfect example of the garden art of yesteryear, conceived by masters, kept up by humble me."

"So why," Grijpstra asked, "stop short of the pond?"

"That dirty swamp?"

"Yes, now maybe," de Gier said, "because you paid it no attention. If you had, you could be keeping great crested grebes, cormorants, swans—growing water lilies in between the waving reeds."

Ravelaar looked unhappy. "I don't care for water."

The three of them stepped back as an ambulance, the patrol car, and fire trucks drove past them toward the gates.

"The property borders the river," de Gier said.

"The river can't reach me," Ravelaar said, "and the pond I will fill in. Never mind the hellish dreams . . ."

"Drowning dreams?" Grijpstra asked kindly.

Ravelaar shivered.

"Chilly?" de Gier asked. "Better get back inside. We will be seeing you again, no doubt."

"HERE YOU ARE again," Ravelaar said, "two disturbers of the Sunday peace." He held up a crystal flask, pointed at long-stemmed goblets.

The detectives declined.

"It's all yours now?" Grijpstra asked.

"There were never any children," Ravelaar said.

"All yours," de Gier said. "The mansion is being worked on already; then there's the park, the Mercedes, a million guilders invested by your wife in a mutual fund."

"Another half million," Grijpstra said, "in life insurance. Unusual, rather. Husband collects on dead wife?"

"I had the mutual clause inserted," Ravelaar said, "to raise the policy's sense of justice. In my modern view, both marriage partners have equal emotional worth. In case of death, the surviving party has her or his anguish tempered with cash."

"You've manipulated yourself into a position of perfect freedom," Grijpstra said, looking out of the apartment's window. He smiled. "Luxury, beauty, solitude, no low-level worries."

Ravelaar smiled, too. "I like you, sir. You may not be too far removed from my level of perception. There's still a bit of a gap, but I see a willingness to close it. Can't say as much for your uncouth friend."

"You're my top suspect," de Gier said sharply.

"See?" Ravelaar shouted. He leered at Grijpstra. "I've met your henchman's type before, in the Audit Bureau. Eager nincompoops who never fail to come in from the wrong angle." He glared at de Gier. "You really see a chance to blame me for that mishap? You can't even *think* of charging me with murder here. The facts and circumstances do not add up to a criminal situation. I'll review your so-called case for you, once and for all. My deceased wife, Alicia, unwittingly purchases a live cannon shell in another hopeless attempt to complete her magpie's collection of gleaming objects. The shell somehow explodes. All by itself. I wasn't even anywhere close. My visits to the main house were both rare and brief. How could I have noticed a live shell among all those shiny whatevers?"

"Watch this," de Gier said. He held an invisible object between his legs and moved his free hand in a rubbing manner.

"Are you masturbating?" Ravelaar asked.

"The sergeant is polishing an Oerlikon shell," Grijpstra said. "The faster and the longer he rubs, the more heat is generated. The temperature within the shell rises to the danger point."

De Gier stopped smiling. *"Kaboom?"* he asked softly. "A neurotic lady venting her frustrated energy on an explosive phallic object?"

Ravelaar studied the glowing fluid in his goblet.

"Polish, polish, polish," de Gier said.

Ravelaar nodded. "Yes. You may have something there, Sergeant." He smiled forgivingly. "Alicia was rather a frustrated woman. That activity you demonstrated could be sexual, yes; why not? She didn't have any normal sexual outlets, of course." He gestured. "Not much of a looker, you know. Short. Chubby. Thick spectacles, not much nose. Rather looked like an owl, I thought."

Grijpstra grimaced. "Don't miss her much, do you now?" He opened his notebook. "We did our homework. Your retirement income is less than half of your salary." He flicked a page. "Your marriage contract held you liable for half the estate's upkeep." He put the notebook away. "Character witnesses define you as extremely stubborn, quite incapable of negotiating a better agreement with your estranged wife. You were a soldier during the war; you would know about shells."

"You found one at the flea market?" de Gier asked.

"Yes?" Grijpstra asked.

"Proof?" Ravelaar asked.

"ARREST HIM, I say," de Gier said in the car. Grijpstra grunted while admiring a flock of ducks, coming in low from across the river. A wild goose floated slowly forward between the cattails at the water's near side. "Look," Grijpstra said. "I think I can use that bird. Good model for my next Sunday painting."

"Not now," de Gier said. "I'm working."

Grijpstra grinned grimly. "Work audibly, Sergeant."

"I say, harass the cat-killer," de Gier said gruffly. "Keep dropping in on him from time to time. Send him official little letters, ordering him to Headquarters on a few days' notice. Steam his brain, I say, rattle his conscience. I'll record my cat and have a tape meow in the bushes. Loud Siamese yells? A full moon? I can get a raccoon's tail at a furrier's. Attach it to a line? Dangle it through the mansion's chimney?"

"The suspect killed his wife as well as a cat," Grijpstra reminded him.

"I'm too tall," de Gier said. "You could dress up like her, wait for a foggy night? Dance in the park? On one of those lawns?"

Grijpstra pondered. "Nah."

"Got to do something."

"Yes," Grijpstra said. "But your ice is too thin. Let's stay on decent ground."

"Then do what?"

"Wait," Grijpstra said, rapping his knuckles against the Volkswagen's roof. "Wait for nice justice."

AUTUMN CAME AND went. Rain became sleet; sleet changed into snow. The Volkswagen's windshield wipers protested squeakily.

"Where?" de Gier asked.

"Amstel Dike," the radio answered. "Just this side of the city limits. A car slipped into the river and broke through the ice. Our wrecker hauled it out, but the driver seems to be missing. Try to assist."

"Will do," de Gier said. He pushed the microphone back

into its clip and shook Grijpstra's shoulder. "Are you there, Adjutant?"

"TELL US?" GRIJPSTRA asked a constable directing traffic on the dike.

"Over there," the constable said. "A large Mercedes skidded off the curve in front of that stately mansion, slithered onto the river's ice, and sank, but we managed to retrieve it. The driver must have freed himself, but the body is still missing. See my mate walking on the ice? He could use some help."

Grijpstra moved along slowly, anxious not to slip. De Gier shuffled along. "Thin ice?" de Gier asked. "Last time *you* said it."

"Your turn," the constable on the river said. "Take my broom. Sweep off the snow so that we can look through the ice."

De Gier swept with broad strokes.

"There," Grijpstra gasped.

Ravelaar floated on his back an inch under the ice, arms spread, legs stretched out; his eyes protruded, his mouth hung open.

"Looks crucified," de Gier said softly. "Let's get him out."

The constable had fetched a sledgehammer and was banging on the ice. Each bang produced a jerky movement in the corpse, moving it closer to the area of open water. Grijpstra and de Gier followed slowly. Grijpstra sighed. "I told you we had only to wait."

De Gier nodded, then stepped back as the body suddenly bobbed up, half jumped, and slid up onto the far side of the ice.

"There goes Ravelaar," Grijpstra said.

The Letter in the Peppermint Jar

That night I worked in the communications room, Headquarters, Amsterdam Municipal Police, at Moose Canal. I had been working there for a while, always at night, through to early morning, I liked that—nice and quiet. Calls are often bizarre: ladies who are bothered by singing mice or a retired commando lieutenant who reports that the neighbors are throwing grenades again—not that he minds much but should we have a patrol car in the neighborhood we might check it out. I could have been off sick, with pay, but I never liked playing the system for all I could get. There wasn't much bothering me, except a lame leg that was repairing itself and didn't hurt that much.

An invalid cop on active duty? Why not? It happens in the highest ranks. Our chief of detectives can't walk without his cane, and my problem was only temporary. The commissaris suffers from chronic rheumatism, I had been shot. His rheumatism isn't his fault, my invalidism was caused by lack of professional know-how.

A colleague—we call him Ketchup because things tend to get bloody when the constable is around—shot me during a bank robbery. Two unemployed Arab immigrant laborers, armed with toy guns, had held up a bank at Spui Street. I should have paid attention. I was also out of luck that day. It doesn't do to be riding in a minibus driven by Ketchup, about to pick up some suspects at Warmoes Street Precinct, when foreign gangsters are threatening bank tellers half a kilometer away. Cops are armed with a real good handgun these days, the Walther P-5 (touch the trigger and deadly bullets fly). No safety on the weapon, we carry it loaded and ready. Ketchup aims, Ketchup fires, Ketchup hits two Arabs (lethal chest and stomach wounds) and an extra bullet pierces the muscles of my left thigh.

Ketchup apologized, and he and Karate, his pal (the two have been palling together for years now, in a nice apartment overlooking the Amstel River, that's okay these days), have been taking me out sailing on the Inland Sea in their yacht, and flying me over the islands in their Cessna, and taking me to dine in the better restaurants on their foreign credit cards, and relaxing me with what-not else, until I begged off. Too much hard-to-explain luxury makes me nervous. Now how can two Amsterdam street cops afford that sort of thing, eh? I did ask and Karate said he and Ketchup buy antique postage stamps as a hobby, and make a fortune that way, buying in Amsterdam, selling in the Seychelles (that's between Africa and India, a likely location, but I know they do fly there sometimes, spending time with tax-free millionaires). Okay, we all know that the Dutch Police Force is not corrupt. Right? No protection of drug deals? No ignored arms shipments to bad-guy land? Out of our magical Amsterdam? Never.

The term, I believe, is "denial."

I have no extra income myself, not so much because I believe in ideals, but because I like living the simple life. In those days I rode a bicycle that I carried up three flights of stairs to my two-room apartment. I read library books and I lived on Marnix Street. Ever been there? Marnix Street resembles a long narrow gutter. It's a dark street, even on a sunny day, but it suited my mood then. My only complaint was that the big yellow street-cars were a bit noisy, which interfered with my piano playing. I did have a nice piano, in addition to a bed, a chair, and a table. And a planter to grow white geraniums in during summer (during wintertime they got too spindly and I would cut them down) and I owned a hundred CDs, mostly Miroslave Viteous, the way-out bass player, and my idols: Ornette Coleman, Keith Jarrett. Mostly somewhat difficult music.

Uncle Franz, who dialed the emergency number that night and got me on the line, asked if I was still "spiritually subsisting in my little dark hole." He knew that the skin graft on my thigh was doing nicely and that I worked nights in the communications room.

I became upset—this number is for emergencies only and I suspected that he was going to bother me with his philosophical monologues. But Uncle Franz said that his call constituted an emergency, although "it hadn't happened yet." A future emergency, he would have me know.

I worried that his sobriety had come to an untimely end, that he had gotten into his favorite brand of jenever again, cold syrupy juniper-flavored gin. He assured me everything was just fine. He did talk rather slowly, but he was in his eighties then, and he had always talked slowly. The man lived like a master plays chess, planning his moves, taking his time. Uncle Franz was special, a genius. During World War II he worked in Germany, where he put submarines together, devising and running a faultless web of locations where parts of U-boats—that type of equipment requires a lot of parts—were assembled quickly and efficiently.

Even during the heavy Allied bombing of all of German industry, those submarines were launched out of Hamburg once a week. Thanks to my little old uncle.

Uncle Franz never had ideals and he was uninterested in morals. I honestly believe that he never even thought about what the Nazis wanted to achieve. Uncle Franz liked to juggle large numbers of factors, parts, techniques, play complicated games against the forces of chaos. "To order the all-prevailing mess and thereby create a working pattern that gets things done,

Nephew." The very idea made him smile. He claimed he only worked "for the hell of it," but he also made a personal fortune. He liked to gamble, not with cards or dice, but with practical projects. "With chaos itself."

Uncle Franz was my grandfather's brother. The family is, in origin, German. We used to be called Muller, but my father changed that to the Dutch word, *Molenaar*. Uncle Franz stuck with the old name. He studied physics and mathematics in Hamburg, and later, when my great-grandfather moved to Holland, got his PhD's at the famous technical university of Delft, Holland. Everything *summa cum laude*. The family had Dutch passports by then. When Germany invaded Holland, anybody with German ancestors became German again so Uncle Franz and my dad were drafted into the German army. Uncle Franz got out because he offered his talents to the makers of the dread submarines. My father, a professed anti-Nazi, was shipped off to occupied Norway to service a huge cannon pointed at the sea. He never had any leave and spent five years polishing the useless weapon, confiscated from the former French Army that had managed to lose the juggernaut's ammunition. As soon as the war was over, my father burned his uniform and walked home in clothes he had stolen off a wash line. I was born in 1961. Father was in his forties by then. My birth killed my mother. Dad struggled along alone, became depressed, swallowed something, and pulled a plastic bag over his head. Uncle Franz inherited the family mansion at Bickers Alley, at the corner of Wester Dock, an antique warehouse that my great-grandfather remodeled into a villa, complete with a roof garden overlooking the harbor. When Dad died, I moved in with Uncle.

After the liberation, back in Amsterdam, Uncle Franz was charged with treason, but the case didn't hold up in court. The Nazis had forced him to become German during the war; now how could a German *betray* Holland? Of course Uncle

Franz defended himself, he made the judge laugh. He made me laugh, too. Often. I won't say it wasn't fun to live with the old lunatic, but I didn't mind leaving the house on my eighteenth birthday. Uncle Franz wanted to pay for my studies at Amsterdam University's School of Music, but I never wanted to be a professional piano player. I applied for a scholarship to the Police School. After graduation I became a regular cop, starting as constable, moving up to constable-first-class, aiming to be a sergeant.

As soon as I got my badge I found the Marnix Street apartment and did my best to evade Uncle Franz's efforts to oversee my career. It seemed that he felt sorry for his occasional neglect, and frequent abuse, at the Bickers Alley villa. I didn't avoid Uncle totally, however. I did owe him some gratitude. He did, in his own perverse way, mean well, I'm sure.

He really was an asshole, my dear little uncle. He looked bad, too. "A bald dwarf," he called himself. His baldness was hidden under a huge curly wig that sat askew on his oversize head.

"Tell me," Uncle Franz said, that evening when he dialed 911 and I happened to pick up the telephone. "How many of you work the phones there?"

There were four constables on duty that night, with a fifth standing by, making coffee.

"Good," Uncle Franz said. "One out of five and you are the one who answers my call—a good omen, my boy."

I asked what kind of emergency was bothering him. Were there burglars in the house? Knowing Uncle, surely he would have trapped them with one of his inventions and had the unfortunates in chains by now. Did he want us to send a bus to pick up suspects?

Bickers Alley at the corner of Wester Dock, is part of one of the mysterious black holes of the city of Amsterdam. Human flotsam likes to congregate in the area, to sleep under the bridges, especially during the warm season. We were having a mild summer and drug and tourism were rife. A rich old hermit living on the waterside, between unguarded warehouses and offices—the situation is an invitation to evildoers.

"I am calling the emergency number," Uncle Franz said, "in connection with a future murder slash manslaughter."

I said I would send a patrol car right away.

"No need as yet, my boy."

"You're sure you've not been at the bottle, Uncle Franz?"

Uncle Franz protested. The famous reformation date was mentioned again: the fifth of November 1987, the day that uncle joined Alcoholics Anonymous, Haarlemmer Street branch. He told his fellow converts that he had decided to quit "because of practical reasons." Uncle was an athlete as a youth and was able to defend himself when sober, which he was not while out on the town. With old age adding to his handicap he was helpless at times. A gang surrounded him near the Harbor Building, took his wallet, and, when he offered resistance, broke his nose and glasses and damaged his expensive dentures. He was in the hospital for a while. "Life, when subject to unforeseeable periods of alcoholic weakness, gets complicated, so I quit," he told me sadly.

"Walter," Uncle Franz had said, patting my arm, "your loving only relative, thoughtful caregiver and staunch significant person is, from now onwards, sober." He was too damaged for me to tell him I only agreed that he was a relative, and that I didn't believe him anyway. He did, however, quit drinking. Thinking back now, I have to admit that he always took his promises seriously. Normally, he didn't commit himself to anything—in spite of my pleas and protests when, as a child, I was at his mercy. His lifestyle always irritated me. I didn't like being a judge of female beauty when he had ladies he'd picked up in a bar strip on the grand piano in our living room. I preferred to do my homework rather than help construct a symbolical maze in the basement, with philosophical obstacles and spiritual downfalls. I got upset

when I had to join Uncle and his current rooster (yes, rooster—
they got drunk sometimes and fell to their death) in concert (I
sang and played harmonica, Uncle took care of percussion and,
sometimes, slide guitar) in the roof garden. Uncle, when suffering
from hangovers, never promised he would better his ways, but
when he said that we would do something nice for a change he
did comply. When we celebrated our birthdays (August first for
both of us) he always thanked me profusely for whatever I bought
him and he would give me something that I really wanted. There
was the bicycle, the electric train, and the annual membership
that got me into the movie museum. When I was ten years old
he bought me a round-trip ticket to New York and came along
to show me the Museum of Natural History and have me listen
to the Miles Davis quintet in a concert hall.

He was pleased the enormous revolving globe in the museum
interested me.

"Those are the real colors, Walter; the ones in your atlas
are all made up. See, there are no frontiers on the real globe?"

"Yes, Uncle."

"But you can see the stains, can't you? The stains are us. We
are the sickness of the earth, but soon we will choke ourselves
and the planet will be like new again, for some better beings
that will come after us."

"Like who, Uncle?"

"Like us again, Nephew, but we'll be part starlight then."

We had dinner in New York's Chinatown, and when I lost my
cool because I couldn't find my kind of Amsterdam / Chinese food
on the menu, he told me how fortunate I was that I could now see
things from a different angle. He ordered something weird that
tasted great, I wish I could remember now what it was.

The flip side of his genius was that I was often left alone in
the villa at Bickers Alley, for days and nights on end sometimes,
with only Dizzy Gillespie, the rooster, and Nietzsche and
Nisargadatta, the cats, for company. If the food ran out, I ate

cat food on moldly bread, or a chicken-feed soup of my own invention. On other nights I might have unexpected company if Uncle pushed a drunken lady into my bed: "Move over, my boy." I sometimes wore the same underwear for weeks. Uncle never came to Parents' Night at school. When Miss Bekker, the mathematics teacher I was in love with, showed up at the house once, he tried to seduce her. There was the night that I had to call the fire brigade. He had kicked over the barbecue on the roof and the wind had blown sparks into our curtains below. He didn't want to phone himself because he couldn't take time out from watching the flames licking through the villa. He kept drinking while the firemen stamped about, waving their hatchets and hose nozzles.

And now he bothered me at work. August the first. Four A.M.

"Are you in the roof garden, Uncle?"

He was. "It's going to be a lovely day, Walter. So it should be, seeing that it's our birthday. There's that deep red glow on the river and the gulls are soaring over my head quietly, dark silhouettes against the lightening sky. Wish you were here, Nephew." He grunted disdainfully. "But no, you have to be a mole, in that dark windowless bunker."

I knew he wasn't referring to my place of work, or even my dark apartment in depressing Marnix Street. He was telling me, once again, that I lived in spiritual darkness. He would say that when I was a little boy. He was always trying to manipulate me into some kind of *breakthrough*.

"Your limited point of view saddens me, Walter."

I protested, and he said he wouldn't give up on me, that it was his duty, as my heaven-appointed mentor, to try and get me to see the light.

"Uncle Franz, this is the communications room of the Amsterdam Municipal Police. You are blocking an emergency line, you'll get me fired."

"I tell you, this *is* an emergency, my boy."

"Are you home alone, Uncle?"

The rooster was keeping him company. He maintained that all his successive Dizzies were the same "familiar," a term he had picked up while studying medieval magic. A familiar, I understood, was a kind of protective spirit, and Uncle had taken the liberty of programing his with a liking for bebop jazz. It was true that the bird would start strutting around as soon as Uncle put on certain types of jazz on the record player.

Dizzy clucked at me through the phone.

"Dizzy," I said, "tell Uncle to hang up."

Uncle was on the line again. He swore that any moment now—in any case, before the sun had properly risen—a violent situation would occur at Bickers Alley. "There will be beauty confronted with evil. There will be blood on the cobblestones. This is the sort of event that will delight your cop's soul, Walter."

"That's it, Uncle, I am about to hang . . ."

"Don't do it, Officer."

His voice was cold and precise. He told me that breaking the connection would not prevent what was about to happen there. But I could help take care of the aftermath. It was like the six o'clock news—nothing the viewer can do about it, but as long as he knows he can help pay for blankets to be helicoptered to the refugees.

My voice was cold and precise too. I told him I was about to turn off his channel.

He thought that sounded funny. He imitated the voice of the black communications officer in *Star Trek* who was always talking about closed channels to Captain Kirk.

I told him he was stuck in the past now, that Kirk had been replaced three times already.

"Remember," Uncle asked, "how we would laugh when that stupid Dr. McCoy said, '*He's dead, Jim!*'"

"Uncle Franz, please," I said kindly.

He chuckled. "That's better. Keep talking, Officer. You forget you told me yourself that it is better to have crazy folks talk themselves out over the phone, it releases their tension." He lowered his voice. "Prevents crime."

"You admit you're crazy, Uncle?"

He told me others were crazy, dangerously crazy, lethal, others who were about to show up down there in Bickers Alley.

I had to laugh. Uncle might be crazy but he wasn't dangerous, he wouldn't harm a soul, except unwittingly. During the war he had constructed those efficient U-boats, but he wasn't trying to kill then, he was just creating fascinating toys. Besides, as far as police procedure goes, he was right. We don't hang up on bizarre calls. Quite often the bizarre is true. There was the apparent madman who screamed, *"Frogs on the speedway, millions of frogs on the speedway."* It was early in the morning then, too. I did believe something was up and directed a patrol car to the speedway where the constables saw a square kilometer of baby frogs, oozing out of the wetlands and slithering across the tarmac. The constables managed to block the way in time and prevented an overloaded tractor-trailer, which came thundering along, from skidding and turning over and spilling its inflammable cargo across four lanes.

"Walter," Uncle asked, "did you read the Charles Willeford books I left on your doorstep?"

"Yes, Uncle."

"How does Willeford, America's most analytical crime writer, define a psychopath?"

"As someone who knows the difference between good and evil, but doesn't give a shit. Uncle. This is it. Bye now."

He raised his voice. "You should know by now that I am a possible psychopath, Officer, and you have to let me talk to you."

"Uncle, dear, please tell me the nature of the future happening."

Too early to tell, Uncle said. He was prepared to fill me in on the actual situation. He was in the roof garden on the fifth floor, and the roses were ready to open in the light of the soon-to-be-rising sun.

"Are you alone?"

"Me and Dizzy."

"I know what the problem is," I said. "You are constipated again because of an overdose of codeine you took for your painful knees. You are going nuts because of bad cramps, and you are hallucinating because of the dope. Just like last month. Want me to come over with an enema, Uncle?"

"Maybe," he said, "you should send that car now."

I knew Grijpstra and de Gier were on duty that night. This wasn't a case for rookie constables in uniform, and Grijpstra and de Gier were experienced detectives operating in civilian clothes out of an unmarked vehicle. I knew them. We play music together. Grijpstra is a drummer with a talent for side percussion and de Gier plays mini-trumpet. They say they like my "thoughtful" style on the keyboard. De Gier isn't a half bad composer. I have never understood why he and Grijpstra are policemen. Grijpstra is a good painter, too; he could sell his work. His girlfriend owns a hotel. De Gier is a minimalist/loner like I used to be, doesn't even want to own a car. He could make a living playing jazz in the city's bars. Live off all the beautiful women who pursue him. The rascal is quite handsome. Looks like a hussar officer, with his handlebar mustache.

"Okay, Uncle," I said. "I'm sending a car, to see what's what, and I'll be along later. Just a few more hours and I'm done."

The information seemed to please him. "To celebrate our birthday, Nephew? The day of the roaring lions? Today the world is ours, you know. How about sharing my dinner tonight?"

I thanked him for the invitation.

"So are you coming?"

"Yes, Uncle Franz."

"You would have come anyway, right?"

Trying to be polite, I said, "Of course," but if he hadn't

reminded me I would have forgotten both his and my birthdays completely.

"And you have already bought me a present?"

"Yes, Uncle."

"You're lying through your teeth," Uncle said angrily, then changed his tone of voice again. "It doesn't matter at all. Your company is enough, my boy."

I felt relieved. "So the cop car isn't necessary anymore, Uncle Franz?"

"Not just yet." He was using his cordless phone. I heard his shoes crunching through the roof garden's gravel. "Downstairs on the street level, I hid two microphones in the ivy on the alley wall. You want to hear a good radio drama play, Nephew? Like in the old days? The cowboy series you liked so much?"

"Damn it, Uncle . . ."

"This is an important call," Uncle Franz said. "Believe me, you are trying to pacify a true public enemy. Bear with me and there will be blood in the street, Officer, ladies will yell, a sports car will growl, bullets will be fired, there'll be tension galore."

I sighed. "Uncle, what claptrap is this?"

"There they are," Uncle said. "I was looking for the coconut shells. I knew they had to be around here somewhere. You know Dr. Portier has me eat coconut to strengthen my heart muscles? Listen to this, Nephew."

I heard the sound of cowboy horses, trotting along. *Clippety-clop. Clippety-clop.*

"Uncle!"

He read my thoughts. "This is no lie, Walter. Ten long years have passed by. Not a drop of alcohol has touched my lips. I wouldn't dare. I promised the AA boys that I would be back the day I slipped, and I can't bear the idea of ever doing that. Of all the boring judgmental assholes I have ever met . . ." I heard him click his dentures in desperation. "Never again, dear boy."

I tried loving kindness. "In an hour and a half I can leave here. I'll swing by, Uncle. Would you like me to do that?"

"No, no," Uncle said pleasantly. "Now listen to this, Walter, the microphones will amplify the coming sounds of horror just beautifully. Navy quality. I still have my connections. Here is a sample."

I heard a thrush sing, a complete cantata, to accompany the first rays of the morning sun.

"What do you think, Walter?"

"Wonderful."

"I call him Miles," Uncle said. "I'm up here every daybreak, just to hear that bird chant. You know I only believe in a system of happenstance, but that system did create birds that sing like this, and that *is* proof of divinity, Nephew."

I began to understand something. "Uncle? Are you helping divine happenstance perhaps?"

Uncle Franz giggled.

"I thought you had told me you were retired," I said desperately, "that there was no need for any extra bullshit anymore. What are you *doing,* Uncle?"

I head a loud chuckling, no doubt leading to a majestic cock-a-doodle-doo, but it ended abruptly.

"Dumb Dizzy," Uncle said. "He was ready to explode ahead of time. I covered him up with the teapot warmer. Aha! There we go now. About time."

I heard, first through Uncle's phone and then through the microphones down in the alley, the mighty growl of an expensive sportscar's engine.

"A golden cabriolet," Uncle Franz said, "dreamed up by no one else but my old friend Dr. Porsche."

"Are you expecting visitors?" I asked.

"Me?" Uncle asked innocently.

I heard car doors slam and the clicking of high heels on cobblestones. I also heard a drunken male voice. "Time for a cold one, what do you think, Arlette?"

The voice that answered made my spine vibrate. I was reminded of Billie Hobday's voice, or maybe Betty Carter's.

"No," the magical voice answered. "Not after all that sweet champagne at the club. Please. No."

The male voice snapped. "Since when does Fastbuck Freddie pour cheap bubbly in his exclusive nightclub?" The voice became sarcastic. "You were kidding, weren't you, dear? Okay. Now, let's see that beautiful present you bought me for my birthday, with the money that stuck to your slender fingers at the club, eh, my sweet?"

Birthday? Uncle was right. This was serendipitous happenstance indeed. Uncle Franz and I, and now this arrogant pimp, all celebrating our birthdays on the first of August.

"It's already in your car, Fred," the wonderful voice said. "The old mechanic installed it this afternoon."

"Since when do you know an old mechanic?" Freddie snarled. "Are you entertaining a client in your time off? Without telling me about the old codger? You're not generating extra income, are you?"

"And we tried it out at the parking lot behind the club," Arlette said. "It'll sound even better here, with the river next to us. There is a button under the dashboard. You'll have to press it."

I noticed that I was shaking my head anxiously. Maybe Uncle Franz no longer drank alcohol but he still frequented the city's nightclubs. Did he have designs on the woman or her pimp? What was that button connected to? Some hellish device?

I wrote the address on my notebook *1, Bickers Alley,* added *Grijpstra and de Gier,* and moved the note to the officer at the next phone. She made the connection and passed her second phone to me so that I could listen in.

"Bickers Alley?" Adjutant Grijpstra's hoarse voice asked. "That's near Wester Dock, isn't it? We are at the other side of the area, near the Orange Locks. A woman in the river, but the Water Police got her. Is this Bickers thing urgent?"

My colleague raised her eyebrows at me. I wrote another note, passed it along, and made a fist.

"Old gentleman and rooster about to bother a nightclub owner and his passenger. Look for golden Porsche. Parties celebrating mutual birthday."

"Let's have that again?" Sergeant de Gier said.

My colleague repeated the message.

"What about the rooster?" de Gier asked. "Is he having a birthday, too?"

I shook my head.

"Not the rooster."

I heard Uncle Franz laugh in my other ear. I asked if the pimp and the lady were the people who were, according to his prediction of a little while ago, going to cause the trouble? Or suffer it?

"No need to whisper, Officer," Uncle said. "I only have microphones in the alley, there are no speakers down there. They can't hear me either. Not unless I shout down at them. From the roof here."

"Who are those people?" I asked.

"Fastbuck Freddie is a royal pain," Uncle Franz said. "Arlette is the sweetest thing around. Nice looking, too. The longest legs ever, Officer. Marlene Dietrich from Nigeria, with the mouth of a voodoo goddess. You couldn't dream up Arlette, not even if you used all your hidden talents."

I began to have a bad feeling about all this.

I heard a beer can clatter on the pavement. "Don't litter, Freddie," the female voice said.

"And why not, dearest?" Freddie asked in a stage whisper, telling her to leave the can be, "or the street cleaners will have nothing to do."

I heard him curse because he couldn't get his birthday present to work.

"Uncle?" I asked.

"I told you he was a pain," Uncle Franz said, "stupid, too.

Pressing that button isn't enough, he has to turn the dashboard key first."

"Is Arlette a stripper, Uncle?"

"Really," Uncle Franz said, "that Freddie is dense. No wonder he has to live off women. What was that? Stripper, you said? Arlette is a very nice young lady who I happened to meet in town."

"You're still addicted to watching T&A, Uncle?"

He grinned. "Nothing more interesting was ever created, Nephew. Admiring female breasts and bottoms even beats putting submarines together. But there is a connection. The sea is female. U-boats are male, of course. What submarines are trying to do to the unlimited sea is admirable but hopeless."

I heard muffled noises. "Poor Dizzy," Uncle said. "Still wearing that stupid teapot warmer. There you go. Feeling better, dear?"

Dizzy clucked happily.

"Arlette is a fabulous cook," Uncle Franz said. "The lady creates a fish soup, my boy, that surpasses anything I ever cooked for you on Thursdays."

I had to admit interest now. Uncle was a gourmet cook and the dinners he put together most Thursday evenings were the highlights of my youth. He excelled at a mussel soup with curry, Oriental shrimp dishes, and there was the cod or haddock dish with mustard sauce and parsley. There was home-baked bread, butter he bought from a farm, and a pineapple and cream pudding.

"And for thanks you let the woman be publicly abused by her employer."

Uncle Franz grumbled. "Freddie still hasn't got it. Does he really expect an electrical gadget to work if he doesn't switch on the current?"

"What is he trying to get going?" I asked.

"A surprise. One of my better ideas," Uncle said, "but Freddie is even more ignorant than I expected . . . bah."

"Why don't you employ Arlette as your housekeeper, Uncle?"

"I am too old."

Nonsense. Uncle Franz was never too old for anything. Or too ugly. Or too crazy. It had been quite an effort to get away from him. He was an amusing genius, too overwhelming for a slow soul like mine.

Uncle activated his microphones again. I heard how Freddie knocked his drunken head against the Porsche's low roof. "What the fuck is the matter with the damned gadget? Nice present, Arlette. The gizmo doesn't work, you know."

"You have to turn the key, Freddie."

"My little sow," Freddie said, "What do you know about technical stuff? The car lights burn without me having to turn a key, right?"

"Why don't you try turning the key, Fred?"

He imitated her voice. "*Try turning the key.* Just because you are a jungle bunny with a tight little ass you think you excel in the brains department too?"

Arlette sounded sad and tired. "When the old gentleman put it together it worked just fine."

"Sure thing," Freddie said. "He probably had screwdriver fingers, and a computer for a brain. I know the type. They touch a machine and the damn thing starts purring. Ouch, Christ almighty." He knocked his head against the roof again. What on earth had happened to Grijpstra and de Gier, my infallible detectives?

Arlette suggested going home.

"Please," Freddie snarled. "Who wants to go home now? I thought we wanted to share the sunrise. Okay, I am going to turn that stupid key now. There we go . . ."

A siren began to wail loudly.

"Yoho!" Uncle Franz shouted. "Dizzy, do your job, my fine beautiful bird."

Dizzy's cock-a-doodle-doo pierced my ears.

"Arlette? You hear that? A rooster! Haha!" Freddie kept pressing the siren button and Uncle kept cheering Dizzy on.

Dizzy was shut up by the teapot warmer. Uncle shouted,
"Hey! You down there! Idiot! You know what time it is?"

Freddie was shouting, too. "Don't you have a clock, you old
buzzard? Haha, Arlette, watch that clown up there. Hey, can you
cock-a-doodle-doo, too? Old man?" The siren howled.

Sergeant de Gier, on the radio, asked what he could do for us.

"What is keeping you, Sergeant?"

"We got stuck," de Gier said. "I tried a shortcut but there is
road work here and we are bogged down in sand."

"So?"

"So we radioed for a cab and it's on the way."

Fool. De Gier outranked me so I couldn't say it. "Yes,
Sergeant."

I got back to the phone. "Uncle?"

"Nephew?"

"How is it going at your end?"

"Freddie is leaning against his car, drinking more beer. You
want to hear him?"

Not really. I could call another patrol car but the matter was
too delicate for uniforms to deal with.

"Isn't this fun?" Uncle asked. "I can switch Freddie on and
off. The way it should be, Walter. You are still in the midst of
things but as you get older you will realize that we create our
own universe, where we can move things."

Typically lionesque. I have been listening to it for as long as I
have known Uncle. It irritates me that there seems to be some
sense behind his cryptic monologues. I even get it at times.
Maybe because I was born on the first of August, too, and am,
astrologically, a lion, too. A lion's arrogance is hard to put up
with. We really believe that the world will come to an end as
soon as we get off it. I remember that as a toddler, I was taken
to the zoo by Uncle, and he claimed that the thousand animals

we saw there only existed while we observed them. He proved his theory by taking me to a spot where we couldn't see the elephants. After that we walked to their quarters. "See?" Uncle asked. "When you can't see them, they don't exist. As soon as you see them, they do, however. You know what you are? You're Walter the Elephant Creator. Now that you have dreamed them up you better get in there and climb upon their backs, make them do what you want, dear."

I started crying but I was amazed, too. The gigantic animals needed a small child so that they could exist? And I could really ride them?

"The universe," Uncle Franz said, "needs *me* to *be*."

"You know, Arlette," Freddie was saying in a beery voice, while kicking another can around in the alley, "this is an important day. August first. Today I have looked at my creation for exactly forty years, and you have viewed yours for twenty-six."

I pride myself on my modesty. I appreciate modesty in others, too. The grandiose statements made by Freddie below in the alley and Uncle Franz up on the roof were irritating to me. I couldn't get at Freddie but Uncle was on the telephone.

"Uncle," I said, "you know what they say?"

"What do they say Nephew?"

"That pride leads to a fall."

"They say a lot," my educator said. "You know who they are? *They* are three obese Zen monks who live at the North Market. They are former disciples of Master Dipshit, an American Zen master with fake Japanese papers. Although they are not related, all three happened to be called Polsen. Because they keep repeating each other, they think they are in agreement."

I had heard him say things like that before. I laughed.

"Maybe," Uncle said, "you will get it one day, and to help you along I herewith appoint you as my successor and in order to give you the means to complete my quest you will also be my heir. Of everything." He laughed. "Which is nothing."

I had heard that before, too, but in the old days he needed alcohol and nude women to reach a state of illumination. What worried me was that he was now stone-cold sober. It also worried me that he might be serious about making me his heir. I had no need of his money and four stories filled with complete collections of what-nots. Why make life complicated? In my present state, I might not be happy but at least I wasn't cluttered.

It seemed he was reading my objections. "I wasn't altogether successful in my quest, Nephew, but maybe you, as my successor, have a chance to go further. You are young, strong, not given to attracting demons, sensitive enough to share, so you won't have to be lonely like me."

"Share?" I asked furiously. Who wants to share? Share misery? Why did he think I was living alone, trying to be minimal, to live as emptily as I could?

"Whoa," Uncle said nervously, "things are going wrong here. That cop car of yours . . . where is it, Walter?"

I heard what was going wrong down in the alley. Freddie was beating Arlette, Arlette was crying.

"Gimme me that key, bitch. Let me try that siren again."

Arlette was sobbing. She told him that he shouldn't bother that poor old man up on the roof. She got her cheeks slapped for her trouble. Loud wailing. Uncle Franz was yelling down from the roof. Dizzy was crowing at full volume. Freddie was screaming that everybody better shut up so that the cops wouldn't hear everybody, resulting in their useless interference. But what the hell, Freddie was screaming, what did *he* care? Everything he ever did was illegal. His permits at the club hadn't been renewed. The Porsche wasn't licensed because he hadn't been able to show his driver's license because it was suspended. Good thing he was a mighty astrological lion celebrating his own creation, for if anyone else had caused all this bullshit anyone else would be in deep shit. Yessir.

The microphones clicked off.

"Walter?" Uncle Franz asked. "Did you notice that Freddie is a lower lion?"

I asked if there were higher lions.

"Higher lions," Uncle Franz said, "are majestic, lower lions are caught up by ego. You and I are of the higher type. We make good kings."

"Do we love and respect our subjects, Uncle?"

"We serve and protect them, my boy."

"And Freddie abuses his subjects?"

"Don't ask stupid questions, my boy."

As usual, Uncle Franz wasn't altogether wrong. He, Freddie, and I, all three of us, obviously were leaders. Uncle Franz himself had always manipulated powerful forces optimally. Freddie drove a golden Porsche and had beautiful women dance in the nude on the stage of his nightclub. I directed police cars through the streets of one of Europe's major cities. I wondered how Arlette deployed her royalty. Right now she was in exile but I could hear, in the energetic undulations of her jazzy voice, that she wasn't planning to stay in exile for much longer.

"Uncle?"

"How can I help you, Nephew?"

"You have thought up this entire situation," I said. "You are the good king, Freddie is the bad king, he caught the beautiful princess and abuses her. That idea of having the siren cut up the quiet night is yours."

"You flatter me," Uncle said.

"Siren," I said. "There is symbolism here. The beautiful mermaids of the Rhine were called sirens. Their chanting caused sailors to wreck their ships on shoals."

"You know," Uncle Franz said. "I never thought of that."

"You are setting Freddie up to have a bad accident," I said, "so you can have the beautiful princess. Arlette."

"Close," Uncle said. "Damned close, Nephew."

I heard Dizzy cluck.

"Sure, Dizzy," Uncle said, "but Walter isn't quite where we want him as yet, is he now? It's better that way. He needs to be surprised or he'll miss our ultimate meaning."

My colleague held up her phone for me. Adjutant Grijpstra was on the line.

"We are lost," Grijpstra said.

"Is the cab driver lost, too?"

"The cab driver is from Turkey," Grijpstra said. "You know I often get lost and you know that Sergeant de Gier often gets lost with me. We can usually find our way by asking pedestrians, but it's too early for pedestrians. Now what?"

Fortunately I am a born director. "Where are you, Adjutant?"

"Realen Canal."

I was glad he knew that much. Realen Canal is close to Bickers Alley.

"Tell your driver," I instructed my superior, "to switch off his engine. Okay? Good. Now all three of you, listen." I used the other phone. "Uncle? Can Dizzy do his thing, please? His specially loud crow?"

Dizzy was good and loud. Freddie, having extracted his car key from Arlette's grasp, accepted the bird's challenge. The siren howled for all it was worth. The racket reached the listening ears of Grijpstra, de Gier, and their Turkish cab driver. The car rolled into Bickers Alley. Uncle Franz activated his microphones in the ivy-covered wall.

"Police," Adjutant Grijpstra said.

"Sure thing," Freddie said. "In a cab?"

"Police in a cab," Sergeant de Gier said. I surmised that the detectives showed their identity cards and, possibly, their weapons, by unbuttoning their jackets and leaning back a bit, so that their guns would show in their armpit holsters. I do the same thing when I patrol out of uniform and happen to walk into a situation.

"My girlfriend and I," Freddie said, "are enjoying the sunrise over the river. We are totally legal, Friends and Detectives."

I could hear him kick beer cans around. "And while you are enjoying yourselves," Grijpstra said morosely, "you're making a bit of a mess here?"

"Shut the fuck up, Fats," Freddie said impatiently. "Who is *we*? *We* did nothing at all, we didn't abuse substances, we didn't mess up the street, nothing."

"Your name?" Grijpstra asked peacefully.

"Listen here," Freddie said. "I'm a gentleman and a scholar. I happen to have a Leyden University *summa cum laude* degree in criminal law. I am an a-ca-de-mic, okay? You have heard of the term? Yes? And I'll have you know that the law says that there is no need for a subject to identify himself if the subject is not a suspect."

"You are a suspect," Grijpstra said peacefully, "and I now formally place you under arrest."

"Suspected of what?"

De Gier sounded angry. "Of drunk driving, littering, disorderly behavior, pollution, refusal to show some ID, showing disrespect to an officer of the law—want more?"

The microphones clicked. "You hear that?" Uncle asked me through the telephone.

"Yes," I said. "Would you mind calling Detective-Adjutant Grijpstra and asking him to arrest you too, while he's at it?"

"Suspected of what?"

"Of provoking a fellow citizen to commit crimes."

"Please," Uncle Franz said. "No proof. And there is my age, Walter. Dr. Portier would never permit my arrest. My heart condition . . ."

The microphones were activated again.

Freddie was holding forth. "I do admit that you may have a few points there, but you'll have to admit that it's thin stuff.

You never saw me drive this vehicle. Arlette . . . first of all, say 'Good morning' to these nice policemen, please."

"Good morning, Officers," the delicious voice said.

"So Arlette drove my Porsche into his picturesque little alley," Freddie said. "Please scratch your drunk driving charge. What else? Littering? You never saw me drop these cans. If they offend you I'll have Arlette pick them up and put them in the car, and then she'll fold her lovely long legs behind the driving wheel and I'll get in nicely on the passenger side, and off we go. Nothing ever happened. Okay?"

I heard his footsteps on the cobblestones.

"Not okay," Grijpstra said. "Open the hood of the Porsche now."

"Never," Freddie said.

"Last chance," de Gier said.

Freddie laughed. "You can't make that case either. You know a judge said that opening the hood of a vehicle equals empty-ing out one's pockets, and that neither can be ordered in our free country, unless there is proof that there is a connection to a criminal act."

"We do have a complaint," Grijpstra said, "about your oper-ating an illegal siren, hidden under the hood of that vehicle."

Freddie was laughing. "Excuse me, Officer Overweight. Are you referring to Old Alzheimer on the roof up there? Who was getting jealous of me and Arlette schmoozing down here in the alley. Now what would a harmless citizen like me be doing with a siren?"

I began to worry. Freddie could be dead right. Circum-stances might not warrant either an arrest or the opening of the Porsche's hood. The detectives definitely needed more weight on their side of the seesaw.

"The siren is hidden under the Porsche's hood," Arlette said.

Freddie lost it. "What? Arlette, have you gone crazy on me now?"

"Sergeant," Grijpstra said, "you see that metal bar leaning against the garbage can over there? Would you please force the hood?"

Freddie preferred to open the hood himself. "There you go," he said. "And what do we see here? Yes, indeedy, one siren. So what, eh? A toy that my sweet girlfriend gave me for my birthday and that we were trying out here. Sirens sound nice across water. And then my sweet girlfriend got pissed off with me, and now she is causing a bit of trouble, but we are at the end of it. Right, Arlette? My darling? Look, I am on my knees. Please forgive me my trespasses, yes, my angel of justice?"

"Adjutant?" Arlette asked. "Please look at my cheeks for a moment."

Grijpstra must have seen that Arlette's face was badly swollen. We were definitely into crime now. Playing with a siren is one thing, beating on a woman's face is something altogether different. Freddie's tone of voice had changed. "Adjutant, this isn't what it looks like. I'm sorry to have to tell you but Arlette is a masochist. She can't, eh, well, how to say that nicely . . . she can't get to where she would like to go unless she gets beaten up a bit."

"Is that right, ma'am?" Grijpstra asked quietly.

"No, Adjutant," Arlette said quietly.

"You are sure about this?" Grijpstra asked.

"I am sure," Arlette said.

Freddie was apologizing seriously now. He swore that he would never touch her again. He was close to tears. Arlette was not. Her voice was cool and even. "I hate it when you abuse me, Fred." Freddie (Grijpstra told me later) was moving around her on his knees now, touching the cobblestones with his forehead. "Please, please, please, Arlette. Let's go home. Please?"

"This man," Arlette said, "has beaten my back with his belt."

"The belt that he is wearing now?" de Gier asked. "With that metal clasp in the shape of a skull and bones?"

"Yes," Arlette said.

"Sergeant," Freddie pleaded, "you know that this kind of complaint is always withdrawn later. Don't get yourself in a mess here. You are wasting time and energy. You're getting into a terrible hassle."

"Miss Arlette . . ." Grijpstra said.

"Arlette Sanders."

"Miss Sanders. Unfortunately the suspect is right. Complaints regarding physical abuse in a sexual relationship are usually withdrawn. Are you sure you will stick to your complaint?"

"I am sure," Arlette said.

"Your name, Suspect?" Grijpstra asked in his most official tone of voice.

Fastbuck Freddie sounded tired. "Frederic Ruyter."

Suspect Ruyter was ordered to turn around, put his hands on the Porsche's roof, and spread his legs.

I could hear Dizzy start on a song of victory. Uncle whispered in my ear, "Isn't this fun, Nephew? Pimps are always psychologically unbalanced. And therefore uncommonly dangerous. Did you know that? Isn't my research paying off?"

De Gier was yelling at Suspect. "Hands on the roof. *Now!*"

"Freddie is armed," Arlette said.

"Now!" Grijpstra yelled.

"Careful," Arlette said. "He has shot people before."

"Pay attention," Freddie said. "You think you can intimidate me but I have nothing to lose. I am the wonderful warrior. I am completely vulnerable, and therefore invulnerable. Can you follow that, nitwits?"

What happened afterward was reported to me by Grijpstra. Freddie pulled a gun, a small revolver that was clasped to his belt. In a case like that we officers of the law don't have to fire a warning shot. De Gier aimed his huge Walther P-5 at Freddie's chest and shot him through the heart. Freddie must have left his body instantly. Our new "stopping" bullets are effective.

After the sound of the gunshot, it became quiet in the alley. Uncle Franz whispered that things had gone well, hadn't they? "So I'll see you tonight, Nephew?"

I walked home, made a mushroom omelet, served it with a balcony-grown salad, made a pot of strong coffee, took a shower, and slept until late in the afternoon. I shaved with a new blade, put on my ironed jeans and the Indian cotton shirt I had found at the thrift shop, put on the necktie with the turtle design that Uncle had given me for my previous birthday, bought a box of gift-wrapped mint-liqueur-filled bonbons at the boutique across the street, found a dozen golden tulips, and rode my bike to Uncle's harborside mansion.

I rang the doorbell. There was no reaction. The door was ajar. I thought I should have brought my service pistol. Now what? An intruder maybe? But the lock hadn't been forced. I tiptoed into the corridor. There was a tantalizing fragrance of freshly baked sole.

I shouted my "Happy Birthday" through the closed door.

"Please come in, Walter," Arlette answered.

She was everything I had been dreaming of recently, but better. I blushed, stuttered, and trembled behind my tulips. She said she knew me. "Franz" had showed her photographs in the family album.

In spite of a painful attack of acute jealousy, I looked about the kitchen happily, rubbing my hands. The table had been prettily set, just like in the old days, when Uncle and I celebrated something. But weren't we supposed to be three for dinner? Why had Arlette only put down two plates?

She pointed. "Sit over there, Walter, please."

"Aren't you having dinner, Arlette?"

She said we were to drink some jenever first, Uncle's favorite brand. Arlette poured me a glass but gave herself some dry white wine. We toasted each other. I thought this was a great idea, just Arlette and me, but what had happened to Uncle

Franz? Had he gone for a walk around the block? Or was he out
buying vanilla ice cream with ginger sprinkles?

Arlette said Uncle had died. She suggested that I sit down.
No, not on the easy chair, that's where he had just died. She said
she had seen the ambulance drive off that afternoon, when she
came to visit. Dr. Portier was still at the house. He said Uncle
had telephoned him urgently, because of heart trouble.

I sat down. Arlette said that this had to be a bad shock to me,
since he and I had always been so close. She also said that she
didn't just know me from photographs but that she had seen me
in the music store, listening to a Chet Baker CD. She smiled.
Let's Get Lost. And, of course, in the park early Sunday morning
where I had fed bread to the giant carp.

I didn't get that. "Why were you there, Arlette?"

She said Franz knew my routines. He had wanted her to
observe me, as I was to be his successor.

"He planned it?" A stupid question again. Of course Franz
had planned it. Including his precious heart attack, taking all
his pills in one gulp, so they would bring on the attack instead
of preventing it. Arlette quoted a note Uncle had pinned to
his jacket. "This body is getting too old, dear people. And the
brain is slowing. I am going to recuperate for a short while
in the inspiration spheres. I'll no doubt see you again. Avoid
babies for the next few years. One of them just could be me,
haha."

"The police came to check?"

Yes. Everything was in order. "Letter present," the constables
wrote in their notebook.

"What else did the note say, Arlette?"

"Thanks," Arlette said.

"For what?"

"Franz didn't say. Everybody, for everything?" She smiled
again.

That was the sort of thing I had heard Uncle say often. I hated his wise utterances. There was too much wisdom in them. I asked Arlette if she knew Uncle would do away with himself.

"Just with his body." Arlette's slender hand was stroking my hair. "All he told was that there would be dinner tonight and that everything would be ready so that I could start cooking when I came in." And he had left her a note, in the peppermint jar. Uncle knew she would always go for the peppermint jar when she got to his kitchen.

"So what was in the letter, Arlette?"

"Instructions."

First we had to eat: his famous fish soup, the freshly baked bread, the fresh farm butter. In spite of, or because of, the tension, I was quite hungry. We ate quietly until she asked whether I thought she resembled Marlene Dietrich. I nodded but said I had no interest in resemblances really. She was Arlette, she had her own inimitable beauty. Unique. New. New and everlasting. I told her "Arlette" meant "renewal forever." In what language, she asked. In Sanskrit. Uncle, most likely, stood behind me, prompting me. Normally I'm not much of a raconteur.

Arlette arranged the tulips in a crystal vase and opened the box of chocolates.

We talked of birthday presents. The tulips were my present to Uncle, the chocolates my present to Arlette, the meal was Arlette's present to me. What would Uncle give Arlette and me?

She smiled suggestively.

Well, of course, there was the house, the money, the stocks and bonds, but I wasn't sure any of that would make me happy. I didn't need to be loaded. I had everything I wanted in the Marnix Street apartment. I was a happy man. I had a sign on my door that said "No thanks."

"You didn't look too happy when I saw you in the park and the music store," Arlette said. "You mostly looked lonely."

That could be, I had to admit.

"You don't mind being lonely?"

Well, perhaps, I did mind, some.

Because if I didn't mind, Arlette said, I might not be in need of the present Uncle Franz had thought up for me, and she wouldn't get Uncle's present to her either.

Right, I said, for I was beginning to understand the final phase of Uncle Franz's plan. Arlette took me by the hand and guided me up the stairs, to the roof garden where Dizzy was waiting next to the automatic coffee maker, with a time mechanism, that had been set by Uncle Franz. The coffee started to perk as we sat down on the garden chairs and Dizzy started to crow. "You sure all these steps were mentioned in the letter in the peppermint jar?" I asked.

She laughed. "Yes. And we have to kiss."

I got up and stretched my arms toward her. She shook her head. "The note says we should have coffee first."

Java mocha, with my mint chocolates on the side. Dizzy was strutting around proudly, showing off how perfectly he fitted into this optimal situation.

This was good. A good universe. Thanks to me. *The universe needs me to be.* It was the first time that I was content with the universe I had created. Maybe Dizzy was a little loud but otherwise everything was pretty perfect.

Arlette showed me the letter from the peppermint jar. It had taken Uncle several sheets to list all his instructions. The final note said, "Put tea warmer on Dizzy, press button I installed under the coffee table."

Arlette hooded Dizzy, I pressed the button.

The microphones below in the alley clicked on and amplified the thrush's evening cantata. Arlette slipped onto my lap. She whispered, "You know that all this is because I thought it up, don't you?"

I knew that.

We kissed.

Heron Island

"You want me to confess?" Professor Suzuki asked through his interpreter, Toshiko. "I wasn't here in Amsterdam, Holland, when it happened, commissaris-san, I was in Kyoto. And confess to what? To a crime? But the crime is the murder of my own son, my only child, and it was the French couple that did that, the skinheads, arrr . . . Ninette, and arrrr . . . Pierre, yes, *yes,* commissaris-san?"

"Mere instruments?" the chief of detectives, a neat little old man, asked politely enough.

He was at an advantage, of course, entrenched behind his huge antique desk. He was at home, so to speak, at Amsterdam's Police Headquarters, a far cry from his visitor's Kyoto, the exotic temple city, the pure heart of Japan; although, Suzuki had told him just now, industry was polluting even Kyoto, darkening the sky above perfect copies of Tang Dynasty Buddhist buildings, extinct in China since the Cultural Revolution, but duplicated perfectly in the land of the Rising Sun.

"Saaah," Suzuki said, admiring a giant blue heron, preening blue-and-silver wings on a branch of a century-old elm tree outside the commissaris's open window, stretching its snake-like neck, croaking musically. "A rare bird."

"Herons aren't rare," the commissaris said. "In fact, they're a pest. All over the city. They get so bad that we put up signs to warn our good people not to walk under their trees. A good splat ruins clothes. It's the canals that attract our thousands of herons, and the recession, of course. You see, we have all the unemployed now, who like to fish, so Amsterdam stocks her canals with minnows and the unemployed yank the fish out and feed them to the herons."

"So desu ka?" the motherly young Toshiko twittered, too surprised to translate. "Is that so? Herons are *very* rare in Japan."

"I thank you, commissaris-san," Suzuki said, "for solving my son's murder. It is terrible indeed when a man's sole biological successor is killed criminally, and his body is cut up, and found in a trunk, floating in . . . arrrr . . . Brewer's Canal, was it?"

"Yes," the commissaris said, sharing a relaxed coffee ceremony with his guests, handling the heavy silverware deftly: pot, jug, bowl and handing out cookies.

"Oishiiii," Suzuki and Toshiko said, "tasty."

"Brewer's Canal," Suzuki said. "It may be fitting that my son departed life there. He did like beer."

"You drink alcohol yourself?" the commissaris asked.

"What?" Suzuki stared over the rim of his coffee cup. "Oh . . . no, don't care for drink . . . but Koichi had the bad gene, his mother's. You know"—the professor spoke in an exaggeratedly youthful voice, which Toshiko immediately imitated in English—*"Out of beer, out of luck . . . All beer is good beer."'* He spoke in his own voice again. "My son's favorite sayings."

The commissaris glanced at Polaroids on his desk. Some were of a dismembered corpse, one showed Koichi alive, standing on an Amsterdam gabled house's stone steps, between sculptured granite lions, squinting awkwardly. The commissaris thought the young man's sullen looks might be due to more than being hungover. Koichi looked disturbed—the way his head was held to the side, as if someone was about to slap him—with defensively raised hands, a too eager smile. *The underdog*, the commissaris thought, *the pathetic creature rolling over on its back signaling:"Please don't hurt me."*

"What should I confess to?" Suzuki asked. "Please, commissaris-san, tell me what happened, from the beginning, if you please . . . oh . . . Koichi, my son . . ."

"I told you," the commissaris said.

The heron in the elm tree half raised his huge wings, as if intending to float down easily to cool its feet in Moose Canal below, then croaked musingly. The elm tree offered shade. The summer day was hot. He could claim his fish later.

"I tell you, yes?" Suzuki said. "Koichi didn't like to travel, he just drank, in bad bars, so I wanted him to expand his mind, to travel. I sent Tadao with him, Tadao, youngest son of my colleague Sakai . . . arrrr . . . Sakai and I are professors, medical men."

"You paid for the trip for both your son, Koichi, and your colleague's son, Tadao," the commissaris said.

Suzuki shrugged. "I am well off. I invested and locked in my profits a long time ago." He stared at the heron, folded his hands, bowed to the creature.

"There are no Japanese herons?" the commissaris asked.

"We only keep Japanese people on the islands now," Suzuki said. "Other life-forms are dying out in Japan." He looked down at the commissaris's Oriental rugs, then up at oil portraits of ancient Dutch constabulary captains, smiling down with red faces.

There was a silence, first soothing, then disturbing. Toshiko broke it. "Not all wildlife is dead. There are sanctuaries, commissaris-san. The professor owns Heron Island on Lake Biwa, close to Kyoto. It is very famous."

"The snow monkey sanctuary in Hokkaido is famous," Suzuki said, "nobody ever heard of my insignificant effort."

"Your son, Koichi," the commissaris said, shaking a pathology report from a plastic file and arranging its pages neatly next to the Polaroids, "died of an overdose of pure heroin."

"A new vice," Suzuki said. "To add to the drinking. I worried about my son. I thought a change of environment . . ."

"Amsterdam heroin," the commissaris said, "is often pure."

"Well," Suzuki said, "so you're saying my son's unnatural death was an accident? I don't think so. Dealer Pierre knew that Koichi wouldn't be able to handle that injection. Malicious foresight, *neh?* They robbed him, *neh?* Pierre and Ninette. You jailed that bad couple?"

"Pierre is dying in the jail's hospital now," the commissaris said. "Withdrawal sometimes does that. Users are in bad shape, they haven't eaten for a while, living on the drug only, and then, when the drug is withheld, the shock kills."

"Ninette, too?" Suzuki asked.

"Holland is short of jail space," the commissaris said. "We released her to the custody of her family, in Paris. Pierre prostituted Ninette. She's in a clinic, recovering nicely."

"A good girl at heart?" Suzuki asked suspiciously.

The commissaris lifted a thin, almost transparent hand, smiling gently. "What's *good?*"

"What's good is what's good for *us,*" Professor Suzuki said, thumping his chest.

The commissaris smiled. "For the surviving life form?"

"Hai," the professor nodded.

"The polluting life form?" the commissaris asked.

"Arrr . . ." Suzuki said.

"Arrr . . ." the commissaris said kindly. "I don't believe holding Ninette will be for the common good."

The heron outside, alerted by the professor's loud voice, lifted a wing and croaked loudly. Suzuki's face twitched as he moved forward in his chair. "Listen, police-officer-san. Ninette bought the trunk with a traveler's check taken from a dead body to get rid of that same body. My only son's dead body. You yourself told me so. That's how you caught Pierre and Ninette. They killed Koichi Saturday night in their loft on Blood Alley, and Pierre, a butcher by trade, bled and dismembered Koichi's corpse. You told me that the stores here are closed Sundays and Mondays. The trunk, found floating in Brewer's Canal late Monday, was new. Your detectives traced the vendor at the street market, which is open on Monday. He'd taken a hundred-dollar American Express traveler's check in payment from a French female skinhead. You knew, because Tadao told you, that Koichi and he had been drinking with a French skinhead couple in Blackbeard's Bar in Blood Alley the Saturday night when Koichi disappeared. The connection is clear. Your detectives traced the French couple to their loft and their search produced more of Koichi's traveler's checks." Suzuki's voice squeaked indignantly. "Yes, commissaris-san, *yes?*"

The commissaris coughed. "Please. I'm sorry, Suzuki-san, I really want you to make a confession." He blew his nose. "Excuse me. It's better for you. You will feel relieved."

"You want to arrest *me?*" Suzuki asked. "You're kidding . . . arrrr . . . you can't hold me for anything. I was halfway across the globe when Koichi died. How could I kill him?"

The commissaris smiled. "I won't arrest you."

"I'm a medical man," Suzuki said, "I serve the common good. Why do you blame me? For sending my only son to Amsterdam, with a friend to protect him?"

"I just want you to clarify your motivation," the commissaris said. "I am not blaming you. Besides," he gestured gently, "you did nothing illegal."

Suzuki held up his hands. His eyes blazed. "So why demand a confession?"

"To clear your mind," the commissaris said.

"For the common good?" Suzuki asked.

The commissaris nodded.

"I don't follow you," Suzuki said. He turned to the pleasant-faced Toshiko. He muttered furiously. "Suzuki-san," the interpreter, stepping out of direct-voice mode, said briskly, "says he doesn't follow you."

"Tell Suzuki-san," the commissaris said, "that he does. Tell

him I want his confession. Tell him I won't arrest him. Tell him
he can go home." Suzuki got up.

"Confession first," the commissaris said. Suzuki sat down.

"Perhaps, if we go through the events again . . ." the commissaris said.

"Okay . . ." Suzuki said. "Where are we now? My unemployed
son, Koichi, and his friend, Tadao Sakai, a medical student, vacationing in Amsterdam, visit a bar. Koichi drinks. Tadao abstains.
Blackbeard, who tends bar, sells Koichi marijuana. Koichi
smokes a joint. Tadao does not. A French couple, in leather
clothes, with shaven skulls, enters Blackbeard's Bar. The couple
indulges too, sidles up to the rich Japanese tourists. Pierre offers
drugs that he keeps in his loft. Koichi leaves with the French
couple. Tadao returns to the hotel alone. Koichi doesn't show
on Monday morning. Tadao informs our ambassador, a Kyoto
native who happens to be an acquaintance of mine. The ambassador alerts the police."

"More coffee?" the commissaris asked.

Suzuki's trembling hand made his cup clatter on its saucer.

The commissaris poured.

"What do you want of me?" Suzuki asked. "Yes, I know I
accused Tadao of kidnapping Koichi, when the ambassador
phoned me in Kyoto. I overreacted. I've explained the situation:
my colleague Sakai has been losing a fortune on the stock market. He's back in debt, his house is mortgaged to the hilt again,
the continued studies of his four sons are in jeopardy. I'm the
rich guy. I first hear my son is missing, then that his dismembered body has been found floating about in a trunk. I don't
know about a French couple. I do know about Tadao. Maybe
Tadao had Koichi tied up in some basement here and wanted
me, in return for my son's release, to pay for his, Tadao's, studies, or maybe I was to pay off Tadao's father's debts. I imagined
that Tadao might have killed Koichi by accident, by binding him
too tightly. It could be, couldn't it? And Tadao studies surgery,

he knows how to cut up a human body . . . to get rid of the evidence.

"Really . . . " the commissaris said, shaking his head. "Really, professor . . ."

"Far-fetched," Suzuki said. "I know. Tadao is a good boy. Besides, my hypothesis was unlikely, as you explained. There are no empty basements in Amsterdam, the city is overcrowded. Besides, Japanese are conspicuous foreigners here. How could one conspicuous foreigner molest another? Wouldn't someone have noticed? Wouldn't you have been informed?"

The commissaris sipped coffee.

"You didn't arrest Tadao," Suzuki said. "You want me to confess to accusing an innocent party? My motive is jealousy? Very well. I confess." Suzuki thumped his knee. "Why does my associate professor Sakai, my inferior, Sakai the foolish gambler, have four excellent sons who study hard, four heirs to have pride in, and why am I cursed with a misfit, Koichi?"

"Thank you," the commissaris said.

"Can I go now?" Suzuki asked.

"That was only the first part of the confession," the commissaris said.

Suzuki was shouting. "You want me to admit to manipulating Koichi by sending him here to Amsterdam, a magic city of sin, where dangerous drugs were bound to reach him? That I was sure that Koichi would go for heroin? That he would surrender to that evil French couple? Show them his roll of traveler's checks? Set himself up to be murdered?"

"We dropped the murder charge," the commissaris said. "There is no evidence of conscious planning. These things mostly just happen, you know. There's no proof that Pierre knowingly injected an overdose into a willing client. We have Tadao's testimony: Koichi bragged that he was used to heroin."

"Pierre should have noticed that Koichi didn't inject," Suzuki said.

"You think Pierre checked Koichi for needle marks?" the commissaris asked. "In a dark loft in the early hours? Everybody is drunk and stoned already, and Pierre has just wandered all over Amsterdam looking to buy heroin and needles, not easy products to purchase, even here?"

The heron was looking at Suzuki. Suzuki covered his eyes.

"*Kudasai . . . kudasai . . .*"

"Please . . . please . . . " Toshiko translated. Suzuki dropped his hands. He stared at the heron. "I protected you, remember?"

"You're almost there," the commissaris said.

Suzuki was calmer, sitting back, hands clasped on knees. "It hurts too much to tell you my truth."

The commissaris smiled helpfully.

"You know why the truth hurts?" Suzuki asked.

"Because we cover it up by lying to ourselves?" the commissaris asked. "But lies are transparent. The truth moves underneath, it keeps wanting to get out."

"It twists about in pain," Suzuki said.

"So?" the commissaris asked.

The heron had flown away. The commissaris looked out of the window, beckoning his guests to join him. Six stories below, the bird stood next to a man in a red hat, dangling a fishing rod above Moose Canal. Man and bird.

"I love birds," Suzuki said. "Koichi hated me. He wanted to hurt me. He was drunk, he was on my island, shooting my birds."

"What had you done to him?" the commissaris asked.

"I didn't marry his mother," Suzuki said. "She gave him to me after my wife left me. Koichi's mother hates me, too, but she thought I would pay for a good education. I paid for everything. Koichi wasn't grateful."

"Should he have been?" the commissaris asked.

Suzuki raised a shoulder. "Maybe I pressured him, eh? Pushed too hard, maybe? Wanting him to do well? Wanting to show off a good son?"

"Thank you," the commissaris said.

Suzuki danced, using the commissaris's large Oriental rug as a stage floor. First he danced Koichi, drunk, crazed, firing an automatic shotgun. Then he danced a wounded bird, flopping about between the pine trees and ornamental bushes, shrieking in agony, trying to stretch its broken wings. The commissaris noticed how heronlike Suzuki was himself, with his wavy silver hair brushed up over his ears so that it tufted backward, with his long arms that perfectly imitated wing movements, with narrow trouser legs and tall-shafted tight boots, stepping about stiffly.

The shot heron died, falling into the professor's chair. The professor sat up painfully, croaking, "Arrrr . . ."

"I see," the commissaris said.

"See what?" Suzuki asked.

"I see what you mean," the commissaris said. "I'm very close to my pet turtle, a dear little fellow who lives in my garden and is closer than I am to humanity, perhaps."

"Now your son shoots your turtle," Suzuki said.

"Now I kill my son?" the commissaris asked.

"So now what do I do?" Suzuki asked.

BOTH PARTIES MET once again, at Suzuki's invitation, at a restaurant facing the southern gate of Amsterdam's Vondel Park, a conglomeration of large ponds surrounded by clusters of trees and shrubbery that provide an optimal habitat for the capital's many species of birds.

"Commissaris-san," Suzuki said, "I thank you."

"Are we done?" the commissaris asked.

Suzuki bowed. "My mind is clear."

"I'm glad," the commissaris said.

"So am I." Suzuki smiled. He touched Toshiko's arm. "My adviser here tells me that it's time to move ahead intelligently.

She also tells me that intelligence is the capacity to make the best use of a given set of circumstances. I still have the island with a recovering population of splendid birds. With Koichi gone I have no heir. You told me that your detectives, when they visited Tadao at his hotel, found him developing photographs of herons, taken while he was hiking about in Vondel Park."

"Tadao told Adjutant Grijpstra," the commissaris said, "who likes to paint waterfowl as a hobby."

"What style?" Suzuki asked. ". . . Arrrr, Hondecoeter's style perhaps, the old master . . . ?"

"The old master," the commissaris said. "Tadao told my adjutant that herons, in Japan, symbolize the ability to fly off to higher spheres."

Suzuki nodded.

"A sensitive boy," the commissaris said, "this Tadao."

"My colleague Sakai might agree," Suzuki said, "to give me one of his four sons. It would be beneficial to all parties. I would pay for Tadao's education, and maybe lend his father some capital with which to sort out his present mess."

The commissaris, limping slightly due to a rheumatic condition, leaning on a silver-tipped cane, walked Professor Suzuki and Toshiko back to the city's center through the park.

A giant blue heron, its long neck curved back gracefully, broad wings stretched wide, hovered effortlessly above them.

Letter Present

I just had a look at the visiting card again, after I found it in my file. It was neatly glued to a sheet of clean paper and put away under the letter G. Evidently, I knew I would need it sometime. The tiny document is filed under G because the person it refers to is called Grijpstra, Henk Grijpstra, adjutant of the Municipal Police, Murder Brigade.

The adjutant, a paternal type with short grey hair that sticks up like the bristles of a well-worn brush, came to see me to inquire, as he put it, "about your father's untimely demise." That's the way the old bird of prey likes to express himself. I would choose my words differently, but then I'm a bit of a scholar in my time off and a publisher of literature by trade.

"Sorry to disturb you," Adjutant Grijpstra said kindly after he lowered his bulk into the easy chair reserved for visitors. For a moment I felt relieved, as respected citizen of our free country. That the police were visiting me, the adjutant explained, was due to a regrettable fact, the possibly unnatural death of Dad. The authorities protect the citizen in a true democracy. The adjutant pointed out that I, as the bereaved party (isn't it terrible when a son loses his beloved father?), could be sure of receiving help. Isn't the state a father, too? I could rest assured. I felt immediately threatened again, however, not so much by the polite and well-mannered adjutant but by his companion, a quiet detective-sergeant, who had also given me his card. The sergeant's card found a place in the wastepaper basket after they left. One hint of conscience was sufficient in my case. The sergeant's name was Rinus de Gier.

Gier means "vulture" and both officers reminded me of deadly, powerful birds. There I was, stretched out on the glowing white sand of a desert, helpless; there they perched on the branch of a dead tree flapping their transparent batlike wings; just another few seconds *and the vorpal blade goes snicker-snack.* I read too much and always remember the wrong passages, which frighten me, and which grow in horror in my sick but fertile imagination. The sergeant himself didn't really resemble a bird at all; he is a much too handsome hero, in his early forties, with the mustache of a romantic cavalry officer of days gone by and the profile one finds in the expensive advertisements of fashion magazines. A movie projection, an exaggerated female dream; did I have to become all nervous because of his glossy image? Couldn't I just shrug my shoulders while I observed the sergeant's smart casual wear, the well-fitting suit cut out of denim, the gay (I didn't think *he* was) baby blue silk scarf knotted loosely under his strong but not uncharming chin? Couldn't I define his presence as merely irritating and meanwhile keep listening to what the adjutant was saying? The adjutant spoke with just a touch of the musical Amsterdam accent and looked at me sympathetically from pale blue, deep-set eyes. He had a second chin and voluminous cheeks. Adjutant Grijpstra was regretting my father's sudden heart attack and mentioned that he thought it "embarrassing" that untimely death had grabbed Dad from the arms of a woman he wasn't married to. He thought I might know my father's girlfriend—the lady who left Dad in the grip of fate, who ran away without even calling a doctor.

I tried to control my trembling lower lip. Surely, I might be a little nervous. Wasn't I Dad's only child, and couldn't I be expected to feel lost and alone? But if I lost my cool altogether, these sleuths, whose eyes were now drilling into my face, might be led to all sorts of dangerous conclusions. The interview, as the adjutant had said, was a formality, no more. They expected me to provide them with short and exact answers; if I could satisfy their curiosity briefly, this painful interlude would come to an end.

"Yes," I croaked. "She's an acquaintance. Her name is Monica and she's really my friend Hubert's, well, eh, sort of mistress. I've known for a while that she rather liked Dad. He liked her, too. Dad was discreet, of course, but my mother died many years ago" (I didn't tell them how Mom met her end, for information should never be too complete) "and Monica is rather attractive and does prefer older men" (I tried to smile in a know-it-all way, for this is Amsterdam and we're all supposed to know what's what in our wicked city.)

The adjutant was decent enough to accept my words in silence, but the sergeant opened up. He saw a contrast between reality and my glib talk. Monica and Dad? An intimate relationship? And Monica was my friend Hubert's girl?

"Quite," I said firmly. Maybe it was my turn to throw out a question. "Isn't reality rather complicated at times? Look here, Monica is extraordinarily attractive. Hubert likes beauty—to admire, so to speak. He collects works of art and some of them are allowed to be alive. But she should never touch him, if you know what I mean. He allows Monica to be his companion; if there's anything more intimate she can offer, he doesn't want to know." I didn't mention that Hubert is fond of boys. Like Dad, I can be discreet. That conclusion could be theirs.

The detectives kept looking at me while they digested my information. What were they seeing? That I'm most intelligent? My IQ is high and I'm a sensitive person. If there are other assets to my character, I haven't noticed. I'm short, bald (only thirty-two years old), somewhat bent over, shy to a fault, and seem rather slavish, but I only project that modesty. Under my servility hides a dictator and I can, in a roundabout way, be ferociously aggressive. Know thyself, Socrates said. He also said that self-knowledge is almost impossible to achieve; but others, unfortunately, can see my self most easily.

I attempted to fathom what the gentlefolks of the Murder Brigade were thinking, while they tipped their small cigars and stirred their coffee. They theorized that if Monica loved my father with Hubert's permission, Hubert was giving instead of taking, even if Dad's passion did finally kill him. In my case there could be motivation. Wasn't I Dad's sole heir? All his possessions passed to me, to wit, one profitable publishing company, one regal mansion just outside of the city, and one sixteenth-century restored gable house on the Emperor's Canal, complete with a luxurious apartment on the upper story, where Dad took his naps and occasionally spent the nights. There was also cash, bonds, and shares. Hubert wasn't getting any of the loot. Now why should Hubert, this collector of beautiful objects, so far unknown to the detectives, instruct Monica in such a manner that she, by showing off her luscious lines of living flesh, might increase Dad's blood pressure to the point where a vein would burst and stop his works?

It's pleasurable to try and analyze the others' hidden thoughts, but only if the observer is a disinterested party, for if he's part of what's going on, he may be eliminated by the equation, and knowing that, fear makes him sweat.

Were Adjutant Grijpstra and Sergeant de Gier trying to prove intent on my part? Princes are forever trying to usurp the crown. I had read widely in the genre of crime literature and knew that heirs are the first to be suspected. But really, was I a British prince in a Shakespearean tale or some ungodly shadow figure in an early Greek play? Nothing exotic, if you please—weren't we in the flat Netherlands, where nothing out of the way is ever imagined behind our all-protecting dikes? Were these solid policemen really prepared to soil their placid minds with foreign poetry?

How much attention could they muster for that one single suspicious circumstance? Monica wasn't present when the detectives answered the emergency call and entered the apartment furnished with antiques, but she did leave a trail. Her bag was found next to the bed. *She* was found that same night, in the bar at the Brewer's Canal, where she had stupefied herself with alcohol and the weed of forgetfulness. Noteworthy: why hadn't Monica called a doctor? Why did she run when Dad had trouble breathing, grasped his neck, groaned in agony? Yes, she said, she had been unnerved and had escaped to the trusted support of her favorite tavern.

"But, miss! Mr. Habbema was obviously ill. Didn't you think you'd better be of help?"

"I thought he was angry with me."

Right. How clever to pretend to be drunk, stoned, and silly. But it could be genuine. Dad wasn't altogether comatose, for he did manage to telephone his friend, the M.D. in his suburb. The doctor did show up, even if he had to leave a jolly party with friends.

Can death from a heart attack be a murder? Isn't the connection a little far-fetched? Not to me, for I read literature. Tanizaki, in his subtle novel *The Key,* makes a young wife excite her husband to the point of death. Was it accidental that the sergeant was playing with his key ring while he kept watching me, stealthily, through his long lashes? Hubert would have been excited if he had been the victim of such quiet, veiled interrogation, but I'm sexually normal and felt severely harassed by the implications the sergeant's mime provoked.

So how about this Hubert, the sergeant wanted to know.

The police like straight lines. What do we have here now? Girlfriend of third party, in bed with the victim. How does the accusing pencil connect the given points? How well did I know this Hubert?

I replied in detail, for the line had missed the important

point. Certainly, I had known Hubert for many years; we started school together and were joined right through university. Together we started our careers in publishing, but Hubert joined another firm, which didn't compete with Habbema & Son Incorporated.

Hubert's company publishes scientific work, and we're more in the popular sector, in herbs and health food and the mystical meadows. While I write this essay, our latest project is on the table, an inane survey of telepathy in animals: *Do You Know That Puss Can Read Your Thoughts?* That's pure nonsense, because cats can't read. They can't even think; at the most, they can feel a little. Whoever owns an animal knows that human moods can be sensed by animals and that they will react to the impulses we emit. This silent communication is the subject of our book. The author, who, commissioned by my firm, fills two hundred pages on this simple subject, can't do much more than repeat himself in vague terms and quote some examples that are "clarified" by unprovable imagination. That's exactly what he did, and we took care of a striking jacket, illuminating illustrations, and some artful photography. The reader will see what he should have known for some time confirmed in clear print, and supplier and client can continue in peace. The book is meant to be a suitable Christmas present and can't do much harm, but for me it's depressing. Dad's trusted pussycat is still alive and determined on revenge. The pliable, animated plaything of the past is turning into a hellish tiger, and hisses and snarls even when I bring him his food.

Hubert's firm prints science for the universities and we entertain, but the positions that Hubert and I filled, before Dad's death, were about equal. We both served the capitalists above. Routine tasks humiliated our brilliant minds. Two PhD's checking spelling mistakes. We demurred volubly during the many drunken hours that we wasted in the bar at the Brewer's Canal, and Monica pretended to listen to our variations on the theme of self-pity. Her only gift was her beauty, and we allowed her to fasten onto us so that we could have something to pride ourselves on. Her seductive presence confirmed our faith in ourselves and the possibility of eventually improving our positions. How? By increasing our status. And what would we eventually do? Publish books ourselves. Which firm would give us our chance? Habbema & Son. What was in the way? Dad's everlasting presence.

Hubert and I came up with the same idea simultaneously, after discussing Tanizaki a little. The sexual urge can destroy a man and make him a willing victim. Would my father be willing? Tanizaki evolved no new thought; the urge has been around since the Creation. There is no novelty in the basic themes, but variations and combinations are, fortunately, endless. The genetic codes are given and can, once they're understood, be used. Our joke would be another way of manipulating what circumstances offered so freely. Dad's high blood pressure, Monica's beauty. $1+1=0$. We ordered fresh drinks and winked at each other, Hubert and I. The zero of Dad's death amused us no end. While we were at it, we worked out the future.

Hubert, who likes to reach out and knows how to ensnare potential clients, would be our commercial director, earning top wages and entitled to invest his savings on purchasing stock; I, with the majority of the shares, would stay in the background, control the final choice of work to be published, and be responsible for artwork and the appearance of the product. Hubert would sell my creations. A deal? Hubert was delighted. "And I?" Monica asked.

"You want to work?" Hubert asked.

"Well, work——"

"You'll be on the payroll," I said at once, because we would need her and she had to stay around. "You'll be our hostess," Hubert said, "or something like it." He underlined his statement with a lopsided grin. We raised our glasses. She'd be worth every penny we would send her way, with her long slender legs, tipped-up bosom, tight waist, ever slightly opened moist lips, and the eyes of an angel.

That's what Hubert was thinking; he's the expert of good taste. I'm a little more gross. My line of thinking always ends in a climax.

Dad's climax this time. Dad was overweight, his hands trembled, and he walked with some trouble. He should not excite himself; his doctor friend kept repeating the warning. I was forgetting at that time that Dad was also a kind old man, not just a fat fence that had to be kicked down to open our way.

"But," I said, "would a man of his age and condition still be capable of fullfilling his desire?"

Hubert, slurring his words, held forth on the power of positive thinking. Monica admired her delicate hands; so did I. I knew her hands quite well; they had been all over me often enough, with Hubert's approval. Hubert, my good friend, always willing to share. He only wanted Monica as a decoration, I needed her to play my sneaky little games. Waiter! More to drink. We did enjoy ourselves in our ghoulish way. I can see that now, a little late.

Demons from the nether spheres: me, in a dirty sweater and frayed jeans with a zipper broken by belly pressure. Hubert, in his leather outfit set off with thin bright chains. Monica, the living mannequin, a painted pawn pushed around by our smudgy hands. How clever we thought we were.

I'm writing all this down to analyze the goings-on and to formulate a clear confession; read on, Adjutant Grijpstra and Sergeant de Gier. As you see, I'm behaving properly in the end, for he who says good-bye should do everything in his power to cause the least trouble to those who remain on the human battlefield. I know the rules because I once heard two cops talking to each other, with me in the backseat of their patrol car, arrested for drunken driving. The officer at the wheel recalled that the previous night he had visited a home where a suicide had taken place. "Letter present?" the other cop asked. "Yes, he knew how to behave, the sucker." A decent chap who hadn't broken the last rule. Their man hung himself but pinned a note to his chest first: "Good-bye. Couldn't take any more of this." Signed and all. No blame cast on anyone else. That's why I'm typing away tonight; I'm expressing my error. I've failed sufficiently; when this envelope with contents reaches you, you can close your file.

Who is to blame? Monica had a bad youth. Abandoned as a child, she was raised in state homes, abused to a level where she could only withdraw into the remnants of her self, and even to us, her companions of a latter day, she could open up only a little. She selected Hubert, whose perversion created distance, and me, whose ugly exterior matched the sadness of her soul.

I'm trembling now because I'm seeing more than I can stand and because the end is slipping into sight. The end of the torture, of my pain, but first I have to take proper care of the final formality. I'll have to call you and press the trigger afterward. I first intended the tiny projectile to enter my brain between the eyes, but I read somewhere that a .22 bullet—the instrument that's waiting so patiently next to my telephone—isn't much more than an improved toy: could be too light and might get stuck in the bone of the forehead. It would be better to direct the shot through the mouth, with the barrel pointed slightly upward; then the mind can be reached easily from within. Oral and ultimate satisfaction. Not too tasty. I sucked the barrel just now—pistol grease is sickly sweet.

Read on, upholders of the law. A son who murders his father is no good, I quite agree. We should be more careful, chipping away at our taboos, but people in your profession aren't too easily shocked. You'll take care of this, won't you? You'll write me off as a sinner who'll have to put up with his just reward?

Dad was a good guy who looked after me well, and after

Mom, too, but Mom paid no attention to traffic that afternoon in the past; no, please, I had nothing to do with that, I was in summer camp, at a safe distance. Dad's only weakness was his overeating. I inherited the trait and even the pets picked up the habit. Dad's weakness mattered to us conspirators, it came up during that fateful conversation in the bar that I haven't visited since then. "Where can your father be hit?" Hubert asked. "We've got to know, if we want to pull this off."

Dad fancied his snacks but he could manage the problem— during the day, that is—when he followed doctor's instructions. At night he slipped into the kitchen—the dog would wake him. Together they sneaked about and emptied the refrigerator. Cheese, fat slices of ham, olives, pickles, buttered toast covered with sardines, creamy soups—the parties lasted for hours. To counter the results, Dad exercised a little and the dog climbed a stepladder. In the old days he could get off, but throughout the last year Dad would have to pick him up and put him carefully on the floor. Then they returned to bed, after a visit to the bathroom and some intake of medications. The dog got some, too.

Hubert had seen the movie *La Grande Bouffe,* a melodrama in which elderly gents, suffering from incurable disease, exploded themselves with previous intent. "Something like that," Hubert said. "We arrange the final feast and he'll pop."

"Too difficult," I answered. "You underestimate Dad's defenses. We have religious genes, so guilt slows us down. If we're too coarse, he'll smell the devil. Don't forget that Albert Habbema, my grandfather, was able to start the publishing firm thanks to the sale of a collection of valuable antique Bibles that he inherited from *his* dad. A little subtlety, old pal."

"Sex is subtle," Monica said, posturing gently.

Hubert moved an inch away from her. "Your father fancies women?"

"Sure," I said brightly, paying no attention to his expression of disgust.

Dad didn't practice sex, of course. A proper widower, well in control of lower lust. "However . . ."

"Yes?" Hubert asked eagerly, trying to dry his hands on the smooth leather of his jacket. "Let's have it, comrade."

He knew that this approach always caught me off guard. To call me "comrade" meant a direct appeal to the core of our friendship. We had been comrades at kindergarten when we defended ourselves against the gang of bullies. We were both minorities; all the others were healthy and sane. Together we managed through the early and later formative years. Friendship? I'm not so sure anymore. Fear kept us together, and we became each other's shadow, which darkened through the years, a composition of black shades to which Monica joined hers later.

I told Hubert what I knew about Dad's sex secrets. There had been a family gathering and Dad, drunk, had beckoned me over and made me sit at his feet. We mellowly discussed erotic pleasures. The next day he avoided me, but by then I knew more. He always liked to squeeze tea bags, looking naughty. That evening he explained why. They reminded him of breasts, of course, which, when properly handled, emit the feeding fluid. "Nothing in this world," Dad said dreamily, "excites me more than the female bosom." He told me about his very early youth, when, as a caged baby, he rattled his fence when his nurse stripped slowly to titillate her captive audience. Toddler Dad would get so frantic that he was attacked by hiccups and had to be lifted out and fondled, and he would fondle in turn. "Amazing," Dad said, "such a strong memory, and the very first; I wasn't two years old."

I thought that was it and wanted to rejoin the party, but Dad's heavy hand restrained me. The nurse stayed with the family and later, when Dad was in puberty, lured him to her attic, for the game wasn't over. The fondling continued but was never fullfilled, for she was religious, too, and believed that complete enjoyment had to be reserved for the heavenly spheres. A little of the way was perhaps all right, so here we see the ripe woman and the forming youth together between the sheets, feeling away but not quite . . . well, yes.

Until the couple were caught, by furious Granddad, and Nurse was thrown out, sobbing, dragging her bursting cardboard suitcase.

"I had to let her go," Dad said, "but the desire clung."

And now the clash of cymbals, clanging into my ears, after Dad had tipped back his umpteenth glass of jenever. "Son, Nurse looked just like Monica."

"*Right,*" Hubert shouted. "Where's there's a will, there's a way. Good luck is with the relentless pursuer. Right away the solution jumps out at us. Our adventure is blessed."

Dad knew Monica well; I often took her home, with Hubert, and the four of us would dine together. Dad was always most polite when addressing our companion. How could I ever have guessed that she resembled the lurid influence of his early days? If he hadn't told me, he might still be alive. But did we have a choice? I often wonder.

Hubert instructed Monica in the fine art of seduction. I assisted his efforts. I suggested to Dad that our garden needed a new design and that my friends would like nothing better than to join the project. While we dug—Hubert and I, for this was manly work, and Dad was too old and Monica too tender—and carried rocks, raked gravel, constructed a bamboo gate, Monica was left with Dad. On the back porch, well out of our sight, Monica displayed her curves, accentuated and not in any way hidden by the smallest of bikinis. She kept up the show, even when she dressed, and Dad wasn't given a moment of respite. She did a good job, even if she couldn't play with the pets, for neither dog nor cat wanted to join her when she enticed them to frolic with her on the Persian rugs, so that she could continue her act.

"This is like Nazi Germany," Hubert said, lugging bags filled with soil, or sinking more lilies in the pond. "Much beauty was created there before the Power showed its true face."

Imbeciles we were, knowing full well what was impelling us but never pausing to reflect.

Hubert developed some muscle and I lost a large number of pounds. We heard Dad laugh and Monica titter from the seclusion of the back porch. Except for the howling and hissing of the pets, working conditions were most pleasant. Hubert wanted to hurry, while I preferred to slow down; the status quo seemed to suit me fine.

Dad didn't want to give in, but he was sorely tempted. The seduction took a month. Meanwhile, the garden developed nicely. Hubert egged Monica on. Autumn was on its way, and we were chopping wood for the open fire by then. Monica finally managed to convince Dad of her sincere longing for his elderly caresses. The merriment on the porch gave way to deep sighs. Then they became absent, for Dad preferred the privacy of his city apartment. Sin shies away from an audience. Dad died in secret, and Monica's panic made her run away, leaving her telltale bag that invited the Murder Brigade into my office.

"So your father had an affair with the young lady," Adjutant Grijpstra said. "I can't say the situation is too clear to me, but I think we have bothered you enough for today." He left, followed by the impeccably attired sergeant, who turned in the doorway to scan me with his steady gaze. *Today.* The word they left hung heavily between my walls. There was always tomorrow, as they intended me to understand. The suspicion, the charge in the sergeant's gaze, was clear enough. I understood that he almost understood my motivation. For look here, something was wrong, although the facts still underlined my innocence. Monica was Hubert's girlfriend. Hubert was gay. Monica was most attractive and I was not. Dad's death transferred all his property to me. The case smelled foully on all sides, but the catchers of ghouls were short of proof, as long as my resistance lasted. Cops catch the wicked, but their power is restricted, and it doesn't often happen that they meet the perpetrators while they're actually doing wrong. Their main task is preventive; they are around and they stay around, making sure you won't ever forget their presence. And while they're around, the sinner may weaken.

Grijpstra and de Gier visited me twice again; afterward they stayed away. Insufficiency of proof—and what did they care anyway? Detectives of the Murder Brigade are always ankle-deep in a quagmire of sticky evil; they could put up with the little I was adding. Whenever they visited, they allowed me to talk and observed me meanwhile, informing me wordlessly that they thought I was a slimy example of everything they abhorred. As if I needed their quiet attack. Of criticism I had a sufficiency and it was all my own. Their pointing fingers were visible, especially the adjutant's stubby index, and it hurt me that this paternal figure refused to show the slightest understanding.

Fine. Dad's dead, the company is mine. Hubert showed up the very next day to remind me of my promise, and I made him a director. Monica appeared and lay down on the visitor's couch. I tried to convince them that some patience might be better, but Hubert called me "comrade" and Monica became erotic.

I knew then I would have to be rid of them; the friendship, if our connection was ever friendly, reminded me of what we had done wrong together. How does one remove nasty people? For once and for all? A good beginning is half the work?

To separate myself from Hubert was easy enough. Hubert always underestimated me, a mistake that has terminated many a criminal mind. When you grow up together, there's enough opportunity to weigh the other. He should have remembered that my PhD was *cum laude*, that I never lose a game of chess, and that in confrontations I always slide out unscratched in the end.

What was Hubert's weakness? Which circumstances needed to be combined? I had money, Hubert hadn't. Hubert had expensive tastes, and his worst was his longing for rough male company. He liked to be around motorcyclists with bulging biceps. Bullies can be bought, especially when they're on expensive drugs, and I found just the type in a junkies' café, who, in spite of his lack of brain, further reduced by addiction, did grasp fairly quickly what I wanted of him. I didn't tell him that Hubert's skull was thin and that, as a kid, he almost died because he fell off his bike and cracked his head. I did mention that Hubert liked to be hurt, especially on the head, if possible with a chain.

Hubert does get rather drunk at times. I took him along to the miserable quarters where the leather boys hang out and introduced him to my burly acquaintance. I gave money to the tough. "Have a good time, boys; you'll get along well." Amazing how easy it all is. Hubert was found in the morning, dying from a fractured skull; he had been nicely arranged between two piles of garbage. He mumbled as he died. A prayer? The alley is called Prayer Without End, for it's circular and bites its own tail.

Monica was a little trickier, but as Hubert used to say, where there's a will, there's a way. I knew her inside out and *her* weak spot was obvious. Monica was allergic to monosodium glutamate, the taste-improver professional cooks use so that they can serve appetizing leftovers. The chemical also tenderizes meat. MSG never fails to upset Monica's stomach. It also makes her dizzy, and when she consumes a lot, she's apt to faint.

I bought a little bright red can filled with MSG.

With Hubert gone, his share in Monica became mine, too. Our more intimate relationship brought along more duties. She asked for presents, and I bought her an Italian sports car with a long dainty nose. Monica liked to race in traffic. As she was a good driver, my hope wasn't fullfilled too soon. I was in a hurry; hence the can of the weakener of Monica's defenses.

Monica was vain.

All factors were available, and the day came that they would connect. We were on holiday in Paris, and I took her to a three-star restaurant, close to the circular road that spans the inner city. Monica just loved to race that highway, all day if need be, and she would change lanes, with inches to spare from the others' fenders.

During the day I was friendly enough and for dinner ordered her favorite delicacy, a filet mignon topped with rare mushrooms. "What's wrong with your hair, dear?" I asked, just when she was ready to dig in.

"Doesn't it look right?"

"No, it's all blown about. You look ridiculous, you know."

She repaired to the rest room to see if I was right, and I sprinkled the glutamate on her little steak, pressing it in with my fork so that the white flakes wouldn't show. Monica returned, ate the filet mignon, and got irritated by my sarcastic remarks. Monica hardly ever lost her temper, but she was sensitive to criticism if it referred to her grammar. Never having been to school much, she expressed herself poorly. I said that it was very nice if a woman was attractive, but that beauty was only skin-deep and that a man did appreciate intelligence after a while. She became furious and left. I had placed the car keys on the table so that she could grab them as she stalked out. We were staying in a hotel around the corner; she knew where she could locate me once her anger passed. I got up, shouted another insult, sat down, and ordered cognac. She must have been squashed while I was on my second refreshment. The gendarmes showed me later how the accident must have taken place. "Madame was speeding." Well over a hundred, they thought; apparently, experts can determine speed from measuring tire tracks. They were short and cut through the railing that supposedly protects the highway. Monica's car made quick work of it and then flew down, landing eventually on a crossing and a Parisian in a Renault, father of four kids, on his way home after working late in his office.

That nice, dead, harmless *monsieur* got to be too much for

me; he appears in all my dreams and keeps asking whether I couldn't have arranged my personal problem a little better. "Four little children, Monsieur!" I might have taken them into consideration. Who would look after them, *hein?* My dream demon isn't angry; he just inquires politely.

Dad's pets pursue me, too. The dog is off his food and suffers from a neurotic itch, and the cat waits for me, in hidden corners, to leap out and hiss and claw. That cat used to be my pal once; she would bring me crumpled papers and expect me to throw them and then would bring them back. Siamese cats do that, if they truly like you. I need medication to fall asleep, and instead of resting, I then keep murdering my father and my friends. Each night they die again, out of breath, clutching their broken heads, flattened in a wrecked sports car, and the French office worker keeps returning to tell me about his starving kids.

ADJUTANT GRIJPSTRA LEFT me his visiting card, with the request to call him if something cropped up. Very well, something has. I won't disturb you personally, Adjutant, although your private number is printed on your card, but it's evening now and I imagine your wife has just brought you your coffee and you're about to watch a nature film on TV. I'll call your communications room. The officers who will take care of my conclusion will deliver this note.

REPORT OF THE COMMUNICATIONS ROOM, POLICE HEADQUARTERS, AMSTERDAM

—January, 198–. Time: 19:37 hours.

Dialogue as taped:
"Hello, the police?"
"Listen. My name is Peter Habbema and I'm phoning

from my office, Habbema and Son Inc., Emperor's Canal 610. I'm going to . . . eh . . . shoot myself."

"Don't do that, sir."

"What was that?"

(repeat)

"Don't do that? Come on, Officer. This is a neat city. Garbage has to be cleared away."

"Mr. Habbema . . ."

"No, just a minute, please. There's a letter all ready for you, addressed to your detectives. I've left nothing out. Motivation. Why it's gotten as far as this. Complete. Crime and punishment. All I have to do now is pull this little trigger." *(clicking sound)*

"What's this now? Just a click? Aha, I see it. Safety is still on, I'm never handy with technical stuff. This way now, up she goes, and ready to fire. See this? The red dot is visible. There we go."

(sound of a shot)

REPORT OF A PATROL CAR. Number 6-7. Time: 19:54 hours . . . and we found the lifeless body of a male. Letter present . . .

Houseful of Mussels

"One dead professor," the girl operator at Amsterdam Municipal Police Headquarters said into the telephone. "Nice job for you, Adjutant. Close by, too. A five-minute walk."

Grijpstra was still trying to claw through the fog of deep sleep. "Whuh?"

"Where? Okay. He lives—eh, lived, isn't it sad, poor chap—at 143, Leyden Quay. Isn't that close?"

"Yuh."

"Are you asleep, Adjutant? It isn't eleven yet."

"I've been up and about all day," Grijpstra said. "Off duty now. Tired. Phone Sergeant de Gier. *He's* on duty."

"He's there now, Adjutant. The commissaris says you'll have to go, too, because of the corpse being a professor. Makes it more involved, don't you agree?"

"Nuh." Grijpstra replaced the phone. He looked, unhappily, first at his three-piece dark blue suit, then at his pistol belt, before putting it all on. He pushed an almost toothless comb through short white bristly hairs that kept standing up as he stared at them in the mirror. "What's up?" he asked his heavy image. "Suicide? That'd be better."

He repeated the thought as he strolled under elm trees that answered by rustling their leaves in the soft warm breeze. Ducks, hoping to be fed and talked to, followed alongside, paddling furiously in the canal. *Professors overthink*, Grijpstra thought. *They know the world is about to fade or fold. They're too intelligent; they can figure out the future. They anticipate this environment's total destruction. Can't bear their insight—I'll confirm that in my report, which de Gier can then type out and sign on my behalf. Meanwhile, I will be in bed again, enjoying the oblivion due to me because of higher status and rank.*

He stumbled and almost fell, tripping over a mostly-dachshund, squatting unobtrusively in weeds. "Oops." The dog yapped kindly. They walked on together to the dead man's house, marked as such from afar by the sweeping blue lights of two patrol cars. A crowd had gathered, lusting for blood. "Away," Grijpstra said, pushing through slowly. Constables guarding a mighty oak door saluted smartly.

"Suicide?" Grijpstra asked cheerfully.

"Murder."

Grijpstra frowned. "How so?"

"We found no weapon. Subject was shot in the forehead. A neighbor lady heard the shot and telephoned at once. Ten thirty P.M. this happened. We arrived at ten thirty-five."

"Were you expecting the mishap?" Grijpstra kept frowning. "Patrol cars are supposed to be slow. Did anyone see anyone leave?"

"No."

"How did you get in?"

"The neighbor lady had a duplicate key, Adjutant."

"No crying wife or live-in love?"

"Just a million mussels, Adjutant," the constable said. "In aquariums. All over. Even in the bathrooms. And this ghastly green light, and little bubbly tubes, and pumps that thump and suck, and the mussels opening and closing, yawning and gaping. Scary. *Yeech.*"

"Mussels," Grijpstra said. "Right. Just what I expected. My sergeant is in here?"

"Yes, Adjutant."

"And the technical gents?"

"On the way, I'm sure."

Grijpstra read a name, hand-lettered nicely on the door's gleaming green surface: HANS STROOM.

"A mussel professor," said the policeman who talked. The policeman who didn't nodded.

"Mussels have been getting pricey lately," Grijpstra said.

"That's logical," the policeman who didn't talk said. "Once the elite get into something, the price goes up, right? Mussel-ologists must be earning a fortune."

The door wasn't closed. De Gier was waiting in the hall. Sergeant Rinus de Gier was a tall man, wide-shouldered, narrow-hipped. He wore tailor-made jeans and jackets that he cheered up with multicolored silk scarves. His curly hair shone softly and his huge handlebar mustache was carefully brushed. High cheekbones pushed his kind brown eyes upward. His age was hard to guess, although he knew it to be close to forty. Grijpstra was close to fifty, also from the down side. De Gier didn't have a female friend at the moment; Grijpstra was separated. De Gier was reputedly still searching for happiness. Grijpstra reputedly no longer cared.

"So?" Grijpstra asked.

"So," de Gier said, "our man is dead. The doctor will confirm his total absence." He pointed.

Grijpstra walked through the indicated door and bowed down. "Oh, dear." He put his hands in his pockets. "Nicely laid out. On his back. Mouth closed. Eyes open." He raised his voice to make himself heard, for the water pumps bubbled loudly. He also raised his hands, as if to protect himself from the green light illuminating the aquariums' wavy water.

"Makes the little fellows grow," de Gier said. "Stimulates plant life—maybe the mussels eat the algae? Our professor is an oceanographer. This is a mussel farm, government funded. He lived here, sharing his life with the black-and-blue chappies."

"TV?" Grijpstra asked, indicating a screen.

"A computer monitor. Must have been working with it. Those figures seem to be some mussel-food formula."

Grijpstra sat down on a yellow plastic case. "Tell me more."

"The neighbor lady was here when I arrived. She phoned the police when she heard the shot, then came to visit. An older lady—the professor's present state upset her, so she went home to take half an overdose of Valium."

"A suspect?"

"Unlikely."

"But she had a key."

"So that she can take care of the place when the professor has to leave. She feeds the mussels, checks temperatures, oxygen, whatever. She gets paid for her troubles."

"Nice-looking laddie," Grijpstra said, bending down toward the corpse. "Good beard. Great tan. Athletic."

"A scuba diver," de Gier said, opening up a cupboard. "See the equipment? I checked his passport—it's on the desk over there. He'd reached the age of thirty-nine. Unmarried. Lives alone, according to the neighbor, but he does have girlfriends, two, both his assistants, one junior colleague and a much-better-looking student.

"Who exactly?"

De Gier checked his notes. "Bakini Khan, late twenties, and Truus Vermuul, a lady of uncertain age. I got addresses." He tapped the notebook. "Phone numbers, too. Both of them live in the area."

"Listen here," Grijpstra said. "This will be simple." He scratched his chin. "Just before the shot there was an argument. Someone heard it."

"Nobody heard an argument," de Gier said. "The neighbors on the other side are on holiday, and my witness is somewhat deaf. She did hear the shot. She also heard the front door slam. I agree with you, though. This student, Bakini, is probably exotically attractive." He pointed at the corpse. "This professor used his chance. They lusted together. Bakini wants to transform the emotion into love. The professor seems to love mussels better. Bakini now hates the forever-opening-and-closing little beasts. She makes her friend a proposition he couldn't possibly refuse, yet he did. So he died."

Grijpstra squatted. "Classical, don't you think? A truly murderous wound, Sergeant—I haven't seen one in a long while. It's all automatic these days. Remember the Chinese last week, with the sixteen wounds? Half an Uzi's clip, fired at random. This is professional. I like this better."

De Gier squatted, too. "Bull's-eye, all right. First prize. I say, do you think he looks like a professor?"

"More like a pirate," Grijpstra agreed. "Including the golden earring. Dashing, very. Women like pimps and pirates better. They help themselves and run off smiling. Women like that, you know, but they get them later."

"Love-related," de Gier said. "So you think so, too. This corpse abused a vengeful woman."

"Are the sleuths done sleuthing?" a gentleman asked, leaning through the open door. "Can my colleagues and I now apply science?"

"We left some fingerprints," de Gier said, "but we haven't found the cartridge yet."

The gentleman found the cartridge. "Thirty-eight caliber."

"A ladylike weapon." De Gier rubbed his hands. "Can be hidden in a handbag. Coming, Adjutant? We can phone from the pub."

"Just a minute," Grijpstra said. "You, sir. That's a Polaroid, right? One gruesome photograph, please, of this gruesome corpse. Don't spare us the blood."

A flashbulb popped. The snapshot became more detailed as they watched. "Nice," Grijpstra said. "Blood coming out of his nostrils and mouth. Just what I wanted."

⸜

GRIJPSTRA USED THE café's telephone while de Gier sipped coffee and drew diagonal lines on a napkin. Line 1: a dead professor. Line 2: a million mussels. Line 3: two unknown female suspects. The gun didn't deserve a line of its own—it was merely the extension of a killing arm. What else?

"Miss Khan," Grijpstra asked the mouthpiece in his hand. "I'm sorry to bother you this late. This is the police, Adjutant Grijpstra, Murder Brigade. Something quite unpleasant has happened and my sergeant and I would like to call on you, yes? . . . Right now? That's nice."

"That's nice," Grijpstra said half a minute later. "No coffee for me? Then I'll have yours. Thank you—very nice coffee. The nice lady's nice street address is just around the nice corner. We can walk. Nice weather outside. Ha-ha."

"Like your job, do you?" de Gier asked grimly.

"No," Grijpstra said.

"I was thinking again," de Gier said. "Did you notice the hard yellow plastic boxes at the professor's?"

"I sat on one, didn't I?" Grijpstra asked. "So what? So nothing."

"Those boxes didn't look right," de Gier said. "I thought. A hard commercial color amid all those soft greens and blues."

Grijpstra pushed the empty coffee cup away. "You see colors? I am the artist."

"You are?" de Gier asked. "Maybe you should paint those mussels. The pure white sands, those swaying dark shapes. And then those ugly yellow boxes, with Chinese characters stamped on their sides. And the neighbor lady says the professor had just returned from Taiwan."

"The boxes are connected?"

"The boxes are contrasted," de Gier explained. "Crime is associated with contrasts. Remember the junkie driving the

Rolls-Royce? Remember the classy lady running barefoot around the queen's palace? Our best cases of that year."

"Boxes?" Grijpstra repeated.

"Never mind." De Gier paid for the coffee.

Grijpstra mumbled as they walked. "Hi," de Gier said to the mostly-dachshund. The doggie wagged its tail. "Friend of ours?" de Gier asked.

Grijpstra nodded. "You know what we are? I wonder about that at times, now that I'm older and more aware. We're ghouls. And we like it. Just now, when I spoke to the nice lady on the phone? I was *scaring* the nice lady."

"I heard you," de Gier said, stooping down to pet the dog. "'The *Murder Brigade*'; 'something *very unpleasant* has happened.'"

"We're werewolves," Grijpstra said sadly, "creeping around being weird, to freak out nice ladies."

"So she is innocent?" de Gier asked.

"Of course," Grijpstra said. "Why would a lovely young lady shoot her very own lover/teacher? Because of the horrible spell that he cast on her? She wasn't getting straight A's anymore because she refused to humble her tender spirit, because she wouldn't give in to his lustful whipping and sexy kicking?"

"Right," de Gier said. "My idea entirely. Perhaps she did do away with him, but she can be excused. I didn't like the chap myself. Sinister, rather. If anyone is to blame, it's *us*. Corruption and liberal laws have weakened the police so that the citizens increasingly rely on self-defense. She knew that her situation could only worsen if she called us. So she shot him herself."

Grijpstra tripped. "Damn dog." He wagged his finger. "What's with you? Your bladder too small? Stop squatting in front of my foot. Get lost." The mostly-dachshund limped. Grijpstra picked it up, felt the sore paw, scratched the dog's neck, and put it down again.

"Faker," de Gier said gruffly. The little dog grinned.

"Ugly yellow boxes," de Gier said. "Subdivided inside, with spirals everywhere. What for?"

Grijpstra rang a bell. The door clicked open. Dainty naked brown feet appeared on a steep staircase, lengthening into slim ankles and long legs. A young woman presented herself. She would be in her early twenties. She had doe eyes and long black hair, cascading down her slender shoulders. A sarong of batik cloth was wrapped around her body.

The detectives showed their IDs, which she carefully studied.

I do sometimes like my work, de Gier thought as he followed Bakini up the stairs. Crime is usually unattractive. Suspects mess up society and we hold our noses and are forever trying to arrange things neatly, making it worse. We deal with monstrosities spawned by perversity, but there's always the exception. Now look at this. A graceful suspect, descending from an Oriental heaven. Aren't our private surroundings projections of ourselves? Well? What about these tasteful rooms?

"Tea?" Bakini asked sweetly. She poured from a red copper kettle into little cups without handles. "No sugar or milk, I'm afraid, but they would only spoil the jasmine fragrance. Would you mind taking a cushion and sitting on the floor? I don't have chairs."

She doesn't even want to know what's up, de Gier thought. A truly polite spirit. The quiet acceptance emanating from Far Eastern philosophical solutions. Here we come clodhopping in, intending to misuse her for our egotistic goals. Wouldn't we like to clap her in irons and drag her to our lair? She knows it, but she keeps quiet, nicely. Good strategy—true kindness is a most fearsome weapon. He sniffed at the incense that reached him from an altar on a low table, next to an aquarium where mussels quietly opened and closed. Bakini had seated herself, tucking her legs under her, hiding them under a fold of her sarong.

"Good tea," Grijpstra said.

"I love your rooms," de Gier said, trying to copy the all-encompassing smile of the little Buddha statue on the table.

Bakini smiled back.

"Professor Hans Stroom?" Grijpstra asked.

"Is he dead?"

"He is," de Gier said. "Shot through the head."

Bakini looked at him calmly.

There we go again, de Gier thought. *Easterners have a better way of reacting. I cringe when bad news hits me, but she sits up straight. I flap my hands; she folds them. My eyes go wide; she almost closes hers. It all goes with the smell of the incense, the bubbling of the water pump.*

Grijpstra made an effort to keep looking stern. *Now what?* the adjutant thought. *We can't relax.* "Were you born here?" he asked.

"I was born in your former South American colony, Suriname," Bakini said softly. "My forefathers were indentured laborers from Pakistan. I knew the professor well. I worked at his mussel station on the coast and assisted with the experiments here at his home. We traveled together—earlier this year we were in Karachi."

"Not in Taiwan?"

"No, Truus went to Taiwan. We do a lot of traveling in our department."

Grijpstra cleared his throat. "You're very calm. Don't you want to know how your teacher was murdered?"

"Yes." Bakini's voice vibrated slightly. De Gier apologized to himself for feeling a pleasurable shiver down his spine.

Bakini bowed her head. "Death is part of life. Scientists especially should accept that. Life and death flow from each other. It would be unthinkable to hold on to either."

"Why did the professor travel?" de Gier asked, trying to keep his voice flat and cold.

"We visited mussel farms mostly."

"Were you here all night?"

"Yes."

"You spoke to him?"

"By telephone." She nodded. "He wanted me to come over, but I said it was no use."

"An affair?" de Gier asked.

"Yes."

"When did it stop?"

"Yesterday," Bakini said quietly. She rose in one supple movement, without touching the floor with her hands. "More tea?" She poured it into the little cups, respectfully held up by the detectives. "I broke up with Hans because I thought he had become too greedy. Scientists should serve society. Our world is three-fourths water. The oceans could feed all of humanity if they were managed properly, but we selfishly rob and steal, pollute, don't replace what we take out. Less food is available each day. But scientists could reverse the process."

"Didn't the professor share your ideals?" de Gier asked.

"No." Bakini replaced the teapot daintily. "Hans was paid quite well as a university professor, about the maximum income that this rich country can provide, but he still had to be a businessman, too, buying cheap mussel seed from Karachi and selling it here through his own company at a huge profit. When he and Truus came back from Taiwan, he brought plastic starting boxes developed by Chinese mussel breeders. He had taken out a sublicense for Western Europe and was about to have them manufactured here."

"For private profit?" de Gier asked. "And that tainted the relationship? Would you continue as his student?"

"Oh, yes," Bakini said. "I do want my degree. He will continue to teach me."

"He's dead," Grijpstra said.

"I rather doubt," Bakini said, "the linear essence of time. Much that he showed me will continue to work."

De Gier looked up. "I keep forgetting to ask you. Are you a good shot?"

She smiled. "Yes, I think so."

"With a pistol?"

"A spear gun." Her hand swept up and indicated an array of long metal arrows decoratively arranged on the wall. The gun itself was on the floor, looking deadly and in good order.

"What time did Hans phone you?" Grijpstra asked.

"Ten o'clock." She arranged a strand of hair on her temple. "I remember because I was going to watch a nature program on TV. I didn't, after all. I sat here instead."

"You had a feeling?" de Gier asked.

"I felt something was very wrong," Bakini said, "but I had no idea what."

Grijpstra dramatically produced the Polaroid picture. She took it from him and reverently pressed it to her forehead, saying something in a singsong voice.

"Beg pardon?" de Gier asked.

"I wished him a good journey."

De Gier shifted to ease a cramp in his leg. "You know," he said slowly, "in some countries crimes against the people are punishable by death. What sort of fish do you shoot when you're out hunting?"

"Sharks," Bakini said. "I shouldn't, perhaps, but I like the challenge."

"Wasn't Hans a shark?"

"The tribal laws of the Netherlands," Bakini said, "disapprove of doing away with our own species. My own law is to wait, once I've legally done all I can."

"SHE DIDN'T HAVE to wait long," Grijpstra said when they were back in the street. "Nice lady, but I'm glad I'm no shark."

"Hmm?"

"Hello?" Grijpstra asked, thumping de Gier's arm. "Hello? Shall we tackle the other one now? Call first? But the cafés around here will be closed by now."

De Gier checked his notepad. "Let's ambush the lady."

Dr. Truus Vermuul's apartment occupied the top floor of a restored little gabled house in a fashionable mews.

"Both suspects live within a ten-minute walk of the dead man's house," Grijpstra remarked. "A coincidence, perhaps?"

"For sure." De Gier rang the bell. "Did *she* do it?"

"You were right about the boxes," Grijpstra said. "Did she?"

De Gier shrugged. "I don't know. I hope so. I'm not going to arrest Bakini. What's the penalty again for assisting a criminal to escape?"

"Go away," the woman yelled at the top of the stairs. "I don't want to believe in Krishna. Piss off or I'll pour this boiling oil on your heads."

"Police, ma'am," Grijpstra shouted, waving his card.

"The other chap, too? He looks like a Krishna."

"Are you?" Grijpstra asked de Gier. "Do you want to save the lovely lady?"

"I wouldn't save you," de Gier yelled, "if you begged me on your knees."

Grijpstra was halfway up the stairs. De Gier bounded past him, heading for the pot she was holding. "It's all right," Truus said grumpily. "I'm boiling up a mess of mussels, a new recipe. What's wrong?"

"Professor Hans Stroom got himself shot dead tonight," Grijpstra panted. "We're making inquiries. Can I sit down?"

"Do you have a warrant?" Truus asked. She was a big woman, in her forties, amply proportioned. Her large, bulging blue eyes weren't focusing too well.

"I can get a warrant," de Gier said. "Back in a jiffy."

She waved him to a straight-backed chair at the bare table under a high white ceiling. The fairly large room was lit by fluorescent tubes.

"Shot?" Truus said. "You're kidding. I saw Hans today at the university. Who would shoot that fool?"

De Gier asked if he could use the phone. "You guys know anything more about the cartridge?"

"Can't be sure," the ballistics voice said. "Probably a Walther PPK. We have the slug, too—dug it out of the skull. All the nasty little gunmen have PPKs now. The weapon is in vogue. You can buy Walthers through the coffee shops where pot is supplied. Someone must have brought in a truckload of the suckers."

"A Walther PPK," de Gier said to Grijpstra. "Fits in a lady's handbag."

Truus had sat down, too. "Are you planning to blame this on *me*?" she asked. "Are you mad? Hans and I are friends. We've just been to Taiwan together."

"You don't look sad," Grijpstra said.

"Should I?" She hit the table with the flat of her hand. "We'll have a new professor tomorrow. There are plenty of professor-men around. Shooting them doesn't help."

"Friends?" de Gier said. "You were friends, you said."

She pulled up a shoulder. "Friends . . . okay . . . but I wouldn't *shoot* him. I wouldn't get his job anyway. The university uses women only for menial work."

It became quiet in the cool room. Truus fetched plates and forks from a cupboard. "Some mussels, boys? May as well make yourselves useful. I'm trying out new recipes, to advertise our clammy friends. I have white Beaujolais, too—not too clever a wine, but it's got a good wallop afterward."

"Just mussels," Grijpstra said.

She filled her own glass. De Gier gestured his refusal of the wine. He dug into the mussels. "Terrific."

Truus tasted the Beaujolais. "So is this. You sure now? You don't know what you're missing."

"You live here alone?" Grijpstra asked.

"Hurrah." She held up her glass. "To old Hans. Sure I live alone. I don't need you get-in-the-ways here. Polluters of the good planet. Multipliers of the bad seeds. Away with all men. We'll clone ourselves soon. Won't that be fun?"

"Can I hide somewhere and watch?" de Gier asked.

She reached for the bottle. "No pornography, please. Cloning is clean fun. Every time the body gets old, the clone will replace it. Throw the old body out."

"Where was your body at ten thirty tonight?" Grijpstra asked.

"Right here." She peered owlishly at her glass while the fluid level rose. "Cooking the old mussels." The bottle was empty. "Excuse me." She fetched another. The corkscrew didn't work too well. She impatiently slammed the cork into the bottle.

"Do you eat all your mussels yourself?" de Gier asked.

"I sell them to a deli further down the alley," Truus said. "Making a bit on the side. I learned that from Hans, I did. But he did it bigger. Yah-hoo, boys." She drank.

Grijpstra pushed the Polaroid photo of the corpse across the table. She looked at it. "Well, well." She pointed at stacked yellow mussel boxes in a corner of the room. "What's to become of those now, eh? His nice new line of merchandise?"

"Now, my dear," Grijpstra said, "who might have wanted to shoot your superior? Why don't you tell us?"

"Might?" Truus asked. "And have? And wanted? And shoot? A lot of verbs you have there. The Chinese maybe?"

"Please," Grijpstra said. "Do we have to go that far? And there are so many of them. Why the Chinese, dear?"

"Don't *dear* me," Truus bellowed, hitting the table with both fists, making the dishes and her glass hop around. "Those mussel boxes are good business. They'll sell themselves. By the hundred thousand. The Chinese were crazy to sign their rights away for all of Western Europe. They must have realized it by now, so they came over, and *plop?*" She winked. "Eh?"

"That's heroin," de Gier said. "Not mussel boxes. You got yourself mixed up."

"Yes?" The wink became more obvious. "More mussels, my

boy? Mind if I drink by myself? There we go." She stared ahead glassily, drops gleaming on her chin.

Grijpstra leaned over to de Gier. "I think our hostess is nervous," he said loudly. "Why? No alibi perhaps?"

"I don't need an alibi," Truus burst out happily. "It's nice to have one, but there's no need, really. Not if I didn't do it. I live here. This is where I can be, as much as I like."

De Gier nodded solemnly. "You could be right, Adjutant. She knew the professor intimately, traveled with him all of the time, hotel rooms, you know what it's like."

"You do?" Truus asked. She put out her tongue. "Yuck." She tried to stare de Gier down, but her eyes kept slipping away. "I always had my own room and Hans always knocked on my door and I never opened. Ha."

Grijpstra pursed his lips. "Yeah."

"Yeah what?" Truus shouted. "More mussels?"

"Jealousy?" Grijpstra said. "The great motivation of most human mistakes. We keep running into jealousy, eh, Sergeant?" He held up the photograph. "Hans doesn't look too good here, but we can still see that he was handsome. And intelligent— must have been intelligent, a professor . . . And this older woman wanted him, and that young thing in the way, that exotic young thing. What a beauty—Bakini, right?"

"What?" Truus shouted. "Me? In love? With a *man*?"

"A woman scorned," de Gier said sadly.

"More mussels?" Truus yelled.

"No thank you, ma'am," Grijpstra said. "Really. They're delicious, but I'm quite full. What about you, Sergeant?"

"Not right now," de Gier said.

"Jealousy," Truus said. "What nonsense. Moral outrage, you mean. It's hard to tolerate a swindler like Hans, but we're still downtrodden—it doesn't do us any good to rebel." She brightened up. "Come on. A little glass? Such a nice evening. So good of you to come. Shall we . . ."

She thought.

"Tell you what," Grijpstra told de Gier. "This probably isn't even murder. She went to see her beloved. She was, once again, refused. She doesn't know the terrific strength of her own sexual longing. She had a gun. It went off."

"Yes?" de Gier asked. "Got him right between the eyes? Wow. Some urge."

". . . celebrate," Truus said. "Couldn't think of the word. Want to celebrate, boys? Okay, now you have some motivation. I've been reading this book on detection. What comes next again? The weapon?"

"Fingerprints," Grijpstra said. "You must have left some."

Truus laughed. "Of course. I often work there."

"Maybe we should go home," de Gier said. "Got to play this fair. A drunk suspect?"

"I'm fine," Truus said. "Don't pity me." She grinned. "You really think I'd get drunk if I was guilty?"

"Good." De Gier folded his hands. "The weapon comes next. You're right. Where is it? Where is the horrible tool used in *la crime passionnelle?*"

"*Crime* is masculine," Truus said. "*Le crime.*"

"The gun?" Grijpstra said. "It's here. She could have thrown it away, but there's only one short stretch of canal between the professor's house and here. Our divers could find it. No, it's here, don't you think?"

"A Walther PPK is expensive," de Gier said. "She would also want it for self-defense. Better watch her, Adjutant. Drunk. Violent. A loaded semiautomatic high-quality murder machine may pop up any moment."

Grijpstra looked around. "Oh, dear."

"Mussels?" Truus asked, looking into the pot. "There's plenty left. Don't you like my herbs? Don't they bring out the flavor?"

"Remember how you lost the tip of your toe?" de Gier asked.

"Let's see now. Suspect hides his gun in your coat. We look everywhere. We don't look in your coat. Then suspect helps you into your coat and takes the gun out. I saw that. I hit his wrist. The gun dropped to the floor and went off."

"I'm not wearing an overcoat today," Grijpstra said. "Neither are you."

"I don't understand you two," Truus said. "You know what the street stalls are asking for fried mussels these days? Four-fifty a scoop. Mine are free." She leaned her head on her hand. Her elbow slipped. Her head dropped, then jerked up again.

"Watch it," de Gier said. "I'm sorry. You kept telling us and I wouldn't hear you." He took the spoon from her hand and dug about in the pot. There was a clank of metal.

"Go easy," Grijpstra said. "We don't want the shells to explode in that hot brew. Easy now."

De Gier turned the pot over. Grijpstra wiped the pistol clean with a dishcloth. He shook his head. "Really, a scientist who doesn't respect a tool. Look at this. Fully loaded, cartridge in the chamber, safety off. There. That's better." He had removed the clip and ejected the chambered cartridge. "She must have dropped it in when she heard me ring the bell."

"I won't come with you," Truus said. "You'll have to drag me."

De Gier telephoned.

TWO POLICEWOMEN CLIMBED the stairs. "Where's the patient?"

"Inside," de Gier said.

"Couldn't bring her in yourself?" the older constable asked. "Shame on you."

"Didn't dare," de Gier said.

"Charge?"

"Manslaughter. She shot her boyfriend. Murder maybe."

"She's drunk," Grijpstra said as the constables marched in.

Truus looked at them sleepily, then pushed over the table.

She ran into the kitchen and came back with a long knife. The constables pulled their guns.

"No, no," de Gier said. "Truus?"

She swung the knife at him in a wide arc, and he blocked it, turned to the side, wrapped his arm around her arm, clamped his hand on her wrist. A sharp twist and she yelled. The knife clattered onto the floor. De Gier stepped behind the suspect and handcuffed her smartly. "There you go."

THE MOSTLY-DACHSHUND HAD been waiting outside. Grijpstra stumbled. De Gier caught him. "Dumb doggie," Grijpstra said, "are you teaching me awareness?"

De Gier picked up the little dog, turned it around, checked, put it down on its legs. "The female mind," de Gier said, "is both devious and relentless. She's offering herself and I would advise you to accept."

"Yes?" Grijpstra asked the mostly-dachshund. The dog held her head to the side, waved her long tail once, barked inside her long snout.

"Poor Truus," de Gier said.

"Poor Bakini," Grijpstra said.

"Why Bakini?"

"Won't you be after her?" Grijpstra asked. "To comfort her?"

"She might comfort *me*," de Gier said. "She has access to heaven."

"She might," Grijpstra said. He began to sigh and grumble.

"Don't be jealous," de Gier said. "See who'll be comforting you." He pointed down. The mostly-dachshund was sitting up, offering both paws. Grijpstra squatted and shook them. The dog wore no tag and looked like she had been living an irregular and needy existence.

"A stray?" Grijpstra asked.

"Yours for the taking," de Gier said. "Sleep well, you two."
He turned and strode off.

The dog woofed invitingly and made a believable attempt to frolic.

"You sure?" Grijpstra asked. "I'm not an easy man."

The little dog's ears waved, her tail wagged.

"You're not into mussels? You won't get fat? You won't watch TV?"

They each waited.

"Be my guest," Grijpstra said. They walked off.

Holiday Patrol

"I thought the Inner City rape/murder was being taken care of," the police dispatcher said on the radio. "Constables Ketchup and Karate were going out there in their bus, but they haven't reported back and now I can't raise them. Anyone else available to take over?"

De Gier grabbed his microphone. "Detective Patrol fourteen-six here. Our position is Emperor's Canal, corner Deer Alley. What's up, Dispatcher?"

"Tourist female," Dispatcher said, "speaking some kind of German, charges a tourist male with abusing her. Tourist female escaped from tourist male's rented holiday apartment. She is in the street now. Female tourist claims male tourist has a gun."

The radio voice was female, too—a warm voice, melodious, with lilting tones slipping into affectionate innuendos.

Detective-Sergeant de Gier, of the Amsterdam Municipal Police, on surveillance duty, behind the wheel of an unmarked vehicle commanded by Detective-Adjutant Grijpstra, groaned his appreciation. While the dispatcher's vocal femininity filled the small car, he even closed his eyes for a moment.

"Hey!" Grijpstra shouted.

De Gier woke from his trance. Their white unmarked Fiat Panda narrowly missed driving into Emperor's Canal.

"I knew that dispatcher's voice would cause trouble." Grijpstra took the microphone from the sergeant as the Fiat veered back from the canal's edge.

EARLIER ON THAT evening, Grijpstra had commented on the dispatcher's voice.

"All that lovey-doveyness gets in the way. I bet you there's nothing to back it up either." Grijpstra cleared his throat furiously. "Just like in that late-night nude show on AIR, your favorite station, Sergeant."

"Amsterdam Illegal Radio?" de Gier asked. "That wonderful silver voice talking about what she does in Art Deco bedrooms, in the elegant Old South district?"

Adjutant Grijpstra's forefinger prodded Sergeant de Gier's biceps. "You know I checked that radio show out? That I located a bunch of derelicts using secondhand equipment in a drafty loft in Mad Nun Alley? That I threatened to shut their operation down? That I didn't because the outfit is pathetic? You want to know why? Are you ready to accept the fact that the voice of your nude show's star performer, she with the naughty little-girlie / Lorelei tones, belongs to a lumpy fifty-year old with fogged-up glasses?"

"Mature and sexy," de Gier said. "So?"

Grijpstra grunted furiously. "The voice may be sexy, the reality is pure *dog*."

"I like pure dog." De Gier smiled happily. "And I am adult enough to appreciate older women."

They drove in silence for two blocks.

"You should read *Police Weekly*." The sergeant kneaded Grijpstra's shoulder. "Last week's issue had an article on *What the Adult Male looks for in his Search for a Partner*."

"Bah," Grijpstra said.

"Bah what?" De Gier smiled. "You're still stuck on firm flesh? The prime sexual desire, Adjutant, in the mature male, isn't for physical penetration of a junior madonnaesque body. In the older male, interest in spiritual aspects appears. It's love and affection men like you and me are after. It's the safe feeling we cherish, it's mutual caring we are in want of . . ." De Gier's smile widened. "It's the ability to caress the beloved's feet with our own before falling asleep that we crave. The arm around her shoulder. Leaning our tired head against her bosom afterward."

The idea seemed to surprise Grijpstra. "You mean cuddling, Sergeant?"

"HELLO?" THE CUDDLY radio voice now asked while it filled the Fiat with loving-care vibrations. "Are you there, fourteen-six? I know you're Special Assignments only, but the uniform patrol has let me down here."

"Location of alleged victim?" Grijpstra asked, while nudging de Gier, who, listening to the dispatcher, was about to swoon again.

Grijpstra switched off the microphone. "Try to keep the car away from open sewers." He switched the microphone on again. "Location of incident? Dispatcher? Hello?"

"Just a minute," the dispatcher said. "It's in my data bank, but the computer is malfunctioning."

"Open sewers?" de Gier asked while waiting. "You heard about the eighteen-centimeter-long minnow caught in Straight Tree Ditch? Did you see the photo of boys diving into the Amstel?"

"Prince Canal," the radio voice said. "Corner of Brewer's Canal. Please let me know what happens. New police policy wants us dispatchers not merely to direct but to support all colleagues on patrol. I can't help you with finding cell space but I can connect you with NASSAD." There was the ticking of a keyboard. "Just a moment, let me check this . . . I don't think NASSAD is open on weekends. It *is* Saturday, am I right?"

"That's affirmative," Grijpstra said. "What's NASSAD again?"

"New Age Shamanic Society Against Denial. It employs psychologists to diffuse ego assertion."

"Right," Grijpstra said gruffly. "Sergeant! Let's go. Corner of Prince and Brewer's."

De Gier had the Fiat Panda going already. Rape and attempted murder are defined as serious crimes and warrant the use of flashing blue light and siren. Police rules prescribe that excessive speeds may be used and traffic signals may be ignored with caution.

The sergeant's long arm reached through the window and stuck a magnetized blue light on the car's roof. The light flashed. The Fiat's hidden two-toned horn was on. De Gier sang along with the TEEH-TOOH TEE-TAH TEEH-TOOH of the siren. He held a black belt in Assorted Unarmed Combat and habitually won contests in the police shooting gallery. Perhaps this would be an occasion for testing his skills.

Grijpstra clicked on his safety belt. The pistol's butt caressing his armpit heightened the adjutant's increased awareness. He restrained the grin that he could feel twisting his cheeks as he tried not to enjoy de Gier's reckless driving. Did he really want to wrestle a murderous rapist on Brewer's Bridge? Was he looking forward to shoving a shackled psychopath into a dank cell?

Not that there were any cells, dank or dry, available these days.

In spite of a marked increase in crime and street warfare, official Amsterdam police policy was unchanged. The capital's chief constable kept urging his subordinates to maintain a low profile. All personnel were requested to make as few arrests as possible. Even so, since drug abuse was affecting unstable citizens' behavior, Amsterdam's limited jail space was in much demand.

Saturday, two A.M.—the speeding Fiat careered through empty alleys and quaysides. A flock of starlings twittered, lifted themselves from a tree, panicked, fluttered down in front of their windshield. When de Gier could see again a lone drunk loomed into view. The drunk was pushing a bicycle, stolen a minute ago. He released his loot. The bicycle carried on alone until it splashed into the canal. The bereaved thief watched his sinking loot being replaced by growing circles reaching out toward the canal's far shore.

Rats, disturbed by the siren's wailing, squeaked angrily while scurrying for cover between elm roots.

Another drunk, a man with a white beard, climbed a lamp post as the Fiat approached. The man's fear changed to cheer. He fell off the post when he lifted his hat to wave.

A few late prostitutes and drug dealers faded into their respective doorways.

The car turned east at Brewer's Canal. A woman in a shimmering low-cut black gown, silhouetted against the white wall of a houseboat, performed exaggerated dance steps on Brewer's Bridge. Grijpstra noticed the dancer's hat, shaped like a silken butterfly, with large drooping orange wings.

The Fiat skidded.

"Hey!" Grijpstra shouted.

Tires complained as the car turned around briskly. "We just passed our destination," de Gier said. "The corner of Prince and Brewer's Canals. I see no other female complainants about. That must be her, Adjutant."

The detectives wished the dancing lady a good evening, then stood back.

"I dance," the woman said in accented German, "because I am nervous."

The month was July, holiday season, and most Amsterdammers had vacated the city. After inquiring ahead for the latest news on civil wars, contagious disease, raging bushfires, lethal mudslides, currency-value changes, availability of wildlife, and discounts on amenities, the citizens had gone. Quite a few had managed to rent their apartments to tourists. The city had filled up with foreign guests, served by Turkish waiters, Moroccan maids, Russian topless dancers, Filipino prostitutes.

Most of Amsterdam's police personnel were on holiday too, except for the multilingual ones who were kept back to protect the tourists. Multilinguals would enjoy extra holiday time later. Grijpstra spoke some English. De Gier, who liked reading, could make his way in German, Spanish, and French. The sergeant's English was acceptably fluent.

"Pay attention," the woman said, gently gyrating her body to prepare for her next impressive stance. "My rapist has a gun." She pointed at a gabled house on Brewer's Canal. "Up there, he sleeps, he drinks, he wants to shoot me with a big cannon. I escape dancing."

Grijpstra bent down. His twitching nostrils noticed no fragrance of cannabis products. He checked the woman's pupils but did not notice dilation. Her long stylish dress was clean. The high-heeled shoes looked new. The butterfly hat was pinned down neatly to long, thick, cared-for hair.

"Are you a sniffer?" the woman asked.

Grijpstra looked abashed.

His discomfort pleased the woman. "Good. You nice cop. Yes?" She breathed into his face. "Me not drunk. Herr Engländer yes drunk. Dutch alcohol-shit. From fridge." She extended a leg, danced away, turned, danced back.

Complainant was possibly a little crazed, Grijpstra concluded. Perhaps nothing serious. Her lover got drunk. There was an argument. Now Lover was asleep in the slender silver-grey gabled house she had indicated. Maybe his charming sergeant could talk this nice lady into rejoining her Herr Engländer, and he and de Gier could tiptoe out of this case.

"What do you think?" Grijpstra asked his sergeant. Maybe it was time to go eat something. Colleagues had told him about a new all-night deli in Vijzel Street. Veal-ragout croquettes, shrimp rolls, and the house brand of Gouda cheese were recommended. Now, if de Gier could take care of this complaint in a tactful and speedy manner . . .

To bolster his optimism, Grijpstra remembered the previous night's case, which had also involved foreigners.

Driving about town, he and de Gier had been called to Leyden Square Police Station, where a Japanese man had showed up in distress, demanding that the desk sergeant perform an urgent, but until then incomprehensible, action.

"*Moshi moshi,*" the Japanese complainant kept wailing.

"Just one doggone minute here, sir," the desk sergeant had said, picking up his phone to call the communications office.

The dispatcher put out a general call. "Anyone speak Japanese?"

The fourteen-six responded. "My sergeant speaks Japanese."

"Hey!" de Gier protested. "What are you getting us into? Nobody speaks Japanese. It's an impossible language."

"Japanese speak it, don't they?" Grijpstra asked. "You spent time in Kyoto, didn't you? You had girlfriends and all. You must remember some of the lingo."

The complainant turned out to be an older, well-dressed male who was very upset.

"I thought all Japanese were Buddhists," the Leyden Square Police Station's desk sergeant said. The desk sergeant had attended a police academy evening class entitled *Behavior and Attitudes of Asian Tourists.* "Aren't Buddhists supposed to cultivate a relaxed attitude? Don't Buddhists know how to step back from what appears to be the general fuck-up?" The desk sergeant's grimace showed his disappointment. "Just look at Moshi Moshisan here. Can't we get him to calm down?"

"*Moshi moshi,*" the Japanese man cried.

"That means 'hello,'" de Gier said. "He's trying to make contact."

Grijpstra had calmed the complainant by putting a protective arm around the gentleman's frail shoulders, guiding him to a chair, setting him down, addressing the man in a sympathetic low rumble. "There, there, there," Grijpstra said in English, "you're safe, my dear sir. You've come to the right place." He patted the complainant's shoulder. "Just tell my colleague here what you want us to do." He lowered his voice to a confidential level. "Feel free to speak your own language, sir."

De Gier bowed. "In Japanese, dear sir. In Nihongo. Nihongo okay. Japanese *yoroshii desu.*"

The Japanese man was still distressed. "*Watashi no okusan wa. Doko desu ka?* Huh?"

"Your wife?" de Gier translated. "Lost her way?"

The man tried to pantomime what had happened. He made circular movements and imitated the sound of a train. He bent forward as if peering into a window. He tried to explain what he saw.

"You were looking at toy trains," de Gier said. "At the Beehive Department Store? I've seen the new electrical models in their toy window on Dam Street. You were admiring the product, right? With *okusan?* With your wife?"

"*So desu.*" The Japanese gentleman's effort to get through to 'outside people' made his eyes bulge and his nostrils flare. "*So desu ne. Nah?*"

De Gier translated so that Grijpstra and the desk sergeant could follow the conversation. "Means *'That's right, isn't it'?*"

"I am right?" de Gier asked the Japanese man cheerfully. "Good for us, Mister Tourist. Turistu-san. Then what happened?"

The man opened his mouth widely. He inhaled. He exhaled, closing his eyes, stretching his arms. "*Okusan wa.*"

"Yawning, was she? Your wife got bored? Because you kept watching those goddamn toy trains?"

"*Goddammu.*" The Japanese man's mood improved. "Ha! *So desu ne. Nah?*"

His mime continued. He was looking into the store window again, where the little trains entered and exited, forever passing little buildings set in a plastic landscape.

"As you kept watching *goddammu* trains," de Gier asked. "Your wife, *okusan,* went *pffffttt?*"

"*Sooo desu, ne? Nah!*" Complainant relived the awful moment. The Japanese tourist's features now showed sudden insight into a serious situation. His gestures projected horrified sensations of bewilderment, of feeling lost and alone forever. Here, his gesticulating limbs and feverishly working features told the sergeant, was the last intelligent being surrounded by the void of a meaningless universe.

Turistu-san flapped his hands. He wailed.

"Oh dear, oh dear, oh dear." The desk sergeant sympathized with the agony of another conscious being.

The desk sergeant addressed Grijpstra. "Such a neat-looking gent, too. Can't Buddhism help out? Weren't you taking that class, too, Adjutant? What was that shit about *koans* the professor kept raving about? Illogical riddles that break the bubble? How about *The Sound of One Hand?*"

The desk sergeant held up his right hand. "Sir? You get this?"

The Japanese man looked unhappy.

"YOU STAY RIGHT here. Not to worry." De Gier bowed. "*Shimpai ga nai yo.* Not to worry now. *Tomodachi?* Friends?" He pointed at his colleagues. "*Tomodachi* here. They'll take care of you. Friends. Okay?" He caressed the old gendeman's cheek. "I'll be back in just one minute."

The desk sergeant had a constable serve coffee and butter cookies. Grijpstra sat next to the tourist.

"Your *okusan* will be just fine," Grijpstra reassured the Japanese gentleman.

"That's what you get when you depend on a woman," the desk sergeant said. "Find yourself a wife and she gets herself lost and causes pain. The trick is to avoid pain in the first place. Don't have a wife. Take me, now. I live with a bunch of red-beak finches. They all look the same. Easy to replace, you know? I keep them in a big cage, feed them well, and they hoot their little thank-you's. They all have those cute little beaks, you know." The sergeant squeezed his nose shut with thumb and finger. "Thank you. *Peh-PEH!*"

The Japanese looked up. "*Soooo desu, ne? Nah!*"

"*Peh PEH?*" Grijpstra asked.

De Gier, having made use of the Fiat's siren and flashing blue light, was back within twenty minutes. His assumption had been right. The lost wife—upper class, aristocratic, an intelligent lady—knew enough not to start wandering through the inner city's alleys. She had gone back to the Beehive Department Store, where she was now waiting with her back to the toy train showcase window.

De Gier wished her good evening. "*Komban wa.*"

She returned the greeting haughtily.

De Gier smiled. He showed her his police badge. He pointed at the blue light flashing above his car. He escorted Okusan to the passenger side. He stood at attention while she daintily folded her small shape into the Fiat.

Okusan spoke some English. "Police-san?"

"Hai hai," de Gier said. "Yes, ma'am."

"My husband . . ." she paused, she took a deep breath, she exhaled sharply, "like all men, is *i-di-ot.*"

De Gier agreed. "*So desu ne? Nah!*"

"Police-san? Men are *stu-pid.*"

De Gier bowed his head deeply. "*So desu ne? Nah!*" His response didn't defuse Okusan's anger. Okusan screamed in fury when she saw her husband, who yelled back in defense.

The desk sergeant stepped between the warring couple. "None of that in my station, folks."

"Now, now, now," Grijpstra said. "It can't be that bad."

"VERY BAD," husband and wife screamed back at him.

Adjutant Grijpstra wouldn't let the couple call for a taxi until they resolved their problem. The adjutant explained, using de Gier as his translator and his own acting as illustration, that it is the task of the Amsterdam Municipal Police to protect its clients from themselves. Extreme stress during a holiday, the adjutant ventured to make clear, in a mindscape where normal defenses are absent, can lead to lasting trouble in a relationship. He wouldn't want these nice folks to initiate trouble, not in Amsterdam, the magic city.

"Kiss and dance," the adjutant ordered.

The Japanese couple did not wish to understand.

It was de Gier's turn. He said that holidays are fun. Holidays aren't designed to split up happy and harmonious couples.

"Kiss and dance?" Okusan asked sternly. "*Wakarimasen.* No understanding. Please. Show me?"

Grijpstra and de Gier danced and hugged.

"No kissing?" Okusan asked.

"Not in my station," the desk sergeant said.

The Japanese woman resisted but Grijpstra and de Gier urged, her husband bowed, and the uniformed desk sergeant kept saluting. She finally had to laugh.

The Japanese couple danced and kissed before going back to the Hilton in a taxi. They bowed. "Thank you, *arigato*, goodbye, *sayonara.*"

Miss Tango's case might turn out okay, too, Grijpstra was hoping. *Not to worry.* He asked complainant for her name.

"Eira-Liisa."

"Take over, Sergeant," Grijpstra ordered.

De Gier interrogated the complainant. Grijpstra, watching the woman, noted details to be mentioned in a report that might not have to be written. He noted that complainant was an elegant forty-year-old, five feet six inches, with a lithe body, weighing some one hundred and forty pounds. Eira-Liisa's hair was a natural white-blond. Her face was triangular. Grijpstra noted that the subject's eyes were large and blue, slightly slanted.

"Eira-Liisa?" de Gier asked meanwhile. "What happened?"

The woman was dancing slowly again, moving around the detectives. "He rapes." Her voice became anxious. "Me AIDS perhaps now?"

"No condom?" de Gier asked.

She looked embarrassed. "He, no. Me, diaphragm. Woman alone. Better have protection." She insisted. "Me raped. He,

Mr. English, points at me with cannon." She made a fluid move, sweeping up both arms to beg the heavens for instant justice.

"A weapon?" de Gier asked.

"Penis?" Grijpstra asked.

"Both," Eira-Liisa said.

She looked away.

"Eira-Liisa," de Gier asked pleasantly. "Please?"

She refused to make eye contact. She shrugged. "Penis."

"You and Mister English, you shared a rented apartment?" de Gier asked.

But it wasn't that simple. Few things are. In her excitement the woman was using another language now, more foreign than German, confounding even the linguistic sergeant.

"Come again, please?" de Gier asked.

A police siren, approaching rapidly, complicated things further. A minibus raced down Brewer's Canal's southern quayside, its brakes squealing, and slid toward the Fiat Panda. Two uniformed constables tumbled out of the dented and blood-spattered Volkswagen. Both men were small-sized, both had their right hands close to their fast-draw holsters.

The two little constables, both shouting, took turns delivering clipped sentences.

"Hello," Karate yelled.

"What's up?" Ketchup yelled.

"There was a bar fight on the way that we couldn't pass up."

"We lost some time beating up drunken sailors."

"Kicking them into Realen Canal."

"Hahahaha." They both laughed.

"Sorry, Adjutant."

"Sorry, Sergeant."

"We came as soon as we could, though," Ketchup said.

"Here we are."

"At your orders," Karate said.

Both men stood to attention, saluted, stood at rest.

"Hello, Ketchup," Grijpstra said.

"Hello, Karate," de Gier said.

"Finnish," the woman was saying. "I am Finnish. I rented room here. I came to listen to Bach on organ, in Church of Saint Nicolas. Mr. English hired own room. Own front door. Not me and Mr. English together. Just same house."

"Mr. English has name?" de Gier asked.

"Mr. English is Michael."

"How do you know his name, Eira-Liisa?"

"First we dance." She slid into another long step, humming a tango tune. "In stairwell. On landing?"

"Adjutant?" Karate asked. "Did we get that radio call correctly? This lady says she was raped? A gun was used to threaten her? There is an armed perpetrator in a house nearby?" Both constables smiled eagerly. "Can we get him for you? He's a drug dealer, right? We'll get both stash and cash while you interrogate . . ."

"Hahahaha," Ketchup said.

Karate laughed, too. ". . .this attractive addict in the privacy of her own apartment."

"He threatens with cannon," the woman said. She indicated the weapon's size by keeping her hands two feet apart. She pointed at her head. "Cannon points my head."

"Some kind of Uzi," Grijpstra said.

"We'll get the weapon," Ketchup said.

"We could get in through the roof," Karate said.

"Or climb the gable."

"Can we do that, Adjutant?"

"We'll all go together and use the stairs," Grijpstra said.

Eira-Liisa used her key to open the gabled house's front door.

The party walked up a steep and narrow staircase, de Gier first, complainant next. All the policemen held their guns at the ready. De Gier looked pensive. He visualized a crazed British killer waiting for them upstairs, perhaps akin to another killer he had recently chased, a London-based bank robber who, resisting arrest, had shot an Amsterdam constable after a chase over rooftops.

De Gier shushed Ketchup and Karate, who were chuckling again. Grijpstra plodded behind.

"I go first, yes?" Eira-Liisa asked.

De Gier stepped aside, then tiptoed ahead again, aiming his pistol well above the woman's right shoulder.

"You're the champion," Ketchup whispered. "Aim for the head, Sarge."

"Sarge?" Karate whispered. "Fire the warning shot last."

"Shoot the gun out of his hand, Sergeant," Grijpstra growled.

"Violence," the Finnish woman whispered. She gently stretched a leg, then slid toward the bed.

Grijpstra found a wall switch. Lights glared down from the ceiling. The Englishman's body, wrapped in sheets, didn't move. A snore changed into a rattle, which gurgled away slowly. Then the body snored again.

Karate and Ketchup arranged themselves at opposite sides of the bed, their pistols pointed at the body.

Grijpstra and de Gier put away their weapons.

The company found themselves in a small apartment's bed/ sitting room. "Mr. English rents from agency," the woman whispered. "Me, me rents, too. My room other side. We often meet, on stairwell, yes?"

"Fucketyfucketyfuck," Ketchup and Karate chanted under their breath. Grijpstra growled at them. De Gier smiled at Eira-Liisa. "Tell us more? Please?"

"Nothink fuckink," the woman hissed at Ketchup and Karate. "Just meetink, I says. Yes?" She shook Ketchup's shoulder. "You. Blockhead. You speak Finnish? Yes? No perhaps? I poetess in Finnish. Published poetess. Not published by self, no! By publisher published. You speak Hungarish? No? I speak fluent Hungarish. You speak Estonic? No? Komi language? No? Karelian language? Ludic? I speak everythink."

Grijpstra pushed Karate. "Say you're sorry."

Karate mumbled.

"I can't hear you, Constable."

"Sorry, ma'am," Karate said clearly.

The woman pushed Ketchup. "You, too."

Ketchup apologized loudly.

"Better." She smiled at de Gier. "Mr. Michael and I meet on staircase. He says: 'I don't dare to talk to you, you always so quiet. I curious what you think.'"

De Gier nodded attentively.

"I say, 'Why you not ask?'"

Grijpstra grunted encouragingly.

"He say," Eira-Liisa continued, "'No, then I would know what you thinkink. No fun. The mystery would be endink.'"

She paused dramatically. "I say, 'Maybe the mystery's beginnink?'"

De Gier raised an eyebrow. "You encouraged Mr. Michael?"

Eira-Liisa laughed sadly, shaking her head. "Me blockhead, yes? Beginnink of what? Beginnink of end, yes? He ask me to come eat. We eat in café. I come to his room after eatink. He drinkink. I dancink.'"

The policemen studied the shape of the accused, still asleep, head hidden in rumpled sheets.

"Hello?" de Gier asked loudly.

A head appeared, with one bloodshot eye staring under tousled hair. "Never mind," the mouth said quickly, "I am dreaming. Must be that jenever I drank." The head disappeared. Lips smacked while the body, safely tucked away into its dark void, rearranged itself for maximum comfort. "Neo-Nazis," the voice mumbled. "Next episode in the nightmare."

The Englishman snored.

"HELLO?" de Gier bellowed.

"Cannon," the lady said. "In bed, perhaps. You look. Better, yes? So he no shoot?"

"Yank the blanket?" Karate asked.

De Gier nodded.

The constables' guns now aimed at a naked Englishman.

"Sir?" De Gier said, showing his identification. "Police. Could we have your gun, please?"

The Englishman covered his crotch with his hands while he awkwardly tried to sit up. "Gun?" He sounded puzzled.

"Cannon," the woman said. "You threaten. I call cops. You now give them cannon?"

"Oh, for fuck's sake," the Englishman said. He smiled. "This is a dream, right?"

De Gier spoke softly but clearly. "It's a serious charge, sir. Apparently you raped this woman and then threatened her life by pointing a large gun at her. If we could have that gun, sir?"

The Englishman looked at the woman. "Eira-Liisa, we only danced."

"Only?" she asked.

"We would like to have the weapon," Grijpstra said. "Where did you put the gun, sir?"

"For fuck's sake," Michael said. "We danced the tango. She told me Finnish women do that. Because they're shy or something. Doing the tango is their pre-mating ritual."

He sang the tune, waving one hand while screening his genitals with the other. "Ta *TA* ta-taahh, teeteeteetee *TAAAH*-ta-TA-tata . . ."

"That's right," Karate said. "I saw that on TV. The tango is big in Finland. It takes place in cafés. They have tango on the jukebox. Women come on to you. You don't talk but you can touch while dancing. Kind of intimate. Saves flirting. Next move is 'Your place or mine?'"

"His place," Eira-Liisa said. "Here. But what is with cannon?"

"Your gun, sir?" Grijpstra asked.

"Oh, *that*," the Englishman said. "But that was an antique. It came with the apartment here. Part of the furniture. I was just showing it to her. What *did* I do with the damn thing? Will you get out of my dream when I find it?"

"Please?" de Gier asked.

The Englishman jumped up and rushed around the room, pushing his way past the policemen, stumbling about wildly. A plate loaded with potato chips was brushed off a cabinet. Magazines and video tapes flew about. A laptop computer was picked up and shaken. The suspect overturned a suitcase and kicked its contents. He looked through drawers. He pushed books off shelves. "There," he shouted. "There is your damn cannon!" He threw a large object onto the bed.

Grijpstra picked up the bulky weapon gingerly.

"It's ornamental," Michael said. "Ancient. Antique. They used them in the old days with ball and powder. I found it behind the books. I am sorry. Okay? I shouldn't have been nosy."

Grijpstra showed the weapon to de Gier. "What do you think, Sergeant?"

"Known as a blunderbuss," de Gier said. "Front loader. A cavalry weapon. Early Napoleonic, I would say. Flint and steel, one of the first handguns equipped with a trigger."

"Illegal?"

De Gier shook his head. "A collector's piece, Adjutant."

Michael walked over and picked up the pistol. He waved it about. "It must belong to whoever lives here. I rented the apartment furnished. I'm a scholar, you see. A historian and sociologist, researching the last war. I was telling Eira-Liisa here about it. My specialty is the British-Dutch sea wars. Weapons fascinate me."

"My specialty Van Gogh Museum," the woman said. "Other specialty Bach on organ. This Sunday concert. In Saint Nicolas Church."

Ketchup held up a hand. "Didn't we have a rape charge?"

"Rrrrape," Eira said, rolling her R, staring at Michael.

"Tango," Michael said. "You explained it to me. You even got the tape from your apartment across the landing. First dance, then . . ."

"Fucketyfucketyfuck," Ketchup and Karate sang softly.

"Hey," Grijpstra growled. "Constables. You were warned before."

Eira-Liisa sobbed. "Now me AIDS."

"No," Michael shook his head. "None of that, dear. I'm clean. I had my nose straightened early on this summer, an accident broke it, the break interfered with my breathing. They checked my blood prior to operating. No sickness. I'm just fine."

"*Huren,*" Eira-Liisa sobbed. "Amsterdam *voll mit Huren.*"

"I wouldn't dare go to the whores," Michael said. "You're the first since my nose got straightened." He smiled. "I really liked it."

"Me no whore." She stamped her foot. "Police! Please arrest!"

"But you got drunk," Grijpstra said, "and then you waved that gun about, sir."

"It isn't just the Finnish who are shy, you know," Michael said. "They tango, we drink alcohol. I don't drink usually, all right? The Agency said I was welcome to use the apartment's supply of food and drink. I found this damned jar. I can handle a few beers but this jenever is liquid dynamite. This is Amsterdam, foreign to me. The local language sounds like the people aren't feeling well. Beautiful women dance on the landing. All this makes me nervous." He opened the refrigerator. "I looked for a beer. Found this." He held up a stone jug. "Looks harmless, doesn't it?"

The Englishman, reliving his adventure, was pulling his hair.

"You got all that?" Grijpstra asked de Gier.

"Yes, Adjutant." He turned to the suspect. "Then what happened, sir?"

"Well, I got drunk. Right? I was telling her that I know things, about antique weapons, for instance, because I'm a historian." The Englishman pointed the blunderbuss at a window. "This thing doesn't even fire. See?"

The suspect pulled the weapon's trigger.

The explosion deafened everybody. Black smoke filled the room. Glass clattered down. The weapon's charge of nails and rusty iron hit the canal's surface and scattered sleeping ducks. The birds flew off quacking. Plaster fell from the wall above the window. The acrid fumes of gunpowder made de Gier and Eira-Liisa choke. Karate coughed. Grijpstra wheezed. The Englishman, still holding the blunderbuss, staggered back. Ketchup got hiccups.

KETCHUP AND KARATE, who shared an apartment overlooking the Amstel River, discussed the Finnish/British conflict during their next morning's breakfast. Karate, recently returned from leave in Torremolinos, made Spanish omelets. Ketchup, who had visited the Dutch Antilles, opened cans of chilled curuba juice.

"More fresh bread?"

"If you please."

"So Grijpstra confiscated Eira-Liisa and Michael's passports," Karate said, "and he will return them today at lunchtime, at the Dobbe Sandwich Shop."

"After making sure there are no bad feelings between subjects," Ketchup said. "A couple of angels. I bet you de Gier will pick up the bill." He shook his small head. "Pity we couldn't take care of the case, hey?"

Karate didn't know. "We couldn't have done much anyway. They were well-meaning folks caught up in a misunderstanding."

"I don't care for well-meaning folks," Ketchup said. "They're hard to shake down."

Karate agreed. "I would have liked that Eira-Liisa."

"Our superiors are crazy," Ketchup said, carrying dirty dishes to the kitchen. "Those two bumblers believe in making things better, but this is a time when things get worse. It's nice when things get worse. You get to take money from robbers. You get to abuse beautiful whores. I like that."

Karate dried while Ketchup washed up. Karate sighed.

Ketchup looked up from the steaming sink. "Going with the

flow. You think Grijpstra and de Gier believe they can reverse the tide?"

Karate pondered the matter. "No."

Ketchup dropped a mug back into the suds. "So what do our so-called superiors believe in? In being good in spite of the fact that this planet is about to shake off its human occupants? Just as we, sincere and therefore cynical observers, believe in doing evil?"

"I don't think those two believe in good," Karate said. "They're too smart to go for an obvious solution. I've heard them talk. They seem to prefer to believe in nothing."

Ketchup grinned. He thought that was amusing.

"What?" Karate asked.

Ketchup said he would like to believe in nothing, too. That nothing was lighter than either Good or Evil. "Totally cool." Ketchup also said he believed it couldn't be done.

"Good luck comes to those who keep trying," Karate said. "Couldn't we try to believe in nothing?"

"Good luck comes to those who keep trying?" Ketchup asked, as he arranged mugs in the cupboard, their ears parallel, every mug shining. "You really think so?"

"What do you think?" Ketchup said, brushing down the sink.

"Good luck," Karate said, "comes to those who are lucky."

LATER THAT DAY Grijpstra watched Michael and Eira-Liisa walk away stiffly. They had their passports.

"Couldn't make them dance and kiss," de Gier said, walking ahead of Grijpstra on their way back to the Fiat. "They're still too shy. Maybe once they're alone together again, eh?"

"Who cares?" Grijpstra asked.

De Gier sang the tango's tune. "Tah-tah-TAH-tah . . ." He danced to the tune. Grijpstra danced behind him. De Gier suddenly stopped and looked around, making Grijpstra freeze halfway in a sliding step.

"I saw that," de Gier said.

Sure, Blue, and Dead, Too

The evening had passed and night was due, but it wasn't quite dark yet. Sergeant de Gier had noticed the mysterious moment of change and passed the information on to Adjutant Grijpstra. "Evening gone, night not quite come." He went further and drew the adjutant's attention to the faint coloring of the sky that curved like a tight metallic blue sheet above the city of Amsterdam, iridescent in its entirety, intensified by the first pulsating stars.

"Quite," Grijpstra answered.

"Blue," Sergeant de Gier said, "but not your everyday blue. A most noteworthy shade of blue, don't you think?"

"So what are we doing here again?" Grijpstra asked.

"We're police detectives," de Gier explained, caressing his full mustache and delicately curved nose. "We're waiting for the heroin dealers to meet and exchange merchandise for money."

"And when are they due?"

"We don't know."

"And what do they look like?"

"We don't know that either."

Adjutant and sergeant, members of the Amsterdam Murder Brigade, were assisting—because no murders had been reported recently—the Dangerous Drugs Department. They were doing so quietly, dressed like innocent civilians, comfortably reclining in an unmarked blue Volkswagen, parked on Brewer's Square, opposite the Concert Building, pointed at Museum Square. They had been reclining for a while now.

"And how do we know that the dealers will meet?"

"Because," the sergeant answered, "Detection passed on the message. Our very own Detection, with the whispering voice of a handsome man like me, who in turn had heard another whispering voice—in the rest room of a better brothel, perhaps. A large quantity of the evil drug will change hands tonight. For us to see. For us to apprehend, together with the hands that exchange it."

Grijpstra spilled cigar ash on his neat pin-striped waistcoat. He also arranged his bristly grey hair. "Bah."

"Bah how?"

"Both in general," the adjutant explained, "and in particular. What can we see? The sky. Numberless passersby. Do you honestly think that we will be able to spot a suspect popping up, parcel in hand, to greet and do business with another?"

"The sky is lovely," said de Gier. "Do look before the blue becomes black. Now is the time to be impressed."

Grijpstra looked up, grunted, and looked down. He grunted again, more emotionally.

"Nice woman," de Gier agreed. "Same color as the sky. Blue summer coat, blue scarf, blue high heels. I can't see her face, but from her general bearing I would deduce she is crying. Why is she crying?"

The woman's hands dropped away from her face. "She's only crying a little," Grijpstra said. "We could investigate the mystery, but we don't want to exceed our authority. A crying woman hardly disturbs the peace of our city."

De Gier sat up. "I feel like working. We were sent on a fool's errand. We aren't fools. I suspect the subject of being a prostitute and want to question her. Are you coming, Adjutant?"

"Prostitution isn't illegal."

"It is, too," de Gier said. "*Here* it is. We are within two hundred feet of the Concert Building, which contains a bar. Prostitution within two hundred feet of a public place where alcoholic beverages are sold is illegal."

"Leave the woman in peace," Grijpstra said gently. "We're after heroin."

"Very well, Adjutant. But now look at that. What do you see? A handcart loaded with rags. Parked under a no-parking sign. And a subject climbing into it. A most suspicious agglomeration of events." He put his hand on the handle of his door. "May I?"

"You may not. Leave Blue Pete alone."

"You know the subject?"

"An old acquaintance."

"Tell me about him," the sergeant said. "I feel a trifle restless. Your tale will calm me down."

"Anything to keep your youthful enthusiasm within suitable bounds.

"Some years ago," Adjutant Grijpstra intoned pleasantly, "when the local station here hadn't been computerized away, I happened to be behind the counter and Blue Pete came in, accompanied by his dear wife, a fat woman, just like mine. Maybe even fatter, if that could be possible. She pushed Blue Pete aside and lodged a complaint. He was part of the complaint, so she had brought him along."

"Yes?" de Gier prodded.

"If you interrupt me, I won't tell the tale."

"Right. But over there goes a gentleman carrying a parcel. Does it contain heroin? No, it's a present for a loved one adorned with a ribbon. Perhaps it's his wife's birthday. Go on, Adjutant."

"Her name was Anne, Blue Pete's wife's was, and probably still is, and she was suffering from a venereal disease at the time."

"That was the complaint?"

"Part of it. She had contracted it from her neighbor and passed it on to Blue Pete."

"Shall I inquire about the nature of the contents of the parcel the gent is carrying? Now look at that, will you? A well-dressed, well-educated gentleman, probably holding an important position in our society, on his way home, where his wife awaits him, is bothering our blue lady. Just because she is crying. Let me arrest the scoundrel."

"He has stopped bothering her," Grijpstra said. "He's still carrying the parcel. Has he perhaps exchanged it for a similar parcel the lady was hiding under her coat?"

"No, I had a full view from here. Nothing changed hands."

"I never have a full view of anything," Grijpstra complained mildly. "Very well, Anne's charge was that her neighbor had given her a venereal disease. She carried proof."

"She showed you her microbes?"

"Her pills. And a prescription for more, signed by her physician. Proof of her affliction."

"The complaint is not clear to me."

"Because you're too young," Grijpstra explained. "You're not familiar with yesteryear's laws. Whippersnappers like your good self gambol about while totally unaware of the great happenings. The present connects with the past. You have no past yet."

"Since when is the spreading of venereal disease prohibited?"

"It was during the war. A German Occupation law, to protect the Nazi soldiery."

"And Blue Pete?"

"A detached personality. Blue Pete drinks methyl alcohol, a well-known killer of microbes, and he only came along to support his wife in her struggle with the paramour next door."

The sergeant looked at the ragman, now settled comfortably on his cart. "You have a marvelous memory, Adjutant."

"Blue Pete showed up again that very same night, the night of the complaint. I was driving a patrol car through an alley and nearly ran into the blighter's cart. No lights. I was going to fine him, but he did have a light, he said. He showed me a candle that he hadn't lit. There was a bit of breeze, you see, and the light might have been blown out."

"Did you fine him?"

"Nah," Grijpstra said. "Mustn't bother the poor too much."

The sergeant looked out of the window again. "Not even when they keep breaking the law? Parking under no-parking signs? How sad it all is. And the blue lady is still crying. What can be the matter with her?"

"Fourteen-six?" the radio under the blue Volkswagen's dashboard asked.

Grijpstra grabbed the microphone. "Go ahead. This is fourteen-six."

"Not correct," the radio said. "Even the Murder Brigade has to adhere to the rules. First you have to confirm your number and then you should ask me for orders."

"Yes, ducks. Sorry, ducks."

"Ducks?"

De Gier took over the microphone. "Fourteen-six here, Marie. Sergeant de Gier. What can we do for you?"

"Darling," the radio purred. "Do go to Headquarters. The constables guarding the building are being bothered by a man."

"We're on our way."

The Volkswagen veered away from the curb.

"And our heroin?" Grijpstra asked.

"Will wait for us," de Gier said. "The communications room is at Headquarters, too, and who knows what will happen if that terrible man penetrates to Marie's whereabouts. She's a constable, of course, but rather vulnerable because of her beauty. Onward at once."

Grijpstra clutched the dashboard. "Please, Sergeant, this is an unmarked car. Nobody knows we're the police. Oh, Sweet Savior—"

"That pedestrian got away, didn't he?" de Gier asked, glancing at his rearview mirror. "Sporty type, climbing a tree now."

"Whoa!"

"I can't slow down for joyriding cyclists. Assistance to endangered colleagues is our most prized emergency."

"Red light ahead."

"Not anymore."

"The streetcar!"

"Police always have the right of way and streetcars have powerful brakes. Ha-ha, look at all those people sliding off their seats. Right, here we are. Headquarters."

"What's happening here?" Grijpstra asked.

"Well," the constable coming from the doorman's lobby said, "we're supposed to guard this building, right? This is no police station, this is Headquarters itself, but this subject walks straight in, drunk and all, and bothers us. What can we do? We can't guard the building and arrest him at the same time."

"But aren't there two of you?" de Gier asked. "You could arrest the subject while your colleague guards the building."

"The subject wants to be subdued by force," the constable whispered.

"Violence," de Gier whispered, "is lawfully permitted under special circumstances. Didn't they teach you that at police school?"

"The subject is somewhat big," the constable whispered.

The subject was in the lobby, well over six feet, barrel-chested, and waving large fists. He was dressed neatly and swayed slowly. He smiled. "You're a cop, too?" he asked the sergeant.

"Sergeant de Gier, at your service entirely."

"Serve me," the subject said. "If you don't, I'll kill you. I've already killed tonight—an innocent bystander. I deserve to suffer suitable punishment. I wish to wither away in a dank cell."

Grijpstra moved forward and addressed the other constable.

"Tell your side of it," Grijpstra said.

The constable backed out of the drunk's earshot. "He didn't kill anyone, Adjutant, he just happens to have been indulging. He says he knocked someone down with his car in Brewer's Square, but we have our radio here and no accident has been reported in that area."

"When would the mishap have occurred?"

"An hour ago, and he has been here ever since, yelling at us. How can we guard the building with the subject distracting us?"

Grijpstra breathed deeply. He reshaped his smile. "Constable, we're of the Criminal Investigation Department. We are highly trained. We learned how to count, for instance. Am I mistaken if I count two of you?"

"I'm not familiar with the ways of the supercops, Adjutant," the constable said pleasantly, "but we regular officers work in couples. My mate and I form just one couple—and couples, we were taught at police school, may never be split. The subject is big. It will need a complete couple to arrest him. If we arrest him, we cannot guard the building."

Grijpstra faced the drunk. "Sir."

The subject continued to sway and to smile.

"You're under arrest. Follow me."

The subject balled his hands into fists.

"Let's go," Grijpstra bellowed.

The subject hit Grijpstra. Grijpstra fell down. De Gier jumped forward. The subject's arm flew up and turned behind his back, yanked expertly by de Gier's arms. Handcuffs clicked.

"The subject is now a suspect," de Gier told the constables. "I suspect him of harassing the police. Watch him." He squatted next to Grijpstra. "How are you doing?"

Grijpstra groaned.

"Ambulance," de Gier said. A constable picked up a phone.

The suspect kicked. De Gier, still squatting, bent sideways and clutched the suspect's leg. The suspect fell over backward and hit the floor with the full impact of his own strength and weight.

"Take him to a cell," de Gier said. The constables dragged the suspect away.

A siren howled in the street. De Gier opened the door.

"Evening," the ambulance driver said. "You guys damaged a subject again?"

"A colleague is hurt," de Gier said. "Be careful with him; he's my friend."

"We're always careful." The driver turned to his assistant. "Ready? Let's pick him up."

Grijpstra opened his eyes.

"Don't relax too much," the driver said. "Otherwise we can't get you on the stretcher. You're a bit heavy, you know."

"I'm not heavy," Grijpstra said, "and I have no intention of cooperating. I was out for a moment, but I'm back again. Where's the suspect, Sergeant?"

"He's in his cell and you're on your way to the doctor."

"No." Grijpstra started to his feet.

"Grab him," de Gier said to the driver.

The driver shook his head. "Not if the patient refuses."

De Gier held his fist under the driver's nose. "Take him along."

He held his fist under Grijpstra's nose. "Be taken along. Your skull hit the stone floor, and I want to know whether it's cracked or not. You can come back if the doctor releases you."

"Who outranks whom?" the driver asked.

"I'm outranked," de Gier said, "but I happen to be more aggressive than he is and I'm good at judo."

"Let's pick him up and get out of here," the driver's assistant said.

"I'll be on my way, too," de Gier said to the constables. "Have a good night now, the two of you."

THE BLUE VOLKSWAGEN was parked on Brewer's Square again, opposite the Concert Building, pointed at

Museum Square. De Gier was at the wheel. He picked up the microphone. "Car fourteen-six."

"Darling."

"I'm back doing what I was doing," de Gier said, "and I have a request."

"Yes?"

"Please ask one of the constables guarding your building to speak to me on the radio."

"Sergeant?" one of the constables asked a few moments later.

"Listen," de Gier said. "The situation was somewhat bewildering just now. What exactly was bothering your suspect when he first approached you?"

"An excess of alcohol," the constable said.

"Anything else?"

"He said he had run someone down on Brewer's Square."

"Details?"

The constable grinned noisily. "He ran down a blue one."

"What does that mean?"

"I wouldn't know, Sergeant."

"Thanks." De Gier pushed the microphone back into its clip.

Over there, de Gier observes, *the blue lady is still crying. Patiently. Into her handkerchief. Seeing that no one is restraining me now*, he thinks, *I'll go and find out what causes her lengthy grief. He got out and walked over.*

"Good evening."

"Please leave me alone."

"I only wanted to ask you something," de Gier said. "I am a—"

A patrol car stopped next to the conversing couple. Two constables got out. They had left their caps in the car. "What's going on here?" one of them asked.

"This man is annoying me," the lady said.

The constables turned to de Gier. "We've been watching you for a while, sir. You were ogling the lady and now you're actually waylaying her. Move along—and be glad that we don't intend, for the moment, to pursue the misdemeanor."

De Gier showed his police card.

The constables edged him along the sidewalk. "Look here," the older of the two said, "even we aren't allowed to bother crying females. It's tempting to do it anyway, I will admit, for when they're in tears, they're easy to push over, but we shouldn't, don't you agree?"

De Gier showed them his digital watch. "You see the seconds change numbers?"

"Yes?"

"Five more numbers and the two of you are back in your car and driving away. I have to talk to the lady. Make yourselves scarce. All right?"

"I don't know whether you recognize the sergeant," the younger constable advised his partner, "but Rinus de Gier has just been declared judo and karate champion of Amsterdam. Let's go. Good evening, Sergeant Champion."

The patrol car drove off. De Gier walked back to the lady. He showed her his police card. "Miss," he said in a low and pleasant voice, "you seem to be unhappy. Did a car run into you a while ago?"

The lady sobbed.

"Let's have nothing but the truth," de Gier said. "Crying only makes your eyes bulge. You have been run into by a car and you had a bad fright. Share your misery."

"No," the lady said. "Do my eyes really bulge?"

"Not really. Would you like a cigarette?"

"I never smoke in the street."

"Smoke in my car."

THE LADY ADJUSTED her skirt and drew on her cigarette.

"Well?" de Gier asked.

"I'll tell you. I'm having an affair with a certain Mr. Dams and he promised to marry me."

"He did?" de Gier said.

"So he would have to divorce his wife."

"He would."

"But he didn't. And I had enough of waiting. Tonight I decided to go to his house."

De Gier waited.

"His wife opened the door. I said, 'I'm your husband's girl-friend and I want to know about the divorce.' She let me in and he switched off the TV and looked at both of us. His wife said, 'What's this about a divorce?' He got up and went to the kitchen and came back with a bottle of gin and drank it all."

De Gier waited.

"And then he left the house and his wife said it was all my fault. I ran out of the house and followed his car, in my own."

De Gier waited.

"He could hardly drive, but he managed to get as far as here and to park it. He walked off before I could park."

"Mr. Darns is a big man?"

"Oh, yes." She blew her nose.

"Three-piece suit? Wide-shouldered?"

"Yes."

"Where's his car?"

"The big Chevrolet over there."

"You saw him park. Did he hit anyone?"

"He drove over the island, where the pedestrians wait for the streetcar."

"Your friend, Mr. Dams," de Gier said, "has been arrested. He hit an officer. He won't be released until tomorrow morning. I would advise you to go home and sleep well."

DE GIER UNCLIPPED the microphone. "Headquarters? Fourteen-six here."

"Darling?"

"Could I speak to that constable again?"

"Sergeant?" the constable asked.

"Go to the suspect's cell and ask him about his accident. Then come back and tell me exactly what he answers."

Heroin, de Gier thought, *brought me here, and I haven't seen any trace of it yet and never will, I'm sure, for soon the Concert Building will empty and there will be thousands of people on the square and they can give each other parcels forever without my seeing any of it. Let's solve puzzles that can be solved. Like what's with the blue lady and her Mr. Dams?*

"Car fourteen-six?" the radio asked.

"Right here."

"Sergeant," the constable said. "Sure, blue, and dead, too."

"What?"

"That's what the suspect said just now."

"That's all?"

"All."

If there's anything, de Gier thought, *that really annoys me, it's a simple situation I can't comprehend. Blue. What blue? Blue what? The lady was blue, but the suspect didn't hit the lady. The sergeant looked out of the car. The cart loaded with rags was still parked under the no-parking sign. The rags were moving.* De Gier got out.

"Is this where you sleep?" de Gier asked.

"I have a bed at home," Blue Pete said, "but my wife is in it and she's watching TV. I'd rather be here. Resting. Drinking a little." He held up a bottle. "Care for a sip?"

"Methylated spirits?" de Gier asked.

"The best Dutch gin," Blue Pete said. "What with welfare on the rise again, methyl alcohol has become too cheap for me. Pity in a way. I really prefer methylated spirits—the taste is a bit sharper."

"But you're still blue," de Gier said.

"That'll never wear off. Sure you don't want a nip?"

De Gier pushed the bottle away. "Tell me, Pete, did anyone happen to run into you tonight with his car?"

"No."

"Are you sure?"

"Yes!" shouted Blue Pete. "Do you think I need to lie to anyone? With my welfare money going up and up and up?"

"Pete," de Gier said. "Relax, it's a beautiful night. But someone drove into 'a blue one' tonight, and you are blue."

"If I'd been involved in an accident," Blue Pete said, "I would have made a fuss. Maybe I'm just a simple textile dealer, but nobody drives over *me,* not even if the millionaire drives a brand-new Chevrolet!"

"Aha," said de Gier. "A Chevrolet, eh? The one over there, perhaps?"

"But it never drove into me," Blue Pete said. "It drove across the traffic island over there. It was stopped by the little pillar with the blue light in it." He laughed raucously. "And it had just been fixed. I watched a uniformed chap fussing with it with a screwdriver and pliers. Fixed it finally and bang, there comes the millionaire with the Chevrolet and bends it all out of shape again. Ho-ho."

De Gier walked back to his car. He thought as he walked. He changed his direction and investigated the pillar. It was bent over a few degrees and scratched, but the light still burned. He walked over to the Chevrolet. Its bumper was dented a little and some of the paint from the pillar adhered to the dent. The sergeant slid back into the Volkswagen, sighing contentedly. Facts once again. Here was Mr. Dams, an upright citizen trapped by a woman. Temporarily insane, Mr. Dams got himself drunk and hit a pillar. How easy everything was once seen from the correct angle.

He released the microphone. "Car fourteen-six."

"Darling?"

"Hello, Marie," de Gier said. "Please don't call me darling. The channel is open—any police car can listen in."

"Yes, my beloved."

"Any news about the adjutant's condition?"

"A sore chin. He's on his way to you."

GRIJPSTRA TAPPED ON the window. De Gier opened the door for him.

"Nothing the matter with me," the adjutant said. "You forced me to make a spectacle of myself."

"I'm sorry," de Gier said. "I'll never do it again. Next time you're out cold on the floor, I will stand on your head."

"Thanks," Grijpstra said. "How's our heroin deal?"

"What heroin?"

"Our original assignment."

"Ah, that." De Gier cursed. "I thought I had it all figured out—and now this." He pointed.

"Are you pointing at the man in the blue uniform opening the little door in the pillar with the blue light in it?"

"I am."

"What could be wrong with that? The man is employed by the electric company and he's checking the pillar."

"I just found out," the sergeant said, "that the light was checked a little while ago. Besides, it's burning. What's he fiddling with the insides of the pillar for?"

"Replacing a fuse?" Grijpstra asked lazily. "Dusting connections? Scraping the socket? Should we care?"

"I think so," de Gier said. "Because he's doing none of that. He's removing some small cellophane packages. You go right; I'll take the left. Pull your gun."

The man in the uniform also pulled a gun. There were two shots. De Gier dropped when the shots went off and kicked the suspect's legs from under him. Grijpstra caught the falling suspect. Handcuffs clicked.

"He didn't hit you, did he?" de Gier asked.

"No," Grijpstra said. "But I hit him. He's bleeding from the chest. I don't think the cuffs were necessary."

ↄ

"COME RIGHT IN," the commissaris said. "The chief is waiting for you. Good work—but it's a pity the suspect didn't survive his arrest."

The chief got up from behind his desk and smiled at his visitors. "Adjutant. Sergeant. My congratulations. The suspect has been identified and important clues have been found in his home that will lead to further arrests. What brilliant reasoning led you to believe that the man masquerading as an electric company worker was your man?"

Grijpstra didn't say anything. De Gier was quiet.

"Well?"

"No brilliant reasoning, sir," de Gier said. "A melody perhaps—one blue note leading to another."

The chief smiled patiently. "Tell me about it."

Grijpstra reported.

"I see," the chief said. "Who put the heroin *into* the pillar?"

Grijpstra shrugged. "We didn't see that. The big dealer presumably."

"And the small dealer took it out?"

"So it seems."

"The pillar merely served as a third party? The dealers didn't want to meet?"

Grijpstra nodded. "The less they know, the less they can tell."

"And the lady in blue?"

"No connection, sir. Neither was Blue Pete."

"Yet the *events* connected," the chief said. "A typical example of proper police work. What do you think, Commissaris? These men are from your department. Don't you agree that they did well?"

The commissaris was standing near the door. He came forward and studied his assistants. His eyes rested on de Gier's brow. "You're pale, Sergeant."

"Blue," de Gier mumbled. "It's such a beautiful shade. It has pursued us all night, leading to death."

The commissaris led the sergeant to the door. Grijpstra followed.

"WHAT WAS THAT?" the chief asked when the commissaris returned.

"An erratic statement," the commissaris said. "It's a while since you and I were assigned to street duty. After a violent death a colleague may tend toward erratic behavior." He looked out the window. The sky curved like a tight metallic blue sheet above the city of Amsterdam, iridescent in its entirety, intensified by the first pulsating stars. "It's the blue hour again," he said to the chief. "Let's go across the street. You may allow me to buy you a drink."

Hup Three

Handsome, successful Frank Nullish and his brand-new super-automatic Volvo had a choice that fateful day. They could take a left turn after leaving the clinic, where Frank's wife, Betty-Baby, wasn't being cured, and go home. Home was Frank's spacious top-floor apartment in a four-story condo in the luxury suburb of Amstelveen. The apartment overlooked a well-kept park lined by ramrod-straight poplars and ever-mown lawns surrounding a clear pool with shiny white Peking ducks on top. A left turn would be nice—the Volvo would sit in its underground garage and Frank, teeth clenched on the old meerschaum, would watch ducks from the balcony, Cat hanging bonelessly across his arms.

Frank smoking, Cat purring, ducks quacking down below. A right turn was not so nice; it meant getting caught up in a web of narrow one-way streets, crescenting alleys and steep bridges that led into the inner city of Amsterdam, originally of seventeenth-century gabled-house splendor, subsequently abused by the greed of commerce, recently revamped as a quaint old-world center, of interest to tourists and pleasure-seeking locals, a region of hup-ho, hanky-panky and goings-on.

There was a choice: left/right. The Volvo turned right. Frank smiled happily for a moment, then worriedly for more moments.

Frank liked to see himself as a detached introvert, a

homebody who'd got it together, a lone watcher of ducks. His wife, Betty-Baby, lonely, watched TV, but that was a while back now, before she got too sickly fat and was hospitalized in the private clinic. A brief daily visit, after work, to his ailing wife was part of the detached, introverted, got-it-together loner's life, which wasn't a bad life at all.

How long had Betty-Baby been away now? Frank calculated, reaching for figures and dates, payments of medical bills going out, insurance payments coming in. While he calculated, the Volvo waited behind a truck that burped up foul smoke.

Frank pulled his sun roof shut. That the truck's rattling exhaust burped oil-smudged air into the Volvo's vents hardly bothered him, of course. No point in fretting about unavoidable aggravations when things are going well. Frank smiled sagely at the truck's enormous rear doors that denied him passage and view.

The truck moved. The Volvo didn't as yet, but then it did, with Frank nodding via his rearview mirror at the angry driver behind. She filled a small car. The car beeped, the truck burped. Frank laughed out loud.

Things still couldn't be better. Wasn't he making a fortune on what Betty-Baby's dad once called "our modest but profitable lines"? The lines consisted of specialized hooks and needles used in art needlecraft by rich ladies with a need to embroider cushion covers, prepatterned wall hangings, bellpulls to summon servants who had left, keyboard covers for pianos nobody played. There had to be quite a few of them, Frank thought: bent-over grannies and aunts in slipping wigs and shoulder scarves, buying the strangely adapted hooks and needles that his company turned out so diligently. All the products had air-tight patents. The machinery making them had been paid for years ago. Yet the quantities sold weren't big enough for Big Business to even consider worrying about. An easy little product, a high profit margin, no competition, a steady, abundant flow of cash into Frank's company.

His company? Well, Betty-Baby's dad's company, but the old man kept forgetting his own name these days. It was okay when Wuffo the dog was alive, for Wuffo brought her doddering master home after walks. But Wuffo herself got old and forgetful, too, and then died, so the old man went to the nice nurses in a nice home, fulfilling nice needs. Frank signed the nice checks with pleasure. With power-of-attorney passing to son-in-law Frank and with only child Betty-Baby ailing, who owns what?

But there was another question just now that got away. Catch the question, Frank. How long has Betty-Baby been sick? Maybe three months? Is she missed? She is not missed. Mostly invisible housekeeper Mrs. Bakker keeps good house. May the good life go on forever. So why the Volvo's wrong turn? Why this almost uncontrollable anger all of a sudden? Wherefrom this glowing desire to step on the gas and ram the smelly truck, shift gears, and reverse into the little beepy car?

Hey, a parking space ahead between elm trees at the side of a canal. Get in there. Don't worry about signals. Ignore the little car's lady's wagging finger. While you're at it, ignore the lady's lips mouthing "Asshole."

Frank, getting out of his vehicle parked inches from the canal's quay, recognized his surroundings. The company was formerly located here, before the inner city exchanged grimy business for glitzy pleasure. Now the refurbished merchant mansions, warehouses, and workshops held cozy bars, tourist hotels, arty galleries behind spiffed-up gables. Frank checked his watch. The galleries would be closing by now, bars would be very much open. What now? Guzzle a gallon?

Frank hadn't guzzled in years. Guzzling requires buddies, good old boys who shout welcomes and thump you around a bit before opening up the inner circle. Frank remembered himself as "Tarzan," raising a tulip-shaped glass of juniper-flavored gin to toast mustachioed and earringed "Pirate," squat, military-dressed "Stinky," and a bartender known as "Saturated Fats."

Twenty years ago, these were important people on Frank's stage. The stage collapsed, the actors wafted away—not quite, though, for Frank recalled running into Pirate again recently, and the new image, bald-faced and with no earrings, cheerfully mentioned one wife, three kids: "The five of us, Tarzan, having breakfast every day."

"The three of us, Pirate," Frank could have said. But Frank, huddled in his British raincoat, with his blown-dry hair wavy in the breeze, didn't say that. It wasn't true, anyway. Betty-Baby and Cat didn't breakfast, but slept in, snoring gently, hand in paw, while Frank gobbled precooked and slurped instant in the living room, one eye checking the paper to see how his stocks were doing. Not that they were ever really doing. Boring beer and banks, electronics, oil. As permanently safe as the royal Netherlandic House of Orange. If the shares dip, wait five minutes. Up they pop again.

"Still drink beer, Pirate?"

"No. No beer." The man had receded into the crowd, on his way to earn, smilingly, more tribal breakfasts.

Frank, standing between the Volvo and a doggie-crusted elm tree, faced a cinema poster showing a nude woman approaching a warty alligator. See the movie? But shouldn't he have dinner first? Grab a nuked bite somewhere close? Why not go home and share one of Mrs. Bakker's filets mignons with Cat? Sautéed chanterelles on the side? Cheese and crackers for a leisurely savory? Real whipped cream on fresh fruit? Java coffee? Cuban cigar? View of the park? Another pleasant evening watching more ducks? What was he doing here in this hellhole?

General Frank curtly ordered himself back into the Volvo. The troops demurred, said "Nah."

Frank wondered whether a woman was wanted, perhaps. There should be quite a few bare-shouldered, bare-legged, bare-bosomed women waiting in the alleys all around, framed by neon tubes, illuminated erotically by pink-or

purple-shaded spotlights hidden under windowsills: a multicolored selection.

Frank muttered a warning to himself. You're not in your right
mind today. You want to get sick?

He tried compromise. Take out a blue movie and stick it
into the VCR at home. But the temptation kept tugging him
along the narrow sidewalks behind the phallic metal posts
installed by the city two feet apart to protect peaceful citizens
from heavy traffic. He touched the posts' smooth tops gently,
begging off that urge. He passed bars filling up with bright
young people. Being forty years old was borderline, maybe?
Wouldn't his clothes make him stand out?

He stopped in front of a small store, put on rimless gold-
rimmed spectacles, and appraised his looks mirrored between
the window's display of high-heeled boots, shoulder bags,
and other leather items for gay tourists. His light-grey three-
piece suit seemed fine. Maroon silk tie? Nice. Button-down
pink pure-cotton shirt? Neat. Hair? Thinning, sure, but still
covering well. Frank frowned. Why would he concern himself
with being accepted by the insignificant little people? Wasn't
he the country's monopolist of profitable needlecraft hooks
and needles?

He walked on, stubbing his toes on cobblestones, limping for
a bit. He recognized the gable he leaned against. It shielded the
patrician mansion where he had started work twenty years ago,
fresh from business school, for Betty-Baby's father. A while later
the building was sold and the company moved to the modern
business park on the city's outskirts where he bossed it around
today, but it was here Frank's career had started.

Frank laughed too loudly, then frowned furiously. Why was
he out of control if he hadn't started drinking yet? He clearly
heard the opening line of a sad jazzy tune. Did the music orig-
inate in a sound system turned on inside the building or was old
Frankie cracking up? He shook his head to get rid of a depressing

but fascinating ballad, played on a row of double basses handled by tall men with hollow eyes.

In order to rid himself of these frock-coated musicians, Frank appealed to the wall he leaned against, feeling it tenderly with his fingertips. He remembered the building as a ruin, but now its surface had been filled in and varnished, its doors repainted, its rotted window frames replaced. The tall mansion's imposing entrance displayed seven brass push buttons with elegantly lettered nameplates, one for each story. So there were apartments here now, instead of Betty-Baby's father's tatty office, the clerks' rooms, and storage for the finished product. The basement, where machinery once thumped and stamped, had become a bar.

Frank rethought himself into the nineteen-year-old bright young fellow finding his gateway to success here: stepping through—stepping right into it. Into marriage, too.

He didn't know about Betty-Baby then, about the sole heiress. Betty-Baby was learning manners at a Swiss college at the time, but about to return to make her debut.

Stepping through.

Did you arrive? Frank asked Frank. How do you like the other side?

I do. I do, Frank told Frank.

Now he was rich, and Betty-Baby was nuts. Frank, waiting for the electricity in his stubbed toes to subside and the gloomy bass players to finish their tune, saw the face of Betty-Baby's doctor. "Physically," the face said, "there's nothing wrong with your wife." The face smiled. "My colleagues are in full agreement, of course." So what about Betty-Baby's itching, stomach cramps, dragging leg, weight problem, breathing troubles?

"I would like to recommend a psychiatrist, Mr. Nullish."

Frank pushed himself off the wall, hurt his toes again, staggered backward into a passerby, turned around, apologized.

"Join AA," the passerby said. "They're boring blowhards, but can be helpful at times."

"Yes," Frank said.

"They sure helped me," the passerby said, pointing at the bar's entrance close by. Frank noticed a strong smell of gin coming from the bar and from the passerby's mouth. "I can resist the attraction now," the passerby said, holding up a stubbly chin. "I don't have to enter those bad places anymore. I can go home." His red-rimmed eyes squinted. "Okay?"

"Yes," Frank said.

Sure Betty-Baby was crazy, just like his brother Pete and his wife Suzie. Another story of success. Pete, through Suzie, stepped into a sole agency for Japanese dike-repairing machinery. Suzie tired of exercising her credit card in shopping centers and started seeing a shrink. Pete was invited to show up, too. Pete came to Frank. There was Pete, in Frank's office, silhouetted against the showcase filled with needlehooks and hooked needles.

Pete's face shone with the sweat of fear. "This shrink wants to make me crazy, too, Frankie. Not me, brother, not me. Liberty for me." So Pete bought himself a plastic replica of a Duesenburg 1931 convertible and picked up girls in the inner city to go sailing with him in his plastic mini-schooner.

We have all gone crazy, Frank thought.

If he could have known then that he would be selling needle-craft hooks for a living—being useful to old ladies at eight times cost. It was a good thing he didn't believe in heavenly justice. As long as he didn't believe, he wouldn't have to amuse Saint Peter.

Saint Peter: What did you busy yourself with down there, sir?

Frank: Eh—with making money.

Saint Peter: Is that so, sir? Specifics?

Frank: Yes. Well, I kind of cornered the market for hooked needlecraft needles, crochet hooks, the kind with those little chromium-plated catches at the end, you know? Mahogany handles?

Saint Peter: What else did you do, sir?

Frank: Eh—nothing.

Saint Peter, leading a choir of angels wielding flaming swords: Hahahahaha.

They probably wouldn't even bother to shove him into hell, but cruelly ignore him instead, let him wander about like he was wandering about now.

Frank wandered into the bar. The bartender reminded him of Saturated Fats, but this was a younger man, although even more blubbery, more overflowing his pants. The bar was antiqued—seats and counter stained in yellowy browns and shot-gunned into wormholes under sagging smoked over-beams bearing a partly white-washed ceiling. Teak wainscoting was added for elegance. A copper rail lined the bar for parking unsteady foot-sies on. There were spittoons in every corner.

"Draft?" Saturated Fats II said, sliding a mug toward a tap.

Frank raised a hand. Beer is for canals, comes out like it goes in, without even being polite enough to change color. "Whoa, Fats. Whiskey. American. Ice, no water."

"Sir," Fats said, "the name is Edmond." He wasn't reaching for the beer tap anymore. He wasn't reaching for anything.

"Edmond," Frank said, gently edging forward to reach a bar stool between longhairs smooching with each other and cleav-age in a lace blouse being stared into by a man with loose teeth. "I am sorry, Edmond."

Edmond's bellies cascaded. "You aren't just saying that, sir?"

"No," Frank said.

"No, sorry?" Edmond asked.

"Yes, sorry."

Edmond poured from a square black bottle and moved ice about with a silver stirrer. Frank smiled. He hadn't been drink-ing for a while. Or smoking. Now he would smoke again, too. He looked at the tobacco display behind the bar and pointed at Black Belgians. Edmond opened a pack, tapped out a cigarette, pushed a candle across.

Frank coughed, waved the loosely stuffed cigarette through dense smoke, and coughed again.

"Being bad?" Cleavage asked, ignoring Loose Teeth's protest.

"Sir?" Edmond asked, half closing his eyes in disgusted disbelief. "Sir? Could you arrange your dentures?"

"What *is* this?" female Longhair asked, watching Loose Teeth's coated tongue frantically trying to correct the position of his overturned dentures.

"Fellini," male Longhair said.

With the third bourbon and the fifth Black Belgian, Frank found himself afloat on pure joy. A flashing insight promised that he could step back to the exact moment that marked the beginning of his wrong turn. The step had to be in time only, for his present location was right. The exact moment happened right here, twenty years ago. Up until then, everything had been fine.

What good times were coming back! Nothing to care about then. Young Tarzan hangs out in his happy jungle, rides the magic streets of Amsterdam on his shiny Harley-Davidson, lives in an attic listening to Dizzy Gillespie on LPs. He wears corduroy pants, a leather jacket, no tie. He goes for Jane.

"Me Frank, you Ravena."

"Ha!" shouted Frank, banging the bar with both hands. "Ha!"

"Sir?" Edmond asked.

"Edmond," Frank whispered, "Edmond, I thank you. This magic third drink, the house drink, is showing me what's what. Thank you, Edmond. Have one on me." He raised his glass. "Hup one." He raised it higher. "Hup two." He put it to his lips. "Hup three." Immediately there was a third flash of insight. Find Ravena. Things had gone wrong after Ravena, so he would have to get back to Ravena to start again. How simple. Bring her magical presence back into his life. Start again. Total turnaround in two easy steps. "Edmond? Got a phone book?"

Ravena wasn't listed.

Frank rested his hand on the page. He was doing well back

then, before turning right instead of left. True to type, daredevil type, young Frank had faced Betty-Baby's dad in his gloomy office. The old man lectured about attitudes, about young Frank's double-exhausted, rumbly, wide-handled, all-victorious American Harley-Davidson motorcycle. Betty-Baby's dad explained that an employee being trained for business management shouldn't be imitating Marlon Brando. Betty-Baby's dad, in his pinstripe suit, made weighty words flow heavily.

But did young Frank Nullish pay attention? He did not. He was looking at Betty-Baby's dad's new secretary's long light brown legs with tightly curved calves, her supple body in a short skirt and tight blouse, elegant hands poised above the Remington's keys, dark eyes, raven black hair.

Frank had met Ravena in the corridor that day. They held hands briefly. He secretly read her application letter in the clerks' room. Born in Borneo? Frank saw palm leaves, heard parrots screech and the slow flap of flying-fox wings, an exaggerated sunset splashed in blood reds and soft orange tints slowly giving way to silver shades as the full moon sails in. Ravena steps out, naked but for a woven grass loincloth. Shell anklets click. The Remington's keys click. Betty-Baby's dad has spoken and Frank is sent off to sell the bike, get a decent suit, behave, think of the future.

But not yet.

Frank stepped out of the past for a minute to enjoy more bourbonically clear insights. "Edmond?"

The square black American bottle poured more clarifying potion.

Frank, inhaling insightful black smoke, reentered the past.

Betty-Baby's dad went off on a business trip. Frank bought six yellow tulips and had a student clerk deliver them to the presidential chamber. The messenger, for a small consideration, promised not to say that the tulips were bought by Frank. Mystery goes with true love.

Next move. Meeting in corridor.

"Would you like to have dinner with me at the Chinese restaurant of your choice?" future executive Tarzan asked secretarial Jane.

"No." She brushed past him. Her huskily vibrant voice made him see birds of paradise spreading brocade wings, a pouched tree kangaroo pogo-sticking across a glade, giant orangutans tossing banana peels, a tiger partly hidden in bamboo shadows.

Of course. This Dayak (he remembered Borneo headhunted from a geography lesson) princess was too exotic to give in easily. His own shameless hurry disgusted him. How could he even dare to expect so much so fast?

Next day, another six yellow tulips.

He waited for her in the street. Offered to take her home on the Harley's saddle, designed for maximal physical contact.

She preferred public transport.

A day passed. More anonymous tulips were accepted but every direct approach was blocked by curt refusals. Maybe she thought he too young. Frank checked Ravena's application again.

She was twenty-three years old, against his nineteen. But what the hell? The mature princess and the ardent young prince. The possibilities were still endless. The form also contained Ravena's address. He rode out on his Harley. She had her own mini apartment with a front door and private steps. She wasn't home.

The clerks were humble people, caught in drudgery, scribbling all day before grinding home on rusty bicycles. Frank refused to laugh at their crude jokes. He wouldn't go out with them for coffee breaks, and chose to read avant-garde poetry at his desk instead. Their resulting hostility exploded into a nasty joke. A clerk sidled up. "Say, Frank, been on the roof yet?"

"No."

"Come with me—you should see the view."

"Okay."

There was a small hinged stepladder leading to a skylight the clerk obligingly unhooked. "You go first, pal," he said.

The minute Frank reached the roof, the trapdoor slammed shut behind him. Below, there was mumbling and laughing. "Nice view, what?" clerky voices asked. The view was not nice. Frank could see other roofs and bare trees reaching up sadly. Ragged washing dried on sagging lines. A rear garden displayed heaped garbage between slimy tree debris. The roofs street side overlooked grumbling traffic, released by a green light.

Frank waited minutes. The skylight stayed shut. Rain drizzled coldly. He squatted so that he could hear better and heard Ravena's soft laugh. She, too.

Angry, he was angry—but anger alone wouldn't free him from this trap. He walked away from the trapdoor to the edge of the roof, where fear of heights stopped him. The laughing voices beneath the skylight egged him on. He jumped to the next roof, across a narrow but gaping passage. His smooth leather soles slid and he almost toppled backward, but managed, by mowing his arms around windmill-fashion, to stay upright. He forced his trembling legs to inch toward the edge of the next roof. Seven stories down, a rear garden covered with junk pushed against a sagging fence. Under the gutter near his feet, a window had been left open. If he—but, no, he couldn't accept the challenge. Say he swung from the overhanging gutter forward and backward once—twice, maybe—trying to work up momentum to propel his reluctant body through the window? What if the gutter broke, and he dropped onto rotted-out boxes and rusted bicycle frames a hundred feet below?

So, back to the skylight, kneel and knock, beg the clerks for mercy?

Never.

Fresh bright orange streaks of fury burst through Frank's brain and burned away most of his fear. Despite his careful squatting he began to slide again, reaching the edge more quickly than he dared to. He hung from the gutter. So far, so good. His fingers had passed through the gutter's gooey contents before grabbing hold. Sooty leaves, creamed in bird droppings. So far, so better. Now for the best part, swinging Tarzan-style. The tension made him grin. Pity he had forgotten the apeman's war cry. But he could make up his own. Yuuu-aayuuuuh? There we go. Hup ONE! Hup TWO!

At hup three, his fingers released their grip on the gutter, his body shot through the window, and his heels aimed for and hit the floor. The room contained a bed, a chest of drawers, a wash-stand. There were no signs of an occupant. A boarding-house room, waiting for the next guest? Frank slid on worn linoleum, slowed down to a casual walk, placed his left hand in his trou-ser pocket, opened a door, followed a corridor, descended the narrow stairs. He lived here and was on his way out for a stroll. If he met anyone, he'd say, "Hello—how are you doing?" noncommittal but friendly enough, and meanwhile keep going.

Descending floor after floor, he met no one. The street door opened easily. Outside, he turned back to the office.

There they were, all the king's men and woman, waiting gleefully for Frankie's pleas from above to open the skylight, waiting for Frankie's surrender.

Frank quietly joined the giggling crowd, maneuvered himself next to Ravena, and took her slender hand. She looked up at him, her dark eyes gleaming. "You! Where did you come from?"

"I flew."

That was all he would ever say about his feat, even to Dayak princess Ravena, the Jane of his private jungle.

Ravena often asked him about the miracle when he lay next to her in the wide bed of her apartment, opened to him after the clerks' defeat. He stayed with her until Betty-Baby's dad trans-ferred him to work for associates in Paris for a while to learn the tricks of the trade. While Frank was away, Betty-Baby's dad sold the building and moved the company to modern premises.

He also got rid of Ravena. She wrote to Frank in Paris, mentioning another lover, a man with a sailboat who might take her far away unless Frank came back at once to take her even farther. He didn't go back at once, and when he eventually did, Betty-Baby's dad made him crown prince.

Rumor reached him that Ravena had been dumped off the sailboat somewhere and had come back to Amsterdam, but Frank didn't see her again. He saw pink, dimply Betty-Baby instead, who bought him the condo. Years slipped by. There had been no reason to hunt about in the alleys of his past.

Until now.

Frank studied the phone book. No Ravena Simons. Sam Simons—would that be Ravena's brother? He dialed.

"Frank Nullish," Frank said. "Remember me, Sam? I used to be with your sister."

"Sure," Sam said. "You're rich now, Frank?"

Frank nodded.

"What?" Sam said.

"Yes."

"I'm poor." Sam gave him her number.

Ravena's voice was low and vibrant.

"This is Frank Nullish, Ravena."

The silence was low and vibrant.

"You remember me, Ravena?"

"I remember you, Frank."

"So how are you doing?"

"Well—," she said. "Okay, I guess."

"That's nice," Frank said. "Meet me? Now? Here?" He gave her the bar's address. She said she needed half an hour.

Frank dipped the tenth Black Belgian into the fifth bourbon and inhaled alcoholic nicotine. Ravena came in. She wore a silk orange-red suit and her hair down, hiding most of her face. What he saw of her skin had wrinkled. She'd be forty-three. The hand that clasped his was clawlike, the claw of the bird of paradise.

So what? Old Ravena. Me old Tarzan. You old Jane.

A lovely lady. A matured exotic. They'd start over, build a gazebo in a banyan tree, turn the lights low, spray perfume. Keep an ape.

Edmond's chins trembled. "What would the lovely lady like to imbibe?"

Ravena ordered whiskey.

Edmond's pudgy hands manipulated the square black bottle with ease and abandon.

"How nice that you phoned," Ravena said.

She needed more whiskey to say more. She told Frank she had a daughter, who'd left home and wasn't doing well, and that she had no man, except Uncle Joe. She lived close by. She hoped Uncle Joe had not followed her.

"Is there an old man looking in?"

Frank asked Edmond. Edmond said there was. "His head shakes."

"Parkinson's disease," Ravena said.

"Very old," Edmond said.

"Eighty," Ravena said. "He gets nervous without me."

"In shirtsleeves," Edmond said.

"He should be wearing a jacket." Ravena excused herself and went outside. Frank saw her admonishing a shabby old man, marching him off. Uncle Joe's bald head shone like a reluctant moon, his arms swung widely.

She came back after a while. "Naughty Uncle Joe. I put him to bed. He'd better stay there." She looked at her empty glass. It filled up again. The bird of paradise claw touched Frank's arm. "How about you, any kids?"

"I married Betty-Baby," Frank said. "No kids. It isn't working out. She's sick all the time."

"The company is hers?"

"In her name," Frank said.

Ravena nodded. "So all your property is Betty-Baby's."

He nodded too. "In a way, in a way, but I'm starting over again." He touched Ravena's shoulder meaningfully. "I phoned you, you know. Can we go somewhere?"

"Uncle Joe will be nervous," Ravena said. "It's better in the morning. He sleeps late. We have a big apartment."

"Uncle Joe's apartment?" Frank asked.

Some gold in her teeth gleamed. "In a way, in a way." She looked up. "There's a hotel nearby. But tomorrow would be better."

Frank overpaid Edmond. Outside, they both stubbed their toes on cobblestones on their way to the Volvo.

Frank drove off carefully, aware of possible police and of Uncle Joe in his mirror. "Which way's the hotel?"

"The other way." She looked over her shoulder. "Oh, dear, he got out again. Stop the car."

Uncle Joe's face pressed against Ravena's window, mouth moving like that of a fish about to die in the bottom of a boat. "Ravena, where are you going?" the fish head asked.

"I'll have to go with him," Ravena told Frank. "Phone me tomorrow morning, we'll work something out . . ."

"No go?" Edmond asked when Frank sat down again. "Last drink? I'll be closing soon."

The black bottle did its job. "You sure you like that lady?" Edmond asked. "I've seen her here before. Got to know her, so to speak."

"Tried her out?" Frank asked. "One morning, Uncle Joe still a-snooze?"

Edmond winked. "Now now, sir, now now."

FRANK STOOD NEXT to the Volvo. A cop car stopped. "You wouldn't be planning to drive?" the cop car's loudspeaker whispered.

Frank crossed the quay again, tentatively pushed the building's door leading to the apartments. The door should have been closed, of course, but wasn't. He climbed all seven flights of stairs, reached the skylight, lowered its steps, walked up the steps, pushed, reached the roof. The roof was still old, with peeling tar sheets showing decayed tinplate and moldy gutters.

Frank was happy. He was back, he had reached the starting point. He would jump to the next roof, slither about, squat down, be a hero again. He would dig his fingers in the juicy contents of the rotten gutter, lower himself, swing his rejuvenated body into the neatly made bed of the boardinghouse room below, Ravena's bed, and they would fly off together on bird-of-paradise wings, away from the battlefield where pathetic clerks' corpses stank pitifully.

Hup one. Hup two—

The gutter broke.

"Yuuu-aayuuuuh!"

"Can we take him now, Adjutant?" one of the paramedics asked the portly police detective. "We haven't got all night."

"Wait," the younger detective with the wide moustache said. "Wait, Grijpstra, tell me again why we shouldn't investigate the corpse and location further. I know you told me before, but you were eating that hamburger." He glared at the paramedics. "You guys wait, okay?"

"Sergeant de Gier," Adjutant Grijpstra said, "you've been upstairs. There are tracks on the roof, the victim's tracks only. The subject jumped off all by himself. Accident? Accidents are okay. Suicide? Suicides are okay."

"The prints say the subject hung from the gutter by his hands," Sergeant de Gier said. "As his swinging broke the window's glass, I may surmise that the subject was attempting to swing himself into the room below. Maybe he was a burglar and a rapist. Maybe he's listed and we can now cross him off our list."

"You checked the subject's wallet," Adjutant Grijpstra said. "Credit cards, cash, valid driving license, papers that go with the Volvo parked at the quayside. Photograph of a large lady. A

Boucheron gold watch. A Leyden House suit. The subject's visiting card calls him managing director of a corporation making needlecraft needles. The company's name is known to me. My own mother and my own ex-wife use those needles. They're good needles. You still say he may be a suspect?"

"There was a woman in the apartment the subject didn't get into because the gutter he was hanging from broke on him," de Gier said. "He tried to enter the woman's room, intending mischief maybe. Perhaps she saw him swing in and pushed him out again."

"Self-defense is kind of okay," Grijpstra said. "But it wasn't self-defense. Why not? Because the woman says so. She was asleep in another room, heard the glass break, heard someone shout *"Aa-yuuuuh,"* opened the broken window, looked down, saw the body, and phoned us. We confronted her with the body. She says she never saw the subject before."

"She lied?" de Gier asked.

"Ugly women have no reason to lie," the second paramedic said.

The sergeant thought. "Yes. So why did he force himself into a fatal accident, this handsome, well-dressed, still youngish, reputable needlecraft-needle-business-owning subject?"

"Who cares?" Grijpstra asked. "Fatal accidents are okay."

De Gier's sensitive brown eyes shone pleadingly. His moustache curled in gentle protest. His perfect teeth showed in a humble smile. "I care," he said.

"Please," Adjutant Grijpstra said pleadingly. "The subject is some forty years old. He is doing fine. He has been making and selling needlecraft needles for years. He is looking at selling even more needlecraft needles for even more years. But why? He already has a Volvo and a Boucheron watch. He is beginning to wonder about his effort, his direction—his destiny even, maybe. One day he goes home, but he doesn't. He comes here. He drinks to cheer up. He cheers down. Events swing him by the arms. We'll ask the bartender in that bar tomorrow. Not that whatever he'll say will matter much maybe."

"Edmond," the first paramedic said. "Fats Edmond, but don't call him Fats or he'll beat you up. We have taken subjects from there that were badly beaten."

"What will Fats say that won't matter much, maybe?" de Gier asked.

Adjutant Grijpstra shrugged. "That the subject got drunk maybe, met a woman maybe, it didn't work out maybe. That he drank more maybe, he was a sporty type once maybe, he was going to show himself he was still a sporty type maybe?"

"That *aa-yuuuuh* the woman heard could be Tarzan's goodbye cry maybe," the paramedic said. "I wanted to be Tarzan, too. I still do maybe."

"Don't drink," Grijpstra told him. "The vine you're swinging from may break."

"I only drink beer," the paramedic said.

"What brand?" de Gier asked.

The paramedic smiled knowledgeably. "All beer is good beer."

"So?" de Gier asked Grijpstra.

"So," Grijpstra said, "Mr. Frank Nullish, married to the bland blonde he keeps a photo of in his wallet, got himself into a situation that reminded him he once was Tarzan, swinging happily from a vine in the Amsterdam jungle. He does that again, Sergeant. Watch this." Grijpstra reached up into an empty and uncaring sky, lifted a huge leg. "Hup *one*."

The first paramedic nodded at his partner. They each grabbed their end of the stretcher.

Grijpstra reached higher into the empty and uncaring sky and lifted a huge leg higher. "Hup *two*."

The paramedics lifted the stretcher. There was a moment of reverent silence, then the stretcher slid into the ambulance while adjutant, sergeant, paramedic one and paramedic two sadly shouted: "Hup *three*."

The Machine Gun and the Mannequin

He sat on the porch in a cane chair dating back to the time the mansion was built, back in the days when the rich still owned plantations in the colonies. He was a little sickly looking guy, smoking a cigar. The cigar didn't function too well either—he had to press the torn leaf on the side to suck smoke out of it.

He wasn't a plantation owner, of course, just another nut, and I was on my way out and ready to walk by him. The mansion was now a home for the disturbed elderly and I had been visiting my aunt, who isn't right in the head. One must be thoughtful once in a while and that's why I was there, but I had been thoughtful enough and wanted to go home. My aunt hasn't a thought in her head anymore—she only clicks her dentures and doesn't know what's what.

The little old guy waved to me and pointed at another cane chair that was ready to fall apart. I sat down. He was all alone on the porch and maybe he had something to say. He looked nutty, all right, with his few long hairs waving around his shiny skull. There were buttons missing on his shirt and his slippers were just about frayed off their soles. The bridge of his spectacles bit into his bony nose and his black raisin eyes stared at me over the round glasses.

"No visitors for you today?" I asked. He wasn't saying anything yet, so I might as well be polite.

"Never have any." It wasn't a complaint, just a statement that loosened more words. "Don't know anyone, "except the woman who used to clean my place. She'll clean for the next guy now, don't you think?"

I nodded. He was there for keeps.

"Yep," the little old guy said. "Willems is my name, but here they call me Gramps."

"Treating you okay?"

He said they were and that the food was fine. And he was allowed to smoke, which was fine, too.

I said it gives you cancer, but he began to cackle and said that cancer is like worms, pretty-colored worms that dig around inside you and finally carry you off.

"You don't mind being carried away?"

He said he didn't. I wanted to go then, but he offered me a cigar. He still looked lonely, so I thought I'd wait.

"I've been lucky," he said. "I'm over sixty-five. If I'd been under, they would have put me in the institution that makes you go to class. Know what I mean?"

"Not quite," I said.

He gave up on his cigar—the leaves kept coming off—and shook the tin. The tin was empty, so he looked at my cigar. I gave it to him. He thanked me. "Class is terrible," he said. "Frightening, too. I was in the institution maybe ten years ago. It scared me, so I became normal and got the hell out." He shook his head. "Such goings-on. They give you wooden shoes and clothes that scratch, and when there's food, they ring a bell and you can't just go and eat—they expect you to play hopscotch in the corridors first." He mused for a while. "There was a big guy who scared me. In class, that was. He would crush cans with his bare hands and look at me like he wanted to do the same thing to me."

"So you got out?"

He showed his brown teeth. "Yes. I told them the urge had gone. It hasn't, but what the hell. I got into the business of the mannequins. It kept me busy, I had to work for a change."

He waved his hands excitedly. "I got up early, went to the fairs, sold them, delivered them myself in the van. I was all over the place."

"And the urge?" I asked—he had me curious now.

"Still there," he said, not too unhappily. "But I took care. I didn't shout 'pow-pow' anymore, and I didn't point at them. I just sort of mumbled. They couldn't hear what I said."

"Mannequins?"

A nurse came. "Visitors' hour is over, Gramps," she said.

I was ready to go, but Willems pushed me back into my chair. "You're cute," he told the nurse. "I wish I'd known you when you were still in the colonies. I would have lured you from the jungle with some beads and then, while you played with them, I would have jumped you. Ha!"

"You would?" the nurse said. She was brown and Indonesian and very pretty.

"Can't he stay?" Willems asked her softly. "I never get visitors and I haven't finished telling him my story yet."

"Right," the nurse said. "I'll go back to the jungle for a while. But don't take too long. We've got to clean up here, and you'll need your nap."

She left the porch and Willems and I looked at her leaving. She had good legs and there were strong supple lines under her tight uniform.

"Nice," Willems said. "I had a mannequin like that once. I sold her in the end. Pity. But the customer offered a good price and she was somewhat damaged here and there. She'd been in the van too long and the van was soft in the springs. If they bounce around too much, they scratch."

"So what were these mannequins?" I asked.

"For shop windows. My deceased uncle used to own that business. He got them from the factory in Germany, slightly damaged merchandise, bought at a discount. I used to help him, and when he croaked, I took over. It was easy, really. If I paid the invoices, the Germans would send more. You should have seen them.

"I went to all the fairs where the storekeepers buy, and I would sit in my own little corner, with all the mannequins around me stark naked, and I would adjust their arms and heads so they could beg the clients to take them away. 'Release us from this wicked sorcerer,' they would scream, and I would sit between them, quietly."

"Were you gesturing, too?"

"Me? Never. I just look pathetic. When I don't make an effort, I always look pathetic." Willems pushed up his glasses and stared at me. His eyes didn't focus. The corners of his mouth hung down—his cheeks, too. "Well? Am I right?"

I agreed.

He was grinning at me again. "The business sort of prospered. Because the mannequins were cheap. I didn't earn much, but I wasn't starving either. Not that I ever needed much money. I lived in my room with a view of Leyden Square. I had a good position—my windows were right above the sandwich shop there. All I ever wanted to do was sit at the window, look at the crowd, and polish the Maxim—oil its works sometimes, tighten a screw here and there, adjust a spring."

I thought I hadn't heard right. "The *Maxim,* Mr. Willems?"

He was distracted by a sudden gust of wind that made the glass doors of the porch rattle, but I managed to catch his attention again. I'm still a policeman, after all, even if I only run the uniform store these days. And a Maxim is a machine gun.

He was nibbing his hands. "Yes. The cops took it away. Good thing, maybe. Perhaps it was time to retire. The cops said the Maxim was too much of a risk. Fully automatic arms are illegal and possession will land you in jail—and in my case it was worse because the gun was loaded, complete with all its parts and a couple of boxes of ammo."

"You mean you had a .50 caliber machine gun?"

"Sure had. But it was easy to get. I served with the RAF during the war, and later with the Dutch air force here. I was even a hero. You want to hear?"

I wanted to hear.

"I escaped to England," Willems said. "In 1943, the Jerries wanted me to work in a factory somewhere, but I wasn't game. I lived on the coast before they moved us to make room for the Atlantic Wall, their bunkers and so forth, but I still knew the way. My brother knew the way, too, and he found out where the Jerries kept their boats. He got us one, engine and all. We dressed up to look like Kraut sailors and one day we went. They saw us, but on account of our clothes they thought we were them. Easy, like eating Momma's pie—it always is when you really want something.

"Once we were out, the British saw us and picked us up. We joined the RAF, him as a pilot. But he crashed somewhere. I flew on a Lancaster, in one of those plastic bubbles. She was a big mother—four engines, guns everywhere, full of bombs. Up and down we went, to Germany and back, me with my Maxim. I was lucky, too—I got one of them Messerschmitts coming right at me. Press the button, there she went in smithereens. That's what I always wanted—know what I mean?"

I didn't, but Willems explained, rubbing his pointed chin, dribbling a little spittle every now and then. As a kid he used to have toy guns, and he pointed them at pedestrians and cars—"*Pow-pow,* you're dead." People laughed then, but they stopped laughing when Willems wasn't a kid anymore and was still shouting "*Pow-pow.*"

"Why did you want them dead, Mr. Willems?"

He gave me a surprised look. "*Because.* Logic argumentation. The only way."

I pretended I agreed, but he didn't seem to believe me.

"No! You don't use logic—nobody does! Listen, Mister Visitor, this world is no good. I knew that from the start. My father used to clean windows and he was drunk most of the time. One day he missed the ladder and *whap,* there he was, out of it. Very clever of him. This life isn't even for the birds. It's a mistake, nothing else.

"Look at us—you ever see anyone smile? Or even take quiet pleasure in what he does? Life's nothing but trouble, hard labor, and misery—nothing works out. Meanwhile, it rains. With death at the end. Notice I don't even mention war. There's that, too, and disease." He shook his head. "Never get into it."

"But you did get into it, Mr. Willems," I said.

His bird's claw grasped my knee. "Could I help it? Did I have a choice? No questions asked, there I was." His small eyes glinted.

"Do you really mind that much, Mr. Willems?"

He laughed. "Maybe not so much, but that's because I found a way out. Here in Holland everybody always builds, always makes things bigger. Better. Healthier even." He raised a finger. "But that's where we are wrong. We've got to think the other way around. We don't have to build, we have to *break.* I thought the Jerries understood—they destroyed a lot when they came. Rotterdam, for instance. I happened to be there when they dropped their bombs. Did that city burn! For days I ran about, fire everywhere I went—bricks flying, beams bursting." And his finger touched my thigh. "I thought it was destroyed. But I was wrong."

"Rotterdam didn't burn?"

"Yes, but not enough. And the Germans wanted to build, too. Destroy, yes, but then build forever—a new world, sky-high, fools that they were." He was whispering now, but a new thought cheered him up. "The British were better. You should have seen what that Lancaster did, and the other planes. All of Germany was burning down.

"Night after night I watched from my bubble on that airplane's belly. Everything below was red with flames, even the smoke. And the Maxim in front of me was always ready to fire, like when the Messerschmitt popped up. Yes, and pop she did, into a thousand bursts and bangs."

Willems was lost in his thoughts.

"And they let you take the Maxim home?"

He laughed and slapped my knee. "Now what did you think? Because I'm crazy I only talk craziness? Never. When the Führer gave in, they sent me back to Holland. I was security sergeant at an airport. When the Maxim arrived in a box, all I did was fill in a form. 'There you are, Sergeant,' the soldiers said. 'Thank you, boys,' I answered."

"As easy as that?"

He shrugged. "Just after the war? With everything upside-down?"

"Where did you take the gun?"

He looked sly. "I stored it safely and then had it taken to my room when they demobilized me. Then I reassembled it carefully, loaded it, and pointed it at the crowd on Leyden Square."

The thought staggered me. "For thirty-five years?"

"Most of the time."

"Loaded and ready?"

"Only during the evenings. Otherwise I locked it away."

"But you were in an institution," I said.

"Only for six months. I kept my room, and the Maxim was in the box."

"But you never fired it."

He scratched behind his ear. His spectacles came undone. "No."

"Good."

"*Bad*," Mr. Willems said loudly. "*Bad*. And weak. To think of the right solution is one thing, to go ahead is another. I've been childish, I know. I should have fired my darling, just once, on a summer night. A long burst, and then another. To prove a point." He produced his handkerchief and dabbed at his eyes. "I only fantasized instead, night after night. And now I'm here. A wasted end of a wasted life."

He was crying and rubbing at the tears impatiently. "The detectives have my Maxim. They came one evening. I still remember the older one's name. Grijpstra, he's called. They took the gun and wished me good night, and the next morning the ambulance came and brought me here. It was my own fault. I'd still be home if I hadn't placed the mannequin on the roof."

The nurse was back and staring at me. "Yes," I said, and shook Mr. Willems's hand.

IT WAS MY day off, but I drove back to Amsterdam. I'm still with the police, although they won't put me on active duty since I lost the use of one leg. I went to Headquarters and found Adjutant Grijpstra in the canteen, together with his sergeant. The sergeant's name is de Gier, but he's often called "the movie star" because of his good looks. Grijpstra is my age—fifty-two. I know him well; we went to police school together. I went and sat next to him and interrupted his argument with de Gier. They were each chiming that it was the other's turn to pay.

When I paid, they calmed down somewhat.

"A Mr. Willems," I said. "Is the name familiar?"

They thought for a while.

"Tell me more," de Gier said.

"A machine gun, and a mannequin."

Grijpstra eyed me morosely. "What's he to you? Not a relative, I hope?"

I described my meeting with Willems.

"Oh—right," Grijpstra acknowledged. "Thanks to de Gier's intelligence, we nabbed him. When the chief-constable heard about it, he came all the way down from the top floor to shake the sergeant's hand."

"So what's the story?"

Grijpstra pointed at de Gier.

"No," de Gier said. "Not me. I should never have interfered with that business. I've told you before, Adjutant, we should have let the suspect be."

Grijpstra is a kindly fellow. He married badly and lives an unhappy life, but if you don't raise your voice and keep pushing, he'll open up.

"Yes," he said now. "You know the Café Tivoli? A big building on Leyden Square? With a flat roof? Went broke a while back and has been empty ever since. Okay. There was a mannequin on the roof a few months back, the kind they use in store windows. But it had been dressed up to resemble a little old guy. He had a bald head, with a bit of fringe left on, and a small nose with spectacles stuck to it. A suit, shoes—very realistic. And beside the mannequin was a machine gun, pointed at the square.

"It was imitation, naturally. The weapon was a stovepipe with a funnel attached to one end of it, the ammo consisting of pine cones sewn into a strip of canvas. The sight was made out of twisted wire. It looked real enough, especially from the square, and frightened the citizens so much the desk sergeant thought he should send somebody to check it out."

"We happened to be around," de Gier said.

"So we went up," Grijpstra explained. "I tore my trousers and got myself dirty and the sergeant almost slipped off the roof—there's a lot of bird dung up there and it was raining, of course—but we did make it in the end. De Gier insisted on a thorough investigation—he even went back to get a camera."

De Gier nodded. "Of course."

"Of course," Grijpstra repeated. "The sergeant is an artist, you see, and a psychologist as well, and interested in furthering his career. We removed the mannequin. It fell apart on the way down, but we still had the photographs, so the sergeant put them up in our room at Headquarters and spent a day or two studying them."

I looked at de Gier. He looked away.

"And finally," Grijpstra said, "our supersleuth came up with this. 'Whoever created this apparition,' he said, 'is crazy, and evil, too. We will make an arrest.'"

"Which was wrong," the sergeant said.

"Which was right," said Grijpstra.

"Yes," I said. "And then?"

Adjutant Grijpstra rubbed the tabletop with his hand. "We found him. It wasn't hard. We knew what he looked like and that he had to be around the square. We ran into him the next evening when I took the sergeant to the sandwich shop to spend some money on him."

"Ha," de Gier said. "The smoked eel was on me. But the adjutant is right. We walked into him easily enough and followed him to his room. The machine gun was there, oiled and greased and fully loaded."

"So you had him removed to the nuthouse," I said.

"Where else?" Grijpstra asked. "How is he now?"

"Fine," I said. "Having his meals on time and being looked after by an Indonesian beauty. Very good of you, Adjutant. A true danger to society if I ever came across one. Not a nasty sort of chap, really, but had he ever pressed that trigger, there would have been a lot of blood on the cobblestones."

"It is the task of the police to protect civilians against themselves," Grijpstra said.

De Gier got up. "We should have let the suspect be. What he explained that evening is absolutely dead right. An original thinker reasoning from a correct point of view. If we learn to destroy the environment and keep at it until there's nothing left we will have done with all misery once and forever. Life is suffering, so it follows that no life equals no suffering. Getting rid of the whole thing is the only way out."

De Gier walked to the canteen's counter and engaged the girl behind it in flirtation. She is a lovely creature, of the same type as Willems's nurse.

"One wonders," I said to Grijpstra, "if your sergeant should really be allowed to be a policeman."

Grijpstra got to his feet. "I have to go on patrol. The Lord only knows what the civilians are up to now."

I repeated my statement.

"De Gier is an excellent policeman," Grijpstra said softly. "Bright and diligent. He has been studying Buddhism lately and contemplating the meaning of suffering. But I don't think he has obtained the right insight yet. Nice to see you again." He started to leave. "Do you think Willems is happy in that home?"

I thought about it. I said he probably was.

The Bongo Bungler

Complainant looked like he had slept in his expensive suit and had cleaned dishes with his silk necktie. As the middle-aged tourist reported his wife missing, the desk sergeant referred Douglas D. Dubber to the Department of Criminal Investigation, better known as the Murder Brigade. At Moose Canal Headquarters of the Amsterdam Municipal Police the disheveled Mr. Dubber saw Adjutant Grijpstra, a burly man with short grey hair, and his assistant, Sergeant de Gier, younger, athletic, handsome, charming, polite.

"You're the good cop," Mr. Dubber wearily told the sergeant.

De Gier said his colleague Grijpstra was the good cop, too. He told the foreign visitor that the bad-cop/good-cop combination is not used much in The Netherlands. All Dutch cops are expected to respect their clients. The practical reason for Netherlandic-cop goodness, de Gier explained in fluent English, was lack of jail space. No use going all out to make arrests if you can't put the bad folks behind bars anyway.

"We tend to try to look at their good sides should they have them," Grijpstra said gruffly in passable English.

Mr. Dubber didn't get it immediately. "You have that many people locked up that you are out of cells?"

"The state gave us few cells to start out with," de Gier said "So we try to mediate, be reasonable, to use the maximum benefit of all possible doubts. Our practice aims at getting people to quiet down a bit, so they can go fishing, watch their savings accounts grow, play with their kids, visit their parents."

Mr. Dubber remained puzzled.

"The Netherlands are a kingdom," de Gier explained.

"Doesn't the king like imprisoning bad guys?"

"The queen, actually," de Gier said.

"Please," Douglas Dubber said, "what does your queens have to do with not apprehending and punishing bad folks?"

"We," Grijpstra said gruffly, showing the visitor his uniform hat, decorated with a bronze crown, "we, the police, represent the crown, which is worn by the queen, and the crown represents the Netherlandic Idea of God, who, we assume, is forgiving rather than vengeful."

"That's the theoretical aspect." De Gier smiled. "It's mostly applied in Amsterdam. In the provinces the Dutch divinity may be seen as sterner."

"Do you have jail space in the provinces?" Mr. Dubber asked.

"Some," de Gier said. "Not too much, though. The provinces are stingy. They build other facilities with the taxpayers' money, a soccer field here, a swimming pool there."

"It also could be that we Dutch are lazy," Grijpstra said gruffly.

"So what are you jokers up to?" Mr. Dubber's eyes were still round with bewildered surprise. "Are you telling me you don't accept my complaint? Am I to be wifeless because you believe in some kind of flaky idealism?"

"We do make an effort," Grijpstra said, a little more pleasantly now that he had seated himself behind his desk. "It wouldn't surprise me if we found your missing wife, Mr. Dubber. Within the next twenty-four hours. We often do find missing persons. Usually because they come to us." He put out a heavy hand. "You have a photo?"

While Douglas Dubber went through his pockets, de Gier pulled up a chair for his visitor.

"Here." Dubber tried to open a passport. His fingers trembled. De Gier took the passport from him and used a scanner to enlarge the photo. He and Grijpstra studied Emily Dubber's attractive face on their computer screens. "Marilyn Monroe," they both said. Dubber smiled tiredly. "She did win a look-alike contest once, but that was way back. This picture is old."

"What do you think happened?" Grijpstra asked.

"She has been murdered," Dubber whispered.

The detectives tsked at such an outrageous idea. "Now, now," Grijpstra said.

"Murders are rare here," de Gier said. "What makes you think such a thing? Really, sir."

"I have not," complainant said, "seen Emily since last Friday night when she walked out on me. She was angry but"—he held up the passport—"she did not take this. She didn't pack any clothes either. Left most of her makeup kit." He weakly thumped his knee. "Where the hell is the woman?"

"Picked up a lover?" de Gier asked. "Bought clothes and other necessities with her credit card?"

"Do you think so?" Dubber asked. "What about her diamond? And her shiner?"

"Shiner?" Grijpstra asked.

Dubber pointed at his eye.

"You hit her?"

"She hit me first," Dubber said. "Where it hurts. She knocked my jenever glass out of my hand. I wanted to hit her on her nose, which was full of coke. Tit for tat, right? I missed I got her eye. It started swelling right away. She wouldn't want to run around town looking like that for several days."

The detectives looked at their computer screens, where Emily Dubber smiled back at them.

"What's this about a diamond?" Grijpstra asked.

"In a ring," Dubber said. "I just bought it for her, twenty thousand dollars' worth of big bauble. And do you think she was grateful?" Dubber found the credit-card receipt for the ring, crumpled in the breast pocket of his elegant jacket. "Look."

"What do you do, Mr. Dubber?" de Gier asked. "For a living, I mean. Are you rich?"

The suggestion cheered the complainant somewhat. He told the detectives he was a Wall Street-based financial adviser, that he sent out a costly newsletter in which he picked stocks for the aggressive investor. He was on vacation in The Netherlands as his maternal grandfather was Dutch-born and had told him tales. He wanted to see windmills spin; drink jenever; eat sole *á la meuniere;* splash, wearing big yellow wooden shoes, through juicy cow pats; see lines of cut willow trees flanking endless ditches between endless pastures; eat smoked eel on fresh white buns. So far, he and Emily, who also had Dutch origins, hadn't gotten around to doing any of that, except for drinking the thick, syrupy juniper-flavored gin that Emily didn't care for, that made Douglas hard to deal with. Or so said Emily, who *he* thought was hard to deal with while stoned on the cocaine she had been buying in the bars around the Tulip Hotel, where they were staying.

"A twenty-thousand-dollar diamond ring, on your credit card?" Grijpstra asked. "How big was that stone, sir?"

"Big," Dubber said. He looked sad now. He said that without his wife he noticed Amsterdam's downside. There was the constant drizzle and a cold summer wind that got to him every time he turned a corner. There was a carillon jingling on the half hour from a church tower close to the hotel. There was the raw herring that he kept eating and that gave him a thirst for more jenever, which, as yet, he hadn't acquired a taste for. There was his rental Mercedes, hauled off by the police because of a parking problem. There was also the public transportation that he couldn't figure out at all. "You have to make me feel good again," Mr. Dubber told the detectives. "I need Emily. We had planned some romance. I need to walk hand in hand with her, along those nice walkways you have here, along the canals, under the elm trees, when the weather breaks again. When you find her for me, I promise we will go easy on the substances and maybe even visit a museum." He gestured. "Van Go!"

"Van *Gogh*" de Gier said. "There's a throat-scrape at the end. And the o is not long like in Ophelia but short like in osprey."

Grijpstra excused de Gier. "The sergeant is a language lover."

"Whatever," Dubber said. "The guy who cut his ear off. Because a whore said it looked pretty and he wanted to give her a present. You know? The painter?"

"Sure," Grijpstra soothed, "Van Go. Just as you say, sir."

"I need my wife," the unhappy Mr. Dubber insisted. "I want to have her with me. She can give me some company in return for the stone. Figure out your streetcar schedules. So I can get around more." He frowned at de Gier. "Do you have a wife?"

De Gier said he shared daydreams with the cat Tabriz, on a rocking chair he'd found in the street, his only piece of furniture, except for a hospital bed, which he kept between potted weeds in the loft he rented from Grijpstra's girlfriend, city weeds that he grew to bushlike heights fertilized by manure he picked up at the police stable.

Dubber wasn't paying attention. "Crazy Van Go, made a present of his pretty ear to a hooker squatting in a picture window!" He laughed out loud. "I tried that, too, you know."

The detectives looked at Dubber's ears.

"Just the whores," complainant said. "The ladies in the windows on the canals here, great lookers, but they don't speak English. Thai, Russian, whatever, how can I order 'specialties' if they don't speak the lingo?"

Dubber began to mumble. Grijpstra went back to studying Emily's face on his screen, de Gier wrote down some of the words that floated in the complainant's otherwise inaudible monologue. *Bitch. Bungle. Bald. Bullshit. Bad. Buddhist. Bar. Bongo.* B-words, de Gier called them when he reported to the commissaris later that day. "Not the MF-word?" the commissaris asked. "You're sure complainant is American? They usually use the MF-word when under stress."

"No, just B-words, sir," de Gier said.

Mr. Dubber's distraught litany came to an end. He looked around the small white-and-grey office. "Hey, you have a coffee machine there. Hey, is that a refrigerator? Any cold beer to spare?"

Grijpstra got the coffee machine burbling and de Gier, using the edge of his metal desk and his hand, chopping, as tools, cracked open a bottle of lemonade flavored with sugared ginger. He smiled an apology. "No alcohol, Mr. Dubber."

"Are you guys on the straight and narrow?" Dubber asked. "Just during office hours, I hope."

"The straight and narrow, at any hour," de Gier said.

"Aren't all good cops bad drunks?" Doug asked.

"Bad drunks shouldn't drink," Grijpstra said.

"Did you go all the way?" Doug looked hurt when Grijpstra nodded. "AA and all?"

"I stay away from AA, too, now," de Gier said, "I just want to quit drinking, I don't want to hear more sob stories. I promised I would go back at the very first slip." He winked. "The thought of seeing those turkeys again should make me stop forever."

"Stop drinking," Doug asked, "or stop listening to other addicts' stories?"

"He combines the two," Grijpstra said, speaking kindly for the first time. "A double negative may make a positive." He looked grave again. "All drunks are crazy, but the craziness doesn't show too much while they're sober." He looked wise before looking sorry.

"That's what his girlfriend tells him," de Gier told Dubber.

"When did you quit?" Dubber asked de Gier.

De Gier looked at his watch.

"That recent?"

"Checking the month," de Gier said. "I quit almost a year ago. Maybe I could go back to AA meetings. Maybe they have thought of a few new stories."

"Don't count on it," Doug said. "The stories never change, even if you shift locations. No matter where you go—LA, Frisco, Chicago, New York, same difference—tattoos on your Johnson that you can't recall having ordered, maxed credit cards you didn't know you carried, cars that have gotten dented overnight and parked where you didn't leave them, lost wallets. The worst is when you can't find your own toilet." Dubber fingered his unshaven cheeks. "And now my own wife is gone. And me out of state." He rubbed with more force. "Out of country. Out of continent, even." He felt his temples gingerly, as if the arteries under his fingertips might burst. "How do I handle this?" His bloodshot eyes stared at Grijpstra's pin-striped waistcoat. "I can't go home without her, can I?" He produced a crumpled set of airplane tickets. "Do you think I can get a credit?"

"Where did you think she might have gone?" Grijpstra asked, gently now.

"Not far, not on her own, that is, certainly not in the dark. She doesn't have good night vision," Dubber said, holding his lemonade up against the light of the room's narrow window. "This is a mystical color, don't you think? Like it is illuminated from within." He swallowed, then inhaled sharply. "Got a bit of a bite, all right."

De Gier refilled Dubber's glass. "The Tulip Hotel is on the Emperor's Canal, at the corner of Palace Street. Did you make inquiries at bars around there?"

Dubber had not. Emily would indeed have gone to one of the nearby bars where he had been told not to return—a matter of a few fistfights and a broken mirror and such. He had found watering holes further afield, and had been spending time with the Thai and the Russian window-ladies, living on street stall bought raw herring, with chopped onions on the side, and taking naps in his hotel room. All that had made time fly, until he noticed that Emily wasn't with him. And hadn't been at his side since Friday evening. "It is Monday now, yes?"

It was Monday morning, de Gier told him. "What was your wife wearing when you saw her last."

"A red dress," Dubber said.

"Had she walked out on you before?" Grijpstra asked.

"Not this trip," Doug said. "In Manhattan she does often, then she comes back the next day. She is pretty, you know, longer legs than Marilyn, real big . . ." He thought for a moment. He shook his head. "Really mammal. A man like me needs that. Don't know why, but there it is. There they are." He sighed, stared at his baggy knees, unpolished and scuffed shoes, dirty fingernails, the stains on his necktie. He sighed again. "I don't feel good. I need a shower." He raised his eyes, not his head. "So can you guys find her?"

De Gier was looking at Emily's face again, which still smiled back at him.

"Notice her cheekbones?" Dubber asked. "Even higher than Marilyn's. They call those 'money bones' in the trade. She is a model. That's how I met her. There are clubs in Manhattan where we financial gurus get to meet movie star look-alike Manhattan models."

"Did she do porn?" Grijpstra asked.

Dubber smiled as he made a fist and shook it in Grijpstra's face. He took a sip of the strong coffee. "If I drank this stuff back home it would kill me. I am a ten-mug-a-day man." The coffee made him talkative again. "Soft porn only, calendar posing, bathing suits, maybe a few movies, a stag party once in a while." Dubber looked wistful. "We made a deal: no charge if I took her to Las Vegas for the weekend. When we went a second time, we came back married."

"And she likes drugs," de Gier said.

Dubber shrugged. "And she cooks. And she puts buttons on coats when I lose them. Give a little, take a little."

"Emily still picks up men in bars?" de Gier asked.

"Uh-huh." Dubber nodded. "When I am mad at her and won't give her money and she thinks the other guys can come up with free cocaine."

"And you mind?"

"Mind, schmind." Dubber frowned furiously. "Sure I mind, but jeez, this is the big bad world, we gotta face that." He gestured widely. "So she stays out a night but that's only the flip side." He got up but quickly sat down again. "There's a flip side to her flip side. I have this big apartment near Wall Street and I mess it up when I am alone. Before Emily, all I had for company was a bunch of starving goldfish. Emily cleans the algae off the aquarium walls, throws out the dead ones, feeds the live ones. Things get better and better every day." He smiled weakly.

Grijpstra rose heavily. "Okay, sir, we know enough to start a search." He pulled a color copy from the printer. "Thirty-five-year-old white female, blond, blue-eyed, tall, with a movie-star figure. One discolored eye. We'll be in touch."

De Gier, maintaining his charming and polite smiles and pleasantly modulated baritone voice, saw complainant off to the open elevator. When he came back, Grijpstra mentioned insurance. "Pushed Emily into a canal, you think?"

De Gier didn't think the suggestion was an impossibility.

The commissaris, chief of the Murder Brigade, a frail older man, fortified behind an antique executive desk, supported by standing lions sculptured in oak, in a high-ceilinged room decorated with geraniums on wide windowsills, picked up on the detail of the twenty-thousand-dollar diamond ring. "Could be a simple case of greed and lack of concern for the other parties," he said brightly. "Which boils down to the same thing, of course." He smiled encouragingly. "Maybe a mugging that turned into a kidnapping?" A sudden ray of sunlight shone between his thin fingers as he raised his hands to urge them into activity. "You two better check on bars where bald bad bungled Buddhists bang bongos. Get Cardozo to help out, and Ketchup and Karate. No uniforms. We may still be in time. Start after dinner tonight, when the district starts cooking."

They were not in time.

An alert sorter at Amsterdam's generator, where the city's garbage is converted into energy, had, by then, noted a human arm dangling from an elongated carton as he operated a crane to hoist inflammables into the incinerator. The carton had been brought in by a garbage barge, one of many stationed on the city's canals during the day, to be hauled to the generator after sunset, weekends excluded. The barges are receptacles for rubbish deposited by citizens living along the canals. All dumping is supposed to be supervised by uniformed officials who guard the barges, but there is only one inspector to each barge and there are the calls of nature, quick trips to sandwich shops, goofing off in the barges' cabins, which provide periods during which the unspeakable can happen. The carton, originally used to pack a standing lamp, had been dumped by an unknown party onto a barge stationed at the intersection of the Brewer's and Emperor's Canals. It contained Emily Dubber's nude and soiled remains.

Grijpstra and de Gier, reached by cell phone, left the interviewing of bartenders and bar regulars to Detective-Constable-First-Class Simon Cardozo, a curly-haired young man in a corduroy suit, and out-of-uniform Constables Ketchup and Karate, while they took a cab to the morgue. Assistant pathologist Herbert Janssen, new to his trade, had vomited next to the dead body and was cleaning up as the detectives came, shivering, into the refrigerated room.

"Bad," Dr. Janssen said. "The autopsy will be later but I can tell you right now that somebody chopped the lady's right ring finger off, and that somebody repeatedly prodded an eighteen-inch-long artifact into her vagina. At this point, I would guess the prodding led to internal bleeding that proved to be lethal."

Sergeant de Gier choked, coughed, covered his mouth, turned on his heel, and ran out of the room. Grijpstra shrugged. "He does that." He turned back to the body. "Coke in the nose? Would you mind checking?"

"There's a white powdery substance in the nose," Dr. Janssen confirmed. He pointed at the corpse's upper arm. "There are fresh needle marks, too." He tried to drop the arm but it resisted gravity. "Rigor mortis," the young doctor said. "I would guess she has been dead for several days." He pointed at something small and white, moving slowly on the blotched skin of a thigh. "That, Detective, is a maggot."

De Gier was smoking a clumsily rolled cigarette outside the morgue's front door.

"You don't smoke anymore," Grijpstra said. "Where did you get that?"

"The doorman hands them out on request," de Gier said hoarsely.

Grijpstra went back into the building and came back smoking, too.

"Nellie will smell that," de Gier said. "You'll yell at each other again. If that keeps happening I don't want to live on top of you guys anymore. It gets too noisy."

"I'll move out with you," Grijpstra said.

De Gier held up his cigarette so the tobacco wouldn't fall out. "A hypothesis, please?"

"Murder?" Grijpstra said, furiously sucking at his cigarette. "Malicious forethought? Premeditated violence? Sickos at large? An onslaught of planned horror?"

De Gier preferred to suppose manslaughter. "We suspects never seem to be big planners. We say afterward that we made all these important decisions but forget that this seems to be true only in hindsight." He contemplated a wisp of smoke rising from Grijpstra's tobacco creation. "Most of us are just foolish." He sang hoarsely, *"Do-ing what co-mes na-tu-ral-ly."*

"It still could be murder," Grijpstra said. "Don't underestimate us too much." He inhaled and coughed. "Some of us sometimes manage to be premeditating assholes."

It was after hours by then, but the detectives, shaken by the confrontation with the corpse of ex-model ex-Emily Dubber, felt in need of guidance again. Instead of facing the home front commanded by Grijpstra's girlfriend at her hotel at Straight Tree Ditch, they took a cab to Queen's Avenue, in Amsterdam's elegant residential district.

The commissaris was in his bath, easing rheumatic pains with almost too hot water, while his wife sat next to the tub, trying to knit her husband a waistcoat for the winter, but hardly able to see yarn and needles in the steamy air. Only the pet turtle seemed comfortable, marching slowly to and fro. The detectives stood at the far end of the large marble-floored room. The commissaris shook his small head, comically decorated with soggy wisps of hair standing up like ghostly ears. "Beautiful Amsterdam, designed to soothe distraught spirits with its Golden Age parks and canalside architecture, and now look what happens."

Grijpstra and de Gier, uncomforted, were mumbling good-byes when Cardozo phoned in on Grijpstra's cell phone. "I am at the Buddha Bar in Bonefield Alley," Cardozo whispered. "I have been interrogating Pirate, the bartender, and Regular, who is a poet. I got some information. Your lost lady, a blonde in a red dress, black-eyed, a cokehead, attractive, was here last Friday. She became friendly with a character called Bungle Bongo, a poet and the bar's main dealer. Bungle's girlfriend, a sunburned woman named Trudi, made a scene when Bungle and Emily Dubber left together. Your complainant, Mr. Dubber, is known here, too. He wasn't here Friday night. He couldn't be, as he was thrown out earlier last week for being a nuisance and told never to return ever."

"Are Bungle and Trudi there now?" Grijpstra asked.

"No," Cardozo said, "but I have an address for them. Houseboat Row at Behind Canal. Supposedly they're neighbors."

"Don't go away," Grijpstra said. He relayed Cardozo's intel to the commissaris.

"Bullshit Buddhists?" the commissaris asked from his bath, remembering de Gier's earlier reporting. He waved away shrouds of steam.

"Bullshit Buddhists?" Grijpstra said into the phone.

"Bald bad bullshit Buddhists," de Gier said.

"Bald bad bullshit Buddhists?" Grijpstra asked Detective-Constable-First-Class Cardozo.

"There are several here," Cardozo said. "Bartender Pirate and client Regular would fit the description but it seems this Bungle Bongo guy defected from Buddhism a while ago. The suspect shifted to the stars."

"Stars?" Grijpstra asked.

"A less subtle philosophy than Buddhism," Cardozo said. "Pirate was telling me that Bungle is weak, he wants to hold on to something. Buddhism believes in nothing. There is this related faith now that holds with star folk, angels, that are due to come and save us. Adjutant?"

"Dear?" Grijpstra asked.

"I think," Cardozo whispered urgently, "we should *move*. Constables Ketchup and Karate want to go to Houseboat Row now. They say this trail is hot. I am trying to restrain them."

"So you have suspects?" Grijpstra asked. "Possible miscreants who were seen with the lady when she was both alive and dressed, wearing a diamond ring?"

"It might seem to appear that way," Cardozo said. "But Trudi spent Friday night with this poet character Regular, she only

left Regular's place late Saturday morning. It looks like Bungle
Bongo is the guy to go after."

"We don't know as yet exactly when Mrs. Dubber died, so
Trudi may be implicated too," Grijpstra said. "Okay, go ahead,
we'll met you at Houseboat Row. In case we are late, make sure
Ketchup and Karate keep their hands in their pockets. Order
them not to show violence to the suspects. Nice and gentle
does it. No arrests if at all possible. Remember our ongoing
problem: zero jail space."

Bungle Bongo, a short, fat street musician whom Grijpstra
remembered having confronted at Amsterdam's central Dam
Square, where, irritated by the man's monotonous composi-
tions, he had suggested that Bungle relocate to Rotterdam,
was not home. Bungle's address was a dented, sixty-foot-long
steel cargo boat, decommissioned at least half a century ago.
Another decrepit vessel, a mastless flat-bottomed worm-eaten
sailboat, was moored next to Bungle Bongo's. A hand-lettered
sign on the sailboat said *Trudi, attack rats trained and kenneled.*
Cardozo was inside Trudi's floating home when his superiors
arrived. Ketchup and Karate, small-sized effeminate-looking
men, were on the cargo boat's deck, hands in pockets, peering
into the boat's cabin through dirty portholes. "Mrs. Dubber was
killed here all right," Ketchup told Grijpstra. "This Trudi says
she tried to get into Bungle's cabin, this one, when she arrived
Saturday morning late, but it was locked, like now. Bungle was
on deck, smoking dope. Trudi looked through that porthole over
there and saw a nude female body in a hammock. The hammock
moved because of the current in the canal, and the body moved
with it, but it had no life of its own. It didn't look asleep, she says,
it looked more dead."

"Trudi recognized Emily Dubber?" de Gier asked.

"It was dark in the cabin," Ketchup said. "The witness is
nervous. Let me at her, Sergeant, me and Karate will slap her
around a bit. We can threaten her with arrest for drug possession

if she doesn't tell us where Bungle Bongo is now. All these boats are loaded with dope. We'll soon find some."

"And," Karate told de Gier, "this Trudi saw Bungle dragging a carton taped shut with lots of silver duct tape into his Volkswagen bus on Sunday morning. The vehicle never came back and neither did the suspect. Maybe Trudi helped him carry the carton. Let me at her, Sergeant. Please?"

"Something about a riding whip that her boyfriend, Bongo, likes to swish around," Cardozo said when he came out of the houseboat next door. "This Bungle likes to ride women like horses. He has composed songs about that, and recites poetry on the subject. Trudi thinks he used the instrument on the tourist lady; she would never play that game with him herself."

De Gier was introduced to Trudi, a woman with a pronounced sunburn, obtained by use of a machine that took up about a third of her living quarters. She told him the rat sign was to keep Jehovah's Witnesses from bothering her. The rats on her boat were neither trained nor kenneled. She said her profession was cook in a halfway house for recovering drug addicts in the inner city. Bungle Bongo worked there, too. He sold drugs to the inmates, to supplement their government-issued rations. Trudi had met Bungle at a meditation class. Bungle had been a Buddhist but had recently removed all his spiritual paraphernalia from his boat. "No more fish-head drums and incense, He is a star child now. He was talking about joining their commune."

"Where?" Grijpstra asked.

Trudi shrugged. "Somewhere in the south I think he said."

"Where is he now?" de Gier asked.

"Who cares?" Trudi asked. "Good riddance. *I* am still a Buddhist." She pointed at a calendar, dated a year back, showing the wrong month, under a reproduction of a Tibetan scroll, depicting a demon waving six arms holding bloody skulls, gesturing from a raging fire in which he sat in the lotus position. "That's what inspired him. He said he had completed Buddhism and that this picture, which I had hung here for a purpose, without knowing it, leads to the next step, which would be this angelic thing. He believes Judgment Day is about to happen. The point of no return has been passed by self-willed humanity and God will send angels to see what can be saved and then burn hopeless sinners."

"Good idea," Grijpstra said.

De Gier studied the calendar picture. "So this image here points to a future, to somewhere where things are going to get better? Once all these skulls the demon/angel holds there are burned?"

"Isn't that silly?" Trudi asked. "I don't believe it. True Buddhism believes in nothing. I believe in nothing. No hope. Nothing gets better. Let go of hope. Bungle is a loser, I kept telling him that. He believes in loss and gain, he is stuck."

"De Gier," Grijpstra asked, "what is the witness saying?"

"Are you saying Bungle Bongo is still stuck in dualism, ma'am?" de Gier asked.

Trudi looked wise, and stayed quiet, to show she was answering him by using Buddhist silence.

"I don't get this," Grijpstra said, after helping himself to a cigarette Trudi offered. "If this Bungle friend of yours, thank you, ma'am"—he puffed contentedly after she had struck a match for him—"if your neighbor and lover is a philosophical man concerned about Divine Judgment, who hopes for this angelic end-of-the-world-as-we-know-it that you mentioned just now, then why would he poke a riding whip into a woman friendly enough to go home with him, and cut off her finger so he could steal her ring?"

"Your colleague," Trudi said, "said it just now. He is stuck in dualism. It makes a loser like Bungle clumsy. It's tricky to be free of things, like I am, but I can do it because I am a pure Buddhist."

GRIJPSTRA AND DE Gier had themselves driven back to the Buddha Bar in Bonefield Alley. "I like these cabs," de Gier said. "I don't miss the old VW patrol car. Isn't it nice not to have to worry about parking space and engine failure and malfunctioning radios and traffic?"

"There isn't all that much traffic anymore," Grijpstra said. "Taking traffic out of the inner city has worked. Some things do go right. It confirms my minimal faith in the possibility of problem solving."

"The inner-city traffic problem got solved by happenstance," the cab driver said. "We merely stumbled into a new set of aldermen who couldn't stand wasting time, on their way to the brothels, while sitting in their stationary cars. Or," the driver said, "it could be that the crisis got so bad that the mayor had no option but to make parking impossible by raising rates and blocking most potential parking space by installing these steel penis poles that even a tank can't push over." He glared at Grijpstra in his mirror. "Don't assume any goodwill. I won't have that in my cab."

"Some of us might be anonymous saints," Grijpstra replied.

"What?" de Gier asked.

Grijpstra apologized. He had merely wanted to keep the dialogue going.

Pirate, the bartender at the Buddha Bar, so called because of an eye patch and a bandanna printed with a repetitive skull and bone motif that covered his bare skull, called over Regular, a small man, also bald, with a third eye tattooed on his forehead, who introduced himself as the poet in residence. Yes, he knew Bungle Bongo, they were drinking buddies. "And Buddhist brothers," Pirate said. That too, Regular said, but Bungle Bongo had recently wavered from a faith that, Bungle claimed, had become, at present levels of insight, unacceptably depressing.

"So he moved on to the star people?" Grijpstra asked. "Would you happen to know where we could locate that organization?"

Regular wasn't sure. All he knew, from Bungle's recent

mutterings—Bungle had been drinking and snorting heavily lately—was that the star folks, or the *angelics,* as Bungle preferred to call his guides, lived in the hills on the Belgian border, and that he visited them from time to time, intending to join their commune, but there was an entrance fee that he hadn't managed to scrape together yet.

"What does Suspect look like?" de Gier asked.

"Oh, it's going to be like that, is it?" the poet Regular asked. "We have labeled the subject of our scorn on mere hearsay?"

"Describe Bungle Bongo," de Gier ordered gently, staring into Regular's eyes.

Regular said that Bungle Bongo looked just like him, Regular, but Bungle was white, a native of the mother country, not of Suriname, South America, the former Dutch colony where Regular himself originated—he thought—it was all so long ago now, another dream, like the present where he seemed to have dreamed himself into Amsterdam.

"Bungle looks like me, too," Pirate confirmed. "I am bald, too, but I have the bandanna and the eye patch. Otherwise, we are birds of a feather."

Cardozo, the next morning, in the commissaris's office, reported on searching Bungle Bongo's houseboat after obtaining a warrant. The riding whip Bungle purportedly used for sexual play was found and confiscated. So was the red dress Emily had been wearing, and a computer. Cardozo had brought the laptop along, got it going, and connected it to the commissaris's telephone outlet.

A list of Bungle Bongo's favorite websites was found: free porno by hobbyists, *The Telegraph*, a newspaper on-line, weather predictions, stock tips.

"Here," the commissaris said, "*Pleiades.* Seven stars, home of the angels who are responsible for creating incarnate life on earth. The place of origin of the Day of Judgment process that will soon interrupt our human degeneration so that the human life experiment can finally be resurgent in the next millennium. Click on that, please, Cardozo."

"How do you know about stuff like that, sir?" Grijpstra asked while waiting for the Pleiades website's home page to appear.

"How could I not know?" the commissaris asked, as surprised as Grijpstra. "Ideas reach me all the time. Don't tell me they don't reach you."

"Reach me from where, sir?"

The commissaris shook his head in amazement. "From everywhere. The papers, the Net, people talking on a streetcar, Katrien coming back from playing bridge, even Turtle is in on it. You mean you haven't heard about the Pleiades, Adjutant?" He kept shaking his head. "You're kidding. That isn't nice, Henk, trying to trick an old man approaching his retirement."

"I suppose you're in on this, too," Grijpstra said to de Gier. De Gier said he had met a woman at a jazz bar who had filled him in on the subject. He had also read about the coming change in essential human development in a Colombian novel. An interesting idea, de Gier told Grijpstra, poking the adjutant in the stomach with a hard finger. The Day of Judgment sorting wasn't, according to this Colombian source, to be a moral affair but just a means of getting rid of useless incarnate life forms. Bad guys wouldn't go to hell. They would simply disappear. The world's population was to be decreased by forty percent at least, more if borderline cases were to be eliminated, too. "In view of our continuing effort to figure things out, you and I might be saved," de Gier said, "but would we want to be saved? The Colombian novelist says this will happen around 2011. We would be too old. Better to get out early and come back in new bodies." De Gier frowned. "Tricky stuff, you know. It has been worrying me lately."

"He reads South American literature now," Grijpstra told the commissaris. "In Spanish. Between his pots of grass in Nellie's loft. It has probably interfered with his perception. It sure doesn't make him happy."

"To be happy is to be silly," the commissaris said. He studied the Pleiades website's pictures and text. "Right, there we are, stars, angels, that scene down there, with the nude blonde being taken from a ship, looks like a detail taken from a Hieronymus Bosch triptych. And over there, a diamond flashing, amazing how it all fits together. Do you see a place where we can contact these visionaries, Cardozo?"

Cardozo brought up an email screen. The commissaris dictated a note. "Dear Pleiades. This is the Amsterdam Police, Murder Brigade, Adjutant Henk Grijpstra, Police Headquarters, Moose Canal. Do you have a recent arrival who brought you a valuable diamond ring as entry fee? Alias Bungle Bongo, real name"—he consulted his notes—"Nicolaas Sieker." Cardozo typed the name in. The commissaris continued dictating. "We have reason to believe that the diamond was cut off the finger of the corpse of Emily Dubber, an American tourist who died because of injuries caused by a riding whip inserted into her vagina. Please make a citizen's arrest of your candidate member and give us your address so that we can pick up Mr. Sieker for questioning. ASAP, if you please. Thanks. Sincerely."

The detectives had coffee while they gave the Pleiades commune time to answer the commissaris's missive.

"Try now," the commissaris said.

"Dear Adjutant Grijpstra," the answering email said, "we abhor violence, but in view of what you describe, our security will hold Sieker if your note turns out to be real. We will look up your number in the book and phone you." The call came in within minutes. The caller identified himself as Piet, elected (for one year) chairman of the democratic Pleiades guidance committee. Piet gave Grijpstra the address of his commune, housed on a former farm near the city of Kerkrade, in the province of Limburg, on the Belgian border.

The commissaris, assisted by Cardozo and Ketchup and Karate, left within minutes, in the commissaris's private old-model Citröen. Grijpstra and de Gier interviewed Mr. Dubber at the Tulip Hotel.

"Rats," Douglas D. Dubber said. "These people are rats."

"Just one rat," Grijpstra said.

"Cutting off her finger," Dubber said. "Really." He opened a drawer and took out papers. "Here, perhaps you can help out. I need a statement from you guys to file a claim."

The papers contained an insurance policy. De Gier mumbled slowly through the text. He looked up. "Life insurance, a thousand dollars for your and your wife's lives each, you are covered for the duration of your vacation."

"Right," Dubber said. "I took it out at the travel agency; it came with the tickets. I say, would you mind giving me a statement on police stationery that Emily is dead? I might as well try to collect this."

De Gier shook his head. "A mere thousand for a man of your wealth? Do you really need to bother?"

"Do you have any more substantial insurance on the life of your wife?" Grijpstra asked.

Dubber didn't seem to hear him.

"Sir?" de Gier asked.

Dubber pointed at the policy in de Gier's hand. "Just that."

"That wasn't true," the commissaris said three days later. Dubber was facing him across the antique desk at Amsterdam's Police Headquarters. "Was it?"

Dubber, looking as disheveled as he had the first time he visited the building, was silent.

The commissaris persisted. "You need our statement in order to collect the real insurance on your wife, don't you? We will find out, you know. We have good contacts with the New York Police Department. As soon as you collect your ill-gained fortune we will be informed. You set up this entire chain of events in order to recapitalize yourself, didn't you, Mr. Dubber?"

Dubber looked at his feet.

"You describe yourself as a stock market adviser," the commissaris said. "But you play the market yourself, don't you? And you are a drinking man, are you not?"

Dubber looked up quickly, before looking at his shoes again.

"Abuse of alcohol goes with impaired judgment," the commissaris said. "Am I correct in assuming that your portfolio is close to zero and that you don't have too many subscriptions to your monthly newsletter, Mr. Dubber?"

"Bungle Bongo killed my wife," Dubber said tonelessly. "You told me that yourself. You have nothing on me."

"Bungle killed the victim with a riding whip," the commissaris said. "You killed her by making a clever play. You had been drinking in the Buddha Bar, listening to Bungle Bongo's ramblings. You learned he liked to torture his sex partners. You also knew your wife, Emily, liked being the masochist in S and M activities. After you hit your wife Friday night, to make her walk out on you, you kept her purse so that she couldn't buy more cocaine and would have to offer herself in order to satisfy her habit. You knew she would go to the Buddha Bar and would be likely to run into Bungle Bongo."

"Bungle killed Emily," Dubber said, "I didn't. Besides, he is dead now, too. The whole thing is over."

"Not quite, perhaps," the commissaris said. "Maybe we only saw one episode when the Pleiades people had Bungle Bongo surrounded in the temple room of their farmhouse. They sat in a double circle, each behind a big church candle in a holder, with Bungle kneeling in the center. Cardozo said the scene reminded him of a scorpion caught in a ring of fire, and like a scorpion, which stings itself to death in such a hopeless situation, Bungle used a knife on himself. The same razor-sharp clasp knife he cut Emily's finger off with. He used enough force to penetrate his breastbone."

"Do you have the diamond ring?" Dubber asked.

"It is yours." The commissaris pushed the ring across his desk. "Please sign this receipt."

Dubber signed. He thanked the commissaris. He pocketed the diamond. "Can I go now?" He grimaced, reminding Grijpstra of a feral cat that had bared its teeth at him when he shone a flashlight at it in Nellie's hotel's courtyard. "I take it I am not under arrest, for lack of proof?"

The commissaris, Grijpstra, and de Gier stared at Douglas D. Dubber, who got up, hesitated, and sat down again.

"Are you arresting me?" Douglas Dubber asked the commissaris.

"I don't think it would work," the commissaris said. "We would have to wait for you to collect your million. It is a million, isn't it?" He smiled. "That's right, don't tell me the exact amount. By that time you would be out of this country. We would have to extradite you. It would all be quite costly."

"We don't have much jail space here," de Gier said.

"And it would make no difference to you," the commissaris said, "whether in jail here, or in your Manhattan apartment there, with your bottles, and the dying goldfish in the aquarium, and Emily's four-fingered bleeding hand in your dreams, and Bungle playing his bongo drums."

"He is not too good a bongo-drum player," Grijpstra said.

"And your million will be invested in speculative stocks," the commissaris said. "You won't be able to resist investing again, and your drinking will make you lose again. The vicious circle keeps turning, Mr. Dubber."

"Maybe it would be better if you confessed," de Gier said kindly. "Would you like to do that? We still wouldn't arrest you, for the case won't hold up in court, but you might seek some treatment."

"Are you torturing me?" Dubber asked. "Is this fun for you? Seeing me squirm? First I lose my wife, and now you accuse me of being behind her horrible death."

"But you were," the commissaris said. "You don't expect us to accept your denial. Passing your wife to a psychopath, taking out that little policy so you could ask for a statement to help you collect the real money in the States, adorning your wife with a jewel that would attract a sadistic killer, setting her up so that she would crave cocaine and not have money to buy it?" The commissaris lowered his voice. "How much money are you aiming to get, sir?"

This time the silence lasted a full minute, uninterrupted by the commissaris's soft voice.

"Maybe two million?" Douglas Dubber asked. "What does it matter? You are right, your case is too weak, you can't make a murder charge stick. Suppose you are right in your assumptions, how about me getting lucky? Pushing Emily off a train would have been easier, but also tricky. The way things turned out, with all these degenerates you allow in your so-called magic city, it was a piece of cake. All I had to do was to make use of what was happening anyway." He tried to rub some dirt off his knee. He had dropped his voice to a confidential whisper. "And don't worry about my future financial situation. This time I will invest in tax-free municipal bonds, with a steady return of five percent. I'll live in Honduras. On a hundred big ones a year, I will be king of all castles." He laughed. "I don't need that much either; a jeep, a cabin with a view, a jetty to fish off of, a cool beer at sunset, the day's catch for dinner. I have picked out the place. This time I will do it right. No gambling. No excessive drinking. No so-called high-class hooker to keep supplied with coke. Daily exercise, swimming, surfing, kayaking, whatever comes up that isn't too exhausting. A local girl once in a while. Watching some satellite TV. No fuss. Just fun."

"Where exactly do you plan to do this?" de Gier asked.

"In El Triunfo." Dubber grinned at him. "A pretty coastal village. Come and see me sometime, I'll be a good host."

⌒

"REMEMBER DOUGLAS D. Dubber?" Grijpstra asked de Gier a year later. They were in a sandwich shop in an alley between the Emperor's and Prince Canals. He read from an article in the Amsterdam morning paper. "El Triunfo, Honduras, hit full on by a killer hurricane with sustained winds of nearly two hundred miles an hour, mud flows, roads taken out, massive devastation."

The commissaris inquired, via his wife's nephew, a relief worker in Honduras, as to what had happened to Douglas D. Dubber. Was anything known about an American millionaire living close to the beach in the idyllic village of El Triunfo?

Mr. Dubber, the nephew reported, was last seen at a second-story picture window in his luxurious beach house. Dubber was shouting for help, but nobody could get to the stylish building, which, having been picked up by a raging river, was rapidly floating toward a boiling ocean.

"You can't win when you won't quit losing," de Gier said.

Grijpstra said he thought de Gier was stuck in dualism. He refused to believe in justice, but he was glad that happenstance tended to even things out, sometimes.

Turn the page for a sneak preview of the first
Grijpstra and de Gier Mystery

Outsider in Amsterdam

Preface

ONCE, SOME TIME ago now, I was a child and my parents would ask me what I wanted to be. I always gave the same answer. I wanted to be an Indian, and a cowboy in my spare time.

When fate, which according to Buddhist thought is the result of previous actions, brought me back to Amsterdam after a trip which took me to a large number of countries and lasted a long time, I received a letter from the army. The letter gave me an address and a name and a date and I found a middle-aged lady behind a desk who told me that I would have to be a soldier. I pointed out that I was over thirty years old but she wasn't impressed.

A little later I received another letter from the army. It told me that I would have to consider myself to be in "extraordinary service." The letter puzzled me and I put it in a drawer. Then there was another letter that told me that I would have to join the "civil reserve." I saw another middle-aged lady and told her that I didn't want to join the civil reserve, whatever it was. She told me to join the police. I told her that I already had a job. "In your spare time," she said.

The idea staggered me. I never knew that one can be a policeman in one's spare time.

But one can, and for several years now I have been a member of Amsterdam's Special Constabulary and serve the Queen in the uniform of a police constable. I have been in a number of adventures in the inner city of the capital and some of them inspired me to write this story. My imagination has, here and there, carried me away and the result is that the police routine as described in this book is not, in every instance, based on established police technique.

Chapter 1

THE VOLKSWAGEN WAS parked on the wide sidewalk of the Haarlemmer Houttuinen, opposite number 5, and it was parked the way it shouldn't be parked.

The adjutant* had switched the engine off.

The adjutant hesitated.

He had arrived at his destination, Haarlemmer Houttuinen, number 5, and the high narrow gable house was waiting for him. He studied the gable house and frowned. The house had a body in it, a dead body, suspended. The body was bound to be turning slowly. Bodies, suspended by the neck, are never quite still.

The adjutant didn't feel like doing anything. He didn't feel like getting out of the car, running through the rain, watching a corpse move slowly, dangling, turning.

"Hey," said Sergeant de Gier, who sat next to Adjutant Grijpstra.

"Hey what?" asked Grijpstra.

De Gier made a helpless gesture. Grijpstra could explain the gesture, the waving arm with its connected stretched-out hand, as he wanted.

But he still didn't move and the adjutant and sergeant listened, peacefully and unanimously, to the fat raindrops

*Dutch municipal police ranks are constable, constable first class, sergeant, adjutant, inspector, chief inspector, commissaris. An adjutant is a noncommissioned officer.

patter from the heavy, juicy spring sky onto the tin roof of the
Volkswagen.

"Yes," the adjutant said, and got out of the car. De Gier had
parked the car on the edge of the sidewalk and Grijpstra was
forced to step into the street, a main thoroughfare, busy at all
times of the day and the night. He didn't pay attention and a
large American limousine approaching at speed had to turn
suddenly to avoid the door of the car. The limousine, suddenly
indignant, honked its powerful horn.

De Gier laughed and shook his head. He got out of the car
as well, on the safe side, and locked the door carefully while
the rain hit him in the neck. In Amsterdam nothing is safe, not
even a police car, and this Volkswagen didn't look like a police
car. No expert would recognize the VW as a means of transport
reserved for officers of the criminal investigation department.
Its radio set was hidden under the dashboard and the antenna
was a mere twig, slightly rusty. No one would suspect that the
backseat contained a well-oiled carbine, neatly wrapped in
canvas and complete with six magazines, or that the harmless
nose of the car was filled with a complete collection of utensils
that police officers think they need during the lawful exercise
of their duties, including such items as a small suitcase full of
burglar's tools, a powerful searchlight, a dredge, gas masks and
a tape recorder.

But nothing was suspected and the officers looked as innocent as their vehicle. Grijpstra is a fat man and de Gier neither
thin nor fat—qualities they share with a large number of
other men in Holland's capital. Grijpstra wore a badly fitting
suit made of expensive English striped material, with a white
shirt and a dark blue tie, and de Gier a made-to-order suit of
blue denim, a blue shirt and a multicolored scarf neatly folded
around his Adam's apple. Grijpstra's hair looked like a well-
worn scrubbing brush and de Gier's curls were beautifully

cut by a proud and highly trained coiffeur taking an almost personal interest in the glamour of his clients. De Gier's curls were so well shaped, in fact, that he could have been mistaken for a woman if viewed from the rear, and only his narrow hips protected him from attacks from that side.

A pedestrian, in a hurry to reach his parked car, bumped into Grijpstra and hurt himself against the large model service pistol that the adjutant carried under his jacket.

"Watch where you're going," the pedestrian mumbled ferociously.

"Yes sir," said Grijpstra kindly.

An ordinary car was parked on the sidewalk and two ordinary men ran through the rain until they reached the porch of number 5 and tried to catch their breath.

Their object achieved, a new period of inactivity began.

"Bah," Grijpstra said and read the sign on the door.

The sign said HINDIST SOCIETY.

Both men studied it. It looked neat, like the door. The text had been written in an unusual script as if the letter artist had tried to create a mysterious atmosphere. It seemed as if the letters had been drawn very quickly; the result was vaguely Chinese, far away.

De Gier produced a comb and arranged his hair while he looked about him.

The porch was old and magnificent in its Golden Age splendor. It had been designed in the seventeenth century for a gentleman-merchant who specialized in expensive timber imported from Africa and the Far East and stored in the first three stories of the tall house, while the merchant himself would have lived in the top three stories where he could see the harbor and his vast stocks of cheaper timber stacked in an area of perhaps a square mile. But that was long ago and the stones of the porch were cracked now and the beams supporting the gable house sagged a little. But the well-built house still retained a good deal of its original stately beauty and the present owner had kept it in reasonable repair.

A small window showed a number of objects and de Gier studied them one by one. Glass jars filled with health grains brown and green tea, and a substance that de Gier, after some thought, determined to be seaweed. A sign in the window, showing the same sort of lettering as the main sign, informed the visitor that the Society went in for a variety of activities. Grijpsira grunted and read the sign in a loud voice.

"Shop, open from nine to four. Restaurant and bar, restaurant open to nine, bar open to twelve P.M."

He looked at de Gier but de Gier was still studying the display.

There were several small cartons filled with incense and a gilded Buddha statue sitting on a pedestal, staring and smiling, with a headgear tapering off into a sharp point.

"A pointed head," Grijpstra said. "Is that what you get when you meditate?"

"That isn't known as a pointed head," said de Gier, using his lecture voice. Once a month, when he taught the young constables of the emergency squad the art of crime detection.

"Not a pointed head," de Gier repeated, "but a heaven-head. The point points at heaven. Heaven is the goal of meditation. Heaven is thin air. Heaven is upstairs."

"Ah," said Grijpstra. "Are you sure?"

"No," said de Gier.

"You can ring the bell," Grijpstra said. "You have a nice index finger."

De Gier bowed from the hips and rang. His index finger was indeed nice, well tapered, thin and powerful.

Grijpstra, as if he wanted to avoid all comparison, had hidden his hands in his pockets.

The door opened immediately; they had been expected.

Both men braced themselves.

"Suspected suicide," the police radio had said, a few minutes ago. "It seems that a man has hanged himself." That was the message, and they had been given the address.

Grijpstra had repeated the address and had said that they would go there, and the female voice belonging to the constable first class of the radio room had thanked them and closed the communication.

And now they had arrived, but they knew no more than the radio had told them.

And now, of course, there would be a great commotion. Several people talking at once. White faces. Fearful eyes. Shouts and screams. Violence affects people.

But the face that looked at them, from the open space where the thick green monumental door had been, wasn't white but black, and it wasn't excited but calm.

The officers studied the man in the door.

"A Negro," Grijpstra thought. "A small Hindist Negro. Now what?"

De Gier hadn't drawn any conclusion. Like Grijpstra he had associated black with "Negro," but he was in doubt. The man was no Negro. "Who else is black?" de Gier thought but the logic line of his thoughts was interrupted by the inquisitive expression on the face of the dark man.

"Police," Grijpstra said and produced his wallet, a large leather wallet consisting of a number of plastic compartments and a notebook. He shook the wallet, the plastic compartments dangled and a small card hung in front of their host's eyes.

The man came closer and concentrated on the document.

"That's a credit card of the Amsterdam-Rotterdam Bank," the small man said.

De Gier laughed softly and Grijpstra looked at his colleague. It was a heavy look, full of criticism.

"I'm sorry," said de Gier.

Grijpstra dug in his wallet and after a while his square, fat fingers found his police identification with its blue and red stripes and photograph of a much younger Grijpstra dressed in uniform with the silver button of his rank on both shoulders.

The dark man bent forward and read the card.

"H. F. Grijpstra," he read in a clear voice. "Adjutant. Municipal Police of Amsterdam."

He paused.

"I have seen it. Please come in."

"Extraordinary," de Gier thought. "Fascinating. That fellow actually read the card. It never happens. Grijpstra always shows his credit card and nobody ever notices anything. He could have shown a receipt from the electricity department and nobody would object, but this chap really reads the identification."

"Who are you?" Grijpstra was asking.

"Jan Karel van Meteren," the man said.

They were in the corridor. There were three doors on the right, heavy oak doors. One of the doors was open and de Gier saw a bar and several young men with long hair and one elderly man with a bald head. Everybody was drinking beer. He had a glance of another young man behind the bar, dressed in a white T-shirt and decorated with a necklace of colored stones. Van Meteren was leading the way and they followed obediently. A staircase at the end of the corridor, again made of oak and recently polished. The floor of the corridor was covered with slabs of marble, cracked but very clean. Near the staircase Grijpstra noticed a niche with an upright Indian figure, made of bronze, life-size and with the right hand raised in a gesture of solemn greeting. Perhaps the gesture symbolized a blessing.

They climbed the staircase and came into a large open space with a high ceiling made of iron, painted white and with a relief of garlands picked out in gold. This was the restaurant, occupying the entire floor. De Gier counted ten tables, six seating four persons and four seating six persons. Nearly every chair was taken.

Grijpstra had stopped while their guide waited patiently. He was admiring a statue, standing on a stone platform attached to the wall. It was a statue of a female deity performing a dance. The noble head on its slender neck seemed to contrast at first with the full breasts and the lewdly raised foot and Grijpstra was surprised that this naked sexual figure represented divinity and that he accepted her divinity. Undoubtedly the figure was free, quiet, detached and powerful. Superior. The thought flitted through his head. Superior. And free. Especially free. The thought disappeared as he walked on. De Gier had seen the statue but hadn't allowed himself to be interested. He watched the guests without fixing any one of them in particular. A fixed stare is aggressive and invites attention. He didn't want any attention and didn't get any. The guests took him for another guest and thought he wanted to join them. One man took his hat and briefcase off a chair and made an inviting gesture. De Gier smiled and shook his head. He noticed that nobody seemed to talk; perhaps they were listening to the music that came from several stereo loudspeakers and was hitting the room in waves. De Gier liked the music; it reminded him of a performance in the Tropical Museum. The heavy rhythmical chords would come from a bass guitar and the dry sharp knocks from a set of drums; he imagined that the wheezing high notes setting the melody itself would be a flute, a bamboo flute probably.

They were moving again, still following van Meteren. He led them through the restaurant and into a long narrow kitchen; through its windows there was a view of a garden full of red and pink rhododendrons. Two girls in jeans were busily stirring pots on a large stove. There was a sharp but not unpleasant smell of weird herbs. One of the girls wanted to object to the presence of strangers but stopped herself when she saw van Meteren.

There was another narrow staircase and another corridor. White walls and several doors. They passed three doors and van Meteren opened the last and fourth door.

De Gier had a feeling that they had now penetrated into the secret part of the house; perhaps the silence of the corridor motivated the thought. The music of the restaurant didn't reach this lofty level. Grijpstra entered the room and sighed. He saw the corpse and it moved, exactly as he had expected. It would be the draft, of course, all phenomena can be explained, but the slow ghastly movement chilled his spine. De Gier had now come in as well and watched silently. He noticed the small bare feet with their neat toes pointed at the floor. His gaze wandered upward and recorded the protruding tongue and the wide open bulging blue eyes. A small corpse that had belonged to a living man. A little over five feet. A thin man, well dressed in khaki trousers of good cloth, nicely ironed, and a freshly laundered striped shirt. Some forty years old. Long thick dark red hair and a full mustache, hanging down at the corners by its own weight. De Gier moved closer and looked at the corpse's wristwatch. He grunted. A very expensive watch, worth a small fortune. He couldn't remember ever having seen a gold strap of such width and quality.

Both officers froze and quietly looked around, noticing as many details as possible. Almost automatically they had put their hands in their pockets. They had been trained in the same school. Hands in pockets cannot touch anything. This silent room was bound to be full of indications, traces, tracks.

They saw a large room, again with a high ceiling made not of cast iron but of plain sawn planks supported by heavy deal beams. There were several bookcases, well filled. There was a telephone in one of the bookcases, and an expensive TV set and a new complete encyclopedia. The furniture consisted of a low settee, a table and three chairs. There were some cushions on the floor, embroidered. The patterns were unusual. "Eastern designs probably," de Gier thought. There was a typewriter on the table with a letter in it. De Gier bent down.

Dear Sirs:
   I thank you for your letter of the tenth and have to inform you

No further text. The letterhead looked expensive. HINDIST SOCIETY, the address and the telephone number.

They saw a footstool lying on its side near the feet of the corpse. They saw a gramophone, a stack of records and a low bed covered with a batik cloth. The woven curtains were closed but allowed enough light to filter through to see every detail of the room.

"What's that?" Grijpstra asked, pointing at another low table covered with red lacquer and serving as a seat for a fairly large statue: a rather fat bald-headed man sitting cross-legged and staring at them with glass eyes.

"An altar of sorts," de Gier answered after some thought. "That copper bowl filled with sand must be an incense burner, and the brown spots in the sand are burnt-out incense sticks."

Grijpstra raised an eyebrow. "You know a lot today."

"I visit museums," de Gier said.

Grijpstra sniffed.

"Incense?" he asked.

De Gier nodded. The heavy sweet smell gave him a headache.

"Who discovered the body?" de Gier asked van Meteren, who was standing near the door.

"I did," van Meteren answered. "I had to ask Piet something and as he didn't answer when I knocked, I went back to my room. A little later I asked the girls in the kitchen if they had seen him and they said he had gone upstairs. I looked into the other rooms; one of them belongs to his mother, and another is the temple. He wasn't there. I thought he might be asleep and knocked again and then I opened the door and saw him hanging there. I telephoned the police and waited for you downstairs. Nobody knows anything yet."

"Why didn't you cut the rope?" asked de Gier.

"He was dead."

"How did you know?"

Van Meteren didn't answer.

"Are you a doctor?" Grijpstra asked.

"No," van Meteren said. "But I have seen a lot of corpses in my life. Piet is dead. Dead is dead. I could feel it. A dead body has no feel."

"Did you touch it?"

Van Meteren shrugged his shoulders. "I don't have to feel a corpse to know it is dead."

"So why didn't you cut the rope?" asked de Gier again.

"I couldn't do it by myself," van Meteren said. "Somebody would have had to hold the body. Besides, I wanted you to find it the way it was. Perhaps it will give you a lead."

De Gier looked again at the corpse. He had an idea that he had seen the man before and searched his memory. De Gier's memory was well organized and he knew his way around his files. After a while he knew that he hadn't seen the man before but that the strong chin, the long hair and the heavy mustache reminded him of a portrait he had seen in a museum in The Hague: a portrait of a Dutch statesman of the sixteenth century, a statesman and a warrior, on his way to battle. The warrior had been sitting on a horse and had a sword in his hand. A leader. Very likely this man had also been a leader, a boss. A little boss in charge of a small society. "Discipline," de Gier thought. "That's it. This house and this room reek of discipline. Everything is neat and clean. The girls in the kitchen are clean too, reasonably clean. Van Meteren is clean. There would be some connection between the corpse and van Meteren. Perhaps van Meteren is an employee of the Society. But why do I observe this?" de Gier asked himself. The answer came immediately. He hadn't expected cleanliness when he had read the sign on the door. HINDIST SOCIETY. He had associated the words with a mess. The new wisdom coming from the East is a messy business.

He thought of the dirty, doped, vague, shadowy people he had arrested in the street and interrogated at Police Headquarters. Petty theft, drug dealing in a small silly way, runaway minors, prostitution. All suspects stank. He had made them empty their pockets before locking them up and had been appalled at the dirty rags, the broken trinkets, the lack of money. He had seen the photographs they carried around with them. Pictures of "holy men," "gurus" or "yogis." Skeletons with long matted hair and crazy eyes. The masters preaching the way.

He had associated the word HINDIST with Hinduism or Buddhism. The religions of the East. Before he had begun to arrest the crazy tramps the words had had a different association. Peace and quiet, some form of detachment. Real wisdom. But gradually "messiness" had crept in.

And now he had to admit that this place, this nest of nonsensical imitation faith, was, after all, clean. And he had been surprised. De Gier's thoughts took only a few seconds and meanwhile Grijpstra had sighed again. The body was dead, no doubt about it, and they would have to cut the rope. They had to assume that the body was still alive. Only a doctor can determine death. He looked over his shoulder and nodded at de Gier.

"You can telephone headquarters, if you like."

There was no need to say it. De Gier was dialing the number already. He didn't have to say much. At headquarters the machine was already in operation. Within a few minutes they would be arriving. Doctor, ambulance and the experts.

While de Gier telephoned Grijpstra picked up the stool and put it right and climbed on top of it. He cut the rope with his switchblade, an illegal weapon that he carried against all regulations. The rope wasn't thick and the knife very sharp. De Gier wanted to catch the corpse but van Meteren was quicker. He put the corpse down, very carefully, on the bed. No one thought that Piet would start breathing again.

He didn't.

Grijpstra bent down and looked at the dead face. "Have a look."

De Gier looked. "Ach, ach," he said.

Van Meteren looked as well.

"A bruise," van Meteren said, "near the temple, slightly swollen."

"You saw that very quickly," de Gier said.

"He has been hit," van Meteren continued, "with a stick, or perhaps a fist. The doctor will be able to tell us."

"What exactly do you do in this house?" de Gier asked.

Van Meteren straightened his back and rubbed it. He thought. The low forehead became wrinkled and the nose seemed to flatten itself even more. Suddenly de Gier knew what this man had to be. Not a Negro, but a Papuan. He remembered the photographs in his geography book at school. Papuan sitting on the beach, sharpening spears. But not a fullblooded Papuan, the nose wasn't flat enough and the face showed other properties. Perhaps three-quarters Papuan or seven-eighths. That would explain the Dutch name. The Papuan's language was pure Dutch, impeccable, overcorrect even. De Gier knew the way the Dutch Negroes spoke and the Indonesians. Van Meteren's way of talking was more guttural.

"I live here," van Meteren said. "That's all. I do nothing here. Piet ran the Society. I think that the girls will take over now, or Eduard or Johan. But Johan is in the bar and hasn't been told yet and Eduard took the day off."

"All right," de Gier said, "in that case I will go down. For the time being nobody is allowed to leave the premises. The cars from Headquarters can arrive any minute now. They'll be sending more detectives and probably uniformed policemen as well. It'll be the usual hullabaloo."

De Gier ran down the stairs. Hullabaloo was the right word. Day after day nothing to do but to drive around and look around a little and now suddenly two corpses in one evening. They had found the first corpse early that evening, or rather, they had seen a body change into a corpse. The woman was still alive when they found her, naked and bleeding in the shabby whorehouse at the canal. A knife in her belly. She died in the doctor's arms; he had come immediately answering de Gier's emergency call. The woman had been able to describe her killer while she kept her hands pressed against her body in a vain attempt to stop both pain and blood. An aging whore, a reasonably sweet person. De Gier had found the young man under a tree, right opposite the whorehouse. The boy was resting his back against an old elm tree and was staring into the canal's murky water. The knife was still in his hand. He confessed at once. A pleasant boy, but not to be trusted with knives and middle-aged women who reminded him of his mother. They had taken him with them in the car and locked him up after they had taken his statement. Another job for the municipal psychiatrist. Most likely the boy wouldn't even have to face court but be taken to an asylum straight away to rot there for the rest of his life while he filled his time making feltdolls and swallowing pills. Or they might release him after a while and put him on national assistance and the state's money would buy another knife and another middle-aged woman would die.

The dead prostitute hadn't taken much of their time and Grijpstra and de Gier had gone out for another ride hoping to be able to fill the rest of their night's shift with peacefully ambling about and stopping in a quiet café somewhere for a cup of coffee. And now this.

De Gier strode into the restaurant. He found the amplifier and turned the knob the wrong way. The loudspeakers screeched and some forty startled faces stared at him. One of the faces, a heavily bearded one, lost its temper.

"Look here," the face said. "Would you mind leaving that amplifier alone? We are listening to that music!"

De Gier walked up to the man and put a hand on his shoulder. "Never mind the music. I am a police officer, I have to request everybody here to stay put."

He raised his voice.

"Something unpleasant has happened in this house tonight. Please remain seated. My colleagues will be here any minute now and we will have to ask some questions. It's only a formality and we won't keep you long. If anyone knows anything about what happened upstairs earlier tonight or this afternoon he can come and speak to me."

The faces began to mumble to each other. The two girls came from the kitchen and approached de Gier.

"What happened?" the oldest girl asked. She was a beautiful girl with large green eyes and pigtails, and would be just over twenty years old.

"You'll be informed in due course," de Gier said.

"Is it about the money?"

"Has money been stolen?" asked de Gier.

"I don't think so," the girl said, "but Piet asked us this afternoon if we had been in his room. Johan had taken the shop's money to Piet and put it on his table at four o'clock and Piet counted it and it was less than he expected. He probably didn't count properly. Did you come because of that?"

"No," de Gier said softly. "We wouldn't disturb the joint for a few guilders. Piet is dead. He was hanging from one of the beams in his room."

"Oh," the girl said and covered her mouth with a shaking hand. The other girl, a fat little thing with glasses, began to cry.

"Okay, okay," de Gier said. "It can't be helped. Any of you two been to his room?"

Both girls shook their heads.

"No," the fat girl said.

"No," the beautiful girl said, "not after five o'clock this afternoon. I saw the money on the table when I went up with Piet. I only stayed ten minutes or so and then I returned to the kitchen to prepare for supper. In fact, he told me to go; he wanted to write some letters."

"He is the boss here, isn't he?" de Gier asked.

"Yes," said the fat girl. "He is the Society's director. The Society is supposed to belong to all of us members but he runs everything. And is he dead now?"

De Gier gave her his handkerchief and she rubbed her eyes.

He looked at the black stripes on the clean white cloth and realized dejectedly that they would never come out in the small washing machine in his apartment.

"You can keep the handkerchief," he said to the girl, "with the compliments of your police force."

Her tears didn't impress him. He has seen the glint in her eyes. Death is sensation. Apparently she liked sensation.

He heard the doorbell and went to answer it. There was quite a crowd on the sidewalk and four parked cars, not counting his own. The colleagues had come quietly, without flashing blue lights or howling sirens. The experts didn't believe in a mad rush.

He shook a few hands and spoke to a fingerprint man, a close friend. He showed them all the way. The doctor and the experts to the dead man's room, the detectives to the restaurant where they started their investigation immediately. All they needed at this stage were names and addresses. De Gier told them to spend a little time on the two girls and Johan the barman, and to ignore van Meteren, whom he reserved for himself.

"Ah yes," he said to the senior detective. "If you find an old lady, leave her alone as well. She is the dead man's mother. We'll see her later."

"Who's 'we'?" the senior detective asked.

"Grijpstra and myself," said de Gier.

The senior detective looked impressed and de Gier grinned at him.

"You are a comedian," he said.

The doorbell rang again.

"Sir," de Gier said when he recognized the chief inspector.

"Suicide?" the chief asked.

"Could be," de Gier said, "but he has a bruise on his temple."

"Hm," the chief said, and went upstairs. He left within a few minutes, and Grijpstra accompanied him to the door.

De Gier looked at Grijpstra.

"Usual behavior," Grijpstra said. "He looked around and grunted a bit. It's all ours."

Peace returned to the gable house two hours later.

Grijpstra and de Gier sat at one of the restaurant tables and smoked and looked at each other.

"Twice in one day," Grijpstra said.

"Too often," said de Gier, "twice too often."

"But what do we make of it?" de Gier asked. "Murder or no murder?"

Grijpstra blew some smoke out of his nostrils; de Gier watched the little hairs wave inside.

"Could be either of the two," Grijpstra said, "but it'll probably be murder. Somebody gave him a nice thump, using his fist, for I saw no possible weapon lying around and the bruise didn't seem very serious. Bam, Piet is on the floor, it doesn't need much to knock a small man over. He is unconscious or dazed. The rope is ready. Rope around the neck. You lift him up with one arm and put him on the stool. Other end of the rope on the hook in the beam. You kick the stool. You leave the room quietly. One minute's work. Half a minute maybe."

"One or two killers?" de Gier asked.

Grijpstra gave him a fierce look and shook his head.

"Why two killers? Two men? Two women? One man and one woman? Why make it involved? One killer, not two or three. Killers are very scarce in Amsterdam so why would we suddenly run into a whole bunch of them?"

"But it isn't an easy job," de Gier said carefully. "He had to be carried around, and put on a stool. It may be difficult if you are by yourself."

Grijpstra got up. "Come with me, we are going to do a little work."

They were busy for several minutes. De Gier stretched out on the floor and relaxed his body. Grijpstra pulled him to his feet, put him on the stool, slipped the noose around his neck.

They tried several times.

"You see?" Grijpstra said. "Nothing to it. Your weight is more than Piet's, you must weigh a little over seventy kilos while he probably weighed ten or twelve kilos less. A very thin little chap. Anyone who isn't a hungry dwarf could have done it."

"Yes," said de Gier.

But later he disagreed again.

"It wasn't like that," he said. "Pay attention."

"I am paying attention," Grijpstra said and opened his eyes as wide as they would go.

"Right," said de Gier. "This Piet of ours is a morose fellow. He wants to die. Life isn't what it should be, he thinks. He can't remember ever having given permission for his own birth. And now he finds himself here, in a room in an old ramshackle house in the Haarlemmer Houttuinen, director of a nonsensical society that isn't going well anyway and gives him nothing but a lot of work and debts. He goes on thinking and works out that he is now over forty years old and that he will soon be an old man who won't be able to look after himself. And it annoys him that he is a *little* man, and that he always has to look up at people. Here he sits, in his empty room. Everything is stale. His ideas are gone and proved wrong. All he has is his own loneliness. It frightens him. He wants to leave, through the white gate which can be opened with the silver key. And he does have the silver key."

"Beg your pardon?" said Grijpstra.

"Imagery from the East," said de Gier. "Comes from my reading and it fits the case for this is a Hindist Society. Death is the white gate and everybody has the silver key."

"Excuse me," Grijpstra said. "I wasn't very good at school and I never read anything. But now I understand. The rope is the silver key."

"Don't excuse yourself," de Gier said. "You are very clever. And books don't give any real information. Words, nothing but words. Hollow words. I read that too. The rope is the silver key but if you have the will to stop breathing for longer than two minutes you are also using the silver key."

"Fine," said Grijpstra. "Piet wants to leave. Through the gate. Or into the tunnel, that's even better imagery. Death must be like a tunnel, I think, a tunnel that leads to the inexpressible. But now what happens? In your story he is still considering."

De Gier got up and began to wander through the restaurant. "He makes up his mind. But that sort of decision takes some doing. We never really decide anything, we take life as it comes and it drags us where it wants to drag us. It's all a matter of circumstances, of powers that control us. But to commit suicide is a decision. He decides but he helps himself by taking a drink. He drinks a lot. He becomes very drunk. Now he has to attach the noose to the beam. He climbs on the stool and he falls. He hurts his head. But he insists. And he manages to hang himself in the end."

Grijpstra scratched the stubbles of his beard. De Gier was still wandering through the restaurant.

"I didn't notice any smell of liquor," Grijpstra said. "Perhaps a whiff. A glass of sherry maybe. But I don't think he was drunk. I didn't even find a glass in the room. I looked out the window but I didn't notice any splinters in the street. I'll check when we go home. He may have thrown the bottle out the window. Drunks often do. But I don't think Piet would have thrown a bottle out the window. I think we agree on his neatness. Somehow I can't believe that a neat man, living in a clean room in a well organized house, and dressed nicely, with combed hair and a beautiful mustache, will commit suicide."

De Gier looked at the statue of the dancing Indian Goddess. "Yes," he said. "Suicidal people lose their self-discipline. They don't shave anymore and have meals at odd times. They have accidents, they drop things. They don't make their beds. I remember the psychologist told us about it at the police school. Could be. But I could imagine a neat man hanging himself using a good piece of rope knotted into a perfect noose, and hung from a strong hook, screwed tightly into a solid beam. Why not? Perhaps there are neat suicides, we'll have to look it up in the library and we can ask the chief. Psychology is his hobby, they say."

Grijpstra went on scratching.

"Yes. And you may still be right. Perhaps he didn't drink anything but used a drug. A drugged person can fall too. There were no marks on his arms and legs but he may have sniffed cocaine or taken a pill. He hadn't smoked, there was no ashtray and no ash in the waste-basket. I asked the girls; he didn't smoke at all, they said. Funny, I had the impression they were lying. Why lie about smoking?"

"Hash," de Gier said. "He probably smoked hash and they did too, and they didn't want us to know."

"Hash doesn't make you fall over and bump your head," Grijpstra said.

De Gier shrugged. "I'm tired. Let's find out tomorrow.

I want to go home but we still have to talk to van Meteren. He is waiting for us in his room upstairs. I sent the girls to bed; if they have been lying we can grill them tomorrow. We have to find out about that money as well. Perhaps there is a connection."

Chapter 2

"WOULD YOU LIKE some tea?" asked van Meteren.

"Coffee," said de Gier and Grijpstra in one voice. They were facing him, sitting on a low bed, with their heads leaning against the wall. It was close to midnight now and de Gier was exhausted; he had visions of his small but comfortable bachelor's flat in the south of the city. He felt the hot water of his shower streaming down his back and the foaming soap on his shoulders. The old gable house with its endless corridors and nooks and crannies began to get on his nerves and the imitation Eastern atmosphere stifled him, although he had to agree that van Meteren's room exhaled a pleasant influence. It was a fairly large room, with whitewashed walls and the floor was covered with a worn but lovely Persian rug. On a shelf along the width of one entire wall van Meteren had displayed a number of objects that interested de Gier. He studied them quickly, one by one, the strangely shaped stones, the shells, the dried flowers and the skull of a large animal, a wild boar perhaps. Van Meteren sat on the floor, on a thick cushion, cross-legged, relaxed and patient, the black hard curls framing his flat skull silhouetted against the white wall, lit up by a light placed on the floor opposite him.

Van Meteren pursed his lips.

"I have no coffee here. The bar will be closed now. The bar is the only place where coffee is served. To drink coffee is really against the rules of the society. Piet always said that coffee excites."

He poured tea from a large thermos flask, decorated with Chinese characters. Grijpstra and de Gier were given a small cup each. They sipped and pulled faces. Van Meteren laughed. "It's an acquired taste. This is very good tea, perhaps the best we can buy in Amsterdam. It's a green tea, very refined, first choice. Tea activates but relaxes at the same time. To drink tea is an art."

"Art?" Grijpstra asked.

"Art. A man who know how to drink tea is a detached man, a free man."

"Detached from what?" asked de Gier.

"Detached from himself, from his greed, his hurry, his own importance. His own suffering."

"That's nice," Grijpstra said. "Did you hear that, de Gier?"

Van Meteren waved a small black hand. "Your colleague heard. He is an intelligent man."

"Thank you," said de Gier. "Could I have another cup of your delicious tea?"

Van Meteren poured another cup, showing his teeth in a wide smile.

"And now tell us," Grijpstra said. "What exactly are you doing in this house? Who are you? What does this Society represent? Who was Piet?"

"Yes," de Gier said. "And do *you* like coffee? Or are you only refusing to drink it because it is against Piet's rules?"

Van Meteren gazed at them. "You are asking a lot of questions at the same time. Where shall I start?"

"Wherever you like," Grijpstra said. De Gier nodded contentedly. Grijpstra was using their usual tactics. De Gier usually asked the unpleasant questions and Grijpstra acted "father," the kind force in the background. Sometimes they changed roles. Sometimes they left the room and only one of them would return, to be replaced by the other. They would do anything to make the suspect talk. The suspect had to talk, that was the main thing, and they could sort out the information as it came. And their tactics usually worked. The suspects talked, far more than they intended to. And very often they confessed, or served as witnesses. And then they would sign their statements and the officers could go home, tired and content.

But de Gier's contentment was short-lived. Van Meteren wasn't the usual suspect. And he didn't say anything. De Gier observed his opponent. A weird figure, even in the inner city of Amsterdam. Small, dark and pleasant. Dark blue trousers and a clean close-fitting shirt with vertical stripes so that van Meteren looked a little taller than he was. Self-possessed. Conscious even. "Do conscious people exist?" De Gier asked himself. People who know what they are doing and who are aware of the situation they are in?

Grijpstra observed too. He saw a man of some forty years old, small and graceful. He had also classified the suspect as a Papuan. Grijpstra had fought in the former Dutch Indies and remembered the faces of a couple of professional soldiers who had joined his unit for an attack in difficult mountainous terrain. Papuans, very unusual types, contrasting with the much lighter-skinned soldiers from Ambon who had made up the bulk of Grijpstra's men. The Papuans revered a colored photograph of the queen, pinned up in their tent. Very courageous they were, but he never got to know them well. They were dead within a few days. They had volunteered for a sniping patrol and the Javanese got them after a fight of a few hours. Two Papuans who had killed nearly fifty enemies with their tommy guns. The Javanese had caught one Papuan alive, they had "tjingtjanged" him, cut him up with their razorsharp "krisses," starting at the feet.

"Your father came from Holland?" Grijpstra asked.

"My grandfather," van Meteren said. "My grandmother was

a Papuan, a chief's daughter. My grandfather worked for the government, he was only a petty official, but a petty official is very powerful in New Guinea. My mother is also a pure Papuan, she is still alive and lives in Hollandia. I arrived here eight years ago. I had to choose in nineteen sixty-five whether I wanted to be an Indonesian or Dutch. I chose to be Dutch and had to run for my life."

"And what do you do for a living?"

"I am on the force," van Meteren said, and laughed when he saw surprise glide over the faces of his investigators. He had a nice laugh, showing strong, even, very white teeth under the small pointed mustache and the flat wide nose.

"Don't let it upset you," he said. "I won't arrest you. I am a traffic warden. All I can do is give you a ticket for parking your car on the sidewalk and you won't have to pay the fine anyway."

"Traffic warden?" Grijpstra asked.

Van Meteren nodded. "I joined the department five years ago. In New Guinea I was a real policeman, constable first class because I could read and write and my name was Dutch. I commanded thirty men. Constable first class is a high rank even there. But when I came out here they told me I was too old for active duty. I was thirty years old. They gave me a job as a clerk in one of their bureaus in The Hague. I kept on asking to be allowed to join the force and eventually they made me a traffic warden and assigned me to street duty. I have two stripes now and I am armed with a rubber truncheon. Every six months I apply for a transfer to the real police but they keep on finding reasons to refuse me."

"A traffic warden is a real policeman too," Grijpstra said.

Van Meteren shrugged his shoulders and looked at the wall.

"What exactly was your job in the New Guinea police?" de Gier asked.

"Field duty. During the last few years I served with the Birdhead Corps, in the South West. We watched the coast and caught Indonesian commandos and paratroopers sneaking in by boat or being dropped. We caught hundreds of them."

De Gier looked at the large linen map of New Guinea that had been pinned on the wall. The map looked worn and had broken on the folds. There were two other maps on the wall, a map of Holland and another of the IJsselmeer, Holland's small inland sea, now transformed into a large lake by the thirty-five kilometer dyke that stops the rollers of the North Sea. "Could I see your traffic warden's identification?"

The little document looked very neat. Van Meteren showed his New Guinea identification as well, yellow at the corners and spotted by sweat, its plastic cover torn right through.

Both Grijpstra and de Gier studied the documents carefully. A Dutch constable first class from the other side of the world. A memento of the past. They looked at the imprint of the rubber stamp and the signature of an inspector-general. They spent some time on the photograph. Van Meteren was shown in uniform, the metal strips had glinted in the light of the photographer's flashbulb. A strong young face, proud of his rank and his responsibility and of his Corps, the Corps State Police of Dutch New Guinea, part of the Kingdom of the Netherlands.

"Well, colleague," Grijpstra said, "and what do you think? Did anyone help Piet when he was being hanged?"

Van Meteren's eyes were sad when he replied.

"It is possible. He may have fallen. I studied the room and I have thought about what I saw but it is always dangerous to come to a conclusion. Piet may have knocked his head against something. And there may have been a fight, it wouldn't be unlikely because he had a very short temper. His state of mind wasn't good, not lately anyway. His wife and child have left him and refuse to return. He has been depressed and he did mention the possibility of suicide. Man is free and has the right to take his own life, I have heard him say it at least three times. He knew he wasn't very well liked but he couldn't make himself likable.

Perhaps someone came to see him, perhaps there was an argument, perhaps someone hit him and perhaps Piet was so upset that he hanged himself after whoever it was left him."

"Who would have argued with him?" de Gier asked.

"You?"

"No," van Meteren said. "I don't argue with anyone. Whenever Piet had one of his moods I avoided him. This is a very big house; there is always another room."

"Were you friendly with Piet?"

"Yes, but I wasn't his friend. I don't believe in friendship. Friendship is a feeling of the moment. Moments pass. I have neither friends nor enemies. The people around me are the people around me, I accept them."

"What are you doing in this house?" de Gier asked.

Van Meteren laughed. "Nothing. I live here. Piet invited me in. I was living in a small room in a boarding house. A cheap place although the rent was high. In a narrow street on the fourth floor, very little light and you can breathe the fumes of the street. The nearest tree was a mile away. I spent most of my free time walking around and had my meals at Chinese restaurants, as often as I could afford to. If I couldn't eat in a restaurant I would have a sandwich in a park. This place has a restaurant and I tried to have a meal here but they wanted me to become a member. I had to go to Piet's office and pay him twenty-five guilders and fill in a form. That's how we met. He seemed to like me straightaway and offered me a room, two hundred guilders a month including as many meals as I wanted."

"That's very cheap," de Gier said.

"Very," van Meteren agreed. "But he may have had a reason. Perhaps he wanted a policeman in the house. I am not on the regular force but I do have a uniform and I am properly trained. There's a bar in the place, clients may be difficult at times."

"Did he ever make use of your services?"

"Once or twice," van Meteren said. "I have taken guests into the streets but I didn't hurt anybody. The grips we were taught are either defensive or merely meant to transport a suspect without causing him any undue pain."

Grijpstra smiled, he remembered the textbook phrase.

"Was Piet a homosexual?" de Gier asked.

It was van Meteren's turn to smile.

"You are a real policeman," he said. But perhaps you are wrong this time. I have thought of it for he often visited me in my room, he was interested in my collection of stones and shells and wanted me to tell him stories about New Guinea. He wanted to know what Papuans eat and what our religion is and whether we used any herbs or drugs and if we danced. But he never bothered me. Whenever he felt that I wanted to be alone he would leave at once. No, Piet liked women even if they caused him trouble."

"Did they?" de Gier asked.

"Always. He wanted to own them, to dominate them."

"I thought women liked to be dominated," de Gier said.

"Yes. But not by Piet. He had little charm and tried to make them ridiculous, especially when he had an audience. So the women became bitter and attacked him and hurt him in his pride. He had a lot of pride. And in the end they would leave him."

"You don't make him sound a very nice person," de Gier said.

Van Meteren shook his head. "No, no. He wasn't all that bad. He meant well."

"No friend, no enemy," de Gier said.

"Yes," van Meteren said. "I try to be detached, to keep my distance. People are the way they are; it's hard to try to change them."

"And that's the reason you drink tea," Grijpstra said.

Van Meteren thought for a while. "I do other things as well."

⌁

"We are getting nowhere," Grijpstra thought, and asked for more tea. Van Meteren filled his cup. Grijpstra took a sip, breathed deeply and immersed himself again in the opaque, sticky substance of an unexplained death of an Amsterdam citizen.

"And this Hindist business, what does it mean?"

Van Meteren felt through his pockets and found a pack of cigarettes. It contained one cigarette only. He offered it to Grijpstra.

Grijpstra shook his head. "It is your last."

"Never mind," van Meteren said. "I have some more somewhere, and if not I can get some downstairs in the shop, I have a key."

"Hindism," de Gier said.

"Yes," van Meteren said. "Hindism. I have been curious too, but I have never quite understood what Piet meant by it. Something between Hinduism and Buddhism perhaps. Piet's own homemade religion. It's quite intricate and bound up with right eating and tea and meditation. The room next door is a temple. There are cushions on the floor and twice a week people sit still on it for an hour or so. Piet is, or was, the priest and had his own special cushion, richly embroidered. He sat closest to the altar. Perhaps he really thought of himself as a prophet, a teacher who had something to show to the new people, the young offbeat types of today. But he was losing interest and he was running short of disciples. Hardly anyone showed up for the meditations and he had to put up with a lot of criticism from the people who work here. Nobody stayed long. The ones you have met, the girls and Johan, and Eduard, whom you'll probably meet later, are all newcomers, they haven't been here for longer than six months at the most and I think they only stay because they can't think of another place they want to go. They'll leave as soon as something turns up. Piet wanted to create an oasis of peace, a quiet place where people can get strength and where they can forget politics and money-making. Find their souls, their real selves. He had invented a special routine, the whole house has been redesigned for that purpose. The bar is an entry; people go easily into a bar. But finally they'll end up in the meditation temple, at least that was the general idea. The barkeeper would have to listen to the guests and direct them, tactfully and gradually, to the higher regions, the restaurant with its clean food and pure fruit and vegetable juices, and the temple with its spiritual air. And Piet would be the divinity in the background, working through others and guiding them without showing himself much. Perhaps he really thought that way in the beginning but he must have lost faith and found himself weak. The arguments must have hurt him and his own lack of strength. I have listened to a long lecture he delivered once; the subject was that one should never eat meat. But afterward he sneaked out and I saw him buying some hot sausages off the street stall around the corner."

"Ha!" de Gier said. "But surely he couldn't have been that much of a failure. This place looks reasonably successful. It is clean for one thing and the restaurant was almost full. He must have been making some money and some people must have admired him one way or another."

"Sure," van Meteren said, "and the atmosphere here is quite pleasant. I have always been reasonably happy here and it would be a pity if it's all over and done with now. And Piet's ideas were all right, but he wasn't the right man to put them into effect. Perhaps if he had admitted that he was a beginner himself and had lost some of his pride. He wanted to be a great master and it must have been a shock to him when people belittled him. His own wife called him a lesser nitwit when she left, the others called him other things. He has been walked over a lot lately . . ." He didn't finish his sentence.

"Who else lives here?" Grijpstra asked.

Van Meteren counted them off on his fingers. "His mother,

eighty-three years old, second door on the right from here, not altogether sound in mind."

"Old age?" asked Grijpstra.

"No, not just old age. A bit mad I would say. Then there is me, you know me. On the next floor there is Thérèse, the girl with the pigtails. Annetje, the other girl, sleeps in the servant quarters, on the other side of the courtyard. She shares her room with Johan. Eduard lives in the little cabin at the end of the garden. He had his day off today but he may have been here this afternoon, you'll have to ask him. Johan has been working; he had the shop today and has been barman during the evening."

Someone knocked at the door. Van Meteren called "Yes" but nothing happened. He got up and opened the door and the detectives saw a very old lady, tall and angular, dressed in a gown set off with lace, a thick woollen scarf hung over her shoulders. Two glinting sharp eyes stared at them. The aggressive nose reminded de Gier of a sparrow hawk's beak.

"What's going on?" the old lady asked. "What are you all talking about? I have been listening to the grunting of voices for hours now. It is half past one, I want to sleep."

Van Meteren put his arm around the old lady. "Come in, Miesje. These gentlemen are police officers. That's Mister Grijpstra and that's Mister de Gier."

The detectives shook the thin hand, dotted all over with dark brown spots.

She sat down, with a straight back, on the edge of the settee.

"So what goes on?" she asked in a brittle voice. "Are they your friends, Jan? Traffic wardens?"

"No, Miesje. They are regular police. There has been an accident. Piet has had a bad fall."

The old lady's eyes, which had been closing slowly, suddenly opened.

"He is dead?" she shrieked.

Nobody answered.

"He is dead," the old lady said and began to cry.

The sound of her sobs grated on the detectives' ears. Her mouth dropped open and Grijpstra shuddered when he saw her tongue flapping and trembling with each fresh howl.

Van Meteren had rushed out of the room and came back with a glass of water and a very small white pill.

"Swallow this, Miesje." The old lady swallowed. The sobs stopped abruptly. She responded to the brief snappy command.

De Gier was grateful; the sudden silence eased his nerves.

The old lady began to talk. She spoke slowly: it seemed that the pill had given her a dry mouth.

"This afternoon Piet told me that I shouldn't complain so much and that the rhododendrons are in bloom. But my eyes are so bad. What are rhododendrons anyway?"

Her voice was gathering volume again.

"Rhododendrons are flowers, Miesje," van Meteren said, still using his command voice. "Like tulips. And now you are going to your room and you are going to sleep. Tomorrow I'll come to see you before I go to work."

He pushed her out of the room.

"I can't stand old ladies," de Gier said, "and I most definitely can't stand them if they are mad."

"You'll have to learn to get used to them," said Grijpstra. "There'll be more and more of them. It's very difficult to find a doctor who'll let old people die nowadays. Haven't you been reading the papers? I wonder what was in that pill."

"An opiate," said van Meteren, who had returned. "It's called Palfium. The doctor prescribes it; she can get as much as she wants. She has been taking these pills for years now and she is hopelessly addicted to them. Piet knew but he didn't mind. It keeps her quiet. Without the pills she would have to go to an asylum and he preferred to keep her here. I'll telephone the doctor tomorrow; he'll probably have her taken away."

"Did Piet take those pills as well?" Grijpstra asked.

"Not as far as I know."

"But he could have taken them, his mother must have a bottle full of them on her bedside table."

Van Meteren nodded thoughtfully.

"I don't think so," he said after a while. "Those pills are very strong. According to the doctor, they will stun a horse but Miesje can take two at a time and stay on her feet. She hasn't got much of a stomach left. She has been operated for ulcers and I suppose most of the stuff goes straight down. If Piet had taken a pill he would have had to sit down and he probably would have gone to sleep. I have never seen him like that. He did drink a bit lately, he would come down to the bar and have a few whiskies. Three glasses would make him drunk enough to be able to laugh and talk to people. I take it you are suggesting that he took a pill today and that the pill knocked him over and caused the bruise on his temple?"

"Yes," said de Gier.

"Perhaps," van Meteren said, "but it would have been the first time that he took a pill. In my opinion anyway."

"Why do you call her Miesje?" Grijpstra asked.

"Ach," van Meteren said. "It's just a trick. Whenever she is hysterical she screams. I thought I might make her calm down if I treated her as if she was a child. She was called Miesje once, when she was a child and wore laced boots and played hop-scotch. When she behaves normally I call her Mrs. Verboom and when I think she will start one of her tantrums I call her Miesje. I take her on my lap and she'll talk quietly and some-times I cuddle her a bit."

"Brr," said de Gier.

Van Meteren grinned. "Yes. It's quite ridiculous. Piet would do it too. I always laughed when I saw that tall skeleton sit-ting on his lap, he was such a small man. Perhaps it looks even funnier when she sits on my lap. But I have done other crazy things. I used to walk for miles with an Indonesian commando on a string. It was knotted in such a way that he would throttle himself if he tried to run away. I would hold the string with one hand and the carbine with the other. And now I have an old crazy lady on my lap and call her Miesje."

There was another knock on the door and a thin young man dressed in jeans and a T-shirt came in. De Gier looked at the long unwashed hair and remembered the barman.

"This is Johan," van Meteren said, and the detectives said, "Good evening." De Gier asked Johan to sit down and made room on the settee.

Grijpstra asked the usual questions but Johan could only shake his head. He hadn't seen Piet after he had given him the takings of the shop at four o'clock. Three hundred and fifty-six guilders and some cents. Piet had phoned him later on the house phone to tell him that there was a difference of some thirty guilders but Johan hadn't gone upstairs; he had been too busy getting the bar in order for the evening's customers.

"What do you think has happened?" de Gier asked.

Johan shrugged his shoulders and didn't reply.

Grijpstra grunted. He had been thinking that he had met the boy hundreds of times already. The inner city was full of duplicates of this boy. Well-meaning, unintelligent and knocked loose from their surroundings, full of protests and questions and wandering in a thin, almost two-dimensional thought-world where they could find no answers. "Maybe they don't really want to find anything," Grijpstra thought. "Maybe they wait for death, or a strong woman who will take them in hand so that they will find a daily routine again and start watching football on TV." He thought of his oldest son and studied Johan without much sympathy. Grijpstra's son wouldn't watch football either. He preferred to lie on his bed, dressed in a striped shirt and an embroidered pair of trousers and watch the cracks in the ceiling.

"Suicide, I suppose," Johan said after a few minutes of silence, which hung heavily in the room. "Who would want to murder Piet? He was a bit of a bore but he didn't hurt anyone. He couldn't if he tried."

Grijpstra changed his opinion. The answer had been cleverer than he had expected.

"You don't seem to be very upset," de Gier said.

"No," Johan said. "I am sorry. Perhaps I should be upset, but I can't generate any feeling. Annetje and I were going to leave next week anyway. This is a commercial enterprise where the goal is money. Piet wanted to make a profit and he wanted the profit for himself. He was the owner of the business. We intended to leave him and find some other place with a bit of idealism behind it, or maybe start one of our own. Piet crooked us. I don't really hold it against him. It's my own stupidity, I should have seen it. He made us work for the great purpose but all we worked for was his wealth. Did you see the gold strap on his wristwatch?"

Grijpstra nodded.

"There are other things as well. There is a new station wagon parked outside. We earned it for him. He was a capitalist but he didn't tell us."

"You don't like capitalists?" de Gier asked.

"I don't mind them," Johan said. "It's a way of life. Free enterprise is a philosophy. It isn't mine. I am against fascism and I would fight it if I had to, but I wouldn't fight capitalism."

"So you think it was suicide?" de Gier asked.

"Yes."

"Enough," Grijpstra said. "You need some sleep. All of us do. Tomorrow is another day. Try and remember anything that may be relevant and tell us about it tomorrow. The peace of the citizens has been disturbed and we, criminal investigators of your police department, have to repair the peace again. And you have to help us. Such is the law."

He grinned, got up, and stretched his aching back.

Within a few minutes the detectives were walking toward their car. A late drunk came swaggering toward them, and de Gier had to jump aside.

"Out of my way," the drunk shouted and grabbed a lamp post.

"Bah," Grijpstra said. The drunk was pissing on the street and all over his own trousers.

"Watch it," de Gier shouted. The drunk had fallen over and rolled off the sidewalk into the street.

Grijpstra, who was getting into the car, grabbed the microphone.

"An unconscious man on the sidewalk of Haarlemmer Houttuinen opposite number five. Please send the bus."

"Drunk?" the voice of Headquarters asked.

"Very," Grijpstra answered. "No need for an ambulance, the police bus will do."

"Bus coming," the voice said. "Out."

"We better wait," de Gier said. "I have pulled him off the street but he may roll over again. He is fast asleep."

"Sure. We've got nothing else to do."

They waited in silence for the small blue bus with its crew of two elderly police constables who dragged the drunk inside, cursing and sighing.

"Nice job," de Gier said, waved at the constables and started the engine.

"So have we," Grijpstra said, "nice and complicated. Murdered innocence dangling from a piece of string, surrounded by dear sweet people of which one is a black cannibal trained in guerilla warfare and another a crazy old female bag of bones."

"I hope his mother has done it," de Gier said.

"You love people, don't you?"

"I don't like jails," de Gier said. "I had to visit some of our clients in their cells this week. Cold, drafty and hopeless. Jail will get you if nothing else does. A day in jail means a year of crime."

Grijpstra turned his heavy neck and stared at his colleague.

"Well, well," he said, "have you forgotten how many people you have directed to the cold, drafty and hopeless cells?"

"Yes, yes," de Gier said and lapsed into silence.

The silence lasted until they entered their office and he had to help Grijpstra to phrase the exact short sentences that framed their report and that they both signed, mentioning in cool print that everything the report contained was the truth as they, officers of the Queen's law, saw it. Grijpstra typed, slowly, with four fingers, without making a single typing error.

De Gier didn't speak when he left but Grijpstra didn't mind. He had been working with de Gier for a number of years and they had never really fallen out.

Other Titles in the Soho Crime Series

Peter Lovesey
(England)
The Circle
The Headhunters
False Inspector Dew
Rough Cider
On the Edge
The Reaper

(Bath, England)
The Last Detective
Diamond Solitaire
The Summons
Bloodhounds
Upon a Dark Night
The Vault
Diamond Dust
The House Sitter
The Secret Hangman
Skeleton Hill
Stagestruck
Cop to Corpse
The Tooth Tattoo
The Stone Wife
Down Among the Dead Men

(London, England)
Wobble to Death
The Detective Wore Silk Drawers
Abracadaver
Mad Hatter's Holiday
The Tick of Death
A Case of Spirits
Swing, Swing Together
Waxwork

Jassy Mackenzie
(South Africa)
Random Violence
Stolen Lives
The Fallen
Pale Horses

Seichō Matsumoto
(Japan)
Inspector Imanishi Investigates

James McClure
(South Africa)
The Steam Pig
The Caterpillar Cop
The Gooseberry Fool
Snake
The Sunday Hangman
The Blood of an Englishman
The Artful Egg
The Song Dog

Magdalen Nabb
(Italy)
Death of an Englishman
Death of a Dutchman
Death in Springtime
Death in Autumn
The Marshal and the Murderer
The Marshal and the Madwoman
The Marshal's Own Case
The Marshal Makes His Report
The Marshal at the Villa Torrini
Property of Blood
Some Bitter Taste
The Innocent
Vita Nuova
The Monster of Florence

Fuminori Nakamura
(Japan)
The Thief
Evil and the Mask
Last Winter, We Parted

Stuart Neville
(Northern Ireland)
The Ghosts of Belfast
Collusion
Stolen Souls
The Final Silence
Those We Left Behind

(Dublin)
Ratlines

Eliot Pattison
(Tibet)
Prayer of the Dragon
The Lord of Death

Rebecca Pawel
(1930s Spain)
Death of a Nationalist
Law of Return
The Watcher in the Pine
The Summer Snow

Kwei Quartey
(Ghana)
Murder at Cape Three Points

Qiu Xiaolong
(China)
Death of a Red Heroine
A Loyal Character Dancer
When Red Is Black

John Straley
(Alaska)
The Woman Who Married a Bear
The Curious Eat Themselves

John Straley cont.
The Big Both Ways
Cold Storage, Alaska

Akimitsu Takagi
(Japan)
The Tattoo Murder Case
Honeymoon to Nowhere
The Informer

Helene Tursten
(Sweden)
Detective Inspector Huss
The Torso
The Glass Devil
Night Rounds
The Golden Calf
The Fire Dance
The Beige Man
The Treacherous Net

Jan Merete Weiss
(Italy)
These Dark Things
A Few Drops of Blood

Janwillem van de Wetering
(Holland)
Outsider in Amsterdam
Tumbleweed
The Corpse on the Dike
Death of a Hawker
The Japanese Corpse
The Blond Baboon
The Maine Massacre
The Mind-Murders
The Streetbird
The Rattle-Rat
Hard Rain
Just a Corpse at Twilight
Hollow-Eyed Angel
The Perfidious Parrot
The Sergeant's Cat: Collected Stories

Timothy Williams
(Guadeloupe)
Another Sun
The Honest Folk of Guadeloupe

(Italy)
Converging Parallels
The Puppeteer
Persona Non Grata
Black August
Big Italy

Jacqueline Winspear
(1920s England)
Maisie Dobbs
Birds of a Feather